Praise For Richard O'Connor's Memoir *Taking A Shot*

"A moving coming of-age-memoir about a kid who made a tough decision, took risks, faced challenges, and wound up scoring big points in life."

—Hubie Brown, NBA Hall of Fame Coach

"O'Connor's story is universal. It's poignant, funny and heartfelt. About a man baring his most vulnerable self by capturing the essence of growing up a superstar athlete in Jersey the way Springsteen captured a poet running on the road of Life. If you don't read this book, you are really missing out. So...take a shot."

—Bradley Siegal, former President of TNT, TBS, TCM, and Cartoon Network/Current CEO Brand New World Studios.

"This wonderful book inspired O'Connor to return to full-time writing. It should gain him a legion of new readers who have never known him as the award-winning sportswriter, Richie O'Connor of years ago. He might even recapture his older fans who lost track of him. A heart-rending and poignant read."

—Pat Jordan, author of *A False Spring.*

"O'Connor's beautifully written book is about paths taken and not taken. From dreaming of being on the cover of Sports Illustrated to seeing his byline in the same magazine, he shares life lessons in perfect prose."

—Ben Guest, author of *Zen and the Art of Coaching Basketball*

"A fast-paced look at a journey from basketball wiz to celebrated writer. At times exuberantly funny and at other times poignantly reflective. O'Connor's story scores on multiple levels, from unveiling the stakes at play with collegiate sports to the joys that come with nailing the perfect paragraph."

—Charles Butler, Co-author of *The Long Run: A New York City's Firefighter's Triumphant Comeback from Crash Victim to Elite Athlete*

"Richard O'Connor's sports story is different, one I've never seen and I'm a former sports scribe. An elite athlete takes a hard look at his sport and all it entails—and walks away. "Willingly," he writes. "Without shame." Sports fans and memoir readers will be captivated by this original story."

—John Capouya, author of *Gorgeous George: The Outrageous Bad-boy Wrestler Who Created American Pop Culture.*

"A young man gives up a chance at stardom in a game he seemed born to play. But instead of "What-if" O'Connor asks "What's next?" Again and again in a life that takes him from elite-level basketball, to writing, to publishing, to business, to fatherhood. It's a template for many who might get stuck at similar crossroads."

-John Hanc, author of *The Coolest Race on Earth: Mud, Madmen, Glaciers and Grannies at the Antarctica.*

Praise for Glenn Stout's Books

"Great storytelling . . . Stout's moving book [*Young Woman and the Sea*] recovers the exhilarating story of a young girl who found her true self out in the water and paved the way for women in sports today."

—Publishers Weekly

"A deft social history of the 1920s--the days of flappers and bootleggers, hot jazz and hot stocks, bloodthirsty thugs and corrupt cops and pols all careening toward the Great Crash . . . *Tiger Girl and the Candy Kid* is a hell of a yarn—worthy of an HBO hoodlum epic like *Boardwalk Empire*."

—Ed Kosner, *The Wall Street Journal*

Tiger Girl and the Candy Kid is a "Rip-roaring account of the Jazz Age's most-feared gangster couple... Stout's fast-paced prose has a Mickey Spillane-like cadence to it that fits his subject matter perfectly... A compulsively readable criminal biography as well as a vivid cultural snapshot of early Prohibition-era America." —*Kirkus Reviews*

"Glenn Stout has done the impossible: With *Fenway 1912* he has put an end to the seemingly bottomless genre that is Fenway Park books. We now need no more. We get not pomp and circumstance, but the bones and blueprint of a legendary ballpark—topped with a star-filled World Series that still endures. He doesn't pretend history is straw hats and cigars, but gives you real people, real baseball and (the best part) real Boston, the way any real writer should."

—Howard Bryant, *ESPN*

"*Fenway 1912* reads like a novel, detailing the trials and tribulations of the quaint ballpark and the team itself ... Stout has made a great story out of history."
—*Baseball America*

"It's hard to have faith, until you read *Nine Months at Ground Zero*. Are there any heroes left? The answer is a resounding yes in this beautiful and poignant and important book. God bless these men so willing to make the impossible possible."
—Buzz Bissinger, author of *Three Nights in August*

"This inspiring story [*Nine Months at Ground Zero*] brings us all to a concrete-and-steel intimacy with a structure, its place, and its people. To know Charlie Vitchers and Bobby Gray is to know New York down to its bones."
—Richard Ben Cramer, author of *What It Takes: The Way to the White House*

Other Books by Richard O'Connor

Foul shot

Gaelic Force

Taking a Shot

Other Books by Glenn Stout

Young Woman and the Sea (also a film from Disney)

Tiger Girl and the Candy Kid

The Selling of the Babe

Fenway 1912

Nine Months at Ground Zero

Red Sox Century

The Year's Best Sports Writing (Founding Editor)

Yankees Century

More Books from The Sager Group

The Swamp: Deceit and Corruption in the CIA
An Elizabeth Petrov Thriller (Book 1)
by Jeff Grant

Chains of Nobility: Brotherhood of the Mamluks (Book 1-3)
by Brad Graft

Meeting Mozart: A Novel Drawn from the Secret Diaries of Lorenzo
Da Ponte by Howard Jay Smith

Death Came Swiftly: Novel About the Tay Bridge Disaster of 1879
by Bill Abrams

A Boy and His Dog in Hell: And Other Stories
by Mike Sager

Eat Wheaties: A Novel
by Michael Kun

Goodbye, Sweetberry Park: A Novel
by Josh Green

Lifeboat No. 8: Surviving the Titanic
by Elizabeth Kaye

Hunting Marlon Brando: A True Story
by Mike Sager

The Sing Sing Follies (A Maximum-Security Comedy): And Other
True Stories
by John H. Richardson

Who She Was: My Search for my Mother's Life
By Samuel G. Freedman

See our entire library at TheSagerGroup.net_

FLAGRANT FOULS

A NOVEL OF BASKETBALL, MURDER AND DESPICABLE ACTS

BY
RICHARD O'CONNOR
AND GLENN STOUT

Flagrant Fouls: A Novel of Basketball, Murder and Despicable Acts

© 2025 Richard O'Connor and Glenn Stout

Cover design and cover art by Sonny & Biddy, WBYK.com.au
Interior design by Siori Kitajima, PatternBased.com

Cataloging-in-Publication data for this book
is available from the Library of Congress.
ISBN-13:
eBook: 978-1-958861-59-2
Paperback: 978-1-958861-60-8

Published by The Sager Group LLC
(TheSagerGroup.net)

FLAGRANT FOULS

A NOVEL

BY

RICHARD O'CONNOR AND GLENN STOUT

To my mother and father who gave me incredible affection, guidance and support, and passed on to me their sense of silliness and gift of humor.

To Peg who was always there.

To Tracey who is always there.

To Glenn Stout for all your patience, energy and smarts. You are, without question, an editorial genius. Can't thank you enough.

And, of course, to my main man, Tim, my son who bestowed upon me the greatest gift one person can give another: He taught me how to love. Unequivocally and fathomlessly. Every day with him is Father's Day.

—Richard O'Connor

To all the writers I have read, worked with, and learned from.

—Glenn Stout

Contents

CHAPTER ONE

I was sitting in my office spinning a basketball on my right index finger when the door opened, and the sorriest looking man I'd seen in years walked in.

"You Elgin O'Brien?" he said in a whisper.

"The one and only," I said, putting down the basketball.

The man took a deep, dejected breath. His eyes were vacant, his skin marshmallow white. A walking cadaver.

"I'm Pat Malone," he said, after licking his cracked lips.

Sitting behind a mahogany desk, I reached over and lowered the volume on my CD player. I'd been listening to Chet Baker. Love his voice. So haunting. I pointed to a brown leather wing chair.

"Please," I said, "have a seat."

Malone, short and potbellied, perched on the edge of the chair and rubbed his hands over and over, as if trying to wash something off. He wore a navy blue sport coat, a wrinkled white shirt, and light gray pants.

"Interesting," he said, his knees jackhammering.

"What's interesting?"

"Your first name."

I smiled. "My father named me after the old Los Angeles Laker star Elgin Baylor."

"Guess your father was a basketball player."

"Jazz musician," I said. "Couldn't throw a ball through a hula hoop. But he was a huge fan."

"Yet you were a great player," he said, referring to my years playing at Duke and for the Dallas Mavericks. "Where then did you get your athletic genes?"

"My father's father, I guess. He played for the Rochester Royals, back when the NBA had only ten teams."

Malone licked his lips again and glanced out the window of my Hoboken brownstone. Fortyish, he had a wedge-shaped face, bulbous nose, and jowls like a bulldog.

I said, "Would you care for some water?"

"I'd . . . I'd love some," he said, still rubbing his hands together. They were as bloodless as his face.

I stood, went to the refrigerator, and grabbed a small, plastic bottle of Fiji Water. I handed it to him. He immediately twisted off the cap, took a big gulp, then wiped his mouth with the back of his hand.

"Thank you," he said.

"You're welcome." Service with a smile.

Malone studied me. I hoped he didn't think I was too laid back. It was early and I was wearing running gear: Vuori shorts, Buck Mason tee, and Hoka sneakers. Nice stuff. Stylish. Not too pretentious, but also not usual PI wear.

I then saw him spy the gun inside the shoulder holster hanging off the coat rack. In it was a Smith & Wesson .38. A nifty little piece, effective at close range. Malone grinned slightly. I assumed the weapon gave me some street cred.

"If you don't mind my asking," he said, "How does an ex-NBA star become a private investigator?"

"By studying the Dudley Do-Right manual."

Malone didn't smile. So much for my sense of humor.

He said, "I guess what I meant is, why'd you choose this profession?"

"The explanation is complicated," I said, thinking how talking about it was too painful, too deeply rooted in the soil of my memory.

"I understand," Malone said.

The room got quiet. The silence was long and uncomfortable. I needed to break it.

"So?" I said, "what can I do for you?" Brilliant opening lines are not my strong point.

"You've been highly recommended."

"By?"

"Sergeant O'Meara."

"How you know Bill?"

"He coached my son."

"What level?"

"Biddy Basketball."

"Was he a good coach?"

"Very good coach."

"He was a good player, too," I said. Bill and I had been high school teammates, he the rebounder and me the shooter. Occasionally, I'd let him take a shot. Very occasionally. He's the closest thing I have to a best friend.

"O'Meara says you're very independent," Malone said, "and that's gotten you into trouble."

"On many occasions."

Malone squeezed the water bottle. It crackled. He said, "I'd like to hire you."

"To do what?"

"Investigate a murder," he said. "You may have heard about the college basketball player who was shot in midtown Manhattan a few months ago?"

"The kid from St. Stephen's?"

Malone sucked air through nostrils so wide they could have vacuumed dust from the floor.

"That . . . that kid was my son," he said, crunching his eyes.

I turned the music off.

"Sorry to hear that," I said.

"His . . . his name was Teddy," he said, his voice breaking.

"If I recall correctly," I said, "the shooting occurred after the season."

"A week after the team lost in the quarterfinals of the NCAA tournament."

"What year was Teddy?"

"A sophomore."

I nodded.

"He was a good player," Malone said.

"A pro prospect?"

"Yes. He was quick and strong and could shoot from three-point range."

"Refresh my memory."

"About?"

"The shooting."

"Teddy . . . Teddy was . . . was shot coming out of a nightclub."

"What club?"

"Infernos."

"The strip joint in Manhattan?"

Malone swallowed hard to lubricate his vocal cords. His Adam's apple bobbed.

"Yes," he said.

"Been there once or twice myself. Back in the day."

"He and two teammates were leaving the club around 2 a.m. when Teddy . . ." He struggled to finish the sentence.

"Just Teddy got shot?"

"Yes. Four times."

I scratched my stubbled chin. It made a raspy sound.

"I assume the police have investigated," I said.

"They have."

"And?"

He shook wildly, as if tasered.

"One detective thinks it was a random shooting," he said, angrily.

"What do you think?"

His face inflated. He crushed the water bottle.

"I think it's BULLSHIT!" he said.

"Why?"

"Because Teddy was the only one shot."

"You saying he was targeted?"

"I am."

"What does O'Meara say?"

"He agrees . . . off the record."

"But?"

"Says there's no proof."

"How about suspects?"

"None."

"Are the cops still investigating?"

"Supposedly."

"You sound skeptical."

"Very."

"You have any theories?"

"About?"

"Who might have targeted Teddy."

"No. Teddy is . . . was a good kid. An honor student. Could've been an academic All-American."

I hesitated to ask the next question, but I knew I had to.

"Teddy have any issues?"

"Issues?" His forehead wrinkled. "What kind of issues?"

"Drugs? Alcohol? Gambling? Girls?"

"No, No. No. Nothing of the sort."

His answer was so quick and so certain I sensed there might be something else going on that he wasn't willing to talk about.

I said, "You sure?"

"I'm positive," he said, his voice sounding constricted, as if an invisible cord was being pulled tight around his throat. "Absolutely positive."

For a moment neither of us spoke. The silence creaked.

I took the moment to center a small plastic cube on my desk. Inside it was a picture of my parents, my White mother and Black father. Growing up Black and Irish I always figured I had the best and worst of both worlds.

"Tell me," I said, after some seconds, "how was Teddy prior to the shooting?"

Malone squirmed in his seat. "What do you mean?"

"Was he scared? Moody? Upset? Depressed?"

He stared at the back of his right hand, as if the veins were lines of information that could be read. "He a . . . he . . . he had been . . ."

"Had been what?" I said, making scooping gestures with my hands, as if trying to draw his words out.

"Distracted."

"Over?"

"I don't know," he said, shaking his head so aggressively his cheeks wobbled. "He wouldn't say."

"Wouldn't or couldn't?"

Malone didn't respond. He stood and glanced out a large picture window, his nose almost touching the glass. He stared across the Hudson River at the tall towers and gothic spires of Manhattan. As glorious as the view was, it always made me melancholy seeing One World Trade Center and thinking of 9/11. One of the saddest days in American history. Lotta haunting memories.

After a minute, Malone turned around and returned to his seat.

He said, "Will you take the case?"

"I will."

"What's your fee?"

I told him. As a friend of O'Meara, I even gave him a bit of a break.

"Seems reasonable," he said.

"It's enough to keep my wine cellar full."

He cracked a grin. Grudgingly.

"I want this shooter found and terminated," he said, his voice hitting high octaves.

"I'll find the shooter," I said, "but I'm not an executioner. I don't deal in revenge."

"What do you deal in?"

"Justice. For everyone. Rich or poor. Black or White. I don't discriminate."

He nodded, pulled out his wallet, and scribbled a check.

Handing it to me, he said, "When can you start?"

"I already have."

"Perfect."

Malone put his hands on his knees, pushed himself to his feet, rising slower than a rusty car jack.

He extended his hand. We shook. His fingers were moist.

I walked him to the front door.

"Thank you for taking the case," he said.

"Thank you for hiring me," I said, wondering how thankful he'd be later if I uncovered something that would rock his world even more. It happens.

Malone left. I went to the window and watched him plod to his Honda SUV like a man who had lost his best friend. I picked up the basketball and once again started spinning it on my finger.

The ball spun off and bounced away.

CHAPTER
TWO

My office was on the first floor of a three-story brownstone reminiscent of the childhood crib I grew up in near Harlem's Mount Morris Park. It had, in addition to the desk and wing chair, a high ceiling, track lighting, and Persian rugs. Against one wall was a floor-to-ceiling bookcase packed with hundreds of hardcover books. My girlfriend, Monique, calls my books my vice. She says I read more than a literary agent.

On the wall opposite the bookcase were framed posters of jazz greats: Miles Davis blowing his trumpet, John Coltrane blaring his saxophone, and Thelonious Monk playing the piano—awesomely talented dudes whose music soothes the soul and nourishes the heart.

Music, you could say, is in my blood. My father, from New Orleans, played the sax. My mother, second generation Bronx Irish, was a pop singer. Her favorite expression was "a life without song is like a walk in the dark." She played records so often neighbors thought we had musical wallpaper.

It was Monique who decorated the house. She invested a lot of time renovating the second floor living room. She had hardwood floors installed. She purchased a big-screen television, sectional sofas, tall lamps, and potted plants. She even commissioned a seventy-year-old Italian mason to restore the old stone fireplace. The guy was expensive. It took him two months to complete the job. But, man, it was worth it. Nothing beats sitting before a fire on a cold winter's night, sipping a cocktail and eyeballing the twinkling lights of Manhattan.

After Malone left, I grabbed my phone and earbuds. I was ready to run. Running was my favorite form of exercise. I didn't lift weights or pedal bikes. Too damn boring. I just ran, long and hard, because guys like me, baby, we were born to run. Or, at my age now, at least jog.

Despite it being the last week in May, the weather outside was uncharacteristically hot, the kind of scorching, oppressive heat that strains air conditioners and turns cars into ovens. Climate change.

For a moment, I thought about bagging the run and heading back inside but decided against it. I wanted time to clear my head and think about the Malone case.

Listening to Charlie Parker, I ran up a hill to Castle Point Terrace and then on to the campus of Stevens Institute of Technology. A small private research university, Stevens had a lovely campus that overlooked Manhattan. The student body consisted of brainiac kids who majored in mathematical engineering and quantitative economics. Stuff way over my head. Compared with them, I can barely add and subtract.

School was still in session. Students streamed in and out of the library. Most were dressed in a colorful confusion of T-shirts, jeans, shorts, sneakers, flips-flops, and sandals. Almost all carried backpacks. Many wore eyeglasses. A hand-holding couple—lanky kid with chopped hair, a heavy-set girl with long braids—stopped outside a Gothic-stone building and engaged in a smoochy détente. I wondered if they learned how to canoodle like that in their bioengineering class.

If you ask me, nothing beats college. I mean, where else in life can you sleep late, party hearty, get laid, and, if you're lucky, get educated? Getting shot, though, coming out of a strip club like Teddy Malone, isn't on the syllabus.

That Teddy was the only person shot that night kept rolling around in my head—as was the thought that his father wasn't being completely truthful. That bothered me. A lot. I was pretty sure he was hiding . . . something.

I ran down Castle Point past Frank Sinatra's childhood home, and later the hall where Frankie's mother, Dolly, nicknamed "Hatpin Dolly," ran an illegal abortion service. She operated a speakeasy and bought booze from the Mob. The church was so appalled at her activities they banned Ol' Blue Eyes from singing in the choir.

Turning a corner, I ran along the dock, the same one where Marlon Brando in *On the Waterfront* played a longshoreman who exposed corruption among local Mob bosses. Can't watch that movie enough. It's a masterpiece.

Increasing my pace, I thought more about Teddy Malone. Experience told me nobody gets shot coming out of a strip club at 2 a.m. for no reason. And that reason usually has something has to do with drugs, women, alcohol, or gambling. Sometimes a combination of all four.

I returned to my apartment, sweating profusely. If I cut down on wine and cheese I could be in better shape. But who wants to give up two of life's greatest pleasures?

I took some oranges from a bowl on the kitchen counter, carefully sliced and squeezed them until I had enough juice to fill a good-sized glass. Drinking orange juice from a container just doesn't cut it. It must be fresh. Tasteful. Done right. Precision matters.

I downed the OJ and put the glass in the dishwasher. I then went upstairs and took a long, cold shower. Feeling refreshed, I shaved, deodorized, and put on Paige jeans, a white Rhone tee, Cole Haan loafers and a linen Zegna blue blazer. Snazzy threads. But not pretentious.

Despite the heat, I needed the blazer to conceal my shoulder holster. The holster was brown. I often thought about getting a new one. Something in blue. To match my blazer. If nothing else, I'd be even more stylish. More *GQ*.

I took a minute to check myself in the foyer mirror. I had on my game face. Looked armed and ready for action. I smiled. Winked. Couldn't imagine being anyone but me. Although George Clooney wouldn't be a bad alternative.

I had one quick thing to do before I left the house. Call Monique.

"What's the story, morning glory?" I said.

"Nice and dandy, like cotton candy," she said, her voice softer than morning mist.

"Wha'cha doing?"

"Just finished running through Central Park. About to make a protein shake. "

I pictured her in the kitchen wearing Lululemon shorts and a white tank top, her blond hair in a ponytail, her slender fingers on the blender.

Many people think Monique resembles the actress Charlize Theron. Putting aside my bias, Theron couldn't shine Monique's Nikes.

"Got to cancel lunch," I said.

"Got a hot date?"

"Got a case."

"Tell me about it."

I told her what I knew. Which wasn't much.

"Are we still on for dinner?" she said.

"Would Romeo cancel Juliet?"

"Only if the Montagues demanded it.

"Even then, he wouldn't. See you later alligator."

"After a while, crocodile."

I left the apartment and walked to my car, a 1989 royal blue Ford Mustang convertible. I just love that car, despite the astronomical repair bills. But who cares? If you love something, or someone, shouldn't you always remain faithful?

A few years ago, I had a top-of-the-line CD player and Bose speakers installed. I'm sort of old school and prefer listening to a CD instead of streaming something from my phone. Monique jokes that I'd put in a turntable if I could, and she's right. I still have all my father's LPs.

I ducked into the car. It was hot. The stuffy air felt like a congested lung.

Checking in with Bill O'Meara was job one. I wanted his take on the murder. O'Meara was a good cop, dedicated and professional. He knew police work inside and out. He paid attention to detail. He followed the rules. There was talk that someday he might make top brass.

Despite our close friendship, Bill and I often disagree, sometimes angrily and sometimes loudly, over policing practices. I feel that there's too much racism, brutality, and dishonesty. Bill feels I exaggerate, although he does admit there is a fair percentage of bad cops.

In the end, after we both calm down, we agree that being a cop is a tough job and that law enforcement, like most big institutions, has its flaws. What's needed, we would agree, is more training, monitoring, and screening of cops. Anything that can help them to avoid unnecessarily leaving more blood from darkening the concrete.

I put the key in the ignition and turned it. The engine farted. The AC rattled. I slid a Sonny Rollins disc into the player and cruised along Hoboken's Washington Avenue, a sizzling stretch of streets that includes Italian restaurants, Irish pubs, Chinese delis, Thai bistros, Spanish bodegas, and Greek diners. It's this culinary diversity that gives the town its heartbeat and thumbprint, its energy and vibrancy, which is why it's so popular now with twenty-somethings who find the rents reasonable and the bars affordable.

I drove through the Lincoln Tunnel and thirty minutes later arrived in Manhattan. Traffic was at a standstill. Too many cars and cabs. Too many double-parked UPS trucks, FedEx trucks, Amazon trucks, Con Ed trucks, garbage trucks. Getting from one block to another was worse than waiting in line for a lousy cup of coffee at Starbucks.

I turned onto Eighth Avenue, Hell's Kitchen. Dozens of bars and restaurants. A crush of people: men in shirtsleeves, women in bright blouses, dog walkers, delivery boys, skateboarders, runners, kids eating ice cream, lovers holding hands. All of them moving quickly, all bumping into one another, all dodging around one another, some waving their arms furiously to signal a cab.

I parked in a garage under the Henry Hudson Parkway and walked a few blocks to the Midtown Police Precinct. The air was thick and heavy. A scythe of steam that cut though my lungs. Barely breathable. Hell on earth.

As I crossed Seventh Avenue, the noise of the city assaulted me. Police sirens, buses braking. Jackhammers drilling. Ambulances blaring. Manhattan is, if nothing else, a place of constant irritation, daily inconveniences, periodic rudeness, corrosive conditions, and ever-present danger. It's clearly not a place for the weak of heart. It's more a place for those who have steel in their soul.

Yet despite its many faults, I could never live far away from New York. For me, the city is magical. It's Oz. It's Xanadu. What F. Scott Fitzgerald once described as "wrapped in its mystery and promise."

The precinct was a four-story, white brick building that had big windows covered with metal grills. Green lanterns flanked a thick bronze circular door. Above the door were a host of American flags. God bless America.

I entered a large tiled room, square, hot, and stuffy. The ceiling was tin, the lights fluorescent. The floor was covered with industrial carpeting and dotted with coffee stains. Uniformed cops—men and women, fat and thin, tall and short—were sitting behind chrome desks, either tapping keyboards or talking on the phone. Low voices, hands gestures. They had shaved faces, bearded faces, scarred faces, pretty faces. The place smelled like ammonia.

I approached the desk sergeant, a middle-aged woman with dirty blond hair and eyes the color of broccoli. We went back a long way.

"Well, well, well," she said in a husky voice. "If it isn't the famous shamus."

"Don't think people use that term anymore."

"What term?"

"Shamus."

"I do," she said. "It's the romantic in me."

"You're romantic, huh?"

"Wanna find out?"

"I thought you had a boyfriend."

"C'mon. You know me. I never put all my eggs in one bastard."

"I take it you're dating a lot?"

"Variety *is* the spice of life."

"So many spices," I said, "so little thyme."

"Clever."

"I thought so."

"At least I get to use my handcuffs."

"Guess your dates like to be restrained."

"Let's put it this way. I boldly take them where no man has gone before."

"Beam me up, Scotty," I said. "Is O'Meara around?"

She pointed skyward.

"He's upstairs."

"Sleeping?"

"No, he's actually awake," she said, kiddingly. "In the interview room."

"Interviewing someone?"

"No," she said. "Eating breakfast."

"At least he's doing something productive."

"For a change," she chuckled.

"Thanks," I said, blowing her a kiss.

She pretended to catch it, then put a hand over her chest.

"Be still my heart," she said, fluttering her eyelashes.

As I was walking up the stairs, a detective named Chaney stopped and greeted me. He and I had crossed paths a few times. He had all the investigative skills of a roast turkey.

A chubby man with a blubbery face, Chaney had piggish eyes, a bad comb-over, and a nose like a pitted potato. He wore a wrinkled flowered Hawaiian shirt that hung over baggy black jeans. I could see the outline of his gun under the shirt.

"Thinking of joining the force, Elg?" he said, his voice a monotone mutter.

"Just stopped by to give you guys some tips on how to do real detective work."

He puffed air like a blowfish. "Don't steal my laptop."

"Surprised you know how to use one."

Chaney gave me the finger and walked away, one hand in his pocket jiggling coins. It sounded like a tambourine.

Taking two steps at a time, I hustled up to the interview room. It was small. No windows. No AC. The flooring was cracked vinyl, the chairs plastic, the Formica table rectangular. A video camera was mounted high in one corner.

Sitting at the table and sweating slightly was O'Meara. He was wearing a crisp white button-down shirt, looking at a laptop, and eating an egg sandwich.

A big man, six feet four and muscular, Bill had forearms thick and taut as power cables. His neck was rounder than a water bucket. I first knew him on the court as a lanky banger under the boards, but now he more resembled an ex-heavyweight fighter: Flat nose and thick scars. Hands so large they could still palm a basketball. If not a moose.

Once upon a time those hands came in handy when we played together in Harlem's famed Rucker Park. Back then Bill had hops. He did the dirty work down low, soaring high above the rim to grab rebounds, then throwing me outlet passes as I sprinted down court. I'd catch the ball, make a reverse dribble and go in for an open layup. We made a good team.

Bill chin-tilted to a chair and said, "Park your keester."

I sat and crossed my legs.

"Little toasty outside, huh?" he said. He had a thick Noo Yawk accent.

"Heat's murder."

"Makes people crazy. Just last night two Franciscan sisters got into a fist fight."

"Sounds like nunsense."

"Funny, Elg, very fucking funny."

O'Meara picked up a mug of coffee and took a sip. The mug had a logo of the perpetually woeful New York Jets. Some fans are just too loyal.

"I had a feeling I'd be seeing you," he said.

"Probably hoping, too . . . seeing how I'm your idol."

"My idol, my ass. When you come around my hemorrhoids flare."

"Glad something lights your fire."

O'Meara finished the last bite of his sandwich, then held up an egg-roll size finger and pointed to an old coffee maker. For such a big man his gestures were oddly precise, even fastidious.

"Want some?" he said.

I shook my head. "Nah."

"Smart. Stuff tastes like STP."

"What can you tell me about the Teddy Malone shooting?" I said.

O'Meara finished his sandwich, then grabbed the crumbled yellow McDonald's wrapping paper and began leveling it out a few times until it began to look ironed.

"I take it Pat came to see you," he said.

"He did."

"I've known Pat for years."

"He a straight shooter?"

O'Meara cocked his head. Even though there was a large fan turning overhead and one window open, it was so warm it seemed as if the walls were dripping sweat.

"Why you ask?" he said.

"Something about his manner."

"His manner?"

"I got the sense he wasn't totally forthcoming."

"You're getting skeptical."

"I'm skeptical of everything. What's his story?"

"He's a mailman, married, and has . . . had one kid. Teddy."

"Good father?"

"I think so. Pretty demanding."

"In what way?"

"He pushed Teddy hard."

"In school?"

"No. In basketball."

"I assume since you were Teddy's Biddy Basketball coach you knew him well."

"I did. Great kid. Worked extremely hard. An overachiever."

I uncrossed my legs, leaned forward and said, "Tell me about the shooting."

O'Meara rubbed his chin. He had a dimple in it the size of a mouse hole.

He said, "Teddy was shot coming out of a strip joint called Infernos."

"Malone thinks Teddy was targeted."

"It looks that way."

"What was he shot with?"

"A forty-five."

"At close range?"

"Maybe ten yards."

"There were two other players with him, correct?"

"Yeah. Teammates. Bobby Rose and Amare Anderson."

"What's their take?"

"They have very little take. Said the shooting took them by surprise."

"They describe the shooter?"

"Said he wore a black hoodie, came out of nowhere, and fired. They hit the ground and when they got up, he was gone."

"How many rounds?"

"Four. All nailing the target."

"Sounds personal."

"It does."

I sucked thoughtfully on my side teeth. "A Mafia hit?"

"Ordinarily I'd say no. But these days anything's possible. We have more gangs than we have names for."

"Any witnesses?"

"Some."

"What did they see?"

"Dingus."

"You're saying they saw nothing?"

"No, *they're* saying they saw nothing. Except for one guy. He said the shooter was tall and muscular."

"Black or White?"

"Couldn't say."

"Got the wit's name?"

"Why should I give it to you?"

"Because you believe in truth, justice, and the American way?"

"Yeah, right. And I also believe in the tooth fairy and Easter Bunny."

O'Meara put on a pair of bifocals, leaned forward on the table, and began tapping the laptop keys.

After a minute, he looked over the top of his glasses and said, "Wit's name is Steven Clark. Late thirties. Registered nurse at Columbia Presbyterian Hospital. Has a girlfriend who's some kind of dancer."

"Got his address?"

"Fifty-five Orchid Street. Lower East Side. My son just moved down there. It's close to his job."

"He like it?"

O'Meara took off his glasses, pinched the bridge of his nose and smiled.

"It's the city's hottest neighborhood, mostly tech kids who've cashed out on Bitcoin and escaped mommy and daddy's hacienda. Says he's either fucking busy or busy fucking."

"Nice to be young," I said.

"Way he's going he'll be footloose and fiancé free forever."

"Were detectives assigned to the case?"

O'Meara sipped some coffee. Made a face as if he had tasted poison.

"Of course, we assigned detectives," he said. "Fuck you think we are here? Brooklyn fucking Nine-Nine?"

"No. But I don't always trust that detectives do their jobs."

O'Meara exhaled loudly. Offended. Even pissed.

"Oh no, oh no, don't give me that bullshit distrust of cops routine again, okay?" he said.

"I only give it because many deserve it, many are incompetent," I said, remembering how the cops mishandled my father's murder.

"That's crap," O'Meara said.

"Like hell it is. One of your detectives told Malone it was a random shooting." I grinned. "You and I both know that's absurd."

"That's just one guy's opinion."

"Who was the guy?"

"What guy?"

"The detective who made the stupid observation."

"Chaney."

"Figures. That idiot couldn't find a vegetable in vegetable soup."

O'Meara snorted like a bear with sinus problems.

"I just wanna know how far your guys have investigated?" I said.

"Look. Trust me when I tell you our guys took it as far as they could, given the huge number of other unsolved murders, and even a little farther, given who the kid was. Bottom line: They got nada."

"No leads, huh?"

"Nothing to write home about."

"Anything worth jotting down?"

He shrugged.

"I'll take that as a no," I said.

"You're very perceptive."

"Aren't I though."

"Truth is, Elg, the case is cold," he said. "And as you well know, a murder case not solved within a few days has less than a 50 percent chance of being cleared." He paused. "This case has been open for months. You'll have your work cut out for you."

"Guess I'll have to consult my Sam Spade manual."

"Thought you only studied Inspector Clouseau."

"Just the parts where he kung fus Kato."

O'Meara rolled his eyes.

"Just a few more questions," I said.

"Is this a quiz?"

"If it was, you'd certainly fail. Did your detectives have any reason to believe Teddy was into anything illegal?"

"Illegal?"

"Gambling? Drugs?"

"Toxicology came back clear except for booze, but when it comes to St. Steve's, drugs are always a possibility."

"Why you say that?"

"The school attracts a lot of out-of-staters, mostly rich, suburban kids who sometimes find themselves getting into trouble with big-city drug dealers."

"Last question," I said.

"Thank God."

"Unofficially, you got any other thoughts on the shooting?"

"Unofficially, huh? I think you've been watching too much *Law & Order*." He pushed aside his mug and clasped his hands on the table. One thumbnail was black, and his knuckles scarred.

"Bottom line," he said. "We got jack shit."

"Sounds like it."

"I gather you're going to start questioning people and making a nuisance of yourself."

"Are you suggesting I annoy people?"

"Yes. Myself included. It's why I recommend you. You're a first-rate annoyer."

"It's what I do best."

I stood. O'Meara stood. We shook hands. His handshake was a bone-popper.

"How's Monique?" O'Meara asked.

"Good."

"You finally thinking about tying the knot?"

"Hey, man, I don't go in for that kinky stuff."

O'Meara shook his head. He then grabbed the McDonald's wrapping paper, crumbled it and tossed it into a trash can.

"Is she working?" he said.

"Yeah."

"Where?"

"Majestic Theatre," I said. "That's Broadway, in case you didn't know."

"Thank you so much for educating me."

"The least I can do."

"Is she appearing in a musical?"

"No. A Tennessee Williams play."

"*Streetcar Named Desire?*"

"*Glass Menagerie*. But I'm impressed you know Tennessee Williams."

"Hey, knucklehead, I went to college."

"Albany State's a college?"

"Bet the girls there were sexier than those southern belles at Duke."

"But not smarter."

"Surely colder. Probably needed gloves to undress them."

I blew into my hands and rubbed them together.

"Not when you have surgical fingers," I said.

"I bet some adoring coed probably lost a tooth nibbling on your ear."

I tugged on my earlobe.

"I always wondered what was stuck in there."

O'Meara chuckled.

"You're a fucking piece of work," he said.

CHAPTER
THREE

left the station. Outside, the air was even hotter. Not a breath of wind. High humidity. Probably ninety degrees. Brutal.

I looked for a cab. None were available.

I thought about getting an Uber, but I like cabs better. Riding in them always reminds me of my childhood, my mother humming tunes and my father telling jokes. Life was fun then. Or so it seemed.

In need of shade, I strolled down the street, passing delivery boys pedaling bicycles, Asian women holding umbrellas, and shirtless teenage boys gulping bottles of water. Anything to beat the heat.

I stopped for a red light. Chuckled at a bumper sticker that read: "Out of work and hungry? Eat a Republican." I wondered if the car belonged to AOC.

The light turned green. I put on Oakley sunglasses and found some relief under a maple tree in front of the old office of my first boss, Sid Meyer. Sid was a private investigator. Really old school. Honest. Knew all the tricks of the trade. Was fanatical about facts, details, and pounding the pavement. A true professional.

I was walking by his office one day when I saw a sign in his window: Help Wanted. I had just ended my ten-year career with the Dallas Mavericks due to a knee injury. Despite having some money in the bank, I was used to spending big and still needed to work, and I wanted something to drive the adrenaline.

It was just my luck that I missed out on the big dough. Today the average player makes more in a year than I made in my entire career. So much for being in the right place at the right time.

I still remember staring at Sid's sign, thinking about my father and the day he was murdered.

I was thirteen when it happened. He was shot coming out of our Harlem apartment. I saw him lying in the street, his face covered in blood, his hand reaching out as if for help. I've never forgotten those hands. Will never forget those hands. Neither will I ever forget the police calling the incident "unexplainable." All I knew was he was dead. My father's murderer was never found.

I didn't accept the police explanation. I pushed for answers. Demanded action. Every week, I'd stop by the precinct and question the White detectives. They'd blow me off. Made me so angry that my hands would clench into fists so tight my forearms spasmed. Once, while waiting outside an office to speak with a detective, I heard someone say, "It's that asshole kid again wanting to know about the shooting of that nigga."

Those words chilled my blood. Put tears in my eyes. I felt as if my lens cap had come off and I could see life clearly. I suddenly disliked cops. Distrusted them. Their inaction got me so incensed I even thought that someday I might want to become a cop myself so I could help bring justice to people who weren't getting it.

My father's death crushed me. The absence of him echoed in every room of our house. His blowing his saxophone. His dancing with my mother. His telling me bedtime stories. His telling me that it's not grades but learning for learning's sake that was the beating, enduring heart of education. If nothing else, my father lived a life bathed in lucidity and light. It took me years to stop missing him, my grief at times turning into a wordless depression.

But at least something positive came out of it. I learned that grief can be an analgesic, the pain a painkiller. Eventually, the acceptance of what happened made me stronger, more resilient, more vigilant. It gave me a reference point for dealing with future hardships, showing me how in the darkest of times, there is always a beacon of hope but only if you follow the light.

At our first meeting, Sid asked me why I wanted to become a private investigator. I thought a moment and said, "I didn't choose this job; I think this job chose me." He said I was worth a shot.

Sid taught me the ropes. He taught me how to shoot a gun, how to investigate and build a case. He said I didn't need lessons on fighting, seeing how one year I led the NBA in starting brawls. That's what happens when you grow up half-White in a Black neighborhood. You deal with every slur, every slight. You have no choice but to defend yourself. Good thing there was a boxing gym around the corner.

When Sid was dying of cancer—he was sixty-eight—he begged me to take over the operation. I gladly agreed. I took over the business and moved it to Hoboken. It's now called "The Baylor Agency."

I'm almost forty now and my mission in life is to make murderers, scumbags, and weasels pay for their crimes. It's what motivates me, gives me purpose. I guess it's payback for my father. Standing up for the dead.

I finally snagged a cab. The driver was a Rastafarian. He was listening to reggae. The cab smelled like garlic.

The cabbie drove straight down Broadway. I got out on Orchid Street. Once a cattle pen that attracted bargain hunters looking to buy cheap goods from the many Jewish shop owners who immigrated to New York in the mid-nineteenth century, the street was now entirely gentrified. Today, there are few Jewish retailers. The area is occupied by fancy boutiques, expensive spas, chic hotels, upscale restaurants, and luxury condominiums. Progress, I guess. But at least Katz's Delicatessen is still there, making those delicious pastrami on rye sandwiches that I love. Score one for the good old days.

Steven Clark lived in a newly renovated six-story brown brick building that had a large glass front door. Three beautiful young women were standing out front, chatting. Swizzle-stick thin, they all wore short-shorts, bare midriffs, and flip-flops. Maybe models or actresses. Maybe even sugar babies or nepo babies.

I flashed them my most becoming smile. None seemed overly impressed. Guess my days of wine and roses have soured and wilted.

I stepped inside the vestibule. It smelled like Clorox. The black-and-white marble floor gleamed. On one wall was a row of tiny gold mailboxes. Across from it was a resident directory. I found Clark's name. I hit a button on the intercom below the directory and within a minute a tired voice said, "Yeah."

"Steven Clark?"

"Yeah."

"My name's Elgin O'Brien," I said. "I'm a private investigator." I always got a chuckle out of saying that. It made me feel like Bogie. "I'd like to speak to you in connection with a murder investigation."

"What murder?"

"Teddy Malone."

"Who?"

"The kid who was shot outside Infernos."

"Look, Mr. Whatever-Your-Name-Is. I've already spoken to the police."

"But you haven't spoken to me."

"Why should I?"

"Because I'm not Frank Drebin and this isn't *The Naked Gun*."

After hearing what sounded like a big yawn, Clark said, "Okay, okay. But I haven't got all day."

"Neither do I."

"I'm apartment 4B."

A second later the door buzzed open.

I walked into the building and hopped into an elevator. Inside, it was lined with white plush cushioning, and attached to the back wall was a gold framed mirror hanging above a wood bench.

The elevator came to a stop as quiet as a falling snowflake. I stepped out into a hallway. A series of oil paintings along the walls, with glass frames. Thick beige carpeting. Art deco sconces. The smell of lemon-scented Pledge.

I knocked on Clark's door.

It opened a crack, held tight by a chain. I saw a side of Clark's face through the narrow opening. In the background, music was playing. Very softly. Billie Eilish.

I heard the chain slide across its holder. The door creaked open. Standing framed in the doorway was a young guy with a massive head and wide nostrils. Short and stocky, he wore round wire-rimmed glasses and had more facial shrubbery than Captain Ahab.

Rubbing sleep from his eyes, Clark was wearing white cotton slippers and paisley pajama pants. No top. He had enough chest hair to qualify as a forest.

He examined my face like a painter about to do a portrait.

"You're not what I expected," he said.

"What'd you expect?"

"I expected a Black dude."

"Really?"

"Elgin's not exactly a White guy's name."

"I am Black."

"You are?" he said, his eyebrows jerking upward like eagle wings. "You don't look it."

"My mother was White."

"I guess then your father was Black."

"Geez, you could be a private detective," I said. "May I come in?"

Clark nodded. He stepped aside. I entered.

He quickly put a finger to his lips and pointed to a closed door behind him.

"Gotta speak quietly," he said, "My girlfriend is asleep. Did too many laps."

"She a swimmer?"

"No. She's dances at Scores."

"Tough job," I said, coughing into my fist. "But somebody's gotta do it."

The apartment had a faint smell of marijuana. There was a navy blue suede couch and two matching suede armchairs sitting atop a braided rug. On the glass end tables were Tiffany lamps, glass ashtrays, and cans of nonalcoholic Heineken beer. Leaning against one wall was a large Banksy print of a young girl releasing a red balloon shaped like a heart. On another wall was a huge dart board. Stuck inside it were three darts.

"You a Billie Eilish fan, huh?" I said, attempting to put him at ease.

"She's the best," he said. "Great pipes."

"What's your favorite song?"

"Of hers?"

"Yeah."

" 'Ocean Eyes.' By far."

"Mine, too," I said, even though I wasn't sure I had ever heard it. Nor is it likely I ever will. My female musical tastes are more along the lines of Etta James, Ella Fitzgerald, Billie Holiday, and Nina Simone. Ladies who sang the blues.

"How about that," Clark said, nodding like a plastic cat in the back window of a car. "A cop who digs Eilish. Who would have thunk it?"

"I told you, I'm not a cop. I'm private."

"What's the difference?"

"Brains."

I took a seat. The armchair was so plush I had the feeling I might sink in it.

"Look, man," he said, making a sweep motion like an orchestra leader about to ignite the band, "I already told the police everything I know."

"I heard."

"So whaddya you want?"

"People don't always tell cops everything."

Clark stared at me for a long moment, rubbing a finger back and forth under his nose.

"I just have a few questions," I said.

Clark puffed his cheeks out and blew out a breath.

He said, "Mind if I smoke?"

"Marijuana?"

His eyes widened.

"Got some good shit, man. Want some?"

"I only get high on music."

Clark opened an end table drawer and pulled out some rolling paper and a baggie. He calmly sprinkled some of the contents onto the paper and rolled with it the dexterity of an electrician splicing together tiny wires. The joint resembled a fat pinworm. He inhaled it as if a doctor had asked him "to take a deep breath."

"You sure you don't want a toke?" he said, taking a seat and extending the joint.

"No, thanks. I'll just breathe the air."

"I just love weed."

"Who doesn't? What can you tell me about the shooting?"

Clark touched fingertips to his temples as if my request was causing him to think deep.

"I went to the club with my girlfriend—she's friends with one of the dancers—and I went out for a smoke—when like . . . like...this guy . . . like came out of nowhere. He had on this black hoodie, raised his gun, fired, and took off running."

"He only aimed at the one kid?"

He frowned.

"Whaddya mean?" he said.

"Did the shooter attempt to shoot anybody else?"

"No. Weird."

"What was weird?"

Clark didn't answer.

"What was weird?" I said again.

Clark took another drag on his joint and held the smoke in his mouth a while before exhaling.

"It was weird that the shooter waved a gun at all three guys but only shot the one," he said.

"I understand you told the detectives that the shooter was tall and muscular. Is that right?"

"Yes . . . yes, he was."

"How tall?"

Clark thought a moment.

"Maybe . . . maybe six four," he said. "Kind of moved like an athlete."

"An athlete?"

"Yeah, man. Had that smooth groove about him."

"Was he Black or White?"

"Couldn't tell."

"You see his hands?"

"His hands?"

"Were they Black or White?"

"He was wearing gloves."

"Was the gun in his right hand or left?"

"Does it matter?"

"Everything matters."

Clark's forehead wrinkled.

"It . . . it was in his, a, a, right hand."

"You sure?"

"I'm sure."

"Okay. Good. You remember what he was wearing?"

"He . . . a... . . . was wearing a black hoodie and black sweatpants."

"Anything on it?"

"On it?"

"An emblem? A logo? A designer label?"

He rocked his head from shoulder to shoulder, thinking.

"Nah . . . his outfit was just plain black," he said.

"Could you tell if he was with anyone?"

He put the joint down.

"Don't . . . don't think so," he said.

"Did you see the gun?"

"No, I . . . a . . . I never did, not really," he said. "Once I heard the shots I took cover."

I put my thumb and forefinger on the corners of my mouth and brought them together.

"Were you with anybody that night besides your girlfriend?"

"No."

"Did your girlfriend see anything?

"No. She was still inside talking with her friend."

"Were you drunk?"

"I don't drink."

"You don't drink?"

"I'm allergic to alcohol."

"My condolences," I said. "Was there anybody else around at the time of the shooting?"

"You mean bystanders?"

"Yeah."

"A few people but they were halfway up the block."

"I see."

Clark's eyes narrowed. A vein pulsed in his forehead.

"Is there anything I haven't asked you that you think I should know?"

His eyes held mine for a long moment.

"Something you may have seen?"

He shifted in his seat, grimaced, as if something had suddenly begun to trouble him.

"C'mon," I said, "talk to me."

"I'm thinking, I'm thinking," he said, suddenly talking faster than an auctioneer.

"Think harder," I said.

Clark rubbed the back of his neck, picked up the joint again and inhaled some more smoke. One toke over the line, sweet Jesus.

"Well . . . I do recall one thing," he said finally.

"Something you saw?"

"No. Something I heard."

"Something you heard. What'd you hear?

"He . . . a . . . he . . . a . . . said . . . "

"Who said? Teddy?"

"No, no. Not the kid. The shooter."

"What'd he say?"

"He . . . a . . . "

"What? Tell me."

"He . . . "

Clark leaned forward, uncomfortably, as if he were experiencing an internal pain.

"What?" I said. "What? Say it."

"Before he shot the kid he yelled, 'hey, you queer-ass bitch.' Said it loud and clear."

I straightened up in my seat and said, "Did you tell this to the detectives?"

"No." he said, his knees fanning back and forth like bat wings.

"Why?

"Because the cops were nasty bastards. They busted my chops, talked down to me as if I had done something wrong."

"Cops do that sometimes."

He looked at me nervously.

"You won't say anything to them, will ya?" he said.

"Hey, I'm a guy who even keeps his mouth shut in the dentist chair."

"Did I do wrong?" he said, his tone wary. "Didn't seem to upset me before but now it kind of bothers me."

I put my hand on his shoulder.

"You didn't do anything wrong," I said. "What we talked about here is between you and me. Understand?"

His mouth compressed into a narrow line.

"Yes," he said. "I understand."

I squeezed his shoulder.

"You did good, kid," I said. "Thanks."

"No," he said. "Thank you."

"For?"

"Easing my conscience a little."

I took a card out and gave it to him.

"If you think of anything else, call me," I said.

He took the card and studied it. It wasn't anything fancy. Just my name and phone number. There were days when I thought about putting a .44 Magnum on it along with a slogan like "Have Gun—Will Travel." Or even "World's Badass Detective." But that'd be corny. Simple is always better.

I stood and grabbed a dart off the board. Aimed it. Fired. Thwack. Bullseye.

"Nice shot," Clark said, raising his hands like a referee signaling a touchdown. "I never saw anybody do that before."

"Probably never saw a guy like me before, either."

"No shit."

I saluted him.

"Enjoy Eilish," I said, walking out the door.

CHAPTER
FOUR

Infernos was located on Manhattan's Upper East Side, not far from the Fifty-Ninth Street Bridge.

A cheesy, boxy looking joint, it had framed pictures of bikinied young women with manufactured bodies decorating the dirty cement exterior. Above the pictures was a large neon sign that said, "Open Until It Closes. Couples Welcome."

I knew from experience that at night the place attracted lots of Wall Street and crypto knuckleheads who thought nothing of splurging on thousand-dollar bottles of watered-down Cristal. Last of the big-time spenders.

Even though it was early afternoon, the place was packed. Rock music boomed, pounded, exploded. Lights flashed. On an elevated stage, a topless brunette with extraordinarily large real ones danced under a red spotlight. The standard bump and grind.

Sitting around the stage lusting after the dancer were a dozen guys of all ages and sizes. They had baby faces, wrinkled faces, lopsided faces. Some had shaved heads, Fu Manchus, or Duck Dynasty beards. A few wore expensive three-piece suits; others sported T-shirts and leather vests. All were guzzling bottles of beer.

One guy with a schnozz like a proboscis monkey was putting dollar bills in the stripper's G-string. She rewarded him by gently swaying her breasts in his face. Grinning like an idiot, his head went back and forth like a windshield wiper.

I took a seat at the bar and a well-endowed almost topless bartender approached. She was young, maybe late twenties, but her eyes looked older. She had fake eyelashes, a symphony of teased blond hair, and colorful tattoos of butterflies that covered her arms and neck.

"What can I get you?" she said in a sexy, sassy voice that sounded like Mariah Carey.

"Got any Guinness?"

"Nope."

"How about Smithwick's?"

She gave me a cockeyed look.

"You got be kidding me," she said.

"Just a bit," I said. "What do you have?"

"Bud and Bud Light."

"Hmmm," I said. "So many choices. Guess I'll go with a Bud."

"Good call."

She popped the cap off a brown beer bottle and placed it on top of a square cardboard coaster.

"Want a glass?" she said.

"Real men don't use glasses."

Her mouth twisted into a faint smile.

"Neither do fake ones," she said.

I grabbed the bottle. It was ice cold. Water dripped down the sides.

"Nice tattoos," I said.

"Got more of them than I do friends."

"Why butterflies?"

"Symbolizes change."

"What would you like to change?"

"My fucking life."

"Anything's possible."

"Not if I keep working in this shithole."

I took a sip of beer.

"You a cop?" she said, squinting.

"I look like one?"

"Yeah. You do."

"Most people mistake me for an actor."

"Which one?"

"Tom Cruise."

She threw her head back and laughed.

"I take it you don't see the resemblance," I said.

"Not really. You look more like Drake."

"Too bad I can't sing like him."

"Few people can."

I nodded. Despite having musical parents, my singing is so bad Monique says I should start a support group for people are as tone deaf as me.

I said, "Is the manager here?"

"Sure is."

"What's his name?"

"Joe Toomey."

"Where can I find him?"

She pointed to a thirty-something bodybuilder type sitting on the other side of the bar. He was wearing a black tee with a picture of Jelly Roll. Old Jelly's done alright for himself, I thought, considering he has been arrested forty times for drug possession, drug dealing, shoplifting, and aggravated robbery. Now he's a big rock star. Only in America. Land of opportunity.

"Thanks," I said, tossing ten bucks on the bar.

"You're welcome, Maverick," she said, flashing a toothy smile as big as a Mercedes grill.

I grabbed a bar stool next to Joe. He was sipping a Bud Light.

"Excuse me," I said. "Got a minute?"

He turned. A suspicious look.

"For what and for whom?" His Brooklyn accent made King Charles sound like Andrew Dice Clay.

"I'm a private investigator."

"Good for you. Didn't catch the name."

"Didn't throw it."

"Ain't cha got one?"

"Doesn't everybody?"

"Yeah. What's yours?"

"O'Brien. Elgin O'Brien."

"The basketball player?"

"Formerly."

"You here to investigate what girls have fake boobs?" He smiled.

"No. I'm here to talk about the murder of Teddy Malone." He stopped smiling.

Toomey had dark skin and thick, black bangs like Moe of The Three Stooges. His hands were gnarled and his nose crooked. Probably broke it breaking up fights.

He said, "Got some ID?"

I took the license from my wallet and gave it to him.

He glanced at it, then glanced at me.

"Doesn't much look like you," he said.

"Wasn't wearing any makeup that day."

He nodded and handed back the license.

"Guess you really are a private investigator," he said.

"Thanks for reminding me. Sometimes I need reassurance."

He shook his head. When he did, his lower jaw shook from side to side.

"Look, man," he said, "I don't know squat."

"Were you here the night of the shooting?"

"I was."

"Anything unusual happen that night?"

"The usual shit," he said. "Jerky young Wall Street types getting out of hand, trying to pinch the girls."

"Just another night in the salt mines, huh?"

"Salt mines, shit. More like a swamp."

He took a sip of his drink, making a small sucking sound.

I said, "You remember seeing the three basketball players?"

"I do."

"Why?"

"Why what?"

"What made them stand out?"

"They were so young looking I had to card them."

"Were they drinking a lot?"

"No more than anyone else."

"Meaning?"

"They were totally shit-faced."

"They cause any problems?"

"The one kid did."

"Which one?"

"The one who got shot."

"Enlighten me."

Joe's attention got diverted. He looked over at the stage where a six-foot blond with humongous breasts was now spinning around a pole. There were table thumps, claps, cheers, whistles, yells. One guy who had teeth like Bugs Bunny screamed, "I'll pay you whatever you want for a blow job."

"I don't eat baby food," the stripper responded.

The guys around the stage stomped their feet and howled.

Joe shook his head and returned his attention to me. "What was I saying?"

"You said the kid, Teddy Malone, caused a problem."

"Yeah, yeah," he said, snapping his fingers. "He got into a beef with some dude in the bathroom."

"Over?"

"Who the fuck knows?" he said. "Probably had to do with one of the girls or drugs. That's what most of these fights are about. Anyway, I heard the shouting, went into the bathroom, and broke the two of them up."

"Can you describe the guy?"

"What guy?"

"The one arguing with Malone."

"Dude was tall."

"So am I," I said. I'm six six, two-thirty. And still capable of dunking the rock. Some days.

I said, "Was there anything else distinctive about him?"

He tapped a fingernail against his glass and said, "He was built, broad-shouldered."

"Young? Old?"

"From the little I saw of his face, I'd say thirties, maybe early forties."

"Black? White? Asian? Hispanic?"

"White."

"Hair color?"

"Don't know. He was wearing a hoodie."

"Eyes?"

"He had two."

"Very funny. What color?"

He thought a moment. "A . . . a . . . I'd say dark."

"Any unusual facial characteristics?"

"Like?"

"A scar. Nose size. Lips. Beard. A cleft chin."

"Not that I recall."

"Think you'd recognize him if you ever saw him again?"

"I doubt it."

"How about his voice?"

"His voice?"

"Did you speak to him? Did he have an accent?"

"No."

"No what?"

"He didn't have an accent."

"So . . . you did speak to him?"

"I guess so."

"Did you or didn't you?"

"We exchanged a few words."

His brow creased into a large V. He finished his beer.

"His voice was clogged . . . like, like he had a throat full of phlegm."

I made a mental note.

"Anything else you can tell me?"

Joe ran a hand through his bowl cut.

"Come to think of it," he said, "There was."

"Was what?"

"Something."

"Let's hear it."

"The guy had something on the back of his right hand."

"What? Like a birthmark? A mole?"

"No, man, not a mark. Art. Some ink. A tat, you know, a tattoo."

"Of what? What did it look like?"

"It looked like a basketball."

CHAPTER
FIVE

I left Infernos, got the Mustang, and headed toward St. Stephen's University. Driving along Third Avenue and Eighty-Fourth, I passed Regis High School, a private, all-male Jesuit secondary school for Roman Catholic boys. It was my alma mater, the place where I first confronted racism. Where I was called "Vanilla Fudge."

The teasing at times was malicious but never hateful. It would have been considerably worse had I not been the team's star basketball player. That designation gave me, for the most part, a free pass.

I had a history teacher, Mr. Johnson, who, like me, was also biracial. We spoke often. He helped me come to grips with my Blackness. He told me, like my parents did, to have pride in my heritage. To stand up for myself. To never let the opinions of others torpedo my self-respect. Don't be fooled, he said, thinking that because you're a revered athlete you're immunized against the prejudice and racism that is often hidden beneath the surface.

He talked a lot about the burden of the Black man in history and how they once lived under the shadow of terrorism and the noose. He also talked about White history and how the Irish endured vehement discrimination when arriving in America in the 1900s. Your history, he'd say to me, *your history*, is embedded in both cultures. Learn about it. Cherish it. Open your eyes to what was and what is and make something good of it.

Mr. Johnson was as much as mentor to me as Socrates was to Plato.

Traffic along Third Avenue was at a standstill, so I turned onto the FDR Drive and soon got onto the Grand Central Parkway. I exited at Union Turnpike, gliding through the village of Forest Hills, Queens, an affluent residential neighborhood housing very wealthy doctors, lawyers, stockbrokers but probably few, if any, butchers, bakers, and candlestick makers.

Most of the homes were magnificent English Tudors, oversized and more than a little garish. They all had perfectly manicured lawns, dogwood trees, and polished expensive automobiles out front. Jaguars, Mercedes, even a few Lamborghinis. It could have been the setting for the next *Housewives* reality show.

As I neared the campus, I grabbed my cell phone and called a former Mavericks teammate, Jamal Roundtree. Jamal was now the club's general manager.

"Hey, Elg, whaddya hear, whaddya say," he said. He had a voice deeper than James Earl Jones.

"I say it's all crazy on the eastern front."

"Still saving damsels in distress?"

"Only on Sundays," I said. "The rest of the week I slay dragons."

"Lots of dragons in the Big Apple."

"To say the least."

"Still amazed you're a detective."

"What can I tell ya," I said. "O'Brien's the name, crime's the game."

After some more silly chitchat, Jamel said, "What can I do for you?"

"Ever scout a player from St. Stephen's by the name of Teddy Malone?"

"The kid who was murdered?"

"Yep."

"Scouted him a few times."

"A prospect?"

"I thought so."

"Thought so?"

"Early last season I thought in another year he could be a second-round pick, maybe even a late first. He had a game like J. J. Redick. A long-range shooter."

"What changed?"

"His game changed. Toward the end of the season, he stopped playing with intensity. He seemed sluggish. He missed wide-open J's. Committed too many turnovers. He played almost zero defense. Had bad games in the NCAA tourney. Almost looked as if he was shaving points."

"That bad, huh?"

"Oh, yeah. Prospect to suspect. It happens."

"Yes, it does. More often than fans think."

"Tell me," Jamal said, "what's your interest in Malone?"

"His father hired me to find his killer."

"Any leads?"

"None so far."

"I have faith you'll uncover some."

"Your words to God's ears," I said. "How's the team look for next season?"

"Need more support for Kyrie."

"Irving's a talent."

"Help is on the way," he said. "Just signed a big kid from Africa named Zareb."

"Zareb, huh? Means guardian."

"How in the name of Zion Williamson would you know that?"

"I read a lot."

"About Africans?"

"J. M. Coetzee is one of my favorite authors."

"Never heard of him."

"He's from South Africa.

"A brother, huh?"

"Nope. Whiter than a marshmallow."

"Guess he ain't Kunta Kinte."

"Far from it," I said. "But, hey, if Zareb he doesn't work out, I could always make a comeback."

"We're not that desperate."

"I can still bury the three."

"In your dreams."

"Thanks, Jamal. Be good."

"Do I have a choice?"

As I neared the St. Stephen's campus, I saw all the places that typically surround a university: used bookstores, discount clothing stores, ice cream parlors, grocery stores, liquor stores, sub joints, pizza parlors, laundromats, a Staples, and a host of pubs. Everything to keep students fortified.

The campus itself wasn't very impressive. Dull, gray-stoned buildings. No tall chapel or big rotunda. No ivy-covered towers. No quads. It kind of reminded me of a small prison. The only things missing were razor wire and bars on the windows.

I parked the car and walked around campus. Students were casually dressed in shorts, tees, and flip-flops. Some were tossing Frisbees. Others were sitting under trees reading, sleeping, or listening to music. There might be a lot of craziness in the world, but show me someone who has a negative thing to say about college and I'll show you a total nitwit.

I strolled past the library. It was small, the student union building even smaller. The only impressive building on campus was the basketball arena.

It was shaped like an airplane hangar. From what I knew, it sat over ten thousand. Every game was SRO, thanks to all the kids who mostly came to St. Stephen's to party and root, root, root for the home team.

Looking at the arena brought back memories of Duke's Cameron Indoor Stadium, college basketball's equivalent of Boston's Fenway Park. For me, playing there was totally exhilarating. Still in use today, it's one of the last gyms in college basketball where the crowd feels as if it's sitting in your lap.

Aside from honing my basketball skills, Duke is where I learned to learn. To study. Though I read a lot at Regis—Hemingway, Fitzgerald, Cheever—it was my Duke professors who introduced me to authors I had never really read before: Albert Camus, James Joyce, Leo Tolstoy. I devoured their books like potato chips. I think I'm the only player in the history of college basketball ever to be suspended for missing practice to go to class.

When I got to the pros, I had plenty of time to continue my education. Instead of playing cards or playing around, I mostly read novels on planes and watched old movies in hotel rooms. I'd like to think I still learn something new every day.

Monique says the only thing I love as much as books and movies is jazz. She says the ultimate pleasure for me would be if I could do all three at one time. I guess that's why when we go to the movies, she won't let me bring books or earplugs.

I entered the gym. The court and the backboards shined. The seats were heavily padded, the overhead scoreboard huge. Hanging from the ceiling were a half dozen championship banners.

I've loved walking into basketball arenas ever since I was a kid. I rooted for the New York Knicks, just like my dad, who used to take me to games at Madison Square Garden. Back in the day his favorite coach had been "Red" Holzman and his favorite player Bill Bradley. He never stopped talking about "Dollar Bill," as he called him. After he died my mother gave me a copy of his favorite book, a biography of Bradley called *A Sense of Where You Are* by John McPhee. He'd read it so often the pages were faded and loose.

A graduate of Princeton and Oxford, Bradley was as much a scholar as a basketball player. He wasn't fast or quick, but he knew how to move without the ball and get open for jump shots. His form was textbook, the squaring of the shoulders, the perfect follow-through. He was what coaches called an "overachiever." A workhorse rather than a racehorse. The greatest compliment I ever received was when Phil Jackson, who'd been Bradley's New York Knicks teammate, once told me "You play a lot like Bill."

The head basketball coach at St. Stephen's, Chris Corsito, was less like the cool and collected Holzman and more like the volatile former coach at the University of Indiana, Bobby Knight. Renowned for temper tantrums, violent tirades, crude insults, tossing towels at referees, and slapping players, Corsito was a volcano with legs. He could explode at any moment.

Chris played his college ball at the University of Carolina, the same years I played at Duke. We were bitter rivals. Got into more than a few fights. I believe I won most of them.

A point guard, only five-eleven, Chris was a tough competitor who had a reputation as a cheap-shot artist. He committed more flagrant fouls than any player in Atlantic Coast Conference history. He was booed regularly. Long time ACC fans who have watched games from infancy claim Corsito was hated even more than Duke's Christian Laettner. Trust me, that's saying a lot.

He barely played one year in the NBA because he was too slow and too small for the pro game, even with his bag of dirty tricks. After getting cut, he went into college coaching, moving quickly from Division II schools to big-time programs, first at DePaul and then Providence. His focus and intensity on the court made a laser beam look like a night-light. His eyes x-rayed the court. He was a player whisperer, a sherpa leading his climbers to the top of Mount Everest. His teams were famous for playing tenacious defense and preci-sion offense. They always made it to the NCAA tournament. Ten years ago, Corsito became the head coach at his alma mater and led the university to two NCAA championships.

He probably would have stayed at Carolina forever had not TMZ done a couple of exposes on his questionable recruiting practices, including outright monetary payments to recruits and the use of prostitutes to seduce them. The NCAA, as weak an organization as the US Congress, investi-gated him and typical of their ineptitude, put the school on probation and let Corsito skate.

Had any other coach broken the rules as many times as Corsito, the writing would have been on the locker room wall: You're fired.

But Corsito, like members of the Supreme Court, has never been truly held accountable.

The story goes, whether it's true or not, that after learning of an investigation into the basketball program, Corsito summoned his players to the locker room. Misty-eyed and putting on a woe-is-me act, he told them, "I've got good news and bad news. The bad news is the school's been put on notice." He then flashed a big smile and said, "The good news is I won't be coaching here next year. St. Stephen's just hired me." A beat. "For a helluva lot more money."

A columnist for the New York *Daily News* nicknamed Corsito "Cor-Cheato," writing that "as long as he wins and makes his college big money it really doesn't matter what offenses he commits. It's as if he's made of Teflon. He rules less like a coach and more like an emperor."

Lately, Corsito had been on ESPN railing about his contract. He's annoyed because University of Kansas coach

Bill Self recently signed a lifetime contract of $53 million over the first five years. Corsito maintains that he's worth just as much, if not more, than Self. He says that aside from him being a better coach than Billionaire Bill, the job has gotten more demanding thanks to the transfer portal, crazy conference realignment, and name, image and likeness (NIL), a term that describes the means through which college players are allowed to receive financial compensation in return for the use of their name, image, and likeness from marketing and promotional endeavors. Bluntly put, it's just a way to bribe a player to play for your school.

Being far less than subtle, Corsito has suggested he will leave St. Stephen's if his demand for a bigger contract isn't met. The grapevine has it that booster gazillionaires are already pooling their wallets to placate him and his players. The joke is that when a St. Steve's player turns pro, they take a pay cut. Only in college athletics can such irrational amounts of money be paid out. Ridiculous.

Understand, I love basketball. Love the feel of the ball, the sound of a swish, the movement and choreography. And, for sure, I really loved playing at Duke. But college basketball, the way it is today? Can't say I like it much anymore. Too many egos, too much hypocrisy, too much money. Sad. Really sad.

Corsito's office was located above the basketball court. When I entered it, a young, busty, and attractive secretary was sitting behind a desk typing. She had hair the color of honey and eyes greener than shamrocks. A saddle of freckles that looked like tiny coffee beans bridged her nose.

"Can I help you?" she said, smiling and chewing gum at the same time.

"Yes, you may," I said. "I'm here to see Coach Corsito."

"Is Coach expecting you?" She had the enthusiastic voice of an ex-cheerleader.

"Only if he's psychic," I said.

She smiled. Her teeth were large and bright white.

"Who should I say is calling?" she said.

"Elgin O'Brien."

She squinted.

"Have I heard of you?" she said.

"Who hasn't?"

She raised her right hand. A jangle of gold bracelets on her wrist made a tinkling sound. "Are you a coach?"

"Heaven forbid."

She scratched her cheek. Her long fingernails were painted pink. I don't think she could type with them, but I don't think she had to. She was purely a decoration. Eye candy for the players.

"Then where would I know you from?" she said.

"I was once the centerfold for *Playgirl* magazine?"

Her mouth dropped open, framing a wad of gum atop her pink tongue.

"I've heard of that magazine," she said. "Were you really the centerfold?"

"Actually, it was for *Psychology Today*."

She giggled and said, "Let me see if Coach is available."

"Thank you," I said. "By the way, what's your name?"

"Anne."

"Of a Thousand Days."

She looked puzzled. Her eyebrows fluttered like lunar moths.

"Don't mind me," I said. "I tend to amuse myself."

She blew a small pink bubble, popped it with her teeth, and chewed it back into her mouth. She then pointed to a chair.

"Please," she said, "take a seat."

I did.

She picked up the receiver and tapped a button on her telephone.

"There's a Mr. O'Brien here to see you, Coach," she said.

She listened for a minute, cracking her gum.

"Yes," she added, "his first name is Elgin."

She nodded, chuckled and said, "No, he isn't being obnoxious." A beat. "Okay, I'll tell him."

She hung up the phone.

"Coach said he'll be with you shortly," she said.

I took a seat. On a table next to me was the team's media guide. A smiling Corsito was on the cover, holding a basketball outside Madison Square Garden.

I flipped through the pages. The guide was slicker than *Vanity Fair* magazine. Great paper stock, colorful pictures, and key statistics. Many, many photos of Corsito, along with a long bio. He was born in Milwaukee, Wisconsin, before his family moved east. Was married to the same woman since college. They had two sons. Neither went into coaching. It wasn't in the guide, but I knew one of them had OD'd. Opiates.

I read some player profiles. Specifically, Teddy Malone's. He'd been an All-American high school player at Archbishop Molloy, a basketball powerhouse located in Briarwood, Queens. He once dropped fifty points against All Hallows High School in Madison Square Garden. Impressive.

I looked at my watch. Twenty minutes passed. I knew Corsito was making me wait. That was his MO—to play games. As if he was God and I was sitting twiddling my thumbs in His waiting room.

I glanced out the window. A group of young women were playing three-on-three basketball. That made me smile. Back in my day women's basketball was no big deal. Now thanks to WNBA stars like Brittney Griner, Sue Bird, Diana Taurasi, Candance Parker, and Caitlin Clark it is. The league is currently drawing sellout crowds and large TV ratings. It's about time.

The only thing left for women athletes is to be viewed and treated equal to men—in terms of endorsements and especially pay. For example, the average NBA salary is $7.5 million a year, while the average WNBA salary is under $150,000. Disgraceful. Unfair.

And, if you ask me, the WNBA is a heck of a lot more enjoyable to watch than the NBA. The NBA has become a three-point orgy. Run-and-gun. No defense. Too much one-on-one. Booooring!

A buzzer sounded. Anne picked up her phone and said "Okay" then hung up.

"You may enter," she said.

"The tabernacle?"

She grinned, stood, and walked around her desk, giving off a strong aroma of sweet vanilla. She wore a skintight button-down white shirt and a maroon leather skirt that barely covered her rear. I made sure to look away. She put her hand on the doorknob and said, "We call it the throne room."

"Funny," I said, "that's what I call my bathroom."

She laughed out loud. Am I a riot or what?

I strolled into Corsito's office. It was the size of a tennis court. There were big casement windows, thick wool carpeting, long velvet drapes, three walnut cabinets, a kitch-enette, a private bathroom, and a teak conference table with enough soft swivel black leather chairs to accommodate an entire basketball team. I'd bet even Elon Musk doesn't have an office this plush.

"Holy shit," Corsito howled, sitting in a throne-like chair behind a walnut desk the size of a roadside billboard. "Look what the fucking cat dragged in."

I did a quick tap step, finishing on one knee, my arms spread out and extended toward him.

"No need to genuflect," Corsito said, leaning back in his chair and clasping his hands behind his head. He was wearing a bright white short-sleeve polo shirt with a blue Nike swoosh. "A simple salute would suffice."

I scratched my nose with my middle finger, then took a seat across from his desk.

"I must say," Corsito said, in his usual disagreeable gruffness, "this is quite the unpleasant surprise."

"I aim to displease."

Corsito smirked. A heavyset man, he had a large head, the protruding forehead of a pit bull, and a face with the sheen of a glazed ham.

"You know, Elgin," he said, unlacing his hands and putting them on the desk. "I'll never understand why your father named you after such a great player like Baylor."

"He knew talent when he saw it."

Corsito hissed like a tire going flat.

"Talent, my balls," he said.

"Remind me again," I said. "How many years did you play in the NBA?"

"I preferred coaching," he snapped.

"Because you couldn't play. At least not at the highest level."

"Whaddya want?" he said, putting his right hand up to his face so I'd be sure to notice his NCAA championship ring.

"Unlike most people," I said. "I wanna talk to you."

"Hardy fucking har har."

I looked at the office walls. On one wall was a big-screen television with a DVD player and dozens of DVDs beneath it. On another were framed photos of Corsito smiling alongside athletes and celebrities. LeBron James, Walt Frazier, Spike Lee, Jack Nicholson, Jon Bon Jovi, Rudy Giuliani, and Andrew Cuomo.

I said, "Actually, I just wanted to stop by and admire your pictures. I'm surprised you don't have one with God."

"Why would I? Here, I am God." For most people that'd be a joke. For Corsito, it's what he believed.

"Know what I think?" he said.

"Not really but go ahead."

"I think you're jealous of my success. Not to mention my salary."

"Let's just say I'd prefer to lose with dignity than win by cheating."

Corsito's face swelled and he pulled back on his neck like a cobra just before it struck.

"I don't cheat!" he shouted.

"Yeah. And neither does Donald Trump."

"Don't knock Trump," he said. "He's a man who does whatever it takes."

"To do what? Hurt people?"

"I'm a true Republican," he said. "I never vote Democrat. How stupid do you think I am?"

"Very."

Before he could respond there was a knock on the door.

"Come in," Corsito yelled.

The door opened and in walked two guys, one short, the other tall. The short one I knew. It was Corsito's longtime assistant coach and chief recruiter, Dave Hunter. Wearing a pair of white basketball shorts and a blue-and-gold St. Stephen's T-shirt, Dave was a handsome, lean man with curly brown hair and big wide eyes, befitting someone always on the look for young talent.

Dave, like Corsito, was in his early forties. A former teammate of Chris's at UNC, he mostly played when games were out of reach. I'd always thought he was an easygoing nice guy, apart from the fact that he sucked up to Corsito so much he often needed his tongue recoated.

"Hey, Elgin," he said, charm oozing out of him like jelly from a donut. "Long time no see, buddy. How you been?"

"Been a rockin' and rollin', a movin' and a groovin'," I said. "You look good, Dave."

"Thanks," he said, after taking a cherry lifesaver from a roll and popping into his mouth. "What've you been up to?"

"Working hard, trying to make a living. How about you?"

"Beating the bushes."

"Recruiting players?"

His smile was brighter than a prison searchlight. "Uh-huh."

"You always get the best ones."

"In my own way," he said, exuding so much energy he damn near gave off sparks.

He smiled, then added, "I see Monique's back on Broadway."

"Sure is."

"She's quite the talent."

"That's for certain," I said. "How's Marie?" Marie was his wife. Thanks to her husband's success, she received a lot of publicity and lucrative perks. Gilt by association.

His face brightened. He sucked on his lifesaver.

"She's great," Hunter said. "Living large. Being wined and dined by fans and alumni. Interviewed on TV. Spending money as fast as I can make it."

"Must be nice being the wife of a celebrity coach."

Dave smiled, then turned to the tall fellow next to him and said to me, "Pardon my bad manners. This is Steve Smith. Our conditioning coach."

Smith was younger, probably early thirties. Tall, maybe six five, with short oily black hair, he had a chest larger than a beer barrel and biceps the size of footballs. I looked at him and thought "steroids."

Wearing tight Bermuda shorts, a tight white tank top, and fingerless gloves, he strolled toward me in a tilting walk associated with gorillas.

"Nice to meet you," he said, his voice sounding as if congested.

"Likewise," I said.

We shook hands. His grip was so strong he damn near broke my fingers.

Corsito interrupted the conversation.

"I hate to break up this goody-goody-getting-to-know-you crap," he said. "But I have a lot of shit to do."

I looked at Smith and rolled my eyes. Smith stared back at me, his smile flickering on and off like a faulty lightbulb.

Corsito looked at Hunter. Hunter looked at Corsito. Baffling couple, I thought. On the surface, they seemed to go together like horseradish and jelly.

"What's up, Dave?" he said.

"Just wanted to remind you I'm leaving for the Memorial Weekend basketball camp tomorrow," he said, bowing his head slightly and looking at Corsito like a servant about to hand the master his slippers.

"The one in the Poconos?"

"Yeah."

"Okay," Corsito said. "Have fun. Find a nice twelve-year-old with a sweet jumper who's about to have a growth spurt and will do anything to play for old St. Steve's ."

Hunter laughed.

"I always do," he said. "Always do."

Dave shook my hand. His fingers were sweaty.

"Take care, Elg," he said.

"You, too," I said.

Smith also shook my hand. Harder even than the first time.

"Pleasure meeting you," he said.

"Same here," I said.

Both men left.

"Dave looks in good shape," I said.

"Best college recruiter in the country," Corsito said. "The players love him. He builds relationships, starts recruiting kids when they're young. That why he still does the kiddie camps."

"What's the story with Smith?"

"Top-notch conditioning coach."

"Where'd he'd come from?"

"Rutgers."

I angled my head and glanced down at the floor.

"Wasn't he involved in a scandal there a few years ago?" I said.

"Ah, that was nothing."

"If I recall it was a lot more than nothing," I said. "Didn't it have to do with him dispensing performance-enhancing drugs?"

"He was never charged."

"But was fired, correct?"

Corsito didn't answer. He just drummed his fingers on the edge of his desk and said, "So why are you here? Whaddya want?"

"Information on Teddy Malone."

"Why?"

"His father hired me."

"To do what?"

"Take a guess."

"Why the fuck would he hire you?"

"He wanted the best."

"You're still the same cocky sonofabitch you were in college."

"Serves me well in my line of work."

Corsito pulled a tiny plastic vial of Visine from his desk drawer, tilted his head back, and squeezed a few drops into his eyes. When he straightened his head, a stream of eyewash rolled down his cheeks.

I said, "Have vision problems?"

"My eyes get scratchy."

"Probably from reading all the NCAA investigation reports."

"Fuck you."

"Tell me about Teddy."

"Tragic, what happened," he said, wiping his cheeks with a tissue. "Very tragic."

"What do you know about it?"

"Only what I read in the papers."

"That's it, huh?"

"That's it," he said, grabbing a rubber band, stretching it between his fingers, then firing it into a trash can.

"You know, Chris . . . "

"Whoa, whoa, whoa," he said, putting up his hand like a cop stopping traffic. "I'd prefer it if you'd call me Coach."

I had to laugh. I love it how coaches think being called "Coach" bestows on them a sacred address, like calling a man of the cloth "Father."

"You know, Chris," I continued, "there's two types of people. Those who reveal and those who conceal."

He lifted his bright white Nike sneakers and placed them on the corner of his desk. "I don't conceal."

"Bullshit. You conceal a lot. And someday you'll be found out."

He turned over his hands like a man showing he had nothing to hide.

I said, "You talk to the police?"

"Of course."

"And?"

"And nothing."

"What kind of kid was he?"

"Who? Teddy?"

"No, Doogie Howser. Yes. Of course, Teddy."

"Good kid. Good student. Good player."

"Easy to coach?"

"A breeze."

"How was he playing?"

"Playing great. Getting better, like they all do when I get them."

"That's funny. I just spoke to an NBA general manager who said Teddy ended the season not playing very well."

Corsito's lips curled into a feral snarl.

"Fucking NBA GMs see a player once and if he has a bad game they write the kid off," he said.

"This GM saw Teddy play a couple of times."

"Then he's either fucking blind or stupid. Teddy was playing just fine."

"How was your relationship with him?"

"Excellent."

"No problems?"

Corsito shifted his sneakers on the desk and wiggled his big butt deeper into the chair. "None. Zero."

"Teddy ever been in trouble?"

"Trouble?"

"Altercations? Drinking? Drugs? Gambling? Girls?"

Corsito reacted like he always did when he didn't like a question. He attacked.

"That's an idiotic question," he said, his voice full of contempt. "What are you suggesting?"

"I'm not suggesting anything," I said. "It's a simple question that requires nothing more than a yes or no."

"No!"

"No what?" I said.

"My players don't do drugs or gamble."

"Right. And politicians don't lie."

Daggers danced in his irises. Looking at them, I thought: Wouldn't it be nice if, somehow, coaches could separate themselves from the lying and the cheating and become more honorable again, more concerned with doing things that elevate the integrity of their sport rather than themselves.

I said, "Aside from having the worst graduation rate of any coach in the country, you've had more players arrested for DUI's, sexual assaults, and drug use than anyone else. So don't give me this innocent shit."

"Yeah, okay," he said, studying his manicured fingernails. "Whatever."

"Don't whatever me," I said. "I'm not one of your players."

"Screw you, Elgin," he said, spitting my name out as if it was an obscenity.

"Just answer my question," I said. "Did Teddy Malone have any issues?"

"Not that I know of."

"Or that you don't wish to acknowledge?"

Corsito made a snuffling sound, like a pig searching for a truffle.

"This conversation is over," he said.

"One more thing."

"We're done here."

"When I say one more thing . . . I mean one more thing."

Corsito pointed toward the door. I fought the urge to toss him out the window and shake him until his teeth fell out.. The thought gave me momentary pleasure. But his fans would probably put a bounty on my head

"Get the hell outta here," he said.

"I told you. I'm not done yet."

"For God's sake . . . what's the other thing."

"Where can I find Bobby Rose and Amare Anderson?"

His black eyes had the look of a moray eel whose lair had been invaded.

"What do you want with them?" he said.

"They were witnesses to Teddy's murder."

"I've talked to them and so have the police. They have little or nothing to say."

"Let me be the judge of that."

"I don't like the idea of you bothering them."

"I'm not going to bother them. I just have some questions."

"Please remember these players have been traumatized. Don't bust their balls."

"I'll leave that to you."

Corsito hit a button on his desk phone and spoke into an intercom.

"Anne," he said. "Call Bobby and Amare and tell them that a . . . a cop named Elgin O'Brien is going to stop by their dorm to talk with them." He then clicked off.

"I'm not a cop," I said.

"Oh, I forgot," he said, smugly. "You're a . . . a what? Oh yeah. A private dick."

"As opposed to you, who's a public one."

"You make any money fighting windmills?" he said.

"Is that a reference to *Don Quixote*?"

"Who?" Could he really be that dumb?

"He used to play for Clemson," I said.

"Don't remember him."

"He shared the backcourt with Sancho Panza."

"What was he? A spic?"

"No, he was Jewish," I snarled. "Of course, he was Spanish, you dickhead."

"I don't care who the cocksucker was," he said. "If I don't remember him, he couldn't have been that good."

"You're still the same moron you were in college."

"What? You expect me to change?"

"Not really . . . though a cockroach can metamorphose."

He smirked, flexed his shoulders, dropping one and lifting the other.

I stood. Corsito stood. We glared at each other like two boxers just before the bell.

"You know, Chris," I said, looking down on him, "sometimes I forget how small you really are."

"Fuck you," he said.

"Maybe you had something to do with Teddy's murder."

Corsito erupted into laughter.

"Me?" he said. "Don't be ridiculous. I'm a coach."

"I rest my case . . . Coach."

CHAPTER
SIX

Bobby Rose and Amare Anderson lived in a fancy-schmancy athletic dorm. It was a meticulously clean three-story white brick building surrounded by rose bushes, cherry trees, and redwood benches. It made a Four Seasons resort look like a flophouse.

Inside it, the hallways had plush gold carpeting, textured paneling, and crystal ceiling lights. On the walls were colorful action shots of former St. Stephen's players shooting jumpers, dribbling basketballs, and grabbing rebounds. A virtual hall of fame.

I took an elevator up to the third floor. Decorating the door of one room was a poster of Megan Thee Stallion in short shorts and a tight T-shirt. Someone had scribbled under the picture the words "I'd ride that horse any day." Somebody else had tried to erase it. It didn't work. But it was worth the effort.

I knocked on a door displaying a different poster—Steph Curry shooting a jumper from the top of the key.

A tall, White kid, thinner than a greyhound, opened the door. He had arms longer than gasoline hoses. His short hair was brown, his big eyes hazel, and he wore blue-and-gold shorts and a LeBron James T-shirt.

I introduced myself.

"Hey, man," he said, "We were expecting you. C'mon in."

The air-conditioned suite had wall-to-wall carpeting, stainless steel appliances, larger-than-normal sized beds, teak desks, a big-screen television, and some bookshelves but not many books. Music was coming from a small JBL speaker. The room would have gone for a bundle at the Ritz-Carlton.

"Bobby Rose," he said, putting up his hand.

I slapped him five.

He then pointed to a long-bodied, muscular Black guy lying in bed, flipping through SLAM magazine. Wearing flip-flops, gym shorts, and a white tank top, his shoulders were the size of watermelons and hands larger than oven mitts. Both forearms were covered with tattoos of spiderwebs.

"That lazy lump is Amare," Bobby said. "Otherwise known as Ambush."

I had read a lot about Ambush Anderson. Only a freshman, he was a six eight lean, mean scoring machine. He had already declared for the NBA draft and was expected to be a first-round pick, if not *the* first pick. The only thing that could prevent him from earning that distinction was his reputation.

Ambush grew up in Hunts Point in the South Bronx. A reputed gang member, he was seen in high school on Instagram with criminals who dealt in drugs, gambling, prostitution—the usual triad of trouble. In one reel he even waved a handgun. He'd already been nabbed in a sting operation and busted for possession of cocaine, only to have the charges dropped. Some colleges refused to recruit him. Not Corsito. He went after Ambush hard, and according to the newspapers, the alumni showered him with a host of lucrative NIL deals. Worth over three million.

"Hey Amare," I said.

Amare gave me a measured look, as if sizing me up. I noticed his yellowed eyes were slightly out of alignment, the right one higher than the left.

"Call me Ambush, man," he said, flipping a hand.

"I like your nickname," I said.

"Got it 'cause I sneak up on opponents and ambush the muthafuckers." His voice sounded like rocks coming down a chute.

"Shoot their lights out, huh?" I said.

"Bet your ass."

I pointed to the JBL speaker.

"Who we listening to?" I said, trying to be congenial.

"Shawn Mendes," Bobby said.

"Any relation to Sergio?"

"Who?" he said, totally baffled.

"He was long before your time," I said. "Headed up Brasil 66."

"Never been to Brazil," he said, nodding like an out-of-control bobblehead. "That's a . . . that's in Europe, right?"

I scratched my cheek. Ah, youth. Oscar Wilde was right. It's wasted on the young.

"Actually," I said. "It's in South America."

"You mean like Alabama?"

"More like Argentina."

Bobby turned a chair around, straddled it, and folded his arms atop the wooden frame.

"You're a cop, huh?" he said.

"A private investigator."

Bobby's eyes lit up. "Like Magnum?"

"Minus the mustache."

"I watch *Magnum* on reruns," he said. "Guy was cool. Living in Hawaii and doing all those gorgeous Hawaiian chicks."

"Not like that for me," I said. "I just walk old ladies across the mean streets of Hoboken."

"Maybe you should move to Hawaii."

"Can't surf."

"Bummer."

"The crosses we bear."

"You're tall," Bobby said. "Ever play hoops?"

"I played for the Dallas Mavericks."

"Wow. Any good?"

"Ten years in the league."

"And now you're a private investigator. Sweet."

"Sweeter than syrup."

"Gotta ask, man," Bobby said. "You pack?"

"Only lunch."

"I mean, you carry a gun?"

"Sometimes."

"You packing today?'

"I am."

"Mind if I check your piece?"

"Maybe another time."

Bobby looked disappointed.

"You ever kill anyone?" he said.

It was a ballsy question, but I thought it deserved an answer.

"No," I said.

"Why not?"

"I believe in the sanctity of life."

"Cool," he said. "I like sanctity. Like it a lot." He paused, then: "What do you wanna know?"

I glanced at Ambush.

He was silent, reading his magazine. Ignoring us.

"I wanna talk about Teddy Malone's murder," I said.

Bobby's face tightened. Ambush looked up for a quick second, then went back to reading. I got the distinct impression he wasn't entirely happy with me being there.

"Sad, man, really sad," Bobby said.

"Let me start with this," I said. "Do you know if Teddy had any enemies? Anybody he didn't get along with on or off campus?"

"Not that I'm aware of," Bobby said. "Everybody liked Teddy. He was quite popular."

I looked at Ambush.

"You agree?" I said to him.

"If Bobby says so, take it to the bank."

"Okay," I said. "Now tell me about the night of the murder."

"Not much to tell," Bobby said. "We came out of Infernos and this fucking dude, like, like, starts blasting away."

"Just at Teddy?"

"Yeah," he said, "Yeah, just at Teddy. No holes in my chest."

"Can you describe the guy?"

"He was, like, taller than me."

"How tall are you?"

"Six two."

"Was he Black or White?'

"Couldn't tell," Bobby said. "Guy wore a hoodie."

"Anything unusual about him?"

"Like?"

"His clothes. His mannerisms."

Bobby placed a finger on the side of his face.

"No, man," he said. "Nothing unusual."

"How about you, Ambush," I said. "You notice anything?"

He glanced up from the magazine. His dark eyes seemed to dilate, and an artery in his neck pulsed.

I waited a minute, allowing him a chance to respond but he didn't.

"Ambush," I said. "Did *you* notice anything?"

"No," he said quickly.

"A witness I spoke with said he heard the shooter call Teddy a 'queer-ass bitch,' " I said. "You guys hear that?"

They both looked at each other and shrugged.

"Not me," Bobby said.

"Me neither," Ambush said, flipping a page of the magazine.

That didn't jive with what Steven Clark had told me. Clark said the shooter yelled the words loud and clear.

"You sure you didn't hear anything?" I said, looking first at Bobby, then at Ambush.

Bobby shook his head. Ambush didn't respond.

"Let me ask you this?" I said, "Do either one of you know anyone with a tattoo of, say, a basketball on the back on their right hand?"

The two looked at each other as if deciding which one should answer first.

After a time, Bobby did. "I know a lot of guys with tattoos but can't say for sure I know one with a basketball tattoo."

Ambush didn't respond. I had to address him directly.

"Ambush," I said. "You know anybody with that kind of tattoo?"

He grimaced, and there came into his face a shred of guilty fear.

"Hey, man," he said, harshly, "I know more guys with more tattoos than you can shake a stick at. But I ain't in the business of studying their fucking hands. You know?"

I let a beat or two pass, then said, "Okay. Moving right along. Was Teddy into any weird shit?"

"What kind of weird shit?" Bobby said.

"Drugs? Gambling? Girls? Guys?"

The players exchanged sideways glances. Neither spoke. Neither moved.

"C'mon, fellas," I said. "Was Teddy using?"

"Using what?" Bobby said.

"Alcohol? Drugs?"

Bobby shrugged. "He smoked weed."

Ambush looked up. His eyes flared for a spilt second.

"Was he using anything else?" I said.

"Like what?" Bobby said.

"You tell me."

Ambush said, "Look, man, the guy smoked some dope. Big deal. Case closed."

There was a brief, heavy silence.

Thinking of what the Mavericks GM had told me, I said, "Teddy gamble?"

"Some," Bobby said.

Ambush glared at Bobby.

"Hey, man," he said with annoyance. "No need to get into that shit."

"It might be important," I said. "Every detail, no matter how small, is meaningful."

Another brief silence. Ambush clenched and unclenched his right hand. I knew he came from a tough place, the South Bronx, a place where showing disloyalty to a friend you could get shot. Was he protecting someone?

"Bobby," I said. "Tell me about Teddy's gambling."

"Whaddya wanna know?"

"What he bet on?"

Ambush gave Bobby the cut sign, but Bobby ignored it.

"You name it, Teddy bet on it," Bobby said. "Mostly online, I think."

"Either of you know if he used a bookie?"

"Can't answer that," Bobby said.

"How about you, Ambush," I said.

A flash of anger, his mouth twisting.

"How about me what?" he said.

"Think Teddy ever used a bookie.?"

"Don't know. Don't care." Ambush appeared to be getting more and more agitated and trying hard not to let it show. He wasn't succeeding.

"Really?" I said.

"Yeah," Ambush said, gruffy. "Really."

I looked at Bobby.

"You think Teddy bet on college basketball games?"

"I don't know, man," he said. "I just don't know."

"Where you think he got the money?" I said.

"What money?" Bobby said.

"To gamble."

Bobby shrugged.

"Got me," he said. "Maybe his old man."

"His father?"

"Yeah. He told me his old man liked to gamble, too. Poker, I think."

I wondered: Is that what Pat Malone was holding back? Did he have a gambling problem? Was he in debt to loan sharks? Had Teddy paid for the sins of his father?

"The manager at Infernos told me Teddy got into an argument there with some guy in the bathroom," I said. "What can you tell me about that?"

Bobby eyeballed Ambush. Ambush stared back, wincing, as if suddenly had a cramp.

"Don't know anything about it," Bobby said.

"Same here," Ambush added.

I said, "C'mon, guys. Are you telling me that Teddy never said anything about it to either one of you?"

They both said no in unison.

"Not a word, huh?"

Again, in unison, "Nope."

"That's hard for me to believe."

Silence. Mendes was singing something about nothing holding him back.

"Either of you think Teddy's argument might have been over a debt?" I said.

"Hey man," Ambush said, sounding annoyed. "Teddy suddenly said he had to take a leak. I don't know if the dude followed him to the head or was already there. For all I know, Teddy pissed on his shoes."

For the next thirty seconds, both players just stared at me. I almost wished I could have stared at me, too. Not having that choice, I stared back at them.

"Is there anything you can think of that might be pertinent to my investigation?" I said. "Anything out of the ordinary. Was Teddy tense? Fearful? Acting strange?"

They both shook their heads.

"How was his relationship with Coach Corsito?" I said.

"It used to be good," Bobby said.

"Used to be?" I said.

"They had a falling out," Bobby said.

"Over?"

"Coach thought he wasn't hustling,"

"Was he?"

"Was he what?"

"Not hustling."

"Maybe," Bobby said. "Yeah, maybe. But I didn't think it was right, Coach calling him 'faggot' and throwing balls at him."

I cringed. I thought of a former teammate of mine at Duke. The coach constantly yelled at him. Embarrassed him. Called him weak and lazy, even a pussy. The player lost confidence. Developed feelings of anxiety and depression. He eventually quit the team. Had a nervous breakdown. The coach could not have cared less. Pathetic.

That same coach once ridiculed me for growing my hair long and having a beard.

"Only losers have long hair and beards," he shouted. "Only goddamn losers."

"Does that include Jesus Christ?" I said.

He glared at me with disgust.

"Okay wise guy," he snarled. "Start doing laps."

He ran my ass off. But I still refused to get snipped or shaved.

"Why do you think Teddy wasn't hustling?" I said.

"I'm not sure," Bobby said. "He just wasn't putting out."

Ambush tossed aside his magazine and straightened up.

"What do you think, Ambush?"

He lifted both his hands before him, the palms turned outward, as if to ward something off, something he didn't like. Or want to face.

"About what?" he said.

"Teddy not putting out."

"No clue, man." He paused. "Maybe he just got tired of Corsito's act."

I rubbed the back of my neck. I knew from former NBA teammates who had played for Corsito that playing for him was like walking into an emotional minefield. One misstep and you were blown clear to the end of the bench.

"You guys like playing for Corsito?" I said.

"He can be tough at times," Bobby said. "But you get used to him. In a way, he's very fair."

"How so?" I said.

"He treats us all like dogs."

"Hey, man," Ambush said. "This is how it be. It's Corsito's world, and we just be playing in it."

"I'm curious," I said. "Why'd you guys chose St. Stephen's? Why not Duke, Kentucky, or Louisville?"

"Two reasons," Bobby said. "I love Coach Hunter and I like that Corsito prepares guys for the NBA."

What he really does, I thought, is take athletic livestock and fatten it up for the pros.

"Why'd you choose St. Stephen's, Amare?"

"I'm from the Bronx, man," he said. "I wanted to go to a school that was close to home so my friends and family could see me play."

"I understand you have a lot of friends," I said. "Interesting friends."

He eyeballed me suspiciously.

"Yeah? So?" he said.

"So . . . it's nice to have friends."

"Yeah, ain't it?"

"Coach told me he offered you guys, shall we say, nice inducements to attend St. Joe," I lied.

"He's takes good care of us," Bobby said.

I said, "Players who've left St. Steve's for the pros say they took a pay cut."

Bobby laughed.

Ambush said, "Bet my deal's better than them guys."

"Oh, yeah," I said. "What's your deal?"

His crooked grin made his dark face into a kind of corrupt crescent.

"Living large off NIL," he said.

"How large?" I said, even though I knew through newspaper stories that his NIL money exceeded $3.2 million. Only in college athletics could such an outrageous amount of money be paid to an eighteen-year-old.

But don't get me wrong. I think it's good college athletes can now earn money off their name and image. They deserve it. I mean, why should the coaches get all the dough?

"If you don't mind, Ambush," I said. "Can you tell me about some of your deals?"

"Let's just say Ambush be doin' solid, thanks to all these Wall Street dudes Coach Corsito hooked me up with."

"Can you give me some names."

"Names? What names?"

"Of the people you deal with?"

"I'll give you just one." He flashed a proud smile. Both his front teeth were chipped, and he was missing an eye tooth. "James Cat-a-la-no." He paused to see if I was impressed.

I was aware of Catalano from occasionally watching CNBC. A graduate of St. Stephen's, he was the CEO and co-founder of Catalano Capital, one of the world's leading investment firms with mega assets. Reputed to come from a Mafia family, Catalano was also known as Corsito's bag man.

"Guess you're in the money," I said.

"Best be believing, brother," Ambush said.

"Must be nice sharing your good fortune with family . . . and friends."

Something moved in the depths of Ambush's eyes, something sharp and cold.

"Yeah," he said. "Yeah."

Before I could ask another question, Ambush stood and stretched. His biceps rippled.

"Gonna go hit the weight room," he said.

"I just met your conditioning coach," I said.

"Good for you," Ambush said, with high sarcasm.

"Sounds like you don't like him?" I said.

"I don't."

"Why?"

"He a hard ass," Ambush said.

"How so?"

"It's his way or the highway. And Ambush Anderson don't take shit from anyone."

"You ask me," Bobby said, "he thinks he's freakin' Conor McGregor, what with all his freakin' muscles."

Ambush scanned me from head to toe and back again.

"You look in good shape," he said. "You lift?"

"Only wine glasses," I said.

They both laughed.

"Thanks, guys," I said. "Appreciate you taking the time. I'm off and running."

"To solve the mystery?" Bobby said.

"No," I said. "To eat lunch."

I shook hands with them and took the elevator down. As I was leaving the dorm, I literally bumped into a half-dozen twenty-somethings, Black and White, wearing red bandannas and sleeveless shirts. They all had tattoos on their forearms. Spiderwebs like Anderson.

"Afternoon, fellas," I said.

None of them replied. A tall, well-built White guy banged into my shoulder. Hard.

"Excuse me," I said.

"Fuck you," he said, his voice a growl.

I snickered.

The guy glared at me, his eyes shining like a wild animal, his lips parting in a malicious smile. He had long canines next to sharp incisors. They were as yellow as kernels of corn.

I took a quick glance at the back of his right hand, thinking maybe I'd see a basketball tattoo. But he moved past me so fast I didn't get a good look.

Outside, I took a seat on a bench that had an advertisement on the back that read: "STRESSED OUT? NEED HELP? CALL REGINA BLAKE AT THE SCHOOL'S COUNSELING CENTER. 516-555-1212. ALL VISITS ARE CONFIDENTIAL." I thought: Maybe I should call her. I sure as hell needed some help.

I crossed my legs and watched students hurrying to class. A few dogs romped around the grounds. Some guys were tossing a football. Campus cops were strolling the pathways. It seems to me colleges everywhere are adding more and more security. And rightly so, given all the random shootings tormenting America.

Uncrossing my legs, I thought: Something's not adding up. Why was Ambush reluctant to address Teddy's gambling? How come neither player heard the shooter calling Teddy a "queer-ass bitch"? How come they didn't know anything about the bathroom altercation? And why was it that Corsito said he and Teddy had an excellent relationship, yet Ambush and Rose said just the opposite.

Who was lying?

If I had to bet, I'd put my money on Corsito every time.

CHAPTER
SEVEN

I drove back into Manhattan and parked the car near Union Square Park. I went to Ray's Pizza and grabbed a quick slice. I love pizza. Especially when it's topped with sausage and peppers. Always sausage and peppers. Never another topping. I'm very persnickety about food.

When I finished, I phoned Pat Malone and asked him if I could stop by. He said sure.

Pat lived in Peter Cooper Village on the east side of Manhattan, a private post–World War II eighty-acre residential community squeezed between Fourteenth and Twenty-Third Streets. Some apartments are still rent controlled. It's about the only place left in Manhattan for the middle class.

Despite the blistering heat, I walked to PCV, moseying through Union Square. Runners, bikers, dogwalkers, roller skaters. Music blared. Mostly hip-hop and rock. I strolled past statues of George Washington, Marquis de Lafayette, Abraham Lincoln, and Mahatma Gandhi.

I always enjoyed looking at Gandhi holding a staff in his right hand and looking toward the horizon, as if to envision a better, more honest world. Most people remember

Mahatma for saying "an eye for an eye only ends up making the world blind." I preferred his line "A man is but a product of his thoughts. What he thinks he becomes."

Sadly, a Great Dane was now pissing on Gandhi's feet. Only in New York can the sacred and profane exist together.

I entered Peter Cooper. Lots of maple and magnolia trees. Dozens of black squirrels running around the feet of residents who sat on wooden benches, fanning themselves, reading books, or scrolling through their phones. There were joggers and bikers. A unicyclist and a guitarist. They were all sweating worse than coal stokers.

I went into the foyer of a building bordering Twenty-Third Street. The foyer had a large mirror on one side and a glass-enclosed directory on the other. I found Malone's name and pressed the button next to it. Pat answered and said, "Yes?"

"Pat. It's Elgin."

"Apartment 7C," he said. "I'll buzz you in."

The buzzer sounded. I heard the door click. I entered the building. To the right were two elevators flanking a mailbox fed by a glass chute. Above the elevators was a brass indicator that lit up the floor numbers as the elevators descended. The door opened. A heavy-set woman with a French poodle got off first, followed by a young guy dressed in tennis clothing. He was carrying an oversized Wilson racquet.

I got on the elevator and rode up to the seventh floor. The corridor was clean. Beige walls and gray carpeting. Fluorescent lighting. Behind one apartment door, I could hear a couple arguing. Behind another a dog barking.

I found 7C. The name Malone was printed in a tiny slot beneath the peephole. I rang the doorbell and waited. Heavy footsteps tapped on the floor inside. I heard a lock turn, and the door opened.

"Thanks for seeing me," I said to Pat. He was wearing khaki pants and a white button-down shirt, sleeves rolled up on his elbows.

He stood aside and ushered me into the living room. It was nicely appointed. Soft brown leather couches and chairs. Rectangular wood end tables. Colorful lithographs. Hardwood floors. The room had a strong floral scent. Maybe gardenia.

"A bit hot out," Pat said.

"And about to get even hotter."

"You believe it's not even summer yet?"

"Even the squirrels are sweating."

"According to the news, the heat index is around 103."

"You know what Yogi Berra once said. 'If it isn't the heat, it's the humility.' "

Pat grinned.

"Want something to drink?" he said.

"I'm good."

He gestured to a chair.

"Sit," he said.

I did. Pat took a seat across from me.

"Sorry my wife, Janet, isn't here," Pat said. "She went on a girls' weekend."

"Where?"

"Bermuda."

"Great place," I said. "Prettiest beaches and best chowder."

"I take it you've been there."

"Many times," I said. "My father used to get these gigs playing at the Southampton Princess."

"What'd your father play?"

"Alto sax."

"Was he good?"

"Great."

"You play?"

"Only CDs."

"Guess you preferred the sound of a basketball."

"Sure did," I said. "How's your wife handling things?"

"Not well. Ever since Teddy's . . . Teddy's death . . . she's . . . a . . . has been struggling. I'm hoping her trip will lift her spirits."

"Let's hope." I said, "I'll tell you what I've uncovered so far. One witness I spoke to told me the shooter called Teddy a 'queer-ass bitch.' "

"I hadn't heard that."

"That's because the wit never told the detectives."

Malone's eyes narrowed. "Why?"

"Said the cops were obnoxious. It happens. Cops intimidate people."

Pat lowered his head. He had a small round patch on the crown. Premature baldness.

"Any idea why someone would call Teddy that?" I said.

"Haven't the faintest," he said, looking up.

"Teddy have any enemies?"

"No. Everybody likes . . . liked Teddy. He is . . . was . . . a great kid."

"How was his relationship with Corsito?"

"Up and down. But, for the most part, good."

"I spoke with Corsito, and he said the relationship was excellent. But Bobby Rose and Ambush Anderson told me just the opposite."

"What'd they say?"

"They said the relationship had deteriorated."

"Really? I wasn't aware of that. Did they say why?"

"Just said Corsito thought Teddy wasn't hustling."

"I don't believe that," Pat said, squirming in his seat. "Teddy was a hard worker."

"You told me Teddy had been distracted before the shooting? Was it days before? Weeks before?"

"Weeks before."

"And you have no idea why?"

His eyes became shifty, just as they had that first time in my office. And I still harbored the feeling that there was something I wasn't being told. Being skeptical is a good trait for a detective. It keeps you on your toes.

"Have you told me everything?" I said.

"I have."

"You're not holding anything back, are you?"

"Not a thing."

"Were you aware of Teddy's gambling?"

His eyes widened. He looked startled, as if the question required major consideration.

"His gambling?" he said, tentatively.

"Yeah. His teammates said he liked to gamble."

"Yes . . . well . . . he . . . a . . . he did gamble a little."

"Were you giving him money?"

"On a postal worker's salary? No, he was using his NIL money."

"Was that substantial?

"Not yet. Only around twenty grand this year." He paused. "I don't get what's the big deal is. Everybody gambles a little. Don't you?"

"I only bet on myself."

I took some time before asking the next question.

"I hear you like to gamble as well?"

His left cheek twitched.

"Who told you that?" he said.

"Do you?"

"Yeah, I gamble."

"A lot?"

"Not a lot."

"What's not a lot?"

"No more than I can afford to lose." He paused and ran a hand through his hair. "What does my gambling have to do with Teddy's murder?"

"I don't know. That's why I'm asking."

Malone looked down at his shoes.

"Well, I can assure you my gambling has nothing to do with what happened," he said.

"Let me ask you," I said. "Why didn't you tell me about Teddy's gambling when we first met?"

"I didn't think it was important."

"Not important?! Are you kidding?! Everything is important."

Malone kneaded his shoulder.

"You know if Teddy owed anyone money?" I said.

"Like who?"

"A bookie."

"Teddy wouldn't deal with bookies."

"How do you know?"

"I know."

"Maybe you don't," I said. "The manager at Infernos told me Teddy got into an argument with some guy in a bathroom the night he was shot. You know anything about that?"

"No."

"You sure?"

"Positive."

"If I had to venture a guess, I'd say it had to do with gambling. Maybe Teddy borrowed money from the wrong guy and hadn't paid it back. Then again, the argument may have been nothing more than two guys who had too much to drink."

Pat cracked a knuckle.

"Tell me," I said. "Who was Teddy's best friend?"

"Probably Amare . . . I mean Ambush. They've been buddies since playing AAU together."

"I assume you're aware Ambush has a history of hanging around with drug dealers, crooks, and gamblers."

"So?"

"So maybe Teddy got involved with some of Ambush's entourage," I said, thinking of the guys with the spiderweb tattoos and bad manners.

Malone's chin slumped to his chest. He didn't respond.

"Well?" I said.

"Well, what?"

"You think Teddy was into something with Ambush's gang?"

"You'd have to ask Ambush."

"I'm asking you."

"Then the answer is an emphatic no." Not sure I believed him.

I took a minute before asking another question. I needed to keep Malone talking, even though I didn't know exactly where I was headed. I was just fishing.

"You know if Teddy had a girlfriend?" I said.

"He had lots of girlfriends."

"Anyone special?"

"He'd been dating a gal named Emma Mitchell."

"She go to St. Steve's?

"Yeah."

"Were they dating around the time of the shooting?"

"No. They had broken up."

"Know the reason?"

"No idea. Teddy didn't want to talk about it."

"Had they been together long?"

"Since senior year in high school, on and off."

"Did you like her?"

"Not really."

"Why?"

"She's a spoiled rich kid, a party girl who once got suspended for a semester for dealing drugs in the dorm."

A red flag immediately shot up in my mind.

"This Emma. She live on campus?"

"Not anymore. She lives in the San Remo. You know it?"

"Who doesn't? It's one of the most expensive buildings in Manhattan."

"Her father's a concert pianist."

Not knowing if that was important or not, I neverthe-less computed it.

I said, "Mind if I take a look through Teddy's room?"

"What for?"

"Never know what I might find."

I stood. He stood.

He said, "We . . . we haven't been in there or touched anything in . . . well since . . . "

"I understand. I promise to leave it the way I found it."

Pat sighed.

"Follow me," he said.

We walked down a narrow hallway and into Teddy's bedroom.

The room was small. It had a queen-size bed, an Ikea desk, a television, and braided rugs. Posters of LeBron and Steph in action covered one wall. On another was a bookshelf filled with plaques and trophies.

The trophies reminded me of the many I had accumulated during my basketball career. I had dozens. As a kid, they meant a lot. When I retired from pro ball, they meant very little. What's the expression? When I became a man, I put away childish things.

"I'll leave you alone," Pat said. "If you need me shout."

"Sounds good."

Malone left. I surveyed the room. The bed was perfectly made, and the pillows carefully arranged against the headboard. I lifted up the mattress. Nothing. I patted down the pillows. Nothing. No hidden diary. No secret compartments. Nada.

On the bedside table there was a clock radio, a small box of Kleenex, and a thin paperback of F. Scott Fitzgerald's *The Great Gatsby*—my favorite novel. Aside from admiring the gorgeous writing, I found the theme fascinating: that the past cannot be repeated. Lotta retired guys I played with never figured that out.

I sat at the desk and took my time going through all the drawers. Papers, pens, highlighters, staplers, rubber bands, loose-leaf paper. Nothing revealing.

I got on my knees and looked under the bed. Dust balls. Some shoes and three pairs of Adidas sneakers. I glanced under the rugs. More dust balls. I sneezed.

I stood and opened the closet door. More sneakers. Along with pants, shirts, and jackets hung on wooden hangers. I went through the pockets of every pair of pants and all the shirts and jackets. I found nickels and dimes, some cough drops and ticket stubs from Madison Square Garden.

Where else to look?

I pulled out the desk chair, stood on it and looked into a ceiling light fixture. Nothing but a dead fly.

I stepped down and went through everything again. The desk, the closet, the clothes. Not a damn thing.

Scratching my head, I looked around again, hoping there was something else I might have missed. Nothing was apparent.

As I was about to leave the room, I glanced down at the three pairs of Adidas sneakers. Two had untied laces. The third one was tied tight and had a pair of sweat socks stuffed inside. I bent down and pulled out the socks. At the back of one of them was a small container with a half dozen pills. The scribbled handwriting on the label read "Apache." I knew that it was the street name for fentanyl. Well, well, well. I found a clue. A goddamn clue. Finally!

I went outside and sat with Pat.

"Find anything?" Pat said.

"I did."

"What?"

I showed him the container.

"What's that?"

"Fentanyl."

"What's fentanyl?"

"A powerful opioid." I said surprised he wasn't familiar with it. Then again, many people aren't. But one of the dirty secrets in sports is how many fathers ignore, enable, or sometimes even demand chemical help for their kids who agree to take the pill to get love and attention from papa. Sports dads. Fortunately, my father was the furthest things from one.

"Where'd you find it?" Pat said.

"In a sneaker."

Pat squeezed his fists against his temples.

"You know anything about this?" I said.

"Not a thing."

"Nothing?"

Pat palmed his heart.

"No," he said. "I swear to God."

I wasn't sure I believed him. Then again, I wasn't sure I believed most people. If I've learned anything in all my years as a PI, it's that people have a tremendous capacity to withhold the truth.

"Any idea where he might have gotten it?" I said.

"Maybe the Mitchell girl," Malone said. "Her father's loaded. And she's always been in trouble for drugs."

"Just in college, or before?"

"Even in high school they found marijuana and meth in her locker. They slapped her wrist."

"I know a lot about fentanyl," I said.

"You do?"

"I had a cousin who was addicted," I said, thinking of John. John was like my little brother. We hung out together. Played sports together. Things happened in his life that ruined it. Made him turn to fentanyl.

Pat still had his hand over his heart. His jaw knotted as if he wanted to speak more but was chewing the words to keep them inside.

"Did Teddy have any recent surgeries?" I said, knowing how some players take fentanyl after getting hurt.

"No."

"Had he been injured? Twisted ankle? Torn ligaments? Cuts, bruises, wounds?"

"No."

"One of the side effects of fentanyl is fatigue. Was Teddy tired? Restless? Having trouble concentrating? Difficulty sleeping?"

"No."

"I know from my cousin John that fentanyl caused him to be depressed," I said. "When we first met you said Teddy was 'distracted.' Was that a euphemism for depression?"

Malone placed the heels of his hands over his eyes.

"Teddy has . . . was never depressed," Malone said. "He was always an upbeat kid."

Looking at Malone, I was convinced he was holding something back. As much as I felt bad for him, I was also starting to dislike him. Worse, distrust him.

"I don't believe this," he said, putting his hands down.

"What don't you believe?"

"Everything you're telling me."

"And I don't believe much of what you're telling me." I just hate it when people lie. In my profession it happens more times than not. Occupational hazard.

"That's unfair," he snapped, his nostrils flaring.

"What's unfair is you withholding information."

"Why would I do that?" he said.

"You tell me."

"I just want my son's killer arrested."

"Then start speaking the truth."

The room got quiet. The only sound came from the rattling of an old window air conditioner.

I said, "You have anything else to add?"

"I . . . I don't."

"You sure?"

He didn't respond.

"Then I guess there's nothing more to discuss," I said. "But if I find out you've been lying, I can assure you I won't be happy."

Pat shifted his gaze to the window. He stared out into someplace far from his living room.

"I gotta go," I said, standing.

"Where to?" he said in a broken voice.

"To see Emma Mitchell," I said, thinking she might have a story to tell and, if so, I needed to hear it.

CHAPTER
EIGHT

The lobby of the San Remo was magnificent: high vaulted ceilings, white marble flooring, black leather couches, blond wood paneling, and colorful abstract art. Very upscale.

It used to be a haven for celebrities, actors, and musicians like Steven Spielberg, Mary Tyler Moore, Robert DeNiro, and Bono. Not so much the case anymore. Today, there are fewer creative types and more titans of industry, venture capitalists who rake in billions. I figured Mr. Mitchell must make some serious coin tickling the ivories. Apartments here sell for astronomical prices. Triple figure millions.

I approached the concierge, an elderly gentleman with a face like baked chicken. Standing behind a black and white high marble desk, he wore a military-style uniform with more gilt on it than a rear admiral. I resisted the urge to salute.

"Afternoon, sir," he said in a proper British accent. "How may I help you?"

"I'm here to see Emma Mitchell."

"Is she expecting you?"

"Only if she's psychic."

He laughed, sounding like a hedgehog with hiccups.

"May I tell her who is calling?" he said.

"Elgin O'Brien," I said.

"Very well," he said, picking up the desk phone and dialing.

"Good afternoon, Miss Mitchell," he said into the receiver. "There's a Mr. O'Brien to see you."

He listened and nodded his head. Then, cradling the phone between his neck and ear, he looked at me and said, "She says she doesn't know you."

"Tell her I'm a private detective hired by Teddy Malone's father to look into Teddy's murder."

The concierge raised his eyebrows slightly then repeated my words verbatim.

Again, he listened, then hung up.

"You may go up, sir," he said. "Twenty-fifth floor. Apartment 25C."

"Thank you," I said and headed toward the elevators.

I pressed the elevator button. The door opened. I stepped inside the shiniest elevator I'd ever seen. Gilded mirrors. Tiled flooring. A strong scent of citrus.

I got off the elevator and stepped into a corridor that had brass sconces, exquisite artwork and plush carpeting. So plush I felt as if I was walking on a Sealy Posturepedic mattress.

I knocked on apartment 25C.

The door opened and a young woman answered. For a moment, I thought I was looking at Taylor Swift. Emma was thin and rangy, with long blond hair and electric blue eyes with a tint of black. A very rare color. Just like Swift's. Her V-neck camisole was pink and labeled Prada, her navy blue shorts had a small polo player on the hem and her shoes were Tory Burch flats. I would have bet my entire Louis Armstrong collection that she wasn't wearing a bra.

"Hello," she said, smiling. It was the practiced smile of someone accustomed to greeting people. A hostess with the mostest.

"Nice to meet you," she said, extending her hand, limp at the wrist. I wasn't sure if I should shake it or lick it. I shook it.

Nice to meet you," I said. "Thanks for seeing me."

Smelling distinctively of lavender, she stepped aside and ushered me into the apartment. Soft classical music was playing in the background. Possibly Beethoven.

"Can I get you anything . . . Mr. O'Brien. A soda? Beer? Water?" Her voice was the stuff of debutante balls and trust funds. High society.

"Please," I said. "Call me Elgin."

She grinned. Her lips were thick as Cupid's, and she wore a little too much makeup.

"You sure I can't I get you anything . . . Elgin?" She smiled. "There's some Dom Perignon in the fridge." Can't beat it, I thought, a little bubbly during an interrogation. Next thing you know she'll be offering me caviar.

"Thanks, but no thanks. Champagne's a little too rich for my blood. I'm more of a Brown's Zinfandel man myself."

A patch of skin above her nose tightened.

"I love wine," she said. "But I've never heard of that one."

"Most people haven't," I said. "Brown's is the first and only Black-owned winery in Napa Valley."

"Interesting," Emma said, "I must say you're the first private detective I've ever met."

"I can assure you the others aren't as handsome."

She giggled.

"You're funny," she said.

"Aren't I though." Mr. Frivolity.

We walked into the living room. It smelled of flowers and floor polish and big bucks. It was half the size of a tennis court. It had a twelve-foot ceiling, large chandeliers, a marble fireplace, and glorious views of Central Park. Fresh colorful flowers in vases were everywhere. Atop a light gray wool tufted loop rug was a modular eleven-seater open-ended U sectional and chaise ottoman. The fabric was a forest green twill. It contrasted perfectly against the white wainscoted walls. In a far corner stood a black Steinway piano. Daddy's, I presumed.

Emma directed me to an armchair upholstered in blue silk and covered with red roses and green leaves. She sat across from me on the coach, her feet tucked under her.

A cute brown and black Yorkshire Terrier suddenly appeared and jumped in her lap.

"This is my girl, Coco," she said.

"Nice to meet you Coco," I said.

Emma hugged and kissed Coco, then placed her on the floor.

Coco ambled over to me and began sniffling my shoes. I patted her head.

"Cute dog," I said.

"The cutest in the whole world," Emma said.

"That covers a lot of ground."

"Coco," Emma said. "Leave Mr . . . leave Elgin alone. Go lie down."

Coco whimpered, then trotted off and situated herself in a heavily cushioned wicker basket.

I pointed to the piano and said, "I understand your father is a concert pianist?"

"Yes," she said. "He often performs at Carnegie Hall."

"My father performed at Carnegie Hall."

"Really? What did he play?"

"The saxophone."

"My favorite instrument," she said.

"Mine, too. I understand you go to St. Steve's. What are you studying? Music?"

She sniffed and lifted her chin. "Drama."

"Wanna be an actress?"

"It's my dream."

"Stage or screen?"

"Oh, motion pictures, for sure."

"Why movies?"

"More people will see me."

"Guess you like an audience."

"Doesn't everyone?"

Emma glanced over at Coco, who was wagging her tail and making soft taps. The music suddenly ended.

"I'd like to speak to you about Teddy?" I said.

"Ah . . . okay," she said with a hint of the dramatic. "What would you like to know?"

"Everything. Anything."

Emma rubbed her right eyelid with her index finger. Then she said, "You mind if I vape?"

"Please. Have all the formaldehyde you like," I said, thinking why in heaven's name would anyone want to inhale toxic chemicals. Makes no sense.

Emma grabbed a vape pen, inhaled, then put the pen aside.

"You dated Teddy, correct?" I said.

"Yes . . . yes, I did."

"For how long?"

She hesitated. Picked a thread from the strap of her camisole.

"Since high school," she said.

"And you guys broke up?"

Emma looked toward a window. Shafts of sunlight invaded the room. She blinked a few times.

"We did," she said.

"Who ended it?"

"Ended what?"

"The relationship."

Emma folded her arms tight across her chest, her neck stretching upward. Swanlike. It was less a gesture and more a pose, as if she was playing a role.

"He did," she said. "This time."

"How long before the murder did the relationship end?"

She put a finger under her chin and looked toward the ceiling like a child who had been asked a difficult question.

"Maybe a month," she said.

"Did Teddy give a reason for the breakup?

"He . . . he said he, a, like, like lost interest."

"Had you guys been arguing?"

"No more than usual."

"Was he seeing someone else?"

She flashed me a wide-eye theatrical stare.

"Not . . . not that I know of. Although I'm sure he had his opportunities."

"Did the breakup anger you?"

"Yes!" The word detonated from her throat.

Wondering if she was a woman scorned, I filed the thought away.

"The weeks before the shooting," I said, "was he acting strange?"

She fell silent, tilted her head back, and raked her long hair. It was a theatrical motion, one that she had employed for so long she probably wasn't even aware of doing it.

"Strange?" she said.

"You know, behaving differently?"

"He was moody, upset."

"Any idea why?"

"He said Coach Corsito was getting on his case."

"Just Corsito?"

She pondered this for a while, closing her eyes briefly. Then she looked at me from under thick lashes. The look almost seemed flirtatious.

"I don't think he was getting along with the conditioning coach very well," she said, her voice softly modulated.

"Steve Smith?"

"Yes."

"What was the problem?"

"I . . . I don't know," she said, before exhaling slowly. "All I know they argued a lot and once got into a nasty shoving match."

"That's helpful," I said. "Could anything else have been bothering him?"

"Not that I know."

"Were you aware Teddy was a gambler?"

"I . . . I . . . a . . . I knew he like to bet on things, if that's what you mean."

"I'm specifically asking if he liked to bet on basketball games."

"I can't really say."

"Can't or won't?"

She pulled her knees up to her chin and locked her arms around her shins.

"I . . . I just don't know. Believe me."

I wasn't sure that I did.

"Let me ask you this," I said, scratching the bulging bone below my right ear, "you know if Teddy was using drugs?"

Her mouth got small and wrinkled, as if she was sucking on a sour ball.

"Why would you ask me that?" she said, defensively.

I pulled out the container of fentanyl.

"I found this in his parent's apartment," I said.

"What is it?" she said.

"I think you know. It's fentanyl."

Her eyes turtled down.

"What do you know about it?" I said.

Half a minute passed. No response. She stared at me the way you look at someone when you're trying to figure out a way to say something you don't want to say.

"What do you know about it?" I said again.

"I know nothing," she said, extending her arms out like a baby asking to be taken out of the crib.

"C'mon, Emma," I said, "don't you want to help me find the person who murdered Teddy?"

She looked at me a long time before answering. Picked up her vape pen then put it down again on the end table. Guess she had enough toxins for one day.

"Yes!" she barked, a verbal slap.

"Yes what?"

"Yes, I knew. He wasn't an addict, but I knew he was using."

"Okay," I said. "Now we're getting somewhere."

Emma lowered her eyes. Her forehead winked. She dramatized even thinking.

"Do you know when Teddy started using?" I said.

She glanced at Coco, as if the dog could provide the answer.

"I'm not sure," she said.

"You're not sure?"

"No."

"Answer me this," I said, "know where he was getting it?"

"I don't know that either," she said, jamming her hands into her armpits.

"You're not that good an actress yet, so I'm going to ask you one more time," I said. "Where'd he get the fentanyl?"

She twisted in her seat. My sense was she's trying to tailor an answer that covers just enough truth that it wouldn't be a total lie.

"Emma, this is tough, I know, but you have to be straight with me."

Her hands dropped and her knees started fanning. She looked away.

"Talk to me, Emma, talk to me," I said. "Where did Teddy get the fentanyl?"

This time a minute passed. Emma sat motionless, looking away. I got the sense she was feeling some kind of embarrassment, some type of shame.

"Look, Emma," I said, "I know you got suspended from school for dealing drugs. That's in the past and it's not my concern. Just tell me where Teddy got the fentanyl. Okay?"

She looked at me with a mixture of surprise and horror.

"How . . . how did . . . did you know about . . ."

"Doesn't matter how I found out. Just tell me."

She put up her hands in surrender and said, "He . . . he got it from me."

"From you?"

"Well, not me exactly."

"Who exactly?"

"A friend."

"What friend?"

"From school."

"St. Steve's?"

"No, Trinity."

"The high school on Ninety-First Street?"

"Yes." She looked stricken. "You won't tell Daddy about this, will you?"

"Certainly not. My work is confidential."

Trinity was the most expensive private coed school in Manhattan. It cost sixty grand a year. Alumni included Humphrey Bogart, John McEnroe, Colson Whitehead, and Alvin Bragg, New York's district attorney.

"What's your friend's name?" I said.

She was silent for a moment while she composed her answer.

"Adam," she said.

"Adam what?"

"Roth."

"Were he and Teddy friends?"

"Sort of."

"Did they hang out together?"

"Occasionally."

"Was he at Infernos?"

"When?"

"The night Teddy was shot."

"I . . . I don't know."

"You don't know?"

"No, I don't. I didn't even know Teddy was going . . . to a place like that."

"Describe Adam."

"He's very handsome."

"Good for him," I said. "Is he tall?"

"Yes."

"Can you be more specific?"

"Maybe six four."

"How's he built?"

"Like a wrestler."

"Where does he live?"

"Gramercy Park."

"Think he's home now?"

"Probably not."

"Where might I find him?"

"He's works late at a photography studio in Greenwich Village."

"What studio?"

"Robert Samuels."

"What street?"

"Bleecker."

"You have an address?"

"It's between MacDougal and Sixth."

Before I could ask another question, Emma put her hands to her face. She was careful not to screw up her makeup.

"I'm sorry to be asking you these questions," I said. "I have to explore every angle."

She put her hands down, pulled a wadded Kleenex from her pants pocket and dabbed her dry eyes.

"I . . . I . . . I loved Teddy," she said, her voice cracking. "I really loved him."

I sat silently and looked for tears. There were none. She needed some classes at the Actor's Studio.

"I'm . . . I'm sorry," she said, still dabbing her dry eyes. Nothing like sincerity.

"No worries," I said.

Emma took a minute to compose herself.

"Look, Emma," I said, "is there anything, anything else, you can tell me about Teddy?"

She called Coco. The dog raced over. Emma picked her up and hugged her.

"Take your time," I said.

She kissed Coco's head and said, "I know one thing."

"What's that?"

"He was seeing a psychologist."

"You know why?"

"No," she said, stroking Coco. "He wouldn't tell me."

"By any chance you know the name of the psychologist?"

"I do," she said. "Regina Blake. At St. Steve's."

I remembered seeing the advertisement for Blake's services on the bench outside Teddy's dormitory.

I had to ask. "You know who killed Teddy? Or who may have wanted to?"

"No," she barked. Even Coco jumped.

I sensed we were done.

"You've been very helpful," I said, standing. "Thank you."

She looked at me with unreadable eyes. There was something in them that was unsettling, but for the life of me I couldn't figure out what it was. Was she acting? Was she truthful? Or was she telling half lies? I wondered if she could even tell the difference.

"Will you find his killer?" she said, leaping from her chair as if she'd been pushed.

"I will."

"You . . . a . . . you sound optimistic."

"To me, a glass is always half full."

"Funny," she said. "I think just the opposite."

CHAPTER
NINE

Bleecker Street was once the heart of the Village. I guess it still is, but the Village has changed dramatically since the sixties. Back then it was a hippie haven. Today, it's all trendy clothing stores, book marts, marijuana dispensaries, stylish restaurants, and jazz clubs. A popular hangout for nearby NYU students.

I know Bleecker well. It's still home to the Blue Note nightclub. My father played there with Dizzy Gillespie, Sarah Vaughn, Lionel Hampton, and Ray Charles. These days the club features more contemporary jazz masters like Wynton Marsalis and Keith Jarrett.

Robert Samuel's studio was a few doors down from the Blue Note. A nondescript brick building, it was squeezed between a boutique hotel and a small café. Students were sitting outside at tiny round tables, chatting on their phones, or playing with their laptops. Some drank bottled beer, others sipped expresso. There was a strong scent of coffee and marijuana.

I rang the studio doorbell. A buzzer sounded and I stepped inside.

I was greeted by a young female receptionist wearing a gray tee under a thick black leather vest. She sported thick black eyeliner, black lipstick, and long black hair that resembled congealed fusilli. Not my style, but it looked fetching on her. To each their own.

"May I help you?" she said. Her voice was squeakier than Betty Boop.

"I'm looking for Adam Roth."

She chucked a thumb over her shoulder and said, "He's in the back."

I pushed aside a velvet curtain and entered a large room with light poles and photo umbrellas. Slithering around them on the floor were thick black extension cords. They resembled fat eels.

A short, slender guy wearing skin-tight red suede pants and a red sleeveless tee was bent over a tripod looking through a camera lens at a pretty girl wearing a bright blue bikini. She was lying on a chaise lounge, flashing a big smile, and holding a red rose in her teeth. Strike a pose.

"Excuse me," I said to the photographer. "Know where I can find Adam Roth?"

He turned quickly. Wearing more makeup than RuPaul, he fashioned red lipstick, blue eyeshadow and fake eyelashes. The name Robert Samuels Photographer was stenciled on his tee.

"What can I do for you . . . handsome?" he said.

"I'm looking for Adam Roth."

Samuels gave me the once-over like a food inspector grading a side of beef.

"You're quite the well-built man," he said, his voice as light as a breeze.

"Just the right size for my clothes."

"Surely you're a weightlifter?"

"I do bench press Buicks. But mostly I lift bottles of wine."

He winked. "Perhaps we can share a glass sometime."

I rubbed a finger under my nose and said, "Is . . . is Adam here?"

He frowned, then yelled, "Adam! Get out here!"

Ten seconds later a good-looking stocky kid, maybe six four with nose rings and a brown man bun, came out from behind a thick velour drape. He was wearing white painter's pants, black combat boots, and no shirt. Hip dude.

"Yes, Robert," the kid said.

"Some guy's looking for you," Samuels said. "Whatever it is, make it snappy. We got work to do."

"Adam Roth?" I said.

"Who wants to know?"

"Me. I'm Elgin O'Brien. A private investigator."

"Whoop-di-do." A real smart ass.

"I'd like to ask you a few questions about Teddy Malone."

His face reeked with distaste. Nobody in the world makes better distasteful faces than superrich prep school kids. I sometimes think that they believe it's a birthright.

"Is there someplace we can talk privately?" I said.

"Why can't we speak here?"

"I'd rather not."

"Why?"

"I have some questions to ask you."

The distasteful face again. It's questioning brats like him that makes you think about leaving the business.

"Just so you know," he said, "you're fucking with the wrong dude."

"Oh, yeah. Who'd be the right one?"

"I'm just saying nobody pushes me around." Guess they make 'em tough at Trinity.

"That's not my intention."

He puffed out his cheeks and exhaled.

"Okay, okay," he said. "I'll give you a few minutes. Let's go to the breakroom."

I followed him into a small room that had photographs of male and female models on the walls. Most of them were naked. All beautiful. Vanity, not love, has been my folly. If I'm not mistaken, I think it was Jane Austen who said that. Then again, it could have been Lady Gaga.

We sat at a small folding table littered with Chipotle wrappers, Starbucks cups, and glass ashtrays. One ashtray held a pyramid of cigarette butts.

"I'm investigating Teddy's murder," I said.

"Hey, man, I don't know much about it."

"But you were with him at Infernos the night of the murder, correct?"

"Yeah, I was. But I left early."

"What's early?"

"Before midnight."

"Can you prove that?"

He put his right hand on the top of his head. I noticed there was a thick raised roundish scar on it, as if from a knife wound. In a way, it did resemble a basketball.

"Why should I?" he said.

"So I can eliminate you as a suspect."

He snorted. "Me? A suspect? What the fuck?"

"Nobody's innocent until I clear them," I said. "Where'd you go after you left Infernos?"

"Groove on MacDougal Street."

"What's Groove?"

"A music bar."

"You with anyone?"

"About a dozen fucking friends."

"Can anybody verify that?"

"Man! You're starting to piss me off."

"It's the least I can do," I said. "Answer my question."

"Maybelline can vouch for me."

"Who's Maybelline?"

"Receptionist out front."

I waited a second before asking the next question.

"I understand you supplied Teddy with fentanyl?" I said.

His eyes snapped wide.

"Who told you that?" he said.

"Emma Mitchell."

His mouth twisted.

"That fucking little bitch," he said. "She should talk. She dispenses more drugs than CVS."

"Are you saying she's still dealing."

"Who the fuck knows. You never know what she does or why."

I stroked my chin.

"Let's get back to you," I said. "Why'd you give him the fentanyl?"

"He said he needed it."

"He say why?"

"No, man. And I didn't ask."

"He didn't say anything else?"

"All he said was that he was stressed out."

"About what?"

"Someone was giving him a hard time."

"He say who?"

"Nah, man, he didn't say, but . . ."

"But what?"

"Whatever the problem was it sure seemed to be taking a toll on him."

"Whaddya mean toll?"

"He seemed depressed. He sure as hell wasn't fun to be around, that's for sure."

I wondered who was giving him the problem. Corsito? Smith? Emma? His father? A bookie? Ambush? One of Ambush's friends? The cast of characters just kept growing.

"Where'd you get the fentanyl?" I said.

"Fentanyl," he said, chuckling, "is easier to get nowadays than weed. I score it in the clubs from whoever has it."

"Last question," I said, "you think Emma had anything to do with Teddy's murder?"

"Nothing Emma does ever surprises. She's a sneaky little bitch. Phony. Conniving. And a lousy lay. I wouldn't put it past her to hire somebody to shoot Teddy. She certainly has the money."

"You know how Emma took Teddy breaking up with her?"

"She went ballistic. Said more than once that she'd love to cap his ass."

"Is that right?"

"Righter than religion."

I thought about his answer and said, "I was under the impression you two were friends."

"Friends, shit! We just fuck. Girl's a nymph."

"I thought she was in love with Teddy Malone."

"She in love with any guy with a dick."

"Let me ask you something," I said. "You ever been in trouble with the police?"

"What the fuck kind of question is that?"

"A good one. Have you?"

"Have I what?"

"Been in trouble with the police?"

"Fuck no."

I took a long look at Roth. Like Emma Mitchell, there was something unnerving about him. Maybe I was imagining it. Or maybe I just flat out didn't like rich, entitled kids.

"Adam!" Samuels screamed, "Get out here! Now!"

"Gotta go," he said.

"Duty calls."

"Fucking guy is a pain in the ass."

"Why do you work for him?"

"Dude is my uncle."

"Appreciate your help," I said.

"Yeah, sure," he said, after taking a minute to study my face as if trying to commit it to memory. I didn't like the look. It was eerie.

I headed back to the reception desk.

Maybelline was toying with a black earring the size of a basketball rim.

"Excuse me," I said. "You remember going to Groove one night a few months back with Adam?"

"I always go to Groove with Adam. It's quite the scene. What night you talkin' bout?"

I knew the next question was a long shot, but I figured I'd asked it anyway. Nothing ventured, nothing gained.

"The night that a basketball player from St. Joseph University was shot?"

She stopped chewing.

"You mean Teddy, Teddy Malone?" she said.

I was flabbergasted.

"How . . . how is it you know Malone's name?" I said.

"I go to St. Stephen's," she said. "I'm a big basketball fan."

"You were with Adam the night of the murder?"

"Sure was," she said. "Me and our whole crew."

"Was he with you all night?"

She stopped toying with her earring.

"Most of the night."

"Most of the night?"

"He left sometime after midnight and returned later."

"You remember what time?"

"No way, José. I was so drunk I could barely pee straight."

"Don't you hate when that happens?"

"Sure do. I tinkled right down my leg."

"You're a real pisser," I said, thinking how in my business things don't ever stay boring for very long.

CHAPTER TEN

I looked at my watch. Eleven o'clock. Time to meet Monique. I snagged a cab and headed uptown. We drove up Park Avenue, then through a tunnel that brought us up on the ramp that swung around Grand Central Terminal and back onto Park. We turned on Forty-Fourth Street and drifted into a crowded Times Square, the lights blazing like a neon and LED purgatory.

I took out my phone and googled Adam Roth. I found a few small newspaper articles about him. He was twice arrested for petty theft and weapon possession. Both times he got a suspended sentence. Most likely his rich daddy got him off.

I scratched my head and thought: It's been a long day of misdirection, redirection, revelation, and information. A typical day in the life of a detective. You question people. You collect details. You sift through them, knowing that what seems unimportant now can become vitally important later when you're putting all the facts under the microscope and magnifying them.

The cab pulled up outside Joe Allen's on West Forty-Sixth Street, otherwise known as Restaurant Row. A Broadway institution, Allen's has been a popular hangout for actors, producers, and directors since it opened in the sixties.

As usual, it was packed. Three deep at the bar. Mostly tourists, talking and laughing loudly. From the overhead speakers, Frank Sinatra crooned about wanting one for his baby and one more for the road. Looking around, I'd have bet my bottom dollar I was the only guy in the place who wore a size 48 XL sport coat and shoulder holster. I grabbed a table in a side room and ordered a beer.

The room had brick walls jammed with framed posters of Broadway plays that had failed. One always caught my attention: A musical called *The Pirate Queen* produced by Les Misérables creators Alain Boublil and Claude-Michel Schönberg. A total bomb.

Ironically, that play turned out to be the best thing that ever happened to Monique. Although she only had a small part, she got the attention of some producer who thought she showed some ability. Next thing you know, the producer hired her for a touring show and her career was launched. She's been on a rocket ever since.

I took a sip of beer and thought about the case. I had leads—too many leads—but none of them leading anywhere. What in God's name, I wondered, was there about Teddy Malone's life or circumstances that made someone want to kill him?

And why was it that no one even had the slightest inking about who that killer might be. Strange. Very strange.

I remembered Sid Meyer often lecturing me on the importance of patience. He said that solving a crime was like trying to reconstruct a broken mirror. It takes time. But once you have all the shards in place, you get a clear picture. All I had now was pieces of broken glass.

I sipped my beer and thought about those pieces. I wondered about Teddy. Was he a big gambler? Was he in debt? To a bookie? To a loan shark? To someone in Ambush

Anderson's gang? Or was he shaving points? Did he screw that up? Seems like every ten years or so there's a big point-shaving scandal in college hoops, and now that you can gamble on your phone . . . anything's possible.

I also wondered about his use of fentanyl. Was it something or nothing? I know some NBA guys take opiates simply to relieve the demons of stress, self-doubt, and tension, the cold hand of fear that bubbles up under pressure. A lot of them wound up in re-rehab. A few even ended up dead.

Had Teddy buckled under the pressure? Was he taking so much shit from Corsito or Smith that he needed medication? A lot of questions needed to be answered. Fast.

But answers, like truth, are often hard to find.

The front door opened. Monique appeared. Heads turned. Conversations stopped. Every time she entered a room, I half expected sustained applause. Sometimes there was.

Monique's tall, almost six feet, with short blond hair, eyes bluer than blueberries and a shape that would make even the pope think about leaving the priesthood.

Walking like a runway model, she strolled toward me, a smile on her face so bright it seemed as if she had swallowed the sun.

As always, seeing her made my heart vault. It's the kind of response you get when you adore someone, when you look forward to ending your day in their arms. Monique brought something into my life that I had never experienced before: true love. It was as if I discovered it the first time we kissed.

Since that kiss, the warmth for me that radiates from her, that flows and vibrates in little glimmers and tremors has produced not only a strong friendship but a tangible rapport that I could never have imagined. Not in a million years.

But the thing I admire most about Monique is that she's an optimist, a person who tries to do good in the world by making personal appearances for charities and working for places like Habitat for Humanity. She is a woman of resolve. Cheerful, always cheerful. Even in the worst of times.

If my glass is always half full, then her glass is always bubbling over.

"You look boffo," I said.

"Is that a review?"

"Just a reaction."

Monique sat and kissed my cheek. She was wearing a thigh-high black dress with white polka dots. Her necklace was white pearls. Her diamond earrings were pear-shaped. She smelled of jasmine.

"You're hired," I said.

"As?"

"My sexy lover."

"I already play that role."

"And I'm the better man for it."

A white-coated waiter appeared and put a martini before Monique.

"Your usual, Miss Montgomery," he said. "With two olives."

"Thank you, George," Monique said, smiling.

George's brown eyes glowed and he lowered his head slightly, as if bowing before a queen. He then backpedaled away. Monique is the only woman I know who can flirt without flirting.

"Every time you smile at George," I said, "I get the feeling he's going to faint."

"You saying I have that kind of effect on men?"

"I'm saying Joel Osteen would go from praising the Lord to praising you, if given the opportunity."

"You are one silver-tongued devil."

"In more ways than one," I said, winking.

Monique chuckled and took a sip of her drink.

"How's your martini?" I said.

"Delicious."

"You know what Dorothy Parker once said about martinis."

"You read Parker?"

"I read everything."

"Is there a book you haven't read?"

"Probably not."

"Okay," she said, "tell me what that wise woman had to say."

" 'I like to have a martini, two at the very most. After three I'm under the table. After four I'm under the host.' "

"Very cheeky," she said. "How was your day?"

I hardly knew where to start and once I did, I didn't know where to stop. I told her about my meetings with Pat Malone, Bobby Rose, Ambush Anderson, Emma Mitchell, Adam Roth, Dave Hunter, Steve Smith, Chris Corsito, and Joe, the manager at Infernos. Monique listened with the intensity of a psychiatrist, her mind following and processing every word.

"I don't know much about college basketball," Monique said, "but isn't Corsito the coach who's always in trouble?"

"He's more nefarious than George Santos."

"That's saying a lot."

"He's an insufferable egomaniac."

"Aren't most major college basketball coaches?"

"Yes," I said. "The thing is they get so much control and are given so much power they think nothing of cheating and breaking the rules. Yet athletic directors and university presidents are reluctant, even afraid, to reign them in when their teams are winning." I paused and sipped my beer. "That is, until the coach stops winning. Then the AD can finally show some balls and fire him."

"Sounds amoral."

"It is," I said, thinking how college sports is all about greed, an epidemic of win-at-all-cost bullshit. Who cares if academic resources are being slashed so long as the lavish, outrageously expensive new arena brings in fans and boat-loads of money? It's a shameful misuse of educational funds. It was bad enough when I was in school and it's a hundred times worse today.

More and more people were now coming into the restaurant, the voices louder, the laughter was fuller. Sinatra had been replaced by Tony Bennett who was now lamenting over leaving his heart in San Franciso. The tourists ate it up. Some tried to sing along.

"Did you talk to Corsito?" Monique said.

"I did."

"Get any insights?"

"Only insights Corsito has are about basketball. Otherwise, talking to him is like talking to Cookie Monster." I grinned. "Get this. His favorite movie is *Patton*. He watches it a dozen times a year. Loves the scene where General George slaps an injured soldier. Calls him a coward. Corsito says watching it inspires him. Need I say more?"

"Did he provide you with anything useful?"

"He said his relationship with Teddy Malone was excellent, but Teddy's teammates said just the opposite."

"Somebody's lying."

"No kidding."

I sipped my beer and thought how people will tell you the truth, their version of the truth, which will often emerge shadowed differently every time they tell it. Fact is, there are many contrasting types of truths. Which one to believe is not always easy to decipher.

"Talking to the teammates was strange," I said. "A witness told me he heard the shooter clearly call Teddy a queer-ass bitch. Yet players strongly denied hearing him. They also denied knowing anything about Teddy getting into an altercation in the Infernos bathroom."

"They could be telling the truth."

"Could be," I said. "But I have my suspicions."

I then told her about the surly guy I bumped into coming out of the dorm, the one who had the same spiderweb tattoo as Amare.

"The guy fit the exact description of the shooter the witness described," I said.

"Did you get a look at the back of his right hand?"

"I didn't. He moved past me too quickly."

"And he's a friend of Anderson's?" Monique said.

"He is."

"From what you've told me, Anderson is a shady guy."

"Very shady."

"You don't think he had anything to do with Teddy's murder, do you?"

"Anything's possible. He and Teddy were tight. But maybe something soured between them. Or maybe something happened between Teddy and one of Ambush's friends. Ambush's friends are, after all, gang members. Drug dealers. Gamblers. Killers. Teddy might have betrayed them, which, in their world, could certainly be a reason for murder."

Monique twirled the steam of her glass slowly without lifting it from the table.

I handed her the container marked Apache.

"What's this?"

"Fentanyl."

"Where'd you get it?"

I told her.

She studied the container.

"Doesn't look like it's a doctor's prescription," she said.

"Sure isn't. Black market, a hundred times more powerful than heroin, probably cut with something else."

She handed the container back.

"What did Teddy's father say about it?"

"He claimed no knowledge."

"You believe him?"

"Not sure that I do."

"Why would he lie?"

"Good question."

"You have any idea where Teddy might have gotten the fentanyl?"

"I know from who."

"Who?"

"A friend of Emma Mitchell."

"A supplier?"

"No. Just a rich kid she went to high school with. A small-time guy who had an alibi for part of the evening Teddy was murdered. Seems he left a nightclub at some point that night and came back later."

"Is he a suspect?"

"Yes. Not only because of his shaky alibi, but when I asked him if he's even been in trouble with the police, he said no. But then I googled him and found he was arrested twice for B&E and weapon possession."

"Is anyone telling you the truth?"

"So far, no. Par for the course."

Monique lifted her glass and held it with her fingertips. Her interest in my case was absolute. She listened with her entire being, her eyes picking up every gesture, every nuance I made. That's why I like talking shop with her. She's perceptive. Little wonder why actors enjoy working beside her. She responds perfectly to their every mannerism.

"Why do you think Teddy was taking fentanyl?" Monique said.

"Could be any number of reasons," I said. "It could be a way of coping with physical pain from an injury while still trying to play. But, according to Teddy's father, the kid had no serious injury. His tox report was clean, and Emma said he wasn't addicted. My guess is he was under a lot of pressure. From what and from whom, I'm not sure."

We both fell silent. All around us we heard clicking glasses and clanging silverware.

"There's more," I said.

Monique looked surprised. She delicately took an olive from her martini glass, put it in her mouth and nibbled half of it.

I said, "It seems Teddy Malone was a gambler."

"What kind of gambler?"

"He bet on sports."

"Is that a problem?" she said finishing off her olive and putting the pit on a napkin.

"Could be. If he owed somebody money or was betting on his own team. Worse, if he was shaving points."

"Shaving points? What's shaving points?" Monique knew as much about sports as I knew about ballet.

"Shaving points is when a player purposely changes the score without changing who wins," I said. "It's typically concocted by a player colluding with gamblers to prevent a team from covering a published point spread, from winning by a certain amount."

"You think Teddy was doing that?"

"Can't say," I said. "I'm just theorizing. Could have easily been prop betting."

Monique wrinkled her eyebrows.

"What's prop betting?" she said.

"It's shorthand for proposition betting, meaning a wager that's not tied to the final score or outcome of a game."

"I'm not sure I understand?" she said. "Give me an example?"

"Let's say a player is averaging eight shots a game. You can place a bet on whether he will go over or under that number."

"Seems silly."

"Prop betting is silly. But it's becoming more widespread. Some people bet on things as absurd as how many times a coach will sip Gatorade in a game."

"Lots of pieces to the puzzle in only one day."

"Oh, but I'm not finished."

"You're not?"

"Nope."

I took a gulp of beer. Monique finished her second olive and sipped her martini. I noticed there was a line of lipstick on the rim of her glass. I wondered what it was like to always have a cherry flavor complimenting your cocktail.

Monique said, "And here I thought *The Glass Menagerie* was complicated."

I said, "Emma Mitchell told me Teddy was seeing a shrink."

"Did she know the reason why?"

"No. Or, if she does, she wasn't saying."

"The plot thickens."

"Indeed, it does."

"Emma also said Teddy had gotten into a shoving match with the conditioning coach, a guy by the name of Steve Smith."

"What was the argument about?"

"She didn't know?"

"You know Smith?"

"I just met him for the first time today. But I remembered reading how he got into trouble some years ago at Rutgers for dispensing performance-enhancing drugs."

"You going to question him?"

"Do dogs bark?"

"When provoked," she said. "I know you won't stop digging until you get to the bottom of all this."

"Don't I always?"

"Yes, you do Sherlock."

"Never compare me to Holmes."

"Why?"

"First of all, he's a Brit. Second, he inhaled more drugs than all the whackos at Waco."

"Remind me again . . . who's your favorite fictional detective?"

"The man who went down the mean streets."

"Dick Tracy?"

"Hell, no. Philip Marlowe."

She tapped her forehead.

"Right, right," she said.

I rubbed the side of her face with the back of my hand.

Trying to sound like Bogart, I sucked down my upper lip and said, "Sweetheart you're so cute you could make a bishop kick a hole in a stained-glass window."

"Is that your Bogart impression?"

"Good, huh?"

"As good as Jim Carrey performing Shakespeare."

I leaned my face toward hers and puckered my lips.

"Kiss me, Angel," I said.

Monique wrinkled her nose.

"You look like a camel," she said.

"I can hump like a camel."

She rolled her eyes.

"Camels don't hump, knucklehead," she said. "Camels have humps."

"I was misinformed."

Monique shook her head lightly.

"You hungry?" she said.

"Only for you." Am I a sweet talker or what?

She put her hand to her cheek and turned in profile.

"How charming," she said, sounding like Scarlett O'Hara.

"Maybe we could just sit here and satisfy our appetites by making out," I said.

"Like teenagers?"

"Tongue and all."

"How decadent."

"It would make for a nice floor show."

"I already performed tonight."

"But not for me."

"You want an encore?"

"Only if it has a happy ending."

She leaned over and kissed my cheek.

"Let me repeat my question," she said. "Are you hungry?"

"Starved."

"Want to eat here?"

"No."

"Where?"

"My place."

"Thai food?"

"Sounds good," I said. "Let's go Thai one on."

"Please tell me you just didn't say that."

ELEVEN

We were sitting by the picture window in the living room listening to Chet Baker sing. Of all the jazz musicians Baker was our favorite. We swore "My Funny Valentine" would be our wedding song when, and if, we decide to get married.

The only reason we haven't gotten married is because we're enjoying the hell out of life. Our feeling is, if it's not broken, why fix it?

On the coffee table before us were open containers of steamed dumplings, brown rice, pad Thai, and Panang curry chicken. The same as always. Consistency matters.

"Don't you just love Thai food?" Monique said. She had changed into an oversized white tee shirt and gray cotton shorts. No shoes.

"I do, except for one thing,' I said.

"What's that?"

"You don't use chopsticks."

"They're awkward."

"No, they're not," I said. "Plus, chopsticks provide nutritional benefits."

"Baloney."

"I'm serious," I said. "Using chopsticks lowers your glycemic index."

Her mouth twisted.

"Let me worry about my glycemic index, if you don't mind."

"Just trying to be helpful."

"You could help me enormously by deep-sixing the dietitian bullshit."

I ran a thumb across my mouth.

"My nutritionist lips are sealed," I said.

Monique picked up a bottle of Singha beer and drank some from the neck. It was one of the things I loved about her. Unlike other actresses I dated, Monique wasn't at all pretentious. Maybe that's because she grew up in a six-story tenement in Omaha, Nebraska, where there was too little heat and too many roaches.

"I know I say this all the time," I said, "but nobody has a voice like Baker. It's so mellow, so sonorous."

"It's almost androgynous."

"Every time I hear him sing, I think of you."

"In what way?"

"Naked."

She rolled her eyes. "Figures. Couldn't you at least envision me in an elegant gown?"

"How about a lace bra, a garter belt, and a pair of spiked Louboutins?"

"Oh yeah," she said, sarcastically, "the Louboutins certainly makes it more elegant."

We ate in silence for a while and listened to Baker. His music was passionate and melancholy. Even sad. The sadness in his voice made me feel for a father who had lost his son.

Using her fork, Monique twirled some pad Thai and chewed it carefully.

I toyed with my chopsticks as if playing the drums, thoughts about Teddy Malone digging at me.

"You seem distracted," Monique said, concentrating fully on me. The experience was, as always, palpable. Her intensity and intelligence a counterpoint to her usual playful self.

"I'm still thinking about the case."

Monique nodded.

"Know what bothers me about it?"

"Besides so many people withholding information?"

"Not one person I've spoken to today has any idea about why someone would want to murder Teddy."

"Why do you think that is?"

"Not sure yet. The only thing I know for sure is, the shooting wasn't random. Teddy was targeted."

"What are you saying?" she said, her eyes wider than those of a kid sitting around a campfire listening to a ghost story.

"I'm saying somebody knew Teddy would be at Infernos and knew he'd be there until late, so that when he was leaving there might not be many witnesses to the shooting."

"But there were witnesses."

"Who saw virtually nothing."

"What's your plan?"

"I haven't connected any of the dots yet, so I'll just have to keep digging some more. Eventually something has got to connect to someone."

"Doesn't it always?"

"Usually. In time."

Monique nibbled on a dumpling, then picked up her napkin and patted her lips.

"At this point," I said, twirling the chopsticks, "there're too many open questions and not enough answers. I need more information before I can come to any conclusions."

"Well, you've moved quickly."

"You must in a case like this. Once you start it's all about speed, keeping the investigation going fast. You slow down, things slow down."

"Time is of the essence."

"When isn't it?"

"With you . . . never."

I pushed around some pad Thai.

"You've hardly eaten anything," she said.

"I thought I was hungry, but I have no appetite," I said, feeling like a jazz musician who can't find the right notes.

"Sorry."

"Don't be."

"Well, I'm stuffed," she said, patting her stomach. "It was delicious."

"Glad you enjoyed."

I stood, took the containers into the kitchen and threw out what little remained.

"Want some dessert?" I said.

"Wha'cha got?"

"M&Ms, Reese's Pieces, KitKat bars."

"What are you, a five-year-old?"

"Satisfies my sweet tooth."

"Well, this sweetie would prefer a Sambuca."

"Good call. Candy is dandy, but liquor is quicker."

"Ogden Nash."

"Bingo!!"

I returned to the living room with two snifters of Sambuca.

She took one from me, looked at it, and said, "That's quite a healthy amount."

"It's a holiday pour."

"Is today a holiday?"

"It is when I'm with you."

Monique raised her glass.

"Here's to staying positive and testing negative," she said.

"Couldn't have said it better myself."

We clicked glass. It made a tiny chiming sound.

We sat in silence over the next few minutes, still listening to Baker. Outside the picture window, the lights of New York were laid out in a place setting of twinkling diamonds and crystals. No matter how many times I've looked at that view I never get tired of it. Nothing in the world is more majestic than the skyline of Manhattan at night.

"You look tired." Monique said.

"I am."

"Maybe you need to be energized." She said the words so sweetly I half expected rose pedals to float from her lips.

She put her drink on the end table and stood, slowly lifting her tee shirt over her head. Her hair shook, her breasts bounced. She then hooked her thumbs into the waistband of her shorts, shimmied them down to her feet and kicked them off like a punter in football.

"You like?" she said, striking a pose like Aphrodite.

"I lust," I said, my voice hoarse. Even though I had seen Monique naked on many, many occasions, the sight of her without clothes always excited me as if it were the first time. It never failed to make my blood percolate.

"Feeling a little energized now?" she said.

"Better believe it," I said, feeling my heart drumming in my chest like a hand pounding a bongo.

"Just lie back and relax," she purred. "This is just the prelude."

I didn't say anything. I just tried to control my breathing.

Monique kissed me; I could taste the Sambuca on her breath.

Then she slowly and adroitly undressed me. Curled lazily into my lap like a Siamese cat. Her body was warm and moist against mine. She smelled seductively of jasmine.

I said, "When does the show start?"

Whispering in my ear, she said, "When your curtain rises."

CHAPTER TWELVE

We rose late the next morning. Strong sunlight was pouring through the window; it was going to be another hot day.

Lying in bed, my head propped in my hand, I looked at Monique and said, "I have a sneaky suspicion you were planning all along to make love to me."

"How intuitive," she said. "You sound like a detective."

"I sure did a lot of detecting last night."

"I'll vouch for your undercover abilities."

"Can I tell you something?"

"By all means."

"Last night was a trip to the moon on gossamer wings."

"Very poetic."

"It's the Irish in me."

"From your deep heart's core."

"Yeats?"

"Yes, Mr. Smarty Pants."

"When you got it, flaunt it."

"And you flaunt it, alright."

I gave Monique a long kiss.

"Anybody ever tell you that you're a very silly man?"

"Yeah. You."

I hopped out of bed singing, "It was just one of those things. Just one of those fabulous flights."

We showered and had breakfast. Monique made herself a healthy shake containing fruits and vegetables, and something called plant-based organic protein powder. That had as much appeal to me as eating cooked cabbage. I'm more of an Entenmann's donut man, along with gallons of coconut-flavored coffee.

We finished breakfast and headed upstairs to get dressed. While Monique blew her hair dry, I sat in a chair, opened my laptop, and googled the St. Stephen's directory. I found a profile for the school's psychologist, Regina Blake.

Her credentials were impressive: a bachelor's degree in biology from Cornell and medical certification at Yale. As an undergrad, she played tennis and volleyball. Her hobbies were running and hiking.

I clicked off the laptop. Monique stopped drying her hair.

"I'm going to see a shrink," I said.

"About time."

"Think I need help?"

"God yes."

"That hurts."

"I'm joking."

"Freud said there are no jokes."

"Freud said a lot of things."

"Most of it crap."

"Who's the shrink?"

"Teddy Malone's psychologist."

"Think she'll talk to you?"

"Who knows? Every shrink I've ever met is a bit screwy. I tend to side with Samuel Goldwyn who once said anyone who goes to a psychiatrist should have their head examined."

"Thankfully, I've never been to one. But my friends who have swear they all peddle the same malarkey: if it's not one thing, it's your mother."

"Good line."

Monique was standing now in front of the bedroom mirror. She was wearing a light blue dress and black flats. Her hair was in a ponytail. Her makeup was expertly applied. Eyeliner, rouge, lipstick. Bobbi Brown couldn't have done it better.

She turned and did a little pirouette.

"How do I look?" she said.

"Prettier than Paris at midnight."

"Merci, grand garçon."

"I bet all the little boys in Omaha lusted after you."

"That didn't happen till my senior year in high school."

"What changed."

"Boobs."

"That would do it."

Monique squinted.

"I get the sense you're checking them out," she said.

"Checking what out?"

"My boobs."

"I'm a detective," I said. "I observe things."

"And what, pray tell, have you observed?"

"That you have first-class breasts."

"Why, thank you."

"You are more than welcome."

Monique then gave me the once-over.

"You look rather snazzy yourself," she said.

I had on AG blue jeans, a James Perse white tee, and Cole Haan loafers. All dressed up and someplace to go.

"I have a flair for dressing," I said.

"With you . . . it's more like a rocket."

"My mother always said men who wear nice clothes live colorful lives."

"You get any more colorful you'll turn into a rainbow."

I patted my stomach.

"I better start cutting back on wine," I said. "I'm getting fat."

Monique pinched my waist.

"You're not fat . . . you're firm."

"Yeah. Firm fat."

She twisted harder.

"I adore every little budge."

I put a fingertip against my lips, then tapped it lightly against Monique's.

"You know what I love about you?" I said.

"No, tell me?"

"Everything."

Monique blushed.

"Flattery will get you everywhere," she said.

"I'm counting on it."

We headed downstairs. I unlocked my desk, grabbed my shoulder holster, and slipped it on. If I have one tip about crime busting, it's this: Never go anywhere unarmed when investigating a murder case. Certainly not in today's world.

I checked the clip. I knew it was loaded, but the one time you don't check . . . I flicked on the thumb safety and put it in the holster.

"Why the gun?" Monique said.

"Psychologists can be dangerous."

"Yeah. They kill people with feelings and emotions."

"That's what I'm afraid of."

To amuse myself, I stood in front of the mirror and did a couple of fast draws. The fact is, I'm a very good shot. Not long after Sid Meyer hired me, I spent weeks and weeks at a shooting range. Eventually, I put in as much time there as I once did in the gym practicing basketball. Trust me when I tell you it's a lot easier hitting a jumper than it is hitting another human being . . . with a bullet.

"Must you always do that?" Monique said.

"Practice makes perfect."

"Sometimes I think you fancy yourself Wyatt Earp."

"Earp couldn't shine my cowboy boots."

"You don't wear cowboy boots."

"Maybe I should get a pair."

"Why don't you, along with a ten-gallon hat."

"Would that be considered ranch dressing?"

Monique rolled her eyes.

"You ready?" she said.

"As I'll ever be."

I grabbed my Zegna blazer. I probably could have purchased a Jaguar for what the jacket cost. But what the hell. You only live once, and if you do it right once is enough.

We left the house and got into the Mustang. Both of us had coffee mugs. I drank mine through the little hole in the cover; inevitably I'd dribble some. Monique sipped hers with the cover off, never spilling a drop. Oh, to have that talent!

As we neared the Lincoln Tunnel, I slipped a Lee Wiley disc into the CD player.

For my money, Wiley's was right up there with Ella Fitzgerald, though she never did get much acclaim. Like me, she was of mixed race, half White and half Cherokee. My mother said her voice was a gift from God.

"Is this Sarah Vaughn?" Monique said as we headed into the Lincoln Tunnel.

"No," I said. "Lee Wiley."

"Never heard of her."

"Most people haven't."

"She's really good."

"One of the best."

"It's a shame when a great artist doesn't get the recognition they deserve."

"Happens a lot," I said. "Look at Margaret Walker."

"Who?"

"See what I mean."

"What's her story?"

"She was a novelist, poet, essayist during the Chicago Black Renaissance. One of the leading woman writers of the mid-twentieth century. Yet she's about as well-known as The Unknown Soldier."

"The things you come up with."

"I came up with you, didn't I?"

"To your great benefit."

After going through the tunnel and fighting midtown Manhattan traffic, we finally got to the Majestic Theatre.

The Majestic is where we first met. I had been hired by an actor to stop a guy from stalking him. The stalker was relentless. I finally had to ram him into a wall, drive a knee into his crotch, and aim a gun between his eyes. He quickly got the message. He pissed in his pants and stopped stalking.

The actor was so grateful he gave me a front row seat to see the play he was in—*Chicago*. He played the part of the shyster lawyer, Billy Flynn. Monique played the role of Velma Kelly.

The minute she walked on stage I was captivated. She had beauty and grace. Presence. Not to mention great legs. To say I was infatuated is an understatement. I was a love-sick fool!

I went backstage after the show, thanked the actor, spotted Monique, introduced myself, and praised her performance.

"I've been working for Matt," I said, referring to the stalked actor.

"He's spoken of you," Monique said.

"I hope well."

"Very well."

"In that case, may I take you to dinner?"

"I . . . I . . . "

"I promise if you go, I'll shower, shave . . . even use deodorant. "

"You would, huh?" she said, flashing a gorgeous smile.

"Yes, madam. I'd even wear a suit and tie."

"Does that mean I have to get all dolled up?"

"You could wear scuba gear for all I care, although a snorkel and tank might be a bit much."

She threw her head back and laughed.

"I have a hunch you could be fun," she said.

"It's my professional opinion that you should always play your hunches."

She nodded.

"Okay, Mr. Detective, you're on."

The first date was great. We had a great dinner at a little Italian restaurant in Greenwich Village. Dim lighting. Red and white checkered tablecloths. Candles. Flowers. Afterward, we went to the Blue Note. Listened to Jane Monheit sing. Her version of "Over the Rainbow" was exquisite. It was a date to build a dream on.

We arrived at the Majestic Theatre.

"Knock 'em dead, kiddo," I said. "There's no business like show business . . . "

". . . Everything about it is appealing."

"Sounds like a song," I said.

I kissed her on the cheek.

"God! You always smell so good. Why is that?"

"Because I wash and deodorize. Maybe you should try it sometime."

"Don't need to. I'm naturally fragrant."

"Yeah. And I'm the Rose of Tralee."

"Catch ya on the rebound."

Monique got out of the car. I watched her walk to the theatre and thought, "Ain't love grand?"

CHAPTER
THIRTEEN

Regina Blake's office was at the far end of campus in a two-story white-shingled building that had warped windowsills and broken gutters. The six granite steps leading up to the black front door were badly cracked. Made me think mental health wasn't a big priority at St. Steve's .

I walked into the office. The anteroom was empty. There were some bentwood chairs and a wood grain desk with brass fittings and cabriole legs. Behind the desk was a credenza. On it was a row of cactus plants. Above the plants were paintings of lakes, the water sage green, a color I once read promoted what shrinks liked to call a calm and relaxing environment. The room smelled of lavender.

The door to the main office was closed. A sign on it read "Do not disturb."

I took a seat. On the table next to me were magazines about health and well-being. I picked up one called "Eating Healthy" and flipped through the pages. The meals described sounded disgusting. Too much kale and too many legumes. Yuck.

After waiting a half hour, the door to the main office opened and a tall, brawny White kid walked out. He was wearing sunglasses, a black hoodie, and black shorts. He glanced at me, seemed momentarily startled, then quickened his pace.

"I'll see you next week," the woman said. "Same time."

"Okay," the kid said. His throat sounded clogged. He gave me another quick glance.

I tried to scope out the back of his right hand, maybe catch sight of a tiny basketball. You never know, right? But the kid rushed out the door too fast.

The woman who had walked behind him was short and slim, fiftyish. She wore a dark pantsuit with a white collared shirt. Sporting a brown bouffant with enough hair spray to stop a bullet, she fashioned large wire-framed glasses that sat crookedly on her nose.

She looked at me with what my father would have called fisheyes: big and magnified.

"May I help you, sir?" she said, in the phony, affected voice of actress Katharine Hepburn, a sort of American-British hybrid that drops "R" sounds and softens vowels to convey wealth and status. Connecticut. Old money.

I stood.

"Are you Regina Blake?" I said.

"Yes," she said, clasping her hands.

"My name is Elgin O'Brien. I'm a private investigator." I flashed her my most winning smile.

She didn't react. Maybe she didn't like my looks. Maybe she didn't like men. Maybe she wasn't having a good day. Maybe I just expected a better reaction. Who knows?

"How may I help you?" she said.

"I'm looking into the murder of Teddy Malone."

"On whose behalf?" All business.

"Pat Malone, the boy's father."

She unclasped her hands.

"I see," she said.

I waited for her to say more but she didn't. She was stiff as sheet rock.

"By the way," I said. "The kid who just left here looked really familiar." I snapped my fingers a few times. "Can't seem to remember his name. Can you remind me?" I was lying through my teeth.

"I'm not at liberty to say." Snotty.

"Aw, c'mon. You can tell me."

"No. I cannot. And please don't ask me again."

"I promise I won't."

"Thank you." Her tone had taken on an even sharper edge.

"I must say I very admire what you do . . . looking after students," I said, hoping to loosen her up. "Must be very rewarding."

"It's quite rewarding," she said. No smile. No grin. So much for my loosening her up. She was tighter than a bale of hay.

"I would imagine it's almost spiritual, the connection and trust you engender."

Her fisheyes widened.

"You said you were a private investigator, right?" she said.

"You sound surprised."

"Well, you . . . you speak so eloquently."

"You speak well, too," I said.

She ran her tongue over her lips, which looked as dry as paper.

"Sorry if I sounded patronizing," she said.

"Apology accepted."

She pushed up her glasses.

"What exactly can I do for you?" she said.

"I'd like to ask you about Teddy."

"What about Teddy?"

"It's my understanding he came to see you."

"Who told you this?"

"His girlfriend."

Blake glanced at her watch.

I shifted my stance and my sport coat opened slightly.

"Are you carrying a gun?" she said in a horrified tone.

"Yes."

"How dare you bring a gun into my office. I abhor guns."

"Who doesn't. But sometimes in my work they're necessary."

"For what? Killing people?"

"No. Protecting people."

She glanced again at her watch.

"Look, Mr . . . "

" . . . O'Brien."

" . . . I have another appointment in ten minutes."

"That's all the time I need."

"Very well," she said, standing aside. "Come into my office."

She followed me in and made a point of leaving the door open.

The office had parquet flooring, a leather wing chair, a leather recliner, a grandfather clock and soft recessed lighting. On a table behind the chair was a fish tank. It was filled with a variety of colorful fish.

I pointed at the tank and said, "Nice touch."

"It's for the patients," she said. "It's what we in the field call a positive distraction, meaning sometimes a glimpse at it can comfort the patient."

"Maybe I should get one."

"You have issues?"

"In my profession, every day."

"Must be stressful."

"Only when people try to kill me."

She put her hand over her mouth.

"Sounds frightening," she said.

"No more than eating at Burger King."

She grinned. Finally.

"Please," she said. "Take a seat."

I sat in the wing chair. The springs creaked underneath me.

"You know, Dr. Blake," I said. "In a way, we're kind of in the same business."

"I take it you consider yourself a problem solver."

"More like a problem eliminator."

"Without the PhD," she said, in a snooty tone. "What can I do for you?"

"Tell me about Teddy Malone?"

"I have nothing to say," she said, picking up a black and gold Montblanc pen. To me, people who use expensive pens are looking to create an image. The successful executive.

"Nothing?" I said.

"That's right. All our conversations are privileged."

"Even though he's dead?"

"Doesn't matter."

"It should matter."

"Why is that?"

"Because maybe he told you something that might help me with my investigation."

She pursed her lips and put the pen down. Outside we could hear cars honking and motorcycles revving.

"Sorry," she said. "I can't help you."

"Can't or won't?"

"Cannot. HIPPA. The Health Insurance Portability and Accountability Act of 1966. Sensitive patient health information cannot be disclosed without the patient's consent or knowledge. It's federal law."

"Gees, I didn't know," I said. But the fact is I did. Sometimes I find it beneficial in my work to look dumb to the people I'm questioning. It often gives them a sense of having the upper hand.

"Suppose I got permission from Teddy's father?" I said.

"Doesn't matter," she said. "Still can't talk to you."

"I may have to investigate that," I said, though I was fully aware it wouldn't make a difference.

"Go right ahead," she said. "Won't do you any good."

"Let me ask you this," I said. "I've been told Teddy was suffering from depression. Can you at least comment on that?"

"No," she said, spitting out the word.

"Is there anything you can comment on?"

"No."

"Were you aware Teddy was using fentanyl?"

Her lips tightened. Sweat glistened in the hollow of her throat. The grandfather clock chimed.

"Cat got your tongue?" I said.

"I told you. I have nothing to say."

"I fail to see what giving me some information could hurt."

"I already told you why."

"I don't buy it."

"Think what you want, Mr. O'Brien."

"A kid's been murdered, and you offer no help. Jesus! Have you no conscience?

"I have a conscience."

"Do you?"

"Yes, I do."

"Then do the honorable thing."

"Don't lecture me about honor."

"What kind of psychologist are you?"

"A responsible one."

"You're not acting like it."

"You're entitled to your opinion."

"I think you know something and you're not telling."

"Maybe because I'm a person with moral and ethical standards."

"Bullshit!"

"Bullshit yourself, Mr. O'Brien."

"Look, lady, I'm not the enemy."

"Then who are you?"

"I'm the guy seeking justice."

"I'd prefer it if you would leave."

"Not till I get some answers."

"I've said all I've got to say."

"Which has been nothing."

"If necessary, I'll call the campus police."

"Yikes."

"Just so you know," she said. "This is a gun-free campus. I suggest you leave before you get in trouble."

"Lady," I said. "Trouble is my business." Can't beat Raymond Chandler for a quip.

"And mine is helping people." A beat. "Now get out."

"I'm giving you an opportunity to do the right thing," I said. "I suggest you take it."

"I certainly don't want and do not need your suggestions."

"Suit yourself," I said. "You may become the shrink who gets shrunk."

"Again, I ask you, please leave."

I stood and said, "With pleasure Doctor Feelbad. With pleasure."

I went to Corsito's office.

"Hello, again," I said to his secretary Anne.

"Hello," she said.

"Is Chris around?

"He's in the weight room."

"Doing what? Eating a hot dog?"

She giggled.

"You think Coach is overweight?" she said.

"If he gets any bigger, he'll qualify as a Macy's Thanksgiving Day balloon," I said. "Where's the weight room?"

"Far end of the gym."

I started to leave.

"Oh, Mr. O'Brien."

I turned. "Yes?"

"Did you hear the good news?"

"What news?"

"Coach was just named the Naismith College Coach of the Year."

"Didn't know that."

"Isn't that wonderful?"

"Yes," I said. "It's right up there with the Razzies."

She looked at me as if I had two heads.

I entered the weight room. It was empty except for Corsito, who was decked out in Nike sweats, a size too small. He was furiously pacing back and forth, a cell phone pressed against his ear. The only thing he was working out was his jaw.

While I waited for him to conclude his conversation, I surveyed the room. It was better equipped than Planet Fitness. The machines—treadmills, ellipticals, stationary bikes, rowing machines, arc trainers, and mountain climbers—looked brand new. Nothing too good for the basketball team.

Corsito got off the phone and immediately got within inches of my face.

"What the fuck is wrong with you?" He shouted, his face swelling and reddening.

"Let's start with knowing you," I said.

"Who the fuck do you think you are harassing the school's psychologist."

"Harassing?

"Yeah, shithead, harassing."

"Blake wouldn't talk to me," I said, "but I have a sneaky suspicion she talked to you. So much for HIPAA."

Corsito's nose was almost touching mine. His breath smelled like onions.

"Back the fuck up," I said.

"Make me."

"What are you? A child?"

"You know, Elgin, you're becoming a real nuisance."

"I'm only doing my job."

"Fuck your job. I should kick your ass."

That did it.

I grabbed Corsito by the throat and rammed him against a wall. His neck elongated and his eyes bulged.

"Listen to me, Chris," I said. "Stop fucking with me. You've been completely indifferent about Teddy's murder . . ."

"What?"

" . . . from the start . . . "

"What are you talking about?"

"Your evasiveness."

"My evasiveness?"

"Where's your loyalty to your players?"

"Where's their loyalty to me? The great ones come for a year, make a splash, then bolt for the NBA, abandoning the program. Is that being loyal?"

"In all my years being around college coaches I don't think I've ever come across one who's as so self-centered as you."

"As if I give a shit what you think."

I took my hands off him.

Corsito rubbed his throat, swallowed hard, and then tried to sucker punch me.

I sidestepped the punch and hit him with a left jab to the stomach. It was soft. He hunched over, but quickly straightened up and came at me again.

I backpedaled.

"Give it up, Chris," I said. "You're not dealing with some college kid. You come at me again, you're going down."

Of course, typical of him, he came at me again. Dumb.

I quickly hit him with a combination of pulled punches to the stomach. He staggered backward. His breathing got heavy and his legs wobbly.

"Had enough?" I said.

"Fuck you, you scumbag motherfucker."

I slapped him with my right hand across the face. It was forceful enough to make him stumble a few steps sideways. He put his forearms up to protect his face.

He started shouting so many obscenities sprays of spittle flew out of his mouth.

I slapped him again. Because his forearms were still protecting his face, I whacked him hard in the kidneys. Once again it rocked him sideways.

"Cocksucker," he screamed.

Just for the hell of it, I hit him once more. This time a powerful punch to the stomach. He grunted and fell to the floor.

"That was a cheap shot," he said.

"I owed you one."

"Fucking bastard."

I stood over him.

"There's nothing I wouldn't enjoy more than beating the ever-loving shit outta you," I said, "but I won't because I want information."

Corsito was bent down on one knee like a batter in the on-deck circle. Gasping for air, he said, "Whaddya want me to say?"

"You told me that you and Teddy had a good relationship, but I've since learned that was bullshit. Truth is, you were riding his ass."

"I ride every kid."

"But you were particularly hard on Teddy."

"He deserved it."

"Why?"

"Because he wasn't playing up to his potential."

"So what? You humiliated him?"

"No. I disciplined him."

"Coaching and abusing are two different things."

"Not in my book."

"Try writing another book."

Corsito started to rise, but like a splayed horse, he had a hard time trying to get to its feet.

I said, "I wanna know what was going on with Teddy."

"Don't know what you mean."

I could almost see lies forming in his eyes. Trying to get the truth from Corsito was like trying to stop snow from falling.

"Let's start with the fact that he was using fentanyl," I said.

"Who told you that?" he said.

"Nobody told me. I found the fentanyl in his room."

"At school?"

"No. His parent's apartment."

His teeth clamped tight.

"I had . . . had no idea," he said, through tight lips.

"No idea of what?

"The fentanyl."

"Really?"

"Yeah, really."

"The use of fentanyl might explain why he wasn't hustling."

"What are you? A fucking doctor?"

"Trust me. I know about the side effects of fentanyl."

"Yeah. You know everything, don't you?"

"I know what the drug did to my cousin. And what drugs did to your son. And I'll tell you what else I know. I know Teddy was into gambling. Maybe he got shot because he owed money and couldn't pay. Or maybe he got shot because he reneged on a deal. Or maybe he was shaving points."

"Shaving points?! Are you crazy?"

"It's been suggested."

"There's no way a player on my team would be shaving points. You don't think I'd know that?"

"There's more than a few coaches who've said the same thing and were proven wrong," I said, thinking of coach Tom Davis and a point-shaving scandal that happened at Boston College years ago. I knew Davis well. We sat together at sports dinners. To this day, he swears he had no knowledge that a couple of his players were in deep with gamblers. I totally believe him.

"I want the truth," I said.

"I'm telling you the truth."

"Who are you kidding? I've known you long enough to know that when it comes to the truth you know only one thing: how it serves your own purposes."

Corsito's face tightened. His neck muscles thickened.

I said, "Try being honest for a change and tell me why Teddy stopped caring about basketball."

"You'd have to fucking ask him."

"I can't, you idiot. The kid's dead, for Christ's sake!"

"Motherfucker . . . Mother . . . I don't know why he stopped caring!" Corsito said, rubbing his cheek. "All I can tell you is he wasn't focused. Wasn't committed. He was lazy in practice and lousy in games. Didn't want to pay the price."

"So you did what? You threw balls at him in practice and called him disgusting names. Is that motivating?"

"I do what I have to do to get the best out of players."

"Who are you kidding? You do it because you're a dictatorial jerk."

"Listen, Elg," he said. "You don't understand the pressure I'm under."

"What pressure?"

"From fans. Parents. Alumni. Social media. The networks. The press. I gotta win."

"You love it. Love the whole fucking circus. The fans, the publicity, the adoration, and the drama. You need it. Want it. It's your oxygen."

"Maybe so. But it's nerve-racking."

"Oh, how I feel for you. You and your seven-million-dollar-a-year salary."

"I earn every penny of it."

"At the expense of the players."

"Players don't come here and play for me unless they want to achieve greatness."

"Ever think they also come to get a diploma?"

"That's up to them, not me."

"No, no, no. It's your responsibility to make them attend class and get educated."

"I'm a coach, not a parent."

"What you are is a fucking phony."

"Think what you want. And let me tell you something. I'm not gonna apologize for my success."

"Nobody's asking you to. I just want answers . . . like what was the problem between Teddy and Smith."

"It was just a misunderstanding. No big deal."

"Tell me about it."

"I just told you. It was nothing."

"Tell me about it," I said again.

"What are you fucking deaf?"

I grabbed his shirt and pushed him against the wall. His face was red with rage.

"Are you going to answer me?" I shouted.

"I don't know how many times I gotta tell you, it was inconsequential."

"I still don't know why or who shot Teddy Malone," I said, "but if I find out you had anything to do with this, anything . . . anything at all, I swear I'm going to do everything in my power to bring you down." I let him go.

"You trying to scare me?"

"Don't need to try."

"Is this some kind of a game with you?"

"Let's just say you better start playing defense."

"Doesn't matter how much offense you play, Elgin . . . I'm gonna win."

"Not this time, Chris, not this time."

He grinned. His grin was demonic.

"Let me tell you something, Elgin," he said. "The game's changed since you played at Duke."

"The game hasn't changed," I said. "It's coaches like you who've changed, who think nothing of breaking the rules."

"That's because in today's coaching environment, it's win or be gone. Play or get played."

"And you certainly play all the angles, don't you, Chris?"

Corsito stared at me as if I was an insect under a microscope.

"Who the fuck you think you're fucking with?" he said. "Don't you get it? I. Never. Lose. I'm a winner. A goddamn fucking winner. You can't beat me. Nobody can. And you better watch your back, Mr. Private Dick."

"Is that a threat?"

"No. It's a fact," he said, snarling. "You've been warned. Get that through your thick . . . thick nigger head."

I knew he was baiting me, but if he thought that slur would bother me, he was wrong. I'd been called that vile name many times before. As a kid, it made me put up my fists. But as I got older, I heeded the words of my father who said, "You can't physically fight racism. But you can use words to give a knockout punch." That's one reason I agreed to serve on the board of the NBA's Social Justice Coalition. In fact, I was one of the guys that pushed the league to establish the Commissioner's Committee on Social Justice.

The snarl on Corsito's face suddenly morphed into a big smile.

"Let me tell you something . . . boy," he said. "At this school I'm king."

"Kings get dethroned."

"Not this one.

"Don't bet on it."

"You know what? If I didn't have a TV interview this afternoon I'd press charges right now."

"For what?"

"Assault."

"The only assault I see here is on my intelligence."

CHAPTER
FIFTEEN

I walked over to the school library. It was quiet. Students sat on lounge chairs, looking at their phones or sleeping. I didn't see much studying going on. A few older men walked by, dressed sloppily in wrinkled linen shirts and baggy jeans. Many had short scraggly graying beards. Big, thick glasses. They looked like dorks. Probably professors.

I strolled up to a lady standing behind the information desk. She looked to be in her mid-thirties, shapely and attractive with long reddish hair, a button nose, and a sweet, sexy smile. No doubt it put male students on a tidal wave of desire.

"Where might I find a computer?" I said, giving her my best hundred-kilowatt Tom Cruise smile.

"Are you a professor?" Her voice was as soft as cashmere.

"God no," I said. "I'm a freshman."

"You look old for a freshman."

"Looks are deceiving," I said, adding another shot of Cruise. "What's your name?"

"Rachel. And yours?"

"Dorian Gray."

She grinned. A fan of thin wrinkles opened at the outer edges of each eye.

"Ah, the man of eternal youth," she said.

"Don't I appear youthful?"

"You appear handsome."

"It's the Botox."

"Yeah, right."

She pointed to a table where a half dozen students were sitting at a high table, working on computers.

"Will you need help?" she said.

"I always need help."

"With?"

"Understanding the mysteries of life."

She cackled.

"I like a man with a sense of humor," she said

"I like anybody with a sense of humor."

"You're interesting. Are you alone?"

"Here?"

"No," she said, lowering her voice " . . . in your life."

"You mean do I have a lady friend?"

"Guess that's what I'm asking."

"I do."

"Is the relationship monogamous?"

"As can be."

"Can't win 'em all."

"Still gotta play the game."

"Unfortunately," she said.

I walked over to the computer table and googled Steve Smith.

He was born in Anaheim, California. He played basketball and football at Cal State, Fullerton. After graduating, he became a Navy Seal and served two tours in Iraq, one in Fallujah and one in Ramadi. He was an expert marksman.

Upon returning to the United States, he got a master's degree in exercise science, including courses in injury prevention, psychology, nutrition, strength, and conditioning. He did a few internships, then took jobs in a variety of small colleges. Then four years ago, he was hired as the conditioning coach at Rutgers University. In 2022, he was fired for allegedly supplying football players with performance-enhancing drugs. Namely, steroids.

Although he never faced legal charges, he subsequently sued the university over his dismissal. He lost. After the case closed, Corsito hired him, which seemed strange given the circumstances.

Obviously, there was a connection between them. I just didn't know what. Despite that, I felt as though I was getting close to the truth.

I got up from the table and stopped by the information desk.

"Did you find what you were looking for?" Rachel said.

"I did. Thank you."

"You ever get tired of monogamy you know where to find me."

"It'll have to wait till pigs fly."

She winked. "Oink, oink."

I strolled over to the weight room. Corsito was gone. He'd been replaced by students running on treadmills, lifting weights, and pedaling Pelotons. Walking around and supervising things was Steve Smith. He was wearing tight shorts, a tank top . . . and fingerless gloves.

"Hey Steve," I said.

"Hey Elgin. How are you?"

"I'm good."

He flashed me a lopsided smile. He looked as if he had just finished lifting weights. His biceps were so swollen they looked like ten-pound hams.

"Wha'cha doing here?" he said, grabbing a towel and wiping his face.

"Just came by for a quick chat."

"Glad you did." He tossed the towel aside.

"This is one helluva nice weight room," I said.

"That it is," Smith said. "You pump iron?"

"Are you kidding? I don't even pump gas. I live in New Jersey."

Smith laughed.

"I understand you were a Navy Seal," I said.

"I was."

"Impressive."

"I was lucky to have survived the program."

"Tough, huh?"

"Brutal."

"I commend you for serving two tours in Iraq. That had to be brutal as well."

"It was."

"You were a sniper, right?"

He regarded me with a quizzical eye.

"How do you know all this stuff?"

"Corsito told me," I lied.

"Chris is something else," he said. "He certainly knows how to light up a room."

"Yeah," I said. "After he leaves it."

Smith cocked his head.

"Just kidding," I said, even though I wasn't.

Smith grinned. His thin, brown lips widened as if they'd been slashed.

"Not sure if you're aware," I said, "but I've been hired by Teddy Malone's father to investigate Teddy's murder."

"I didn't know," he said. He nervously pulled at one of his fingers, as if trying to pull off a ring that wasn't there.

"You know anything about it?" I said.

"Only what I read in the papers."

We fell silent. All around us we heard the clanking of weights.

"Pardon me for asking," I said, "but I was told that you and Teddy didn't get along."

His eyebrows knitted together.

"Who told you that?" he said.

"His girlfriend."

"She's lying," he said, fiercely.

"Is she?"

"Damn right she is."

"She told me you guys had some beef and pushed each other around," I said. "Is that true?"

He gave me an expression of disgust, his agitation rising.

"You ask a lot of questions," he said.

"Occupational habit," I said. "Is it true that you guys had a tussle?"

"Yes," he said, "we did have words and there was some pushing and shoving."

"What was the disagreement?"

"His body."

"What about his body?"

"He was being pushed around down low in the paint. He needed to bulk up."

"Did you suggest he take steroids?"

Smith's face turned a violent shade of scarlet.

"Is that a subtle reference to what happened to me at Rutgers?" he said.

"Not subtle," I said. "What did happen?"

He expelled a breath.

"I got fired," he said.

"Because?"

"I was a good soldier. I followed orders."

"Enlighten me."

"The head coach told me to bulk up some players."

"But you got fired, he didn't."

"That's because he's the coach," Smith said. "You know how it works. Winning coaches never take the heat. I was the fall guy."

"I read articles about what happened," I said. "Why didn't you finger the coach?"

"Because I was told that if I kept my mouth shut, I'd get a great severance package."

"Did you?"

"No."

"Is that why you sued?"

"Damn right."

"But you lost."

"Right, again."

"How is it you came to St. Steve's ?"

"Coach Hunter recruited me."

"Were you and Dave friends?"

"We . . . we had a number of mutual acquaintances."

"Gotta ask you," I said, "where were you the night Teddy Malone was murdered?"

He gazed at me, as if hypnotized.

"Why would you ask me that?" he said.

"You obviously had problems with Teddy . . . and you know how to shoot a gun."

He shifted his weight from his right leg to his left.

"Look, Elgin," he said, "I don't wanna hassle with you."

"Who would?"

Enmity was oozing out of him like molasses from a tree.

"You like to provoke people, don't you?" he said.

"I provoke to get answers."

"Why are you bothering me. What the fuck I ever do to you?"

"Nothing."

"Then leave me alone."

"I don't mean to me rude . . . "

He smiled. It was a weird smile, fierce, almost a snarl. "Oh, no?"

"No. I just want information."

"I don't fucking believe this."

"It's my job to question everyone."

He shifted from his left leg to his right. His mouth tightened and his face got dark. A telltale sign of guilt.

"Can't believe I have to answer this," he said, indignantly.

"You don't. But you should. I need to know."

"Know what?"

"Where you were the night Teddy Malone was murdered."

"Suppose I don't wish to answer."

"I could make your life miserable."

I suddenly got the sense he wanted to rip my heart out.

"How?" he said.

"I could report to you to the NCAA," I said. "Tell them I suspect you of dispensing steroids. I have a lot of friends there."

My words jarred him. He gaped at me open-mouthed but took his time before speaking.

"You're a real pain in the ass, you know that?" he said.

"I strongly suggest you cooperate."

Our eyes held for a long moment. It took a while before Smith responded.

"If I recall correctly," he said, the muscles in his jaw bulging, "I was home."

"Alone?"

"Yes."

"Can anyone verify that?"

"No."

"Not a great alibi."

"I don't need a great alibi. I didn't shoot the kid."

The students around us were oblivious to our discussion. They were focused on biking and running.

"This conversation is over," Smith said.

"Far from it. I know you're hiding something."

He turned and started to walk away.

I grabbed his bicep.

"Get your goddamn hands off me," he said.

"After you do one thing."

"What's that?"

"Take the glove off on your right hand."

He slapped my hand away. The anger in his eyes turned savage and cold.

"Fuck you," he said. He then turned and stormed out of the room.

I thought about running after him and stripping off his glove. But even if he had the tiny tattoo of a basketball, what would that prove?

Nothing. I needed more evidence, a lot more evidence. Hard evidence.

CHAPTER
SIXTEEN

I left the weight room. It was another hot afternoon. I started walking to my car when I noticed Ambush Anderson coming out of the student union building with the tall White guy who had bumped into me yesterday. Strolling between them was . . . Emma Mitchell.

The three of them were having a serious conversation. No smiles, no laughter. She was doing most of the talking.

Keeping a good distance away, I followed them.

When they got to a building named Taylor Hall, Emma hugged them both, then quickly disappeared inside. The two guys continued walking. They walked behind the building and ducked into a shiny Jaguar. Ambush got behind the wheel. I assumed it was his ride. No doubt purchased with NIL money—courtesy of one James Catalano.

Tires screeching, the Jag zoomed off. A velocity of escape.

Unfortunately, my Mustang was parked too far away for me to get it and tail them.

I wasn't sure what to make of that unlikely trio. Were they classmates? Friends? Associates? Partners in crime? Whatever the case, I didn't like it. Didn't like it at all.

I got to my car. Started the engine. Turned up the AC. It made a rattling noise. I drove off.

Despite what I had just witnessed, Smith was still my number one suspect. I had to find out where he was on the night of the shooting.

Putting him aside, I thought about Corsito and Blake. What were they hiding? Were they protecting Smith? Themselves? They sure knew a helluva lot more than they were saying.

And what about Ambush Anderson and his gangster friends? What role, if any, did they, along with Emma Mitchell, play in Teddy Malone's murder? But what could Ambush possibly gain from having Teddy knocked off? What would be his motive? Certainly not money. Ambush was soon to be an NBA first-round draft pick. But even rich guys lose control and get stupid. Look at O.J. Maybe Teddy and Ambush had a falling out? Maybe Teddy wronged one of his friends? Reneged on a deal? Failed to pay a debt? Stole some drugs? All four?

Or maybe Emma Mitchell hired one of Ambush's friends to kill Teddy. Hell hath no fury like a woman scorned. I thought of what Roth told me back in the photography studio—that Emma was more than capable of engaging someone to do her dirty work.

Add to this . . . Teddy's father. What did he know? What was he withholding? Was it something to do with Teddy's gambling? His gambling? Point shaving? Prop betting? Fentanyl? There was a lot of ponder.

I wanted time to think. As my Irish grandfather used to say, "When the going gets tough, the tough drinks Guinness."

On my way back home, I stopped at the Landmark Tavern, one of my favorite places. Founded in 1868 and tucked away on the corner of Forty-Fourth Street and Eleventh Avenue, it's one of the longest continually operating restaurants in New York. Very old school Manhattan:

tin ceilings, brick walls, planked floors, a gold cash register, and a small fireplace. You half expect to see Walt Whitman sitting before the fire rhapsodizing on democracy, nature, love, and friendship.

The place had the sweet smell of beer and burgers. A bartender, wearing a white apron around his waist, was whistling softly and polishing the bar top with a damp cloth.

I took an open seat at the bar. The bartender saw me and grinned. He was fortyish, chubby, and short with reddish hair and a Teddy Roosevelt mustache. On his left index finger was a Claddagh ring.

He sauntered toward me and said, "What can I get ye?" He had a thick Irish accent.

"Guinness?"

"On tap?"

"Sold."

I watched as he grabbed a pint glass, tilted it at a forty-five-degree angle then pulled the spout toward him and filled the glass three-quarters full. He waited a minute for the beer to settle. When it did, he held the glass level and topped it off. It was crowned with a nice layer of foam.

"Masterful job of pouring," I said.

"If ye gonna do sumting, do it right," he said, putting the pint before me.

"Couldn't agree more."

I raised my pint.

"Slainte," I said.

"May ye be in heaven half hour before the devil knows ye's dead," he said, smiling. His front teeth were chipped.

"I'll drink to that," I said.

"I'll drink to anything," he said, extending his hand. "Name's Padraig."

We shook.

"Elgin," I said.

He squinted as if something had ignited his memory.

"Elgin?" he said. "Elgin as in Baylor?"

My eyebrows rose. What's the chance of meeting an Irishman who knows the name Elgin Baylor?

"You're a basketball fan?" I said.

"Fookin' love the game," he said. "Played it in me younger days, for the St. Michael's Club team in Killarney." He patted his ample stomach. "Back when I was leaner and meaner."

"How about that."

"Ye a tall guy," he said. "Ever play?"

"Played college ball at Duke and ten years with the Dallas Mavericks."

"You play with Nowitzki?"

"I did."

"Dirk was one talented German."

"No shit."

We talked hoops for a while, mostly about the old Laker teams. He knew all about Elgin's teammates: Jerry West, Wilt Chamberlain, Rudy LaRusso, Gail Goodrich, "Happy" Hairston.

"I read everything I can about dem guys and watch 'em on You Tube. Dat's when the NBA was great," he said. "Back in dem old days. Today it's all run and gun, razzle dazzle, too many tree pointers. Don't watch it much anymore."

"Me neither."

A young couple entered the restaurant and took seats at the bar. Padraig immediately attended to them.

I sipped my beer. It was cold and crisp. The way a true Irishman favors it. Which is very unlike those batty Brits who enjoyed their beer warm. Maybe the constant rain in London fogs their brains.

I wiped the foam off my mouth with a tiny napkin imprinted with the words "Guinness: Good Things Come to Those That Wait."

I was making some headway, though not fast enough. But that's how it often goes with a case. You go through the motions, you interview people, you do research, collect a certain amount of data, and it might seem like you're not making progress, but eventually the pieces start to fall into place.

Padraig returned and turned on a TV behind the bar. Using a remote, he clicked around the channels, finally stopping at ESPN.

A reporter was in the middle of a taped interview with—who else? Corsito.

"Let's talk about next season," the reporter said.

"It's looking good," Corsito said, grinning ear to ear. "We have veteran players returning, and some great players coming in." I noticed his makeup melting and running down his cheek. His cheek was still red from where I'd slapped him.

"According to the *College Recruiting Report*, you've signed the two of best players in the New York area, Ricky Vasquez and Marius Griffin. Five-star recruits."

"That we did," Corsito said.

"What is it about your program, *or you*, that attracts such talent?"

"Well, for one thing," Corsito said, "we—I—have a reputation for developing players who can make the NBA. Also, players who come to St. Stephen's know they will be treated with the utmost respect."

"Are you concerned that the media still gives you flak about your players not graduating and using drugs, rather than praising you for providing opportunities?"

Corsito flashed his phony, devilish smile.

"First of all, our graduation rate is higher than most people think," Corsito said. "And secondly, every coach has to deal with players who, let's just say, go off the rails. My players have been accused of many things, but not one of them has been convicted of anything." He took a deep breath. "Let's be honest here. A lot of the accusers . . . well, their stories have been a bit flimsy. I take good kids and make them great."

"To my knowledge not one player—not one player—has ever been suspended for their behavior."

Corsito got huffy.

"Why would I suspend a kid based on lies?" Corsito said. "It wouldn't be fair to the players, the team, and the school."

"Gotta ask you, Coach, are you concerned about recent reports that your star player, Amare Anderson—Ambush as he is called—has been photographed lately with some rather well-known gamblers?"

"Not concerned at all."

"Why?"

"Why? I'll tell you why. First of all, Amare grew up in a tough neighborhood in the Bronx. It was inevitable that he'd come in contact with some unsavory people. Yes, some questionable people are friends of his. Friendship means a lot to him. But I've learned never to condemn anybody by the company they keep. Condemn them for who they are. In Amare's case, there is simply nothing about him worth condemnation."

"Well said, Coach. Because accusations are not facts. I get accused of things all the time that are not true. Comes with the throne; someone always trying to take your crown. Congrats, Coach, on you getting so many top recruits."

Corsito put up his hands in the air like the pope giving a papal blessing.

"I gotta give a lot of credit to my assistant, Dave Hunter," Corsito said. "He's the best recruiter in all of college basketball. I wouldn't be where I am without him."

"One last question, Coach," the reporter said. "Your program was rocked this spring by this tragic shooting of Teddy Malone who was murdered a few months ago outside a Manhattan gentleman's club. Can you comment on that?"

Corsito sniffed.

"Look, it was a tragedy. By all accounts the young man was just in the wrong place at the wrong time. And Teddy was just a kid, a real stubborn kid, talented, but a bit of a hothead. He'd even had an altercation with our conditioning coach a few weeks before. When you can't control your emotions . . . well, bad things can happen. May God rest his soul. My thoughts and prayers go out to his family."

The reporter ended the interview. "That was St. Stephen's head coach, Chris Corsito, a Naismith Award winner and a man who, in my humble opinion, is *the* best coach in college basketball and I predict, *right now*, will win *another* NCAA title come next March. *Write that down.*"

The reporter's suck up and Corsito's pious BS almost soured the taste of my Guinness. But the interview made me think that speaking with Dave Hunter might be worthwhile.

Dave wasn't as fiery as Chris. He was more mellow. Laid back. Maybe, just maybe, he might give me something to work with. Like a clue.

I pointed to the TV and asked Padraig to turn the volume down.

"Corsito's a great coach, but a fookin' eejit," Padraig said. "He's so full of shite."

"If lying was an Olympic sport, he'd win a gold medal."

Padraig turned the TV off and music suddenly filled the room—John Fogarty singing about "a bad moon rising."

I finished my Guinness and signaled Padraig for the check.

"Not staying for lunch?" he said.

"Can't. Gotta go visit a basketball camp."

"Where?"

"The Poconos."

"The one in Stroudsburg?"

"Boy oh boy, you do know your basketball."

"I went to dat camp as a kid, after I come over here with me parents."

"I went there, too."

"Fookin' top-notch competition."

"To say the least. Did your game improve?"

"Bet your arse. But it didn't make me any taller."

I laughed, threw some bills on the bar, and shook Padraig's hand.

"Tanks," he said. "May luck rise with ye."

I shot him the peace sign.

Outside, the heat was still pounding down. I got into the car and the leather seat was hot. I cranked up the AC and headed home, wondering why Corsito had just thrown Teddy Malone's memory under the bus.

CHAPTER SEVENTEEN

The first thing I did when I got home was take a shower. The cool water felt great. I let it pound my shoulders.

After fifteen minutes, I turned the shower off, dried myself and put a towel around my waist. I then went into the kitchen, grabbed a bottle of Fiji Water.

As I drank, I couldn't help but think how when I took this case I suspected it might bring me into the shadowy world of college basketball, where money and prestige have become the termites on the game's foundation. But what I didn't expect, and should have, was how Corsito would circle the wagons. His only priority was self-protection. He didn't care anything about either Teddy or finding his murderer. In fact, I was more and more convinced that he knew a lot more than he let on. He didn't want me to find the truth.

I finished the water and opened my mail. Nothing of real interest. Ads from real estate and insurance companies. A bill from my corner liquor store. I couldn't believe how much wine I'd purchased. Geez Louise. There was also another big bill from Zegna. Sometimes I wonder: Do I spend more money on clothes or wine? Guess it really doesn't matter. I get enormous pleasure from both.

I went to the picture window and opened the shade. I glanced out at the park across the street and saw a tall, muscular guy wearing a black hoodie and black shorts. He was pacing back and forth, occasionally stopping and staring up at my building.

Even though I couldn't see his face, his frame resembled the guy who deliberately bumped me coming out of Teddy Malone's old dorm. He was also about the same size of the kid I saw exiting Regina Blake's office. Maybe I was being paranoid. But paranoia for a detective isn't a bad thing. It keeps you on edge.

I quickly threw on shorts, a tee, and sneakers. Then I grabbed my gun. I took three stairs at a time, clinging to the banister for balance. I set a new house racing record.

Gasping for air, I ran outside and started across the street. A cruising bus blocked my path, nearly hit me. I stopped. Waited. The bus passed. The guy was gone.

I looked up and down the street. Didn't see him. I walked into the park, holding the gun tight against my thigh. A crashing noise came from behind me. I turned quickly. Raised my gun. Aimed.

A teenage kid immediately put his hands up and shouted, "Don't shoot! Don't shoot! I . . . I . . . I just knocked over a garbage can."

"For Christ's sake," I said, sighing and lowering my gun.

"Sorry, man, sorry," the kid mumbled.

"Get lost," I said. The kid turned and ran away

I continued walking through the park, looking behind trees, bushes and statues, keeping the gun out of sight near my hip. No hoodie man. Just some old folks on benches and girls walking dogs.

I went back to the house and reholstered my gun. The idea that some guy, whoever he was, might be spying on me was unnerving. For my sake as well as Monique's.

I needed to calm down and take my mind someplace else for a while. For me, music and books are what antianxiety medication is to other people.

I went into the office, put an Ornette Coleman CD into the Bose player and pulled a copy of Zadie Smith's new novel, *Fraud*, from the bookcase. I admire Smith. Her talents are expansive. The book is about a trial that divided Victorian England, exposing deception and corruption at the highest levels. To celebrate opening the book I poured myself a two-fingered glass of Bushmills.

I find Bushmills a great complement to reading. It relaxes the body. Marinates the mind. At least that's what I tell myself.

I took a quick sip, exhaled, and said, "Ah!" I then sat back, legs extended, ankles crossed, and thought of how my Irish grandfather used to call Bushmills the healer, the cure, the remedy, the ultimate pick-me-up. The man was an Irish Confucius.

One of his philosophical tenants was that God invented whiskey so the Irish wouldn't rule the world. What he forgot to add was that they could barely rule themselves. That's the Irish, for ye.

I was twenty pages into the book when the buzzer sounded. I pressed the intercom.

"Yes," I said.

"Elgin O'Brien?"

"Yes."

"Have a minute?"

"For?"

"A quick conversation."

"About?"

"Coach Chris Corsito."

"Who am I speaking with?"

"James Catalano."

"As in Catalano Capital?"

"I'm surprised you know me," he said.

I could recognize the voice of a pompous ass anywhere.

"Occasionally, I watch things on TV other than cartoons," I said.

"I guess you've seen me on CNBC."

"Only when you're being investigated." Catalano had been investigated even more than Donald Trump. And like Trump, he was not a man to cross. The *Wall Street Journal* once wrote that "turning down a demand by James Catalano was akin to jumping up and down on a trampoline with an explosive on your back."

"May I come up?" he said.

"Why not. Maybe you can give me tips on how to fleece a company."

I hit the buzzer. Seconds later, an older, handsome broad-shouldered guy with a globular head and conceited face appeared. He was wearing a bespoke navy blue suit, a bright yellow tie, and a white shirt so crisp I could smell the starch. The shirt contrasted nicely with his moneyed tan. Ralph Lauren would have been impressed.

"Enter," I said.

Reeking of expensive cologne, he strutted into the office as if he expected to be greeted with blaring trumpets and rose petals. He looked around the room at the music posters on the wall and said, "I see you're a jazz fan."

"That I am."

"So am I," he said, pointing to the picture of Miles Davis. I noticed his fingernails were polished and manicured, his cufflinks solid gold, his wristwatch Patek Philippe. The watch probably cost at least a cool fifty grand. No doubt one of many.

"You're a jazz fan, huh?" I said, surprised. "Who do you like?"

"I love Kenny G."

I coughed into my fist. As far as I'm concerned Kenny G is to jazz what James Patterson is to Shakespeare.

"Take a seat," I said. He sat in the leather wing chair, crossed his legs, straightened his tie, and pulled his pant legs up so they wouldn't bag. Mr. Beau Brummell.

"What can I do for you?" I said.

"First, let me tell you about myself."

I yawned. "Do tell."

"As you may know, I run one of the largest investment firms on Wall Street. I graduated from St. Stephen's and am president of the alumni club."

"I'm not interested in making a donation."

"That's not why I'm here."

"Then why are you here?"

He clasped his hands together. His pinky ring was the size of a golf ball.

"I heard about your confrontation today with Coach Corsito," he said. "He feels bad about hurting you."

"Hurting me?" I said. "That's a laugh. Please continue."

"Whatever the case," he said. "He's *very* upset over what happened."

"He should be."

"He knows you're looking into the murder of Teddy Malone, and he's concerned that if you make it into a big issue, that might generate negative publicity that it could hurt his recruiting."

"Breaking the rules could hurt him even more. Maybe he should be concerned about that."

"I admit Coach has at times blurred the line."

"Blurred the line!" I said. "He obliterates it."

"Don't exaggerate."

"Are you alumni so fucking blind you don't see what's going on there?"

Smugly, he said, "Why don't you tell me?"

"Players aren't getting degrees. They're forever getting into trouble. Drugs. Gambling. Drunk driving. Sexual assaults. And now one gets murdered. Yet supporters bribe players like Ambush Anderson with NILs deals just to genuflect in front of Corsito."

"What can I tell you?" he said. "I want to support St. Stephen's, and I think Corsito is a genius."

"So was Ted Kaczynski. The Unabomber. Look where it got him."

"Don't kid yourself," he said. "You know almost every top college coach plays the same game."

"Most do, yes," I said. "But without regulations it's all darkness."

Catalano didn't respond.

"Don't you believe coaches should play by the rules?" I said.

A wide grin illuminated his face. "The only thing I believe in . . . is a great rate of return."

I shook my head. What an asshole.

Catalano reached inside his suit pocket and pulled out a monogrammed silver Tiffany's cigarette case. He flipped open the case. Cigarettes popped up like miniature organ chords. He pulled one out and said, "Mind if I smoke."

"Yeah, I do."

"Worried about secondhand smoke?"

"No. Cancer."

Catalano put the case back in his pocket and stuck the cigarette behind his right ear.

"We assume Mr. Malone is paying you to investigate," he said. "Is that correct?"

"It is."

"And we think it's good what you're doing."

"Thank you for the endorsement."

"But." He paused and gave me his serious I'm a business shark look, the one that probably intimidated investors. "We'd appreciate it you'd stop bothering Coach Corsito and any other member of the St. Stephen's family."

"You'd appreciate that, would you?"

"Very much so."

I rubbed my right eye with my right knuckle.

"In fact," he said, "We . . . I . . . am willing to show our appreciation by hiring you to conduct the investigation for us without involving the basketball program or Coach Corsito. I think we can offer a more substantial retainer than Mr. Malone for what will certainly turn out to be—as the police believe and I'm sure you'll conclude—a tragic act of random violence. Think of it as a gratuity."

"Like you give recruits?"

He ignored my comment.

I said, "It's my understanding you've funneled a lot of money to Ambush Anderson."

He raised his hands and turned them over.

"As you well know," he said, "players can now get paid for the use of their image."

"And you've taken full advantage."

"Only what's within the rules."

"You mean Corsito's rules."

"I just do whatever I can to help the program."

"I'm sure you do, legal and otherwise."

Catalano leaned forward in his seat.

"Would a ten-thousand-dollar retainer be sufficient?" he said.

"Ten thousand. Wow! That's a lot of salad."

He smiled victoriously, his sharp teeth flashing like tiny bayonets.

"May I counter?" I said.

His smile grew even wider.

"Of course," he said. "Money talks."

"In your world, it screams."

"It's what makes America great."

"Don't give me that horseshit."

"It's true," he said. "Capitalism counts."

"For what? Greed?"

"I take it you want to up the price," he said. "I like that. You play an aggressive game."

"I'm naturally competitive."

"And, I would assume, a gambler."

"Depends on the odds."

"I'm going to put the odds in your favor."

Catalano rubbed his palms together, as if warming his hands.

"How much would you like?" he said. "Name your price."

"You can't afford this soul. I'm not Faust and I have no price."

"Believe me, I can offer you a lot more than Malone."

"You can offer me more and more and more, but I ain't taking it."

"Don't be foolish," he said.

"I try not to be, but sometimes I can't help myself."

"Listen, Mr. O'Brien. I truly believe making a deal would be in our mutual interest."

"You think so?"

"Don't dismiss my offer lightly," he said. "Being a former professional athlete, you must remember what it feels like when you have lots of money in your bank account. It gives you freedom and power." He paused. "Bottom line, I can offer you a fortune if you do as I ask."

"Remind me what I'd have to do," I said.

"Keep St. Stephen's out of your investigation," he said. "Let the police do the dirty work and give poor Mr. Malone some peace." He smiled. "I'm certain we can come to a favorable arrangement. Your name would look good on the masthead as my company's chief security officer. And you wouldn't even have to come to the office. Ever."

"I'll tell you what I'll think about."

"What's that?"

I reached over and pulled the cigarette from behind his ear and tossed it to the floor.

"I think I'd like to punch your fucking lights out," I said.

He leaned back in his seat and gave me the kind of cold hard look that one gives an adversary when they're convinced something violent can be leveled on them with a snap of a finger.

"I don't take threats lightly," he said, making a slicing gesture, as with a knife.

"Meaning?"

"I know people who could cause you headaches."

"Like your family?"

Catalano's father and uncles were well-known mobsters. They profited from extortion, prostitution, gambling, and narcotics. The grapevine had it that they ordered rivals killed as easily as most people ordered pizza.

"I see you studied my genealogy," Catalano said.

"What little I know I don't admire."

"That's your prerogative," he said, his pupils lighting up as if given a battery charge. "I do have friends who settle accounts . . . for me."

"I assume you're not taking about bookkeepers."

"I'm taking about people who mop up messes."

"You mean janitors?"

"Funny, O'Brien, funny. The folks I'm referencing do things clean and tidy."

"Like Simonize toilets?"

His face darkened with fury. His lips curled upward in a venomous smile.

"Go ahead, shithead, keep making with the wisecracks. But don't doubt my resources."

"I won't if you do me one favor."

"What's that?"

"Get the fuck out of my apartment. NOW!"

Catalano gave me a smug, self-satisfied smile.

"You'll regret this," he said.

"I regret a lot of things," I said. "Meeting you is now one of them."

Catalano stood. I stood. We looked like two wrestlers taking a break and planning new holds, new strategies.

After a long minute of silence, Catalano said, "I have half a mind to . . . " He raised his hand and shot me with a finger gun.

I laughed. "One thing's for sure."

"What's that?"

"You do have half a mind."

Catalano left. In a huff. I celebrated his departure by finishing off my glass of Bushmills.

CHAPTER
EIGHTEEN

I decided to postpone driving up to see Hunter, if for no other reason than I knew he was Corsito's lapdog and would most likely parrot whatever his boss said.

I quickly dressed, putting on AG jeans, a Vuori polo shirt, and Allbird sneakers. Glancing at myself in the mirror, I looked like an aging preppy. To give myself a more mature appearance, I grabbed an old linen bomber jacket that I purchased back when I was buying clothes from my favorite men's shop, Barney's New York.

Barney's was a great store. Expensive. Had great brands. Great service. Tailoring. But, sadly, like so many fabulous New York institutions—Chumley's, 21 Club, the Oak Bar at the Plaza Hotel—it's gone out of business. Bye-bye Miss American Pie.

I left the house. The air had a gray tint to it and felt heavy and barely breathable. Motorcycles mumbled and the roofs of parked cars gave off a searing sheen.

I ducked into the Mustang. It was hotter than a sauna. I drove toward the Holland Tunnel. For some unexplainable reason, I was filled with a sense of foreboding; I could almost feel it bubbling inside me like some dreadful greasy gruel.

As I neared the tunnel, I looked into the review mirror and noticed a black SUV. After a few blocks, I realized it was following me.

The driver of the SUV was very good. A pro. He remained a few cars behind me and would occasionally change lanes so as not to be conspicuous.

The last time someone trailed me they quickly zoomed up next to me and started shooting. Fortunately, I slammed the brakes at the last minute and avoided being shot. It was a close call. Saved the Mustang, too.

I didn't want that to happen again. You can only be lucky so many times.

I sped up through the tunnel. The SUV stayed close behind. When I got into Manhattan, I made a couple of quick lefts and rights. The moves didn't elude the SUV. I swerved around a bus. So did the SUV. I ran two red lights. The SUV followed suit.

Speeding around Canal Street, I had to jam the brakes so as not to hit an old lady wheeling a shopping cart. Had I not been being followed I would have stopped and apologized. But I didn't have that luxury; a bad guy was on my ass.

I parked on the corner of Grand Street in Little Italy. Before getting out, I pulled my gun from the shoulder holster. If someone was going to attempt a drive by shooting, I wanted to be ready. I opened the car door slowly. Stepped out slowly, my gun at my side. The SUV reduced speed. Crept along. I suddenly heard a blast. It sounded like gunfire. I ducked. It wasn't gunfire. It was a bus backfiring.

When I rose, I watched as the SUV drove past me. The windows were tinted black. There were no license plates.

I walked down Grand Street to Ferrara's Bakery and Café. Opened in 1892, it claims to be the first expresso bar in America. It's one of Marty Scorsese's favorite spots. I'd seen him there a few times.

I went inside. The place smelled deliciously of coffee and pastries. Eclairs, napoleons, and assorted biscotti—chocolate, almond, anise, hazelnut. A crowd of people stood at the cash register wolfing down cups of gelato. Nothing beats cold ice cream on a hot day.

I was at Ferrara's because I knew a "Goodfella" who had an expresso and cannoli there every afternoon at five o'clock: Carlo Romano. He knew more gossip about gangsters than a platoon of FBI agents. I once helped his sister beat a robbery rap—she was actually innocent—and since then Carlo has felt indebted to me. Typical goomba stuff. You do me a favor, I do you one. A pact for perpetuity.

Carlo was sitting, alone as usual, at a small wooden table far in the back. A huge man with a head the size of a buffalo, he had an oily face with more scars than Frankenstein. His hair was curly gray and short. He had a double chin and a waddle dripping from beneath it. Decked out in a white linen suit, he sported a black silk shirt opened to his breastbone. He reminded me of Luca Brasi from *The Godfather*.

He was reading the *Daily Racing Form*. As I took a seat across from him. he folded the paper in half. I noticed he had a big diamond pinky ring and massive solid gold cufflinks. He looked up at me and smiled. His choppers were larger and whiter than Chiclets.

"How you be, Carlo?" I said.

He shook my hand without breaking any bones.

"You play the ponies, Elgin?" he said. His voice had the purr of a diesel engine.

"No. Only fillies I like are two-legged."

"Smart. It's gotten to the point where fucking jockeys are more crooked than bankers."

"Can't trust anyone anymore, can you?"

"Bet your sweet Vanilla Fudge ass, you can't," he said. "World is fucked up. Want something to eat?"

"Got any Guinness cake here?"

Carlo laughed. "What the fuck? This ain't no Irish pub. Try the cheesecake. It's the best in the city."

"Sold."

Carlo, his hand full of liver spots, waved over an elderly waiter—short, thin, olive-skinned—wearing a white apron.

"Give my friend here a slice of cheese and some espresso," Carlo said. "And fill my cup while you're at it."

"Yes, sir, Mr. Romano, yes sir, sure thing, Mr. Romano, right away," the waiter said. I was surprised he didn't kiss Carlo's ring.

"What brings you to this part of town?" he said. pushing aside a half-smoked cigar sitting in a red-and-white Cinzano ashtray.

"Figured I'd stop by and get some gabagool," I said.

"I thought you Black Irish just ate bangers and ribs."

"Only on St. Patrick's Day and Juneteenth."

"You know, Elg, you're the funniest melanzana I know."

"How many melanzanas do you know?"

"Just you."

"Well, I guess I deserve that distinction."

He nodded as if I had just won a point in a major debate.

"There one thing I'll never understand about you," he said.

"What's that?"

"Why the fuck would a guy like you want to become a private dick? I mean if you wanna help people, why not become a social worker instead of having to deal with businessmen like me."

"I like putting guys like you in jail."

He waved a hand. "It's a hell of a way to make a living."

"Ain't it, though?"

He touched his cigar but didn't pick it up.

"How's that hot honey of yours, what's her name . . . Monique?"

"Good as gold."

"I thought she wanted you to quit this crazy racket."

"She does. But she knows I like the job."

"Glad to see you're not pussy-whipped."

"I only get cool whipped, if you catch my drift."

"I fuckin' caught it, alright," he said. "I know this ain't a social call. Now what can I do for you?"

"I need information."

"On?"

"James Catalano."

Carlo snorted.

"I'll sum him up for you in one word: He's a fucking douchebag."

"That's four words."

"Never was any good at math."

The waiter returned with our order.

"Go ahead," Carlo said. "Take a bite of the cheese. Tastes better than half the broads in this town."

I looked at the cheesecake. My nostrils flared. Instead of wolfing it down, I took a tiny, refined bite. Self-discipline. The cheesecake was delicious.

"Best thing I've tasted since Irish soda bread," I said.

He gestured as if throwing something into a trash can.

"You and your Irish shit," he said. "Fuhgeddaboudit. Ask me, you're more a darky than Mick."

"Black's my better half."

"I hope that half includes your schmeckel," he said. "You Irish are known for having shlongs the size of cashews."

"For your information, my shlong, as you call it, is registered."

"As what?"

"A lethal weapon."

"Fuck you kidding?"

Carlo took a sip of his espresso, pinky extended.

"Why you interested in that stronzo Catalano?" he said.

"He's involved in a case I'm working on."

"Let's hear it."

"It's confidential."

"Gwan. You can tell me."

"It's a long story.

"Then just give me a fucking headline."

"He may have something to do with a murder investigation I'm working on."

Carlo laughed. It sounded like cow cackling.

"Catalano connected to a murder! Shocking. Positively shocking. His fucking family has killed more people than the Gotti and Gambino families combined. Whaddya wanna know?'

"I know his history and his family background. What I'm wondering is . . . does he or his corrupt family use anyone in particular to do their dirty work?"

"Meaning?"

"A hitman."

Carlo stroked his chin.

"They employ a lot of guys," he said.

"I'm looking for someone specific. A tall guy with an athletic build."

"Fuck Elg. That describes half the guys in Little Italy. Can you be a little more specific?"

"That's all I got."

Carlo sipped more espresso. Deep in thought.

"You know, there is one guy . . . a young guy . . . got balls the size of truck tires. I think his name's Ant-knee. The Catalanos supposedly use him for big jobs. The guy may even be Jimmy's nephew. If I remember correctly, he's tall, not like you tall, but built, a former Army Ranger who I believe played basketball at Brooklyn College."

"Could be the guy I'm looking for," I said. "Know where I can find him?"

"I don't."

"You know him?"

"Of course. Us wise guys all know each other. We're like a fucked-up fraternity."

"Are members required to pledge?"

"Just take an oath to kill."

"Anything else you can tell me about this Anthony fella?"

"Nah."

I tasted more cheesecake. Just the little I ate probably added three pounds to my waistline.

"Wish I could be of more help," Carlo said.

"You've been very helpful."

Carlo reached into his suit jacket pocket and pulled out a brown leather flask.

"Want a snort?" he said.

"What is it?"

"Strega."

"Never heard of it."

"It's an Italian liqueur. Try it. It'll put hair on your balls."

"Just what I need."

Carlo grabbed two water glasses off a nearby table and poured some bright yellow liquid. He then raised his glass.

"Salut," he said.

"Salut," I said.

We both took a sip. I nearly choked on mine.

"What is this shit," I said, coughing. "Drano?"

"Stop. It'll clear your sinuses."

"More like burn them."

"C'mon Elg. Whaddya getting soft? Next thing you know you'll be asking for a frozen daiquiri."

"I prefer mint juleps."

"Ain't that the crap they serve at the Kentucky Derby?"

"Yeah. But it has even deeper roots in African history."

He smirked. "The shit you know. Fuck's wrong with you?"

"I wish I knew."

I poured the rest of my drink into Carlo's glass.

He nodded, then fired up his half-smoked cigar. Blew a series of smoke rings.

"I didn't think you could smoke in here?" I said.

"Who's gonna stop me? The fucking Mafia?' He let out a belly laugh.

"Good seeing you, Carlo," I said, standing.

"Always good to be seen."

I started to walk away, but Carlo grabbed my wrist.

"Be careful around Catalano," he said. "The guy has the scruples of a rattlesnake."

In my line of work, when somebody like Carlo says be careful, you take heed.

"I will," I said.

"One last thing."

"What?"

"Good luck finding this assassino."

CHAPTER
NINETEEN

As it turned out, I didn't need luck. The guy found me.

Walking to my car, I suddenly felt something stick in my side. I knew from experience it was a gun.

"Keep walking," a voice said. It sounded as if coming through rusty pipes.

"If you insist."

"Make one stupid move and that'll be the last shot you ever take, Mr. NBA."

We proceeded down Grand Street, passing a host of Italian restaurants. Noree. Gelso's. Nino's. The scent of warm pizza and marinara sauce perfumed the air. Made me hungry.

I said, "Wanna stop for a slice?" I said.

"Shut the fuck up."

"Maybe some scungilli or calamari?"

The guy jammed the gun even deeper into my side. Nobody on the street—tourists wearing I Love NYC tees and Asians dangling cameras around their necks—seemed to notice, or care, about my being kidnapped. They must have been in a New York state of mind. Meaning they could give a shit.

"Guess you don't like Italian food, huh?" I said. "How about some Chinese? I know a great place nearby that serves great moo shu pork."

"Clamp it, asshole, clamp it," he said, his heavy footsteps clomping on the pavement like a Clydesdale.

When we got to the corner I saw the black SUV. A back door opened.

"Get in the car," the voice said.

The voice's fingers vise-gripped my neck and pushed me inside. The interior was cooler than a meat locker. It smelled like smoke and whiskey. The voice then slammed the door and stood guard outside.

There was another guy in the front seat, on the driver's side. He twisted around and pointed a gun at me.

I winked at him.

Sitting in the back was a tall, well-built dude, six four, two-forty, maybe late twenties, maybe early thirties. He had a pockmarked face, black wavy hair, and the yellowish-blue eyes of a wolf.

I stared into those eyes for just a second. Then I spied the back of his right hand. It had a tiny tattoo. But the tattoo wasn't a basketball. It was a grotesque eyeball. Had the manager at Infernos mistaken the eyeball for a basketball? Weird. But possible.

"What's your fucking problem?" he said. His voice was harsh and hoarse as if there was something wrong with his vocal cords.

"Lately, it's been finding a great Bordeaux," I said.

"Think you're funny, huh?"

"I have my moments."

"Well, I don't like comedians. In fact, I hate them."

"Jerry Seinfeld will be disappointed."

He shifted in his seat. He wore blue jeans and a red striped bowling shirt. Tattoos of snakes and serpents covered his neck and arms. A small gold heart hung on a chain around his neck. It didn't seem to go with the rest of him.

"What color are you?" he said.

I grinned. "My father was Black, and my mother was White. What color does that make me?"

"Makes you fucking gray as a squirrel."

"Well, I am squirrely, alright."

He winced, and a tide of something deceitful and hateful washed through his eyes.

"Look, asshole, I don't wanna spend any more time with you than I have to," he said. "I'm here to give you a warning."

"I appreciate the heads up . . . Anthony," I said, taking a shot in the dark.

His eyes opened wider than an ostrich.

"How the fuck . . . how the fuck you know my name?" he said.

"I'm psychic."

Anthony glared at me, then took out a crushed pack of Marlboros from his shirt pocket. He lit a cigarette and blew smoke in my face.

"I could fucking rip your fucking tongue out right now and staple it to your fucking nose," he said.

"Nicely put," I said. "Very poetic. You don't often meet people anymore who put the word fucking three times in one sentence. That's an adverb and two adjectives."

"Look, shithead," he said, "Here's the deal. I don't want you bothering my friend anymore."

"Who's your friend?"

"None of your business."

"Let me guess it's . . . James Catalano. And for your information I didn't bother him. He came to my office and bothered me."

He gave me a cockeyed look as if he were confused. Not understanding. Maybe it wasn't Uncle Jimmy who sent him? Maybe it was someone else? But who?

"Here's how it's gonna play, asshole. Keep your nose out of other people's business at the college or you're gonna have a lot of people coming after you, including me."

"I'll try to keep my knees from knocking."

"You unnerstan me?"

"It's actually pronounced understand."

His lips turned into an evil crescent.

"Fuck you talking about?" he said.

"You said unnerstan instead of understand. Unnerstan is grammatically incorrect."

He put his cigarette out in an ashtray, then pulled a gun from his side and aimed it at me. The gun was big and boxy. A Glock.

"I should shoot you right now, motherfucker," he said.

"But you won't."

"Why won't I?"

"Because if you wanted me dead you would have shot me on the street," I said. "My guess is you were told to just give me this warning."

"You ain't scared of me, are you?"

"Nope."

"Most people are."

"I'm not most people."

He flashed a shit-eating grin wider than Kim Kardashian's hips.

"Let me tell you something," he said.

"I eagerly await your next utterance."

"If I'm asked, I will kill you."

"You're forgetting something."

"What's that?"

"I could end up killing you."

"Don't make me fucking laugh."

"No worries," I said. "You don't strike me as the laughing kind."

He pressed the tip of the gun hard against my forehead and curled his finger around the trigger. I had no doubt he was the kind of killer who giggled when murdering someone.

I said, "You think this is the first gun ever pointed at me?"

"No. But it could be the last."

I snickered.

"Better heed my advice, asshole," he said. "Drop the case you're working on . . . or you'll be sitting with the angels."

"Is that the same as swimming with the fishes?"

"One more wisecrack, just one, and I will not only break your fucking nose, but I will knock out all your fucking teeth."

"Then how would I eat my Milky Ways?"

He snorted.

"Are you for fucking real? Ever heard a nose get broken? It sounds a fucking twig getting snapped."

"I do know the sound. Shaq once gave me a vicious elbow."

"Just keep it up, private dickwad, just keep it up."

I grinned.

He scowled and said, "You know what's the worst thing is about me?"

"I would imagine your body odor."

"It's that I like killing people. Love killing people. Love it, love it, love it."

"Even more than pasta?"

He pressed the gun harder against my forehead. I wondered if it would leave a mark. I hate it when that happens.

"Now get the fuck out of the car," he shouted, his face swelling, his spittle coming at me like shrapnel.

"With pleasure," I said. "I never like being in a place where I'm not wanted."

I exited the SUV. It pulled away fast, tires screeching.

I walked to a place called Capo's. An Italian restaurant. Very old school. Dark lighting. Countless green, white, and red flags. Blue-and-white checkered tables cloths. Chianti bottles wrapped in straw. Photos of Sinatra, DeNiro, Pesci, Sophia Loren, Gina Lollobrigida, Rocky Graziano, Jake LaMotta. From ceiling speakers Dean Martin was singing "Volare" ("Nel Blu Dipinto di Blu"). I knew the song well. My mother often sang it.

Since I doubted Capo's had Guinness, I ordered a scotch and soda. I downed it in one gulp and quickly signaled the bartender for another.

"Thirsty, huh?" the bartender said. He was wearing a white shirt, sleeves rolled up, and a white apron. His mustache was long and pointy like painter Salvador Dali.

"Yeah," I said. "For information."

He twisted the ends of his mustache, gave me a funny look, and turned away.

I sat at the bar for a while, nursing my drink. Occasionally, I'd glance up at the television behind the bar. Local news.

I decided not to tell Monique about Anthony. Threats to my being unnerved her. Upset her. She was always worried that some nutjob would, for whatever reason, stab or shoot me. Or worse, kill me.

She often reminded me how much she disliked my working in a world of violence, a world of evil. As much as I tried to allay her fears, nothing seemed to work.

There had been times when Monique literally begged me to quit my job. I told her it would be hard for me to quit, that the job was something I needed to do, something I was good at. Something that gave my father's death a purpose.

Maybe that's why we hadn't gotten married . . . yet.

It's funny how life goes, right? Look at me, a private investigator. In my college and pro days, I never would have imagined that's what I'd do for a living. But I guess it's just the way things happen—our futures don't always turn out the way we expect.

I stood, threw some money on the bar and was about to skedaddle when I saw Ambush Anderson's face appear on the screen.

"Can you turn the television up," I asked the bartender. He grabbed a remote and the sound increased.

A young male reporter was saying, "Last night in a schoolyard in Astoria, Queens, a fight broke out between two rival gangs. Gunshots were fired and two gang members were wounded, but the police moved in quickly before things really got out of hand.

"One witness to the rumble was apparently none other than St. Stephen's star basketball player Ambush Anderson, projected by many to be a first-round draft pick in the upcoming NBA draft.

"Police have not given a reason for the outbreak but say that Anderson remained in a vehicle and was not one of the shooters. However, his close friend and high school teammate Gary Grimes was. According to witnesses, Grimes was carrying a .45 caliber gun, though it isn't clear whether he fired any of the wounding shots. Grimes was detained by police and released last night on his own recognizance.

"Here's some footage of the police taking Grimes into custody."

I recognized Grimes immediately—the wiseass with the spiderweb tattoo who had bumped into me hard coming out of Ambush's dormitory.

I watched a handcuffed Grimes being escorted toward a police car. In the background, there was a crowd of young girls, Black and White. I looked closely at the screen. One blond bore a faint resemblance to Emma Mitchell. But I wasn't certain it was her.

The fact that Grimes carried a .45 caught my interest. It was the same caliber gun used to murder Teddy Malone.

Coincidence? I doubt it. As my Irish grandfather used to say, "There's two things I don't believe in: coincidence and leprechauns."

The reporter came back on the screen and provided some background on Ambush's life. It was Dickensian. First of six children, his mother was an alcoholic and his father a drug addict. Ambush basically raised himself, going to work at age eleven, delivering newspapers and pizzas to feed his siblings. Tough life.

As a high school freshman, he was kicked out of school for bringing a gun into a classroom, only to be reinstated because the school's basketball coach saw Ambush's talent and saw him as a ticket out for both of them. By senior year, Ambush was the best player in the New York Metropolitan area, if not the country.

But he couldn't scrap trouble off his shoe. His best friend, Grimes, a good player himself, was in and out of trouble—robbery and drugs. He was arrested over and over. But Ambush wasn't. His coach, a zealot with a reputation for helping Black kids through sports, used his clout with the police.

The two players, according to the reporter, have remained fierce friends, supporting each other at every turn. Kind of like Affleck and Damon of the underworld.

As I walked out of the bar, I wondered if Ambush was protecting Grimes. Or vice versa.

CHAPTER
TWENTY

"This Catalano guy was too much," I said to Monique. "Thinks he can buy me off. Not a chance."

We were in the Mustang, top down, driving to the Poconos. The sun was hot but there was a little breeze. From the CD player, Lena Horne was singing about an ill wind.

"I'm sure a lot of people would have taken his offer," Monique said. She was wearing white shorts, a light blue linen blouse, and a Yankees baseball hat. Draped over her shoulders was a light, blue cardigan. Her sunglasses were big and black, like Jackie O wore back in the day.

"When I was a kid," I said, "My family purchased a house in Scarsdale. Because my father was Black, some Whites in the neighborhood didn't care for him. They offered him money to move. He said no. Our house was egged. Vandalized. But my father refused to relent. He stuck it out till the harassment stopped. Then we moved back to the city."

"Your father must have been a tough guy."

"He was."

"I guess the apple didn't fall far from the tree."

"I'd like to think so."

"Tell me about the psychologist, this . . . this Regina Blake?" Monique said, her right elbow leaning on the car door.

"Wouldn't cooperate."

"Think she's just a stickler for doctor/patient confidentiality?"

"No. There's a federal law called the Health Insurance Portability and Accountability Act. Basically, she can't talk to me without a patient's permission."

"But Teddy's dead."

"Doesn't matter," I said. "Patients are entitled to the same respect for confidentiality of their personal information after death as they were in life."

"Didn't know that."

"Strange thing is . . . as soon as I left her office, she forgot all about HIPPA and got on the phone to Corsito."

"That certainly showed integrity."

"Yeah. None."

"And what's the story with this . . . this conditioning coach . . . Smith."

"He's hiding something."

"Like a basketball tattoo on the back of his right hand?"

"Possibly. He wouldn't take off his glove."

"Shouldn't you call O'Meara? Loop him in."

"Not yet," I said. "I need more hard evidence."

Horne was now singing about stormy weather.

"What do you make of this Emma Mitchell being seen with Ambush Anderson and Anderson's friend? What's his name?"

"Grimes. Gary Grimes."

"It's not good. Makes me think drugs could be the reason Teddy was murdered."

"Elaborate."

I told her about seeing Grimes getting arrested on TV and the possibility of Emma Mitchell being on the scene.

"It could be Teddy stole some drugs. Or maybe he owed someone money and didn't make the payments. Hard to say."

"Have you discounted the point-shaving angle?"

"Not entirely. These kids today, top players, they got everybody coming at them for everything. With their undeveloped frontal lobes, they don't know how to say no."

We were now in Pennsylvania, on Interstate 80 heading west toward the kids' basketball camp where Hunter coached. Deer were everywhere. Crossing the road or hiding in the bushes.

"It's nice up here," Monique said, stretching her arms upward as if appealing to the gods.

"It is," I said. "Fresh air. Lots of natural and man-made lakes. Ski resorts and water parks."

Monique pointed to my left.

"Look over there," she said.

I lowered my Oakleys and took a quick look. A large lake. People kayaking, paddle boating, and swimming. Surrounding the lake were a host of small log cabins.

"Would you ever stay in one of the cabins?" Monique asked.

"Instead of a fancy-pants hotel with a heart-shaped tub?"

"Might be cozy," she said.

"If you want to be around raccoons and possums."

"That settles it," she said. "Fancy-pants hotel here we come."

I leaned over and kissed her cheek.

"Did you ever vacation up here?" Monique said.

"A long time ago."

"With your girlfriend?"

"Different girlfriends."

"Listen to you. Last of the red-hot lovers."

"Hey, once upon a time women saw me as catnip."

"Excuse me while I hock up a fur ball."

"Ha-ha." Sometimes I think Monique should give up acting and become a comedian.

"Were those women prettier and sexier than me?"

"Let's just say they were younger."

"I'll accept that."

"I forgot to ask," I said. "How's your latest leading man?"

"He's a bit stiff."

"A bit stiff? If I remember correctly, he's a talking tree trunk."

"At least he knows his lines."

"He should . . . for the money he's making."

"That's the theatre for you. Big names get big money."

"Life is a cabaret, old chum."

We drove in silence for a while, inhaling the fragrant air.

"Tell me again," Monique said, "why are we going to see Hunter?"

"Because I don't know who else to talk to."

Monique nodded. I had thought about just calling him, but I knew from experience that things can get misinterpreted and misconstrued over the phone. Plus, you can't read expressions or emotions.

"Tell me," Monique said, "Why is Corsito not being helpful?"

"Because he sees the situation as an inconvenience."

"Doesn't it bother him that one of his players has been murdered?"

"Quite honestly, I don't think so."

"But why?"

"There's nothing in it for him, except bad publicity. And if there's one thing Chris Corsito hates its negative press."

"What a horrible person."

"I'll sum up Corsito this way. As a college coach, nobody comes close to him. As a person, nobody *wants* to come close to him."

Monique shook her head and strands of hair flew in her face. She delicately brushed them aside.

"How much longer to Stroudsburg?" she asked.

"Maybe fifteen minutes."

"Good," she said. "I'm hungry."

I glanced over at her.

"How does somebody who eats as much as you do stay so thin?" I said.

"Good genes, I guess."

"I look at a cheeseburger and I gain ten pounds."

"Maybe you should eat more fruits and vegetables."

"I'd rather be flabby."

Monique put a hand on my shoulder.

"You sure you have time?" she said.

"For?"

"Lunch."

"Of course."

We arrived in Stroudsburg. A mile down the road was our fancy-pants hotel: The Penn Stroud, a three-story structure on the corner of Main Street.

I parked the car, registered at the front desk and took our luggage to the room. It was small. There was barely space for a king size bed, a television, a desk and chair. I had to walk around the bed sideways just to get to the bathroom.

"Far cry from the Four Seasons," I said.

"Don't be a snob."

"Just a comment," I said. "Let's go eat."

We went to a restaurant down the block called Sweet Sue's Street Grill. It had a pool table and a dart board, along with a menu that included everything from sushi to burgers to pasta.

A young freckle-faced waitress in a white uniform came by, holding a pen and pad.

"What can I get you folks?" she said smiling.

"What's good?" Monique said.

"Everything."

"That narrows it down," I said.

Monique studied the menu.

"How's the sesame encrusted tuna steak?" she asked.

"It's served with wasabi mayo and red onion on a toasted brioche roll. Delicious."

"I'll try it," Monique said, closing her menu.

"And you, sir?" the waitress asked.

"Your Tex-Mex burger sounds too good to pass up."

"It's fabulous." Her enthusiasm was genuine. "Has salsa and guacamole. We make it fresh daily."

"I like fresh. Sold."

"And what would you like to drink?" she said.

Monique looked at me.

"Want some wine?" she said.

"Might have whiskey."

"Well, well."

I said to the waitress, "You have Bushmills?"

"No."

"How about Jameson?'

"That we have."

"Great."

"Straight or on the rocks?"

"Straight." Watering down Irish whiskey is a no-no. It's worse than drinking white wine with ice cubes.

The waitress then looked at Monique.

"And you, miss? What are you having?"

"What kind of wine do you have?" Monique said.

"Red and white."

Monique smiled.

"What kind of red?" Monique asked.

"Kind?"

"Merlot? Pinot? Cabernet?"

"Just Cab-Bear-Nay."

"I'll have a glass."

The waitress left.

"Let's hope the wine is drinkable," I said.

"Let's hope," she said. "Why is it you only drink Irish whiskey?"

"It's part of my heritage."

"But you're only half Irish."

"I guess they just don't make good whiskey in Africa."

Monique shook her head. A Bruce Springsteen song suddenly blared from invisible speakers. He sang about "a darkness on the edge of town."

"Tell me about this Hunter person," Monique said.

"He's been Corsito's longtime assistant."

"What do you hope to find out?"

"Something, anything."

"That's specific enough."

"He's sort of my last hope."

Our drinks arrived. Mine was served in a rocks glass, Monique's a jelly jar.

"At least it's not a sippy cup," I said.

"Points for that."

I raised my glass and said, "Here's looking at you, kid."

Monique puckered her lips.

She said, "Kiss me as if it's the last time."

I hummed "da-dy-da-dy-da-dum, da-dy-da-dee-da-dum."

"We'll always have Paris," Monique said.

"And Hoboken."

We tapped glasses.

Monique took a sip of her wine.

I said, "How is it?"

"Kind of like Kool-Aid."

I sang, "Kool-Aid, Kool-Aid tastes great, Kool-Aid, Kool-Aid can't wait."

Monique shook her head and said, "Think you'll ever grow up?"

"I hope not."

The food came. Our meals were delicious. I ordered another whiskey.

I said, "You want another glass of wine?"

"Think I'll pass. The first one may have taken the enamel off my teeth."

"How about a shot of whiskey?"

"You know my metabolism. One shot of whiskey and I'll be dancing on the table."

"You used to get seductive."

"Now I get drunk."

"I like you drunk."

"I'm sure you do."

After we finished eating, we played a game of pool. Monique won.

"You were lucky," I said, hanging up my pool cue.

"Skill, baby, skill," she said.

We left the restaurant. It was hot. But not as blisteringly as Manhattan.

Monique said, "That was fun."

"It was."

I put my arm around her shoulders. We headed back to the car.

Midway down the block I stopped, turned to her and said, "You know what they say?"

"No. What do the all-knowing 'they' say."

"They say it's not the number of breaths you take, it's the moments that take your breath away."

"Is this one of those moments?"

"It is," I said, taking her face between my hands and kissing her on the lips.

"Who would have thought we could find such a moment in the Poconos?"

"Usually when you come to the Poconos the best thing you can find is a mirrored ceiling."

"We don't have one in our room."

"You win some, you lose some."

CHAPTER
TWENTY-ONE

It was a short drive to the basketball camp. It had wood barracks and ten outdoor courts. The courts were nice, well maintained. Glass backboards. Nylon nets. Overhead lighting. The only discordant note was the load of kids' underwear hanging from a clothesline.

"I attended this camp when I was in grammar school," I said.

"Back when you were incubating into a big shot?" Monique said.

"I still am a big shot?"

"In your dreams."

All the courts were in use. Kids of different ages were running and jumping around like eager puppies. We heard shouts and screams, referee whistles.

We walked toward court number one. I spotted Dave Hunter. Standing on the sideline clapping and yelling instructions to his team, he was wearing a St. Stephen's tee and shorts.

I noticed whenever a kid came out of the game, he'd give him a high five and a big hug. Nonstop positive energy.

"Seems like a nice guy," Monique said.

"From what little I know, he is."

"How does he put up with that jerk Corsito?"

"That's anybody's guess."

"Was he ever a head coach?"

"Yes."

"Where?"

"High school and college."

"A big-time college?"

"Division II

"Meaning it's a smaller school?"

"Meaning they don't compete against the big boys."

"Was he successful?"

"Pretty much. Looked to be on the fast track."

We watched the game. The kids, who were no more than ten or twelve, were hustling their asses off.

When the game ended, Dave's team had won. The kids all lined up and shook hands. Dave hugged them, tousled their hair, and patted their behinds.

He noticed us and waved. I waved back. He grinned and headed in our direction.

"Hey, Elg," he said, shaking my hand. "What are you doing here? Trying to take my job?"

"No, no, no. Just wanted to speak with you."

"About?"

"Teddy Malone."

"Sure," he said, running a finger around his shirt collar. "Whatever you need."

I introduced Monique.

Dave looked at her and flashed a smile wider than Kansas.

"Nice to finally meet you," he said. "I've been impressed with your Broadway career."

"Why, thank you," Monique said.

"Gotta ask ya," Dave said. "How the hell did a loser like Elg ever get a winner like you?"

"He sweet-talked me," she said.

"Probably wowed you with stories of how great a player he was."

"He tried," Monique said, "but I let it go in one ear and out the other."

I looked at her and said, "And here I thought you fell for my intellectual rap."

"Think again, big boy," she said, grinning. "Think again."

"So?" Dave said. "Whaddya wanna know?"

I pointed to an empty table under a large striped awning.

"Let's get some shade," I said.

"A little toasty, huh?" Dave said.

"Can't wait till this heat wave passes," I said.

We walked over to the table and sat. The surface was marked with initials and graffiti. One scribbler had written in capital letters: CAN'T WAIT TO FAST-BREAK OUTTA THIS MADHOUSE.

"Gotta tell you," Dave said. "I was heartbroken when I heard about Teddy. He was a great kid."

"Any idea why anyone would want to shoot him?" I said.

Dave shook his head. "Can't imagine."

"Tell me. How was his relationship with Corsito?"

"For the most part, good."

"I was told that Corsito was hard on him."

"Chris is hard on every kid."

"I heard he was especially hard on Teddy."

"That's because Teddy got, well, lazy."

"Why do you think that was?"

"Not sure."

"Did you know Teddy was suffering from depression?" I said.

Dave winced. He pulled out a handkerchief from his pants pocket and mopped his sweaty brow.

"Didn't know anything about that," he said.

"Were you aware he was using fentanyl?"

His jaw dropped. "I'm . . . I'm totally shocked."

"I've also learned Teddy liked to gamble."

"Had no idea. But you know how easy it is today. You can gamble on an app, and if you come up short on some crazy prop bet, you hear all about it online."

"One NBA general manager told me Teddy was playing so bad it looked as if he might have been shaving points."

Hunter's face squeezed tighter than a fist.

"Now that's outrageous," Dave said. "Teddy was too upstanding a kid to do anything like that. Not a chance. No way. He just wasn't playing well. It's as simple as that. You know how it is."

"Do I?"

"Yeah, you do."

I thought a moment before asking my next question.

"You know Regina Blake?" I said.

"Sure. She's the school's psychologist."

"Teddy was seeing her."

"I'm totally baffled," Hunter said, squirming in his seat. "You would think I would know these things." He paused and swallowed hard. "You seem to know a lot more about Teddy than I do."

"I met with Blake," I said. "She wasn't very cooperative."

"She can be a tough nut," he said, "but I've heard that she's helped a lot of kids."

"Didn't help Teddy."

"No?"

"No."

I glanced at Monique. She was following the conversation closely, her eyes going back and forth between Dave and me like someone watching a fast-paced tennis match.

"Sorry to be excluding you," I said to her.

"No worries," she said.

Dave looked at Monique, put his hand on her arm and said, "It's kind of hot. Would you like some water?"

"No thanks," Monique said. "I'm good."

"We have great lemonade here," he said, smiling. "Fresh squeezed. I squeeze it myself. The kids love it."

"Really," she said. "I'm fine."

Dave was sweating profusely. He took a package of Juicy Fruit gum from his shorts pocket and offered some to Monique and me. We declined. He then selected a stick, peeled off the silver foil and folded it into his mouth.

"Kids love this gum," he said, chewing anxiously.

"Bet they do," I said. "By the way, is Marie here?"

"No."

"Is she coming up?"

"No. She's too busy attending fashion shows and spending money."

"She ever come up?"

"No . . . no." He hesitated. "Why . . . why would she?"

"To keep you company?"

"I'm plenty busy with the kids. And Main Street Stroudsburg isn't exactly Fifth Avenue."

In the background, we heard kids shouting and balls bouncing.

"Seems like a nice camp," Monique said.

"It is," Dave said. "I've been coming here for ten years. Love the kids. They make my summer."

A camp counselor called out to Dave.

"Coach," he yelled. "Got a minute?" He was standing next to a boy who was crying, his body shaking.

"Be right there, Tommy," Dave shouted.

Dave stood.

"Sorry I couldn't be more helpful," he said. "You guys staying in town?"

"Yeah," I said.

"Go to Sweet Sue's Street Grill," he said. "Good food."

"We've been there," Monique said.

"Then you already got the lay of the land," he said, flashing Monique a big smile. What a charmer.

Dave and I shook hands. His hand was clammy.

"See you around, Elg," he said. "Nice meeting you Monique."

"Same here," she said.

Dave headed back to the court.

I watched him put his arm around the kid. The kid jumped when Dave touched him, as if an electric shock had passed between them. He squirmed out of Dave's embrace. Then ran away.

"What are you staring at?" Monique said.

"Dave."

"Why?"

"Did you see that?"

"See what?"

"The kid running away from Dave."

With her hand over her eyes Monique squinted at the kid running. "Yeah? So?"

"The kid looked frightened."

"Frightened?"

"As if he were scared of Dave."

We watched as Dave was now massaging the shoulders of another boy. He cupped his hand and said something into his ear and the boy beamed.

I said, "Don't you think Dave's a little too touchy-feely with the kids."

"Aren't all coaches like that?"

"Not like Dave's acting."

"What are you saying?"

"I'm saying I don't think I like his behavior."

"Are you thinking what I think you're thinking?"

"One thing people don't realize is that there are almost as many creeps in sports as there are in the priesthood. Or the Boy Scouts. It just doesn't get reported enough."

"Why?"

"Because it's the one thing in sports nobody wants to address."

"Are you calling Dave a pedophile?"

"Perhaps."

"That seems like a stretch."

"Maybe."

"If he is doing what you're suggesting wouldn't a kid say something?"

"No. Kids, especially if they're athletes, are petrified of admitting something like that happened to them."

"But it isn't their fault."

"Right, it isn't and many of them know that. But molestation strikes at their manhood, and they don't want the stigma of the incident to follow them into high school or college."

"Are administrators aware of how much this goes on?"

"Many are."

"And?"

"And if the coach is powerful and successful, they look the other way."

"That's disgraceful."

"No," I said. "That's sports today."

Monique got quiet.

"You really think Dave could be a child molester?" she said.

"Makes me wonder. But I'm wondering about a lot of things."

"But he seems so nice."

"That's the problem," I said. "Coaches like him can fool you."

"Think Corsito knows?"

"I don't know," I said. "One wouldn't think so because if something like that ever got out his career could be in jeopardy."

"Even if he didn't know?"

"It would be guilt by association,' I said. "But knowing Corsito, he'd plead ignorance, throw Hunter under the bus, and talk his way of it. He'd probably leave St. Stephen's and go to another college . . . for even more money."

Monique scratched her head.

"This is horrible," she said.

"Yes, it is."

"So whaddya gonna do?"

"Think I'll have another word with Dave."

I stood and walked over to where Dave was joking with a freckled-faced kid.

"Excuse me, Dave," I said.

He turned.

"What's up?" he said.

"I have a few more questions."

Hunter turned away from me, patted the boy on the butt, and said, "Go work on that dribbling drill. I'll be with you later and we can play one-on-one." A big smile. "I promise."

The boy smiled as if he'd been anointed.

Dave turned back to me.

"Go ahead," he said. "Ask your questions."

"I'm curious why Teddy never spoke to you about his problems."

He raised his hands in mock surrender. "Can't explain that."

"Can't explain that, huh?"

"No . . . no, I can't."

"But weren't you close to him?"

Two thick veins on either side of his neck throbbed. "We had a good relationship."

"How good?"

His eyes narrowed and all the niceness and playfulness were gone. "Whaddya implying?"

"I'm not implying anything," I said. "Chris said the St. Stephen's players love you and you have a great rep. I'm just asking a simple question."

"Didn't sound like it."

"I mean, I assume you and Teddy talked a lot? Maybe you guys went to dinner or watched films together?" I paused, then: "Just the two of you."

Something registered in Dave's eyes—a flicker of fear. It's what the police and poker players call a "tell." It was all the confirmation I needed. As good as a signed confession, but I had a lot of work to do to prove it.

"No," he said, licking his lips. "We never did."

"Never did what?"

"Hang out together."

"You sure?"

His upper lip was soaked with perspiration. "I'm sure."

"Really?"

"Yeah, really. I was just his coach." He was trying to control himself, but his voice took on an edge.

"Well, either you just got extremely cold or else suddenly developed Parkinson's," I said, pointing to his shaky hands.

He stared at me with predatory intensity. I looked into his eyes and just instinctively knew that behind them was darkness.

I said, "Look, I'm only trying to get to the bottom of things and . . ."

"Listen, Elg, I've told you everything I know. I don't like the tone of this, this . . . inquisition. I don't know who killed Teddy or why."

"This isn't an inquisition," I said. "It's my job to ask questions, even uncomfortable questions."

He glared at me, and I could feel contempt and loathing coming off him in waves.

"I don't like the insinuation. In fact, they make me sick. Chris told me you were gonna try to bring him down. . . . Is this what this is all about? I thought we were friends."

As upset as he was, he was trying hard to regain control.

"Listen," he said, his voice soft again, his eyes going back and forth from me to Monique. "My job is to help these kids. I take that responsibility very seriously. I have work to do."

Before I could say another word, Dave abruptly turned and walked away.

As he approached the kids, it was as if he flipped a switch, suddenly all smiles again. He didn't seem shook up at all. He clapped his hands and whistled. "Alright, alright," he called out, "who wants a little one-on-one?" A handful of kids came running his way like puppies after a piece of meat. I wanted to puke.

I returned to Monique, who was standing by the table.

"Well?" she said, hands on hips.

"He's dirty," I said.

"Are you sure? How can you tell?"

"I just can."

"How?"

"First-hand experience."

"You were molested?" she said, her voice rising.

"No, no, no," I said. "But when I was a freshman in high school, there was this coach who was in his late thirties and never married. He was a great coach and very popular. But after practice he'd hang out in the locker room and was always trying to get me to wrestle him. Said I was soft, and it would 'make me hard.' Then he'd give me this look. A weird, creepy look." My body involuntarily shook. "I never did wrestle with him, but some teammates did. Athletes are trained to please their coaches. Anyway, one day he got caught fondling a player in the shower. Next thing you know he quit and moved away. But a year later, he was coaching again . . . in another high school."

I swallowed hard.

"You know who that player was?" I said. "The one who was fondled?"

"No idea."

"You remember me telling you about my cousin John?"

"The one who was like your brother and who got addicted?"

"Yeah." I rubbed a knuckle under my nose, took a deep breath before speaking again. "The kid in the shower was John."

Monique put a cupped hand to her lips.

"Oh, my God. I am so sorry."

I nodded, thinking how John, and guys like him, spend the rest of their lives trying to climb up a greased pole but always sliding down.

"He never recovered from what happened," I said. "He tried to get past it but couldn't. His problems snowballed, and he turned to oxy and then fentanyl. He's been a drug addict ever since. In and out of the rehab so many times . . . with little or no success."

Monique hugged me.

"The things bad people can do to good ones," she said.

I nodded again.

"There's one thing I don't get," Monique said. "How does what happened with your creepy coach connect to Hunter."

"His eyes."

"Whaddya mean . . . his eyes?"

"Hunter gave me the same creepy look as my old coach."

"You sure you're not imagining this?"

"I'm not."

"Let me get this straight. You think Hunter may have molested Teddy Malone?"

"It's a working theory."

"Okay, let's say he did. What's that got to do with Teddy's murder? You don't think he shot him, do you?"

"Not him personally."

"Who then?"

"No idea. But it goes to motive."

"Motive?"

"Someone wanted to keep Hunter's secret, a secret."

CHAPTER TWENTY-TWO

We drove back to my house early the next morning, trying to beat the holiday traffic. Years ago, I would have started my day by knocking on doors. Not so in today's investigative world. Today the two most important tools are laptops and cell phones.

After finishing my coffee and toast, I started work by logging onto my computer and doing a deep dive on Dave Hunter.

He'd been in the coaching business for a long time, and there was quite a paper trail—feature stories, podcast interviews, and speeches. I learned a lot. I learned Dave grew up in Astoria, Queens, the only child of a garment worker mother and alcoholic father. His parents divorced when he was five. He attended St. James High School where he was a star basketball player. He received a scholarship to the University of Carolina but rarely got his rear off the bench.

He began his coaching career at St. James and after a few years married his high school sweetheart, Marie Ruggiero. They had two boys, a year apart. Both attended a year-round boarding school. I thought it strange that a guy who spends so much time with kids sent his own boys away.

I slowly scrolled down his coaching history. After St. James, he had some assistant coaching gigs before becoming the head coach at a D-II school—Gladstone College. Despite a winning record, he resigned in 2010. No reason was given for the resignation. A year later, Corsito hired his former Carolina teammate.

Hunter quickly made a reputation for himself as a top recruiter. *The New York Times* profiled him, stating that he was "the Pied Piper of high school talent, a sweet and fast talker with an enormous gift of persuasion." The Irish would call it the gift of gab.

I stopped reading and grabbed my cell phone. I called a number of basketball coaches I knew, both college and pro, and as subtly as possible asked them about Corsito and Hunter.

When they asked me why I was asking, I lied and said I had a neighbor's high school kid who was sorting through college basketball offers.

Most of the coaches praised and condemned Corsito. They called him everything from a genius to a crook, usually in the same sentence. Pretty accurate.

Hunter, on the other hand, was applauded by everyone for his ability to recruit, his knowledge of basketball and his good-naturedness. Mr. Rogers in shorts and sneakers.

After speaking with the coaches, I phoned a few athletic directors and gave them the same line about the neighborhood kid. They parroted the same sentiments about Corsito and Hunter.

I literally spent over three hours researching Hunter on Google and three hours on the phone. And I got nothing I could work with, nothing that confirmed, or even hinted at, Hunter being a pedophile.

Not getting information drove me crazy. I felt like I was back in college studying for an exam in a course I detested. Twice, I left the apartment for short runs—only to come back to research Hunter again and get even more discouraged.

Bottom line: I had nothing to substantiate my suspicions. The anger I felt was monumental.

Monique appeared. She was wearing a long white terry cloth robe and white cotton slippers. A thick towel was wrapped around her head.

"Looking up stuff about Hunter?" she said.

"Yeah."

"How's it going?"

"Frustrating. Very frustrating."

"Why?"

"Because everyone I spoke to had nothing but nice things to say about him."

"Everyone?

"Yeah." I sighed. "Only thing that caught my interest is that he once resigned from Gladstone College."

"Why is that interesting?"

"He had just come off the most successful season the school ever had."

"Don't coaches move around a lot?"

"Not usually after they have a year like Hunter had."

"Maybe he got a better offer someplace else."

"Maybe."

"Where's Gladstone?"

"Sparta, New Jersey."

"Where's Sparta?"

"Sussex County, near the Delaware Water Gap."

"Never heard of the school."

"Most people haven't," I said. "It's a small college, maybe two thousand students."

"Good basketball program?"

"Not since Hunter left."

Monique sat on my lap.

"What's on your agenda today?" she said.

"First, I'm going to St. James High School. It's where Hunter began his career. Maybe I can gleam some information about his past. Then I'm going to Sparta to find out why Hunter resigned."

"Can't you just make some calls?"

"It's harder for people to lie to you in person."

Monique kissed my cheek.

"What's your day like?" I said.

She posed. "I'm auditioning for a movie role."

"Wait a minute. Wait a minute. A movie role? Why haven't you told me?"

"Just got the official invite through my agent. Didn't want to distract you. You've been so focused on the case the past few days."

"What's the part?"

"It's playing a single mother whose daughter accidentally murders someone. The mother hides the body, but a witness to the murder attempts to blackmail her. She takes all her money out of the bank and sells her jewelry but it's not nearly enough to pay the guy off. She ultimately has to figure out of way to deal with him."

"How does it end?"

"You'll have to go see the movie."

"Can you give me a hint?"

"No."

"Okay, be that way," I said. "Who are you meeting with?"

"The producer."

"Hope he isn't a Harvey Weinstein type."

"Let's hope not."

"Does the casting couch still exist?"

"So I'm told."

"Need me to go with you?" I said.

"As what?"

"Your bodyguard."

"You forget, Lone Ranger, I'm schooled in tae kwon do."

"That you are, Tonto."

"Bet your ass, Kemo Sabe."

"I'd rather kiss it."

"You'll just have to settle for my lips."

"Done."

I kissed her full on the mouth.

Monique stood.

"Hi ho, Silver," I said.

She pulled me up off the chair.

"Get dressed," she said. "I gotta be at the Peninsula Hotel in two hours."

I thrusted a fist in the air and said, "With the speed of light and a cloud of dust, The Lone Ranger rides again."

"Then get on your horse and let's go. And, by the way, you watch way too many old reruns."

We both dressed quickly, got into the Mustang and endured ungodly traffic getting through the Lincoln Tunnel.

"Are you getting tired of Broadway?" I said. "Is that why you're thinking of doing a movie?"

"I think I'm ready for a change. I love performing in live theatre, but doing eight shows a week is exhausting."

"I would think. Especially since you've had to break in more than a few different co-leads."

"That's tiring as well. Not all actors, even movie stars, are suited for Broadway. It's a whole different world performing before a live audience as opposed to having many retakes and reshoots."

"I can't wait to see you on the big screen."

"Don't count your chicken before . . ."

"I have full confidence you'll get the role."

She lifted her chin, turned her face in profile and said, "All right then, Mr. DeMille, I'm ready for my close-up."

"Bet you are, Salome."

The Peninsula was located at 700 Fifth Avenue, on the corner of Fifty-Fifth Street. A historic luxury hotel, its limestone and granite façade resembled an Italian villa.

I had stayed there many times, always around Christmas. Aside from the hotel having exquisite holiday decorations, I liked it because it was only a few blocks away from St. Patrick's Cathedral. The cathedral always inspired me to become more spiritual. But not long after my visits, I once again become a lapsed Catholic.

Don't get me wrong. I still believe in God. Or, rather, I believe there is a God. Whether he or she is Catholic, Protestant, Mormon, Jewish, or Muslim isn't important to me. What is important is that there is some higher authority that makes more good people than bad. The only time I pray now is for Monique's safety, for Duke to win the NCAA tournament, and the Dallas Mavericks to capture an NBA title.

"Good luck," I said, kissing Monique on the cheek.

Imitating Don Corleone, she said, "Hopefully, the producer will make me an offer I can't refuse."

"You get the role you might have to go to Hollywood."

"The place where dreams are made?"

"And nightmares. Remember what Brando said."

"About?"

"Hollyweird. He said the most successful people there are failures as human beings."

"I'll keep that in mind when I'm strolling down Rodeo Drive with my boy toy."

I laughed. "Who can give you what? Adoration?"

"More like stimulation?"

"From what I know of the escorts in Hollywood, you'd be better off with a vibrator."

"In that case, I'll stick with you. You're all the vibration I need."

"Keep talking. You're giving me excitations."

"The Beach Boys, right?"

"As rain."

Monique put he hand on the door handle, turned to me and said, "Want me to cook dinner tonight?"

My eyebrows jumped. "*You* cooking dinner?"

The fact is, Monique can't cook worth a lick. She wouldn't know a cutting board from a backboard, or a garlic press from a full-court press.

Not long ago, she made what she called a "special dish."

I tasted it and said, "Very interesting. It kind of tastes like turkey."

Monique whacked my bicep.

"It is turkey, you birdbrain."

She hasn't cooked anything since. Thank God!

"Don't worry about making dinner," I said. "I'll just grab whatever's in the fridge."

She pursed her lips.

"Sometimes I get the impression you don't like my cooking."

"Why would you say that?"

"Because you always want Pepto Bismol afterward."

"I have a sensitive stomach."

She smirked. "Yeah, right."

Monique opened the car door, got out and peeked back in.

"Love ya, "she said, blowing me a kiss.

"Right back at ya."

I put the car in gear and drove off.

CHAPTER TWENTY-THREE

St. James High School is in Astoria, Queens. A large three-story dirty brick building, it had rounded towers at both ends and a campanile between them. It looked less like an academic institution and more like a fort. The only thing missing was a moat.

Entering the building, I was immediately stopped by a security guard sitting at a folding table. He resembled officer Barney Fife from the old *Andy Griffith Show*, his face thin, his eyes wide as if he were in a perpetual state of surprise. I noticed a gun hanging off his hip.

"Can I help you?" he said. His name tag said Vyzas. He had a slight accent. Perhaps from the Baltic region. Maybe Lithuania or Estonia.

"I'm here to see Principal Sanchez," I said.

"Is he expecting you?"

"Yes," I said, having called earlier. "I have an appointment."

"Your name?"

"Elgin O'Brien."

The guard grabbed a black-and-white notebook, opened it, and ran a finger down a list of names.

After a few seconds, he said, "Ah, yes. Here you are."

He handed me a sticky name badge that said "Visitor." I stuck it on my chest.

"Please proceed through the metal detector," he said.

I took everything out of my pockets and slipped off my shoulder holster. The guard's eyes got even wider when he saw it.

"What's with the shooter?" he said.

"I'm a private investigator."

"Can I see some identification."

I pulled out my wallet and showed him my ID.

"Handsome devil, ain't I?" I said.

He made a barely audible snorting sound.

"Okay, pal," he said, pointing. "Go straight down the corridor. It's the last office on your right. Just keep your jacket closed."

"Thank you, Officer Vyzas," I said, gathering my things.

I walked down the corridor. The walls were painted forest green and lined with lockers. The flooring was linoleum. There was a large statue of the Virgin Mary, as well as classrooms and a library. The lingering smell of pencil shavings and chalk made me think of my school days. Thank God there wasn't social media then. I can't imagine the trouble I would have gotten into.

Personally, I find social media disturbing. People who don't know shit from Shinola promote their ideas, mostly anonymously. The ideas can be insane and far-fetched. Hurtful. Mean. Impossible to believe. Once upon a time I thought social media was going to be a good thing. Today, I see it as the exact opposite.

I stopped before a trophy case. It was filled with silver bowls and bronze plaques. Pictures of teams and athletes, both guys and girls, surrounded the awards.

I noticed there were many photos of David Hunter, some as a coach and some when he went back to visit his old school, showing off his NCAA championship rings. In almost every shot he had an arm around a player's shoulder. Both he and the players flashed big smiles.

Two other photos caught my attention. They showed Hunter hugging a small man with ears longer than hot dog rolls.

I bent down to look at the name plate under the pictures: Coach David Hunter with principal Jose Sanchez.

I resumed walking down the corridor, passing a few students—guys in blue blazers and khaki pants and girls in green blazers and plaid skirts—all scrolling on their cell phones. They all walked with that slouching, cool teenage rhythm, a pace they'll probably never again employ for the rest of their lives.

I opened the door to the principal's office. A middle-aged, bespectacled woman wearing a light cotton dress, her hair in a tight bun, smiled at me.

"May I help you?" she said in a cheerful voice.

"I'm Elgin O'Brien. I have an appointment with Mr. Sanchez."

"Yes, he's expecting you." She pointed to an open door behind her. "Go right in."

Sanchez's office was small. It had a metal desk, two oak bookcases, a corkboard filled with notes and a large picture of Jesus, his head topped with a crown of thorns.

Sitting behind an L-shaped desk with computers on each side was a heavyset guy in his fifties, maybe sixties, with thick eyebrows and thinning hair. His complexion was so white he looked as if he had been embalmed. He wore a striped tie and a starched white shirt with paisley suspenders. The shirt had a tiny brown stain. Resembled gravy.

"Welcome, Mr. O'Brien," he said in a nasally voice. "Please have a seat."

I sat in a folding chair. Looked at Sanchez's desk. It was a cluttered mess. A phone. A laptop and a desktop. Different pens and pencils. Scattered sheets of loose-leaf paper. Even a leather-bound thesaurus so old the spine was cracked.

"You said on the phone you wanted to talk about Coach Hunter," he said. "May I ask what this is in reference to?

"It's in regard to an investigation I'm working on."

"Can you elaborate?"

"Sorry, I can't."

He put his elbows on the desk and tented his hands.

"Very well," he said. "How can I help?"

"Just to be clear," I said. "You were the principal here when Dave was the basketball coach, correct?"

"Yes, I was."

"Okay. Good. Tell me about Dave?"

"What specifically would you like to know?"

"How was he when he worked here?"

"How was he?"

"Yeah. Was he liked? Disliked?"

Sanchez grinned. "He was very well liked. Very popular with the students. He coached winning teams and taught gym."

Before I could respond, Sanchez added, "Don't know if you're aware that his wife, Marie, also worked here. She coached the cheerleaders." Another grin. "She was a tough taskmaster. She made sure to keep Dave away from the girls."

I forced a grin. "Let me ask you this. When Dave was coaching here were there any problems, any issues?"

His brow ceased into a dark V. "Regarding?"

"Anything. Anything at all."

He hesitated. Made a slight shake of his head.

"Not that I can recall," he said. "He won and the kids seemed to like playing for him."

"Did any parents ever complain?"

"Complain about what?"

"Dave's behavior."

"No. No. Never. I never once heard a grievance."

"How about the players," I said. "Did any of them have problems with Dave?"

A vein throbbed in his forehead. He swallowed hard. Avoided eye contact.

"The only thing I can remember is a few students grumbling about how David could be a little rough with them when they wrestled."

"Wrestled?"

"Yes. David liked to wrestle. He wrestled in high school and taught wrestling in phys ed."

"Didn't that strike you as odd . . . a coach wrestling with his players?"

Blood seemed to rush into his face and there was a slight tremor along his right jawline.

"No," he said. "Not in the least. It's part of the curriculum. He played basketball with the kids, too."

"I find the wrestling strange."

Sanchez grabbed a ballpoint pen off his desk and nervously began clicking it with his right thumb.

"Strange?" he said, his forehead wrinkling like a venetian blind suddenly being raised.

"I know from personal experience, not my own mind you, that some coaches take physical contact a little too far . . . if you know what I mean."

Sanchez reared back in his seat. He started clicking the pen almost maniacally.

"That's absurd!" he said. "I've never heard of such a thing."

"It's a fact."

"Is it?"

"Yeah," I said, even though I couldn't substantiate my theory.

"Well, okay, if you say so. But I can assure you there was nothing untoward or inappropriate about Dave's behavior while at St. James. As I said, he was very well liked."

"That's the problem," I said. "Coaches that are sexual predators are often attractive, charming, and successful. They're good at hiding things."

"Wait a second. Wait a second. What are you suggesting?" He was still clicking the pen.

"I'm just wondering if Dave took any sexual liberties with a player or players."

Sanchez raised his arms in a hands-off manner.

"Oh my God, no," he said, loosening his tie. "We provide a safe environment here." Very defensive.

"Safe environment?"

"Yes. We are very concerned with the safety and well-being of our student-athletes."

"I'm sure you are."

"If David or any other teacher here made any advances on a student-athlete I'm sure I would have heard about it."

"Maybe not. Kids are too embarrassed to talk about abuse. It's uncomfortable and unpleasant."

"I can assure you that no teacher or coach has ever been accused of making sexual overtures to a student-athlete at this school."

"I don't care about other teachers or coaches. I'm only interested with Dave Hunter."

"Well, Mr. O'Brien, let me put your mind at ease, once and for all. There is nothing to suggest that David Hunter engaged in any improper behavior." He paused. His voice had a hiccup of panic. It took him a few swallows, then he added, "That is my final word on the matter."

"You could be wrong."

He dropped the pen on his desk and put two hands on it like a man in the ocean trying to steady a raft.

"Not a chance," he said, slowly uncoiling upward like a serpent to a snake charmer's flute.

I spread out my arms and raised my hands palms out like a magician who had just finished an incredible trick.

"You know, Sanchez," I said, "You haven't told me what I wanted to hear, but as the expression goes . . . actions speak louder than words. And for damn sure, your actions scream."

Sanchez flinched.

"I think you're being a bit unpleasant," he said.

"I don't get hired for my manners."

He looked at me as if I'd just caught him stealing from the school's missionary box.

"One last question," I said. "Have you been in touch with Hunter lately?"

"In touch?"

"Yeah. Has he phoned you recently?"

His face colored. He didn't answer my question, but his eyes dropped away from mine, and in that moment, I surmised a tell. A confirmation.

"I noticed a few pictures of you with Hunter in your trophy case," I said. "You guys looked pretty chummy."

His eyes got wider than hula hoops.

"What may I ask are you implying?" he said, indignantly.

"I'm not implying a damn thing," I said. "I'm just saying you guys seemed awfully friendly."

"For your information . . . sir," he said. "I'm married with three children."

"Good for you. Glad you could procreate."

That brought a long silence. I refused to break first.

"Are we through here?" he said.

I pointed to the picture of Christ and said, "Bible says a false witness will not go unpunished, and he who speaks lies will not escape."

"Excuse me?" he said.

"It's from Proverbs," I said. "I suggest you read it sometime. Might learn something."

I turned and left thinking, another day, another liar.

CHAPTER
TWENTY-
FOUR

An hour later, I was crossing the George Washington Bridge onto Interstate 80 West. Thankfully New Jersey traffic was light, and I zipped up to the Sparta exit, 34B.

I listened to Charlie Parker the entire trip. "Bird" was my father's idol. He often said Parker was the greatest jazz musician ever. Yet unlike Parker, my father never took drugs and hardly, if ever, drank—a rare accomplishment for a touring musician. The same was true of my mother.

Still, my parents were a fun couple who also had a serious side. They'd grown up in the sixties and believed deeply in truth and liberty and, most especially, civil rights. They were adamant that all people regardless of race should enjoy freedom of speech. No crime, my father often said, was worse than being afraid to speak your mind.

Which he did at every opportunity. He spoke out against police brutality, against discrimination, against racism. And he paid for it. He was arrested twice for protesting; once he was beaten so bad the cops busted his eardrum. But he played a gig that night, and the next morning was back on the street with my mother standing up for justice.

It's a shame my father didn't live long enough to see me become an adult. I think he would have been proud of me. Very proud. Less because I became a professional athlete and more because I live my life on my own terms and fight hard for racial equality.

I still carry in my wallet an index card he gave me before he was murdered. On it is a handwritten note from Tennyson's poem "Ulysses." It reads "To strive, to seek, to find, and not to yield." It is both my personal and professional credo.

I cruised through the center of Sparta, a nice enough commercial strip featuring pizza parlors, candy stores, salons, florists, realtors, and restaurants. I meandered my way around beautiful Lake Mohawk where dozens of small boats were motoring. Some pulled a triangular team of skiers; others dragged kids on innertubes. There were a few fishermen on the dock, casting their lines.

Ten minutes outside town, I saw a sign that read "Gladstone College: Home of the Gladiators."

I pulled into the campus. No quad, no tall towers. Low, flat buildings. No grandiose library. It looked less like a college and more like an old business park. No soul whatsoever.

The basketball arena was brick and had large glass panels fronting the entrance. I walked inside. The court reminded me of the one in the movie *Hoosiers*. It was small. Had limited seating. Worn floorboards. A wooden scoreboard. At least the backboards were glass.

The athletic director's office was in a separate building. A receptionist, a middle-aged woman with a Dutch Boy hairstyle and lots of makeup, greeted me. She wore a pink cardigan over a white blouse. A small nameplate on her desk said Colleen Neeson.

"Morning Colleen," I said.

"Good morning," she said, sounding bright and chipper.

I pointed to her nameplate.

"Any relation to Liam?" I said.

"No," she said. "But I wouldn't mind dating him."

"You and a thousand other women."

She exaggerated a sigh.

"I can dream, can't I," she said.

"Absolutely," I said. "Where would we be without our dreams?"

I handed her my business card.

"Mr. Brady is expecting you," Colleen said. I had called in advance and made an appointment. "I'll see if he's available."

"Thank you."

She stood, slid past me, and opened a door that said "Benjamin Brady."

"Mr. O'Brien is here to see you," she called into the room.

"Send him in," a voice said. "Send him in."

Colleen stepped aside. I entered the office.

It was the size of a broom closet. The carpeting was old. The acoustic ceiling tiles were stained. Large plaques and framed pictures of athletes decorated the walls. Guys throwing footballs. Women shooting basketballs. I was happy to see that Brady believed in equality.

Sitting behind the desk was an older gentleman with a weak chin, sagging jowls, and a gray toupee. He wore an orange polo shirt with Gladiators scripted over his right breast.

He stood and extended his hand. I shook it.

"Nice to meet you, Mr. O'Brien," he said, smiling. He had the overbite of a rodent.

He pointed to a chair across from his desk. The chair was gunmetal gray. I sat. The chair wobbled.

"This is a real treat," he said, after returning to his seat. "I used to watch you play, both at Duke and Dallas. Yes sir, you were one heck of a player. You dang sure were." Brady had a syrupy Southern synthetic accent. He pronounced "I" like "Ah."

"Appreciate the compliment," I said.

"I think I was at a game in Madison Square many years ago when you scored, I believe, forty points in a big upset of St. John's."

"Forty-two," I said.

Brady smiled then leaned forward in his chair. He rested his chin on clasped hands.

"Like your accent," I said. "Where you from?"

"Born and raised in Mobile, Alabama."

"Gateway to the Gulf," I said. "Birthplace of Henry Aaron. What made you come north?"

"I managed the basketball team at The U. After I graduated, I got an internship at SUNY Binghamton in upstate New York."

"In the athletic department?"

"Yes sir. Made me happier than a pig in sunshine." Southern humor, I gathered. Not my cup of tea.

"You mentioned over the phone that you were interested in talking about Coach Hunter," he said. "May I ask why?"

"As you may know a kid from his St. Stephen's team, Teddy Malone, was murdered a few months back."

"I remember readin' about it," he said. "Such a tragedy. Did they ever find the killer?"

"No. That's why his father hired me."

"And y'all is a private investigator, correct?"

"Correct."

"Interesting choice of an occupation for an ex-basketball star."

"It was either that or the priesthood."

"Seriously?" he said. "You considered the priesthood?"

"In the end I just couldn't make the commitment."

"To God?"

"No," I said. "To celibacy."

Brady laughed heartily. A real yuk yuk yuk. Like Curly from *The Three Stooges*.

"I imagine your work must bring y'all in contact with lots of unsavory people," he said.

"No more than in your profession."

Brady chewed his lower lip.

"If I might ask," he said. "How's your investigation going?"

"I'm still gathering evidence. I've spoken to the police, friends, witnesses, and both coaches—Corsito and Hunter— but nobody's been able to shed much light on who the shooter might be or his motive."

"How can I be of assistance?"

"I'm doing background checks on anyone who had a close association with Teddy."

"Is that standard procedure?"

"It is."

"What would y'all like to know?"

"I googled Dave Hunter and read that he had resigned from Gladstone."

"That was a year before I got here."

"I didn't realize that."

"Mitch Mahoney was AD then."

"Is Mitch still around?"

"Sadly, no. He died last year."

"From?"

"A heart attack."

"Sorry to hear that," I said. "You replaced Mitch?"

"Yes, sir. Indeed, I did." he said, rubbing the bottom of his nose. "If y'all don't mind me asking . . . why the interest in Hunter's resignation?"

"Just covering all bases," I said. "Do you know why Hunter resigned?"

"As I said, I wasn't here at the time."

"Was Mitch still alive when you got the job?"

"He was. But he was sick. Though he did stop by on occasion."

"You ever talk to him about Hunter?"

"A little."

"Then you must know why Hunter resigned?"

"Mitch said they had a falling out."

"Over?"

"A parent registered a complaint."

"Against Hunter?"

"Yes."

"You recall what the complaint was?"

Brady looked down and picked at some invisible lint on his pant leg.

"I don't," he said. "I sincerely don't."

"You don't, huh?"

"No . . . no, I don't."

"That's all Mitch told you. That he and Hunter had a falling out?"

"Yes, sir."

"Strange he didn't go into more detail."

Brady stared at me with a blank face. Probably his only genuine look.

"Even more strange is that Hunter would resign after a championship season," I said.

Brady was still staring at me. Behind the blank look was discomfort.

I said, "Do you at least know if Mitch notified the school president?"

"Of?"

"The father's complaint."

"I do not, no."

"You don't?"

"No, I don't."

"How about the campus police? Did Mitch inform them?"

Brady gave me a dead-eyed look and said, "I really wish I could help you, Elgin, but I just don't know much about what happened. I am so very sorry."

I just about had it with the syrup. I leaned forward in my seat and said, "Whoa, whoa, whoa. Wait a second. Are you trying to tell me that you spoke to Mitch about the father's complaint, and yet you don't know exactly what the complaint was? Is that what you're trying to tell me? Is it? Is it?"

"I hate repeating myself . . . I just don't know much."

His evasiveness was only confirming what I suspected. He's lying through his teeth.

Raising my voice, I said, "Don't bullshit me, Brady."

"Now Mistuh O'Brien. Why would I do that?"

"To protect Mitch? The president? The school?"

"Look," he said. "I am a man of integrity telling you the truth."

"Are you?"

"I am."

Brady shifted in his chair. He sighed, heavy and exhausted. I noticed small oval stains were starting to appear beneath his armpits.

"Look, Mistuh O'Brien, I'm trying to be helpful. All I know is all I know. I just don't know the whole story."

I didn't believe him or his dumb hick routine. Then again, I don't believe most athletic directors. They make an art of talking out of both sides of their mouth. When they say the words "student-athletes," believe me, they're thinking "cost-benefit analysis" and calculating their pensions.

"Answer me this," I said. "Do you even know if Mitch spoke with the kid?"

"Again, I . . . I don't know. As I told you, I took over after Hunter left."

"By any chance, do you know the kid's name?"

"The kid's name?"

"Yeah. The one whose father registered the complaint."

"It's . . . it's James Leonard. Round here they called him Jimmy."

"How is it you remember the player's name, but you don't remember the complaint?"

Brady didn't respond. He just stared at me with anemic eyes.

"Cat got your tongue?" I said.

"What would you like me to say?"

"Something intelligent," I said. "Is Jimmy still in the area?"

"I do believe he may be in jail."

"Jail?"

"Everyone round here knows the poor young man has had a rough go of it. Theft, drinking, drugs."

"Know where I can find the father?"

"Yes, I do. Mr. Leonard works at Home Depot."

"In Sparta?"

"Yeah."

"How do you know that?"

"This is a small town. Almost everyone knows everyone. One of the many charms of Sparta."

"I guess I'll just have to go see Mr. Leonard if I want the truth."

"You best be careful," Brady said. "From what I heard Leonard can get angrier than a wet hen."

"You sure know how to whistle 'Dixie,' Brady" I said, thinking that there are Texas stockyards not half as rich in bullshit as this AD's line of crap.

"Tell me about Leonard's anger," I said.

"Mitch told me Leonard physically attacked him."

"You have a very selective memory, Brady, you know that? Attacked him how?"

"He grabbed Mitch by the throat and pushed him against a wall."

"Why?

"Mitch refused to press charges."

"The charges being?"

"I already told you. As the good Lord is my witness, I just don't know."

"Let me tell *you* something I know, Brady," I said, rage building inside me. "I know you know why Hunter resigned. You do. You do. And the fact that you can't be honest about it makes you a sick enabler of a sick person."

Color drained from Brady's face. He shook his head as if embarrassed. I shook my head as well. I had just outed another Hunter protector.

I said, "As they say down South, Brady, you're lyin' like a no-legged dog."

"Why, how dare you . . . you . . . say such a thing, you uppity—" he stopped short. "Sir, you are plumb crazy. Plumb crazy. Now get out of my office and never come back."

I stood. Smiled. That's me, spreading goodwill wherever I go.

CHAPTER TWENTY-FIVE

The Home Depot was crowded. Lots of people carrying air conditioners, hoses, and plants, getting ready for summer.

I walked over to a cashier, a young woman with bleached blond hair and thick black eyebrows.

"Excuse me," I said. "Do you know where I can find a Mr. Leonard."

"You mean Chuck?"

"Is there another Mr. Leonard?"

"Not that I know of."

"Then Chuck it is."

She pointed to her left.

"He works in appliances," she said.

I thanked her and went up an aisle that was packed with ovens and stoves and microwaves.

Leaning against a Maytag refrigerator was a six-foot, buffed man wearing khaki pants, a blue short-sleeved shirt, and brown docksiders. His upper body was covered with an orange apron that said Home Depot.

"Excuse me," I said, tapping him on the shoulder.

He turned. His face was badly wrinkled. The lid on his right eye was sucked into the socket so that only a tiny bit of eyeball could be seen.

"Yes," he said, his voice was gruff, like a bear if a bear could talk.

"You Chuck Leonard?" I said.

"Yeah. What can I do for you?"

"My name is Elgin O'Brien."

His left eye squinted.

"The guy who used to play for the Mavericks?" he said.

"That's me. I'm now a private investigator. And if you don't mind, I'd like to ask you a few questions."

"What about?

"Dave Hunter."

Leonard grimaced. "I got nothing to say about that asshole." His voice was full of contempt and revulsion.

"Let me explain," I said. "I'm looking into the murder of a kid by the name of Teddy Malone. He was a player at St. Stephen's University who was shot and killed months ago."

"I read about that," he said. "But what's that kid's murder got to do with me?"

"It's less about you and more about your son."

His head tilted. A ninety-degree angle.

"My son?" he said, suspiciously. "What's my son got to do with anything? Christ, every goddamn time somebody's paper goes missing, they come after Jimmy."

"Hold on. He's got nothing to do with the shooting. Nothing directly."

"Then I don't get it."

"I'd like to know what his problem was with Dave Hunter."

"Leave Jimmy out of this," he said, clenching his hands so tight his knuckles shone waxy white.

"Can we go someplace more private to speak?" I said.

Leonard rubbed his muscular right forearm. It was decorated with a Harley-Davidson tattoo.

"I'll give you a few minutes," he said.

"Great."

Leonard called out to a co-worker.

"Hey, Jeff," he shouted. "Can you cover for me?"

Jeff saluted him.

"Let's go outside," Leonard said.

Outside, the heat was intense. Ninety-two in the shade. We sat under a potted cherry tree dripping a shower of pink blossoms.

"I understand you registered a complaint against Hunter," I said.

"Damn right, I did."

"Can you tell me about it?"

He paused and took a few deep breaths. "Tell you about it? You want me to tell you about it? I'll tell you about it. The motherfucker abused my son."

"In what way?"

Leonard cringed. His anger radiated toward me like heat from an open furnace.

"The Hunter way," he said.

"Can you be more specific?"

"You really want to hear this shit?"

"Very much so."

"Okay," he said. "I knew Hunter was harassing my kid, so I went to see this douchebag Mahoney, the athletic director. I demanded Hunter get fired."

"He resigned, didn't he?"

"That was a fucking cover-up," he said, sweat popping off his forehead like grease from a skillet.

"A cover-up?"

He wiped sweat from his forehead.

"I'm not sure I wanna get into this," he said.

"I think you should."

"You do, do you?"

"Yeah, I do."

Leonard leaned forward, elbows on the table. I noticed the knuckles on both hands were large and swollen, perhaps from too many neighborhood fist fights.

"Let me ask you a question," he said. "I'm getting the sense that this is something personal with you."

"Whaddya mean?"

"Like it's a vendetta?"

"It's more than that."

"What exactly?"

"A long time ago my father was murdered," I said. "His killer was never found. And my cousin, well, he had some shit happens to him and ended up an addict. I think I got into this line of work so other people wouldn't have to live with the kind of questions I have."

"So now you seek revenge, is that it?"

"No. Not revenge. Justice. Justice in a sinful world."

Leonard studied my face.

"You strike me as kind of a hard guy," he said.

"It's takes one to know one."

Something suddenly passed between us, some kind of connection. He exhaled and his voice softened.

"Okay," he said. "Here's what happened. Jimmy was just a freshman. One day after practice Hunter was alone with him in the locker room. Jimmy already had kind of a bad feeling about the guy, just from the way Hunter looked at him. Anyway, Jimmy had just come out of the shower. He was only wearing a towel. Hunter pulled the towel off him, pushed him up against the wall, grabbed his dick and tried to jerk him off. Jimmy pushed him off. The motherfucker just laughed and said, 'Don't you wanna play?' Jimmy quit the team the next day."

"Did you confront Hunter?" I said.

"Fuck, yeah! He denied everything."

"Did you speak with anyone else besides Mahoney?"

"I spoke to the HR Department."

"What they do?"

Leonard was once again clenching his fists.

"They did fucking . . . NOTHING!"

"Nothing?

"Not a damn thing. Then I went back to see Mahoney. He said he spoke with Hunter and Hunter denied the charges. But Mitch knew he was lying. But instead of pressing charges against Hunter, the asshole accepted Hunter's resignation and, supposedly, gave him a generous goodbye package."

"Why didn't you press charges?"

"Why?" he shouted. "Why?"

"Yes, why?"

"Because my word means shit. I got no pull. Gladstone employs a lot of people here, pays a lot of bills. Almost every cop in this town went to Gladstone." Leonard sucked air through his nostrils. "Fuck. The goddamn chief of police is one of the school's biggest supporters."

"Did Hunter talk about his resignation?"

"Oh, yeah. He went on local TV and put on quite the performance. He said how heartbroken he was to leave Gladstone. How the school and he just couldn't agree on funding for the basketball program. Even had his adoring wife Marie and boys standing next to him, all of 'em crying." Leonard's face seemed to fold in on itself. "What crap!"

I took a deep breath before speaking again.

"Tell me about Jimmy," I said.

"What . . . exactly?"

"I was told he's had some issues."

His brow wrinkled.

"Who told you that?" he said.

"Gladstone's AD."

"Brady?"

"Yeah."

Leonard sniffed. "Another empty suit."

"Can you tell me about the issues?" I said.

Leonard rubbed his left eye.

"I love that word . . . issues," he said, scowling. "Issues makes it sound as if it's a topic for debate. What Jimmy had and has are problems. Serious problems."

"Can you elaborate?"

"Name a problem—stealing, drugs, alcohol—he's had them all, and he's still dealing with them. Every damn day."

"You attribute his problems to Hunter?"

"Hell, yeah," he said, his voice going up an octave. "Hunter derailed his life. Before the episode, Jimmy was a happy-go-lucky kid. A good basketball player. A good student. Had thoughts of becoming a lawyer. My kid, a lawyer. Then that pervert Hunter ruined everything. Sent Jimmy into a tailspin. Dropped out of school and dropped into trouble."

Listening, my jaw clenched tight enough to crack a tooth. How a college could push a kid's problem under the rug to protect a basketball coach is beyond comprehension. But it happens all the time. Shame on them.

"I'm confused about something," Leonard said.

"Confused about what?"

"I know Hunter's a perv, but you're looking into who killed Teddy Malone? Do you think Hunter killed the Malone kid? Or had someone else kill him?"

"I have no proof of that."

"But you suspect something?"

"Let's just say I'm suspicious."

"Is that enough to go on? Your suspicions?"

"No, that's why I need your help."

"Help?"

"I need evidence."

"What kind of evidence?"

"Testimony from abused players."

"Is that why you're here?" he said. "You want to speak with Jimmy?"

"Yes."

Leonard put his hands together, as if in prayer.

"Don't know if he'd agree," he said.

"Could you ask him?"

"I could."

"That'd be great."

"On one condition."

"What's that?"

"Don't pressure him. He's doing okay right now, and I don't want him to have another relapse."

"I won't."

"Won't what?"

"Pressure him."

"I want your word."

"You got it."

"Say it."

"I promise. I won't pressure him."

Leonard pulled a cell phone from his back pocket.

"What's your cell number?" he said.

I told him.

He tapped it into his phone, then said, "I'll text you later and tell you where and when . . . if Jimmy consents."

"Appreciate it," I said. We shook hands.

"Don't thank me yet," he said. "Jimmy may not want to meet."

"We'll see, won't we."

Leonard stood, turned and walked away, swaying side to side like a boxer who'd taken a punch and refused to fall.

CHAPTER TWENTY-SIX

Chuck Leonard called me an hour later. Said Jimmy would meet me at the Sparta Diner. Five o'clock.

The diner was on Woodport Road, just a few miles from the Gladstone campus. The exterior was aluminum and glass. Inside, ten stools fronted a lunch counter, and five leatherette booths lined the opposite wall. Behind the counter were coffee urns, soda dispensers, and a variety of baked goods: muffins, donuts, cakes. The room smelled of warm chocolate and hamburger grease.

People were coming and going. Talking. Laughing. A young couple passed by me holding hands. They couldn't have been more than sixteen. Puppy love.

I slid into a booth by a window. An elderly stoop-shouldered waitress approached. I asked for a glass of water and a cup of tea. I've been drinking a lot of tea lately. Monique got me into it. She calls tea "a hug in a cup."

I glanced out the window. Across the street was a small mall housing a Panera's, a pizza parlor, a bowling alley, a pet shop, and an independent bookstore. I was elated to see it. There aren't many left. Which is a shame. A damn shame.

I grew up with books. As early as age six, my parents started giving me books instead of toys. Their goal was to instill in me a love of ideas and the idea of learning. At first, the books were about sports and music. As I got older, they gave me stories by Black authors Langston Hughes, Toni Morrison, and James Baldwin, as well as the Irish writers my mother grew up with. Samuel Beckett. William Butler Yeats. Oscar Wilde. Their writing was powerful and transformative. Their words, their sentences, their paragraphs all spoke to me. They wrote about human beings, about people who lived and loved, fought and failed, cried and laughed. Though I didn't fully understand them till later in life, they helped me figure out who I was, a kid who struggled at times with being biracial and caught between cultures.

To this day, I can almost quote verbatim Baldwin who wrote "You think your pain and your heartbreak are unprecedented in the history of the world, but then you read. It was books that taught me that the things that tormented me the most were the very things that connected me with all the people who were alive, who had ever been alive."

As a teenager, I thought that someday I might want to become a writer. But as I got older, I was injected with a stronger narcotic: basketball. I did, however, major in journalism at Duke. The coaches didn't like that, but it helped me a lot when I got to the NBA.

The waitress returned and put a mug on the table. Steam floated upward.

"Can I get you something else?" she said. "Cream? Milk? Sugar?"

"I'm good."

"You like tea, huh?"

"My girlfriend calls it a 'hug in a cup.' "

"Wish I could drink it."

"Why can't you?"

"Acid reflux."

"Not good."

"Neither is my life," she said. "

Strangers, I thought, they tell you the darndest things. Yet if I've learned anything from them it's that they all want a place to call home, a place to relax, a place to be at peace. Ideally, with someone they care about and who cares about them. A devoted partner.

I looked at my watch. It was 5:25. I felt like a mourner sitting in a funeral parlor waiting for the funeral to begin. If Jimmy didn't show up in the next few minutes, I'd text Chuck.

I liked Chuck. He reminded me of the tough guys I grew up with in Harlem, guys who learned early in life how to mix it up, slip punches, bob and weave, always staying on their feet, always hanging in there, and never quitting on one's corner stool in the early or middle rounds.

Five-thirty. No Jimmy. I was just about to text Chuck when a skinny guy with eyes that looked as if they'd been zapped by an electrical shock walked into the diner. He wore ripped gray sweatpants and a blue Ultimate Fighting Championship tee that featured the outline of an octagon. He looked around the place. His eyes met mine. He trudged slowly in my direction.

He got to the booth and looked down on me.

"You O'Brien?" he said. His voice was so soft it was almost hard to hear. He sounded like he was in pain.

I looked up at him. In all my years as a private investigator I don't think I ever saw anyone with such a sad face. It was heartbreaking to look at.

"Yes, and you must be Jimmy," I said. "Please sit."

He slid into the booth and clasped his hands on the table. His fingernails were bitten to the quick.

"Nice to meet you, Jimmy," I said, extending my hand.

He looked at it for a long moment as if it were contaminated. He eventually shook it. His hand was sweaty and limp.

The waitress reappeared.

"Can I get you anything?" she said to him.

Jimmy shrugged, staring down at his lifeless hands.

"Gwan," I said. "Have something to drink. It's hot outside."

He glanced up at me.

"Okay," he said. When he spoke his lips barely moved. "I'll have a Coke."

"Either of you care for something to eat?" she said.

I looked at Jimmy. "Hungry?"

"Nah," he said, moving a tiny glass saltshaker back and forth slowly on the table.

"Mind if I have something?"

He shrugged.

"How are your cheeseburgers?" I asked the waitress.

"Juicy."

"I'll have one."

"Want salad or fries with that?"

"Fries, of course," I said. "Gotta keep my weight up."

She forced herself to grin.

"Thank you for coming," I said to Jimmy.

He shrugged. Shrugging seemed to be his favorite gesture.

"You a UFC fan?" I said, pointing to his shirt.

He nodded. At least he didn't shrug. Progress.

"You watch a lot of fights?" I said.

"When I can," he said, moving the saltshaker more agitatedly this time.

"I do, too," I said, even though I had only seen a few pay-per-views.

The waitress returned with Jimmy's coke. She placed the glass on the table. He looked at it as if it were a mirage.

"I think you know why I'm here," I said. "I'd like to talk to you about Dave Hunter."

His face darkened.

"I'm told he harassed you," I said, trying to be sensitive to his feelings.

He shrugged. Maybe I hadn't made progress.

"What do you mean?" Jimmy said.

"You know what I mean."

"No, I don't."

"Yes," I said softly. "You do."

"I don't."

"Okay," I said. After all, I did promise Chuck I wouldn't push him. "Just tell me this. Why'd you quit the team?"

"I got tired of Hunter's bullshit," he said, lowering his eyes.

"Anything else?"

"Anything else?"

"Something he did to you?"

He raised his eyes slowly, as if they were attached to sinkers.

"Why do you care?" he said. His voice was a monotone mutter.

"I care because he may have molested a player by the name of Teddy Malone."

Jimmy put one finger in his Coke and moved the ice around, then took his finger out and sucked off some soda.

"Look, Jimmy," I said, leaning forward, "I know from talking to your father that Hunter took liberties with you. I just need you—you—to confirm that."

Jimmy was quiet. I counted to thirty before I spoke again.

"Chances are whatever he did to you he's still doing to other kids," I said.

Jimmy looked at me. I could see in his wincing eyes that he was remembering things. Bad things.

"If that's the case," I said, "He has to be stopped."

No response.

"We can't let coaches like Hunter get away with this stuff," I said.

Jimmy touched trembling fingertips to his temples as if my words were giving him a massive headache.

The waitress came with my burger and fries. I let it sit.

I said, "Jimmy, whatever you tell me . . . dies right here."

His face was filled with terminal agony.

"I can't," he said, choking on his words. "I can't."

"Can't what?"

"Can't tell you."

"You can." My voice was low. Like that of a priest behind the screen talking to a confessor.

"I can't."

"It's okay. You can tell me." I stopped speaking. I've learned from talking with all sorts of crime victims that you have to give them the space to grapple with their demons, the space to talk.

"I . . . I . . ." he faltered, his eyelids going up and down like broken semaphores.

"You . . . you what?"

"I . . . I . . . His voice stuck like a faulty clutch. "I've . . . only . . . in my life . . . have . . . have told my father about . . . about what happened."

"I know that. Your father is a good man."

He puffed his cheeks out and made tiny plosive sounds. The look on his face was so excruciating, so viscerally painful, it almost forced me to turn away.

"I . . . I did . . . I did . . . because nobody else would have believed me."

I slowly reached out and squeezed his wrist. I hoped the gesture was sending a message; we're in this together. "I believe you."

"You . . . you do?" he said, his mumbled reply barely audible.

"I do."

"But . . . but Hunter's a big-time coach now. He's been written up all over the place. People idolize him. You think if what I tell you comes out people will . . . will take my . . . my word over his?"

"They might."

Jimmy wiggled around aggressively in his seat like someone tied with rope trying to get free.

"In a fucking pig's eye, they will," he said. Under the table, his knees were pumping so hard it shook.

"Just answer one question. Yes or no," I said. "Did Dave Hunter sexually molest you?"

He jerked in his seat. For a moment, I thought he might get up and bolt. But he didn't. He just looked at me, his shoulders shaking, as if he were freezing.

I said nothing.

Jimmy didn't answer. The diner was eerily quiet, as if the place had suddenly sunk into the bottom of a deep, dark, silent sea.

"Jimmy," I said. "Help me, help you."

"You can't," he said, his face drenched in sweat as if he were in the grip of a fever.

"I can. And maybe together we can help other kids. Please, Jimmy, talk to me."

Jimmy's mouth opened into a big O, but no words came forth. It was as if he was suddenly struck speechless.

"Please, Jimmy," I said. "You can tell me."

A long silence ensued. Then, finally, in a voice so soft I wasn't sure I heard him correctly he said "Yeah."

"Yeah what?"

"Yeah," he said, his voice warbling with crushing emotion. "Yeah, he did molest me."

I felt his words shoot through me like a spasm of pain.

"Can you be any more specific?"

"I'd rather not," he said, shaking his head as if being attacked by wasps.

"Okay. Is there anything I can do for you?"

His eyes met mine like lasers. "Find me a way to sleep at night."

Before I could respond, Jimmy slid out of the booth and rushed from the diner.

I sat with my eyes closed in a state of stupefaction, unable to move or, even more, unable to control the rage in my heart.

The waitress appeared.

"Is something wrong with your food?" she said. "You haven't even touched it."

"No," I said, my mind filled with revulsion. "The meal's fine. Its sports that's the problem."

She shot me a funny look.

I pulled some bills from my pants pocket and threw them on the table.

I had lost my appetite.

CHAPTER TWENTY-SEVEN

The next day I was sitting outside O'Meara's office, waiting for him to conclude a meeting.

As I sat there my thoughts turned to Dave Hunter. I was now totally convinced he was a pedophile, even if I only had Jimmy Leonard's word for it. But I still needed more evidence. From others who Hunter molested.

Even if I got that evidence there was still something about this case that wasn't adding up, wasn't quite right. I mean, where did Corsito, Smith, Blake, Catalano, Emma Mitchell, Adam Roth, and Ambush Anderson fit into all this? Were some of them—or all of them—covering up for Hunter's depravity? Even if they were, could they know or have known who killed Teddy? Was it Smith? Was it someone Hunter hired? Or Corsito hired? Or Blake hired? Or Emma hired? Was it Gary Grimes? Or the Roth kid? Or Catalano's nephew, Anthony. There were a lot of pieces to this puzzle, all scattered over the floor. I just needed to dovetail them in place. Like Agatha Christie would.

O'Meara's office door opened. Six uniformed cops, men and women, exited.

Bill saw me and said, "Oh, it's you."

"Who'd you expect? Mila Kunis?"

"One can only hope," he said. "Get your ass in here."

I got up off my chair and went inside. O'Meara was sitting behind his desk, eating an apple. His office was nicely decorated. Lots of framed plaques and citations. Pictures of him with past mayors and governors. A large American flag. And the Irish tricolor.

"Sorry to keep you waiting," he said.

"One always expects to wait for the big cheese."

"Big cheese? I'm more like a chunk of limburger."

"Busy, huh?

"Got a lot on my mind." He grinned. "Which, by the way, is said to be a common mark of genius."

"Only mark you have is the scar on your forehead."

He smirked. "What can I do for you?"

"You used to work in Queens, right?" I asked.

"I did," he said. "Worked in the 115th Precinct, oh, up till the end of last year. Why?"

"How much did you deal with St. Stephen's?"

"Whaddya mean?"

"Problems with the players."

"Plenty. Some of them were out of control."

"Educate me."

He took a bite of his apple, making a crisp, crunchy sound. Behind him, on a credenza, there were framed pictures of kids riding on ponies, jumping in swimming pools, shooting basketballs. Families. Nothing more important.

"Drug arrests, occasional fights, sexual assaults," he said.

"Anything to do with Teddy?"

"Just once. He was pulled over in a car along with Ambush Anderson, and we found drugs."

"Case go to court?"

"Got dropped."

"Dropped? Why?"

"Some big shot St. Joe alumni had pull with the district attorney's office."

"Let me guess. James Catalano?"

O'Meara's eyes widened.

"How'd you know?" he said.

"I have my ways."

"I'm impressed."

"You ever talk to Corsito?"

"About?"

"The players?"

"A couple of times."

"What he say?"

"Always the same shit: 'I'll take care of things.' "

"Did he?"

"Not really."

How pathetic, I thought, college coaches who cover up for their players against any transgressions that might affect their eligibility. Many often use that bullshit line that "boys will be boys."

That, for sure, doesn't help a player mature, doesn't help them understand that in the real world there are no excuses for bad behavior. There are no time-outs, no guardian angels. Nobody gives you a get-out-of-jail-free card. There's only one solution for a coach who winks and nods at bad behavior. He should be benched. Permanently.

"Tell me about Dave Hunter?" I said.

"What about him?"

"You know him."

"Well enough."

O'Meara finished his apple, then tossed it into a trash can. He wiped his hand with a tiny napkin.

"What's your opinion?" I said.

"Of Dave?"

"Yeah."

"Seems like a nice guy. I met him a few times at school events. He comped me game tickets a couple of times. What's your interest in him?"

"The other day I went to see him at a basketball camp. He acted a little too, shall we say, a bit too 'hands on' with the kids."

O'Meara looked at me as if mesmerized.

"What are you saying?" he said.

"I'm saying I didn't like what I saw."

"You serious?"

"Deadly."

"You aren't suggesting what I think you're suggesting, are you?"

I nodded.

He gave a low whistle. "You must be crazy."

"Sometimes I'm afraid I am," I said. "Nevertheless, I spoke with a kid from Gladstone College who Hunter coached. The kid confirmed to me Hunter molested him."

"The kid credible?"

"If you'd seen him, you wouldn't ask that question."

"How long ago did this allegedly happen?"

"Roughly fifteen years."

"Did the kid report it?"

"His father spoke to the athletic director and the HR Department."

"What happened?"

"Nothing."

O'Meara pinched his lower lip.

"Be a hard case to prove," he said. "It would be a he-said, he-said case. Never easy to prove or disprove."

"And, of course, Hunter being a big-time coach, people wouldn't believe the kid."

"Book it."

I pointed to O'Meara's computer.

"Can you look up and see if Hunter has a record," I said.

"A record of what?"

"I don't know. I'm just spitballing. Anything."

"I'd doubt he has one."

"Still. Mind checking? And don't just look under David Hunter or Dave Hunter. When I googled him, I discovered his legal first name is Allen, Allen David Hunter. Might explain how he stayed under the radar."

O'Meara put on his bifocals, turned to his desktop computer, and began tapping the keys. A minute later, he cupped his chin and said, "Hmmm."

"Hmmm," I said. "Is that a police term?"

"Only to those in the know."

"I see."

"You're not dealing here with Officer Krupke."

"I like that. A reference to *West Side Story*."

"You see Spielberg's remake?"

"Yeah."

"You like it?"

"Not as much as the original," I said. "Now elaborate on the hmmm."

He pointed to the screen and said, "Nothing under David Hunter. But it says here a woman once filed a complaint against an Allen David Hunter to the Queens attorney general."

I snapped my fingers. "See. I was right."

O'Meara smirked. "For a change."

"What was the complaint?"

"Seems Hunter was harassing her son."

"Sexually harassing?"

"Doesn't specify. The complaint was withdrawn."

"Does it give the women's name and address?"

"Gives both."

"Can I have it?"

He smirked.

"What am I . . . your secretary?"

"Just a cop who wants to help."

"I will . . . if."

"If what?"

"You buy me dinner at Le Cirque."

"I thought cops only ate at White Castle."

"Perish the thought," he said. "I only eat at the finest establishments."

"I suppose you'll want wine, too."

"A meal without wine is called breakfast."

"Okay. Le Cirque it is."

"I knew you'd see it my way."

"You're a real pal, O'Meara."

"What I am is a real pushover."

"What are friends for?"

O'Meara smiled. He then wrote out the name and the address of the complainant.

I took it and said, "Appreciate it."

"What can I say. A friend in need is . . ."

I stood.

"See you in the funny papers," I said.

"Haven't heard that expression in years."

"It was one of my father's favorites."

"Jazzy."

"That he was," I said. "That he was."

CHAPTER
TWENTY-EIGHT

The complainant's name was Eleanor Lang. She lived at 771 Astoria Boulevard in Queens. Her house was a small Cape Cod. It was missing roof tiles and rain gutters. Weeds spouted out of the cracked walkway. It struck me that a huff and a puff could blow this house down.

I strolled up the wooden front steps. They were rotted. Hanging from the center of the door was an artificial Christmas wreath. It was missing lots of holly and all the cheer.

I rang the doorbell. A short, haggard-faced woman in her late forties opened the door a crack and held the doorknob tight. She was wearing a ripped green robe and dirty white slippers. Her gray hair was jammed with tiny, round curlers.

"Can I help you?" she said, her voice raspy.

I was taken aback by the look in her eyes. They were the eyes of the walking dead.

I quickly regrouped, introduced myself, showed her my ID, and jumped right in.

"I'd like to speak to you about David Hunter," I said.

She winced. Her mouth was slack on one side as if she had suffered a stroke or a mild heart attack.

I said, "May I come in?"

"I . . . I guess so," she said.

She moved aside. I entered. The place wasn't air-conditioned. It was hot, suffocating. There was a strong smell of cat piss and sour milk.

The living room had a rocking chair with broken straw backing. Next to it was a lumpy sofa covered with frayed throw blankets. Above the sofa was a framed photo of Jesus, his shirt open, his heart dripping blood. On the wall across from it were a dozen pictures of a young boy with blond hair. He was smiling and shooting a basketball.

"That your son?" I said, pointing to the pictures.

"Yes," she said. "That's . . . that's my Billy. When . . . when he was in grade school."

"How is Billy?"

She shut her eyes and pursed her lips. An agonizing look.

"Billy . . . Billy is dead," she said, her voice filled with emotion.

"My deepest condolences," I said, wishing I had magical words of comfort, but I didn't. "I'm sorry. I wasn't aware. Was he sick, in an accident?"

She swallowed hard. Her boozy eyes dropped. For a moment, the only sound in the room came from her wheezy breathing.

"He . . . he committed suicide," she said. Her voice was flat, no inflection.

I glanced at the photographs and nausea swirled around in my stomach. I made a fist and silently bounced it on my thigh like a hammer. If you do this job long enough, you learn to deal with a lot of heartbreak. Some more difficult than others. This was perhaps the most difficult ever.

"That must have been awful," I said, cringing and thinking that there can't be any tragedy worse for a parent than having a child take their own life. I wondered how anyone deals with the anguish. My guess is: They don't.

Mrs. Lang grinned slightly, peeling her lips back from a bad set of dentures. She then pointed to the rocking chair.

"Have a seat," she said, taking one herself.

I sat. As I did, I heard a meow and saw a brown and black short-haired cat crawl under the couch.

"I'm here, Mrs. Lang, because I understand you lodged a complaint years ago against Dave Hunter, your son's coach. Can you tell me about it."

She stared at me for a moment, then briefly shook her head like a person coming out of a trance.

"Mind if I smoke?" she said.

"No. Go right ahead."

She grabbed a pack of Camels and lit one with a tiny BIC lighter. She nervously inhaled, coughed, then blew out twin streams of smoke from flaring nostrils.

"I'm sorry to make you relive all of this," I said softly, thinking how I wasn't happy to be causing her more grief than she already carried. "Can you tell me about the complaint?"

Her eyes quickly shut, then just as quickly reopened. She took another lungful of smoke and began to cough so violently she doubled over, her knees jerking upward.

"Sorry," she said. "I know I should quit but I can't."

"I understand."

She took a deep breath and said, "Every summer Billy used to go to that basketball camp in the Poconos. He worked as a waiter there to pay the cost. He loved it. Absolutely loved it. Loved the kids and the coaches." She paused and fell into a silence so prolonged that it began to unnerve me.

Then: "Billy's father died when Billy was four, so in a way his coaches became father figures. He got especially close to . . . to . . ." She struggled to talk, then in a voice that startled me with its mingled tone of regret and hate said. ". . . Dave Hunter."

A moment of silence. So paralyzingly awkward I hope I never have to experience one like it again.

While I waited for her to speak, I glanced at a picture on the end table. It was of a young Mrs. Lang, smiling and holding a baby. Presumably Billy. She was quite attractive back then, had the kind of looks that would have made men do a double take.

"One year after camp Hunter started calling Billy, started coming around. He began taking Billy to movies and McDonald's. I thought it was good for Billy . . . he was having so much fun with him . . . until . . ."

She fell silent again and blew out some smoke, then waved it away as if it were a snarl of cobwebs.

"Until what?" I said.

Mrs. Lang leaned forward and squeezed her shoulder blades together as if she were cold. I got the sense, though, that like many grief-stricken people I had interviewed in the past, she was ready to talk about what happened to Billy out of a sense of motherly duty. She just needed a little nudging.

"Until . . . until . . ."—she bit her lip, blinking from the effort—" . . . until Hunter took Billy to his apartment and forced him . . ."

"Forced him to do what?"

She looked down and mumbled something under her breath. Her hand was trembling so bad that ash dropped off the tip of her cigarette and fell to the floor.

"To . . . to perform oral sex," she said in a whisper.

An icy chill raced through my body like an electric current.

"How'd you find out about this?" I said.

"All of a sudden Billy started to act strange. He wasn't eating right. He wasn't talking much. When Hunter called, he wouldn't call him back, He just stayed in his room. Didn't even go to the park to play basketball anymore. He was very depressed. Very depressed."

She drew on her cigarette, shaking so badly that the cigarette in the corner of her mouth quivered up and down like a diving board after a swimmer jumps.

"I got so concerned I made an appointment with a counselor," she said. "But then one night I heard Billy crying so hard he went into convulsions. I went to his room and begged him to tell me what was wrong." Her voice was beginning to buckle, despite her icy words. "Finally, he told me how Hunter made him not only perform oral sex but . . . but other disgusting things."

"What did you do then?"

"I went to see the Queens attorney general," she said, after lighting a new cigarette with the stub of the old one.

"What did he or she say?"

"It was a he. And he said he'd look into it."

"Did he?"

She cocked her head, eyes fever-bright.

"He talked to Billy and said he would talk to Hunter," she said. "Weeks passed and I heard nothing, so I barged into his office demanding answers. He said, yes, he had talked to Hunter and that Hunter said the boy was exaggerating. Said Billy was mentally disturbed. Had father issues."

Listening to her account, my heart started pounding instead of beating. Her misery reminded me how my mother reacted after my father's murder. She cried for days. Nonstop. What the Irish call keening. Eventually, she suffered a nervous breakdown. Died of a heart attack my first year in the league. For a long time after, conversations about her were unsafe territory for me if I wanted to keep my composure, which, quite honestly, I usually failed to do.

"I then got an appointment with the State attorney general's office," she said, her whole body beginning to convulse with rage. "And he, too, said he would investigate."

"What happened?"

"A few weeks later, I got a call from someone in his office who said the investigation was concluded and that Hunter was highly regarded by the administrators at the basketball camp and that without further collaboration there was nothing they could do about it."

My right hand clenched into a fist so tight the muscles in my forearm spasmed.

"Those . . . those bastards," she said, her words a wet stutter. "They just didn't care."

I could feel my nostrils widening, my jaw tightening. From outside the house, I could hear police cars howling.

"Little by little, my Billy became more and more withdrawn," she said. "He lost interest in school. In friends. In basketball. He wouldn't even watch games on television."

Her chest suddenly heaved, and her eyes filled with tears. Streams of mucus ran down from her nose. She pulled a tissue from her robe pocket. Wiped her eyes. Within seconds, the tissue turned into a wet sponge.

"Then one day Billy went to school. He seemed fine for the first time in months," she said in between sobs. "I was so happy to see him happy. Then when I got home from work that night, I found Billy . . ." she stopped to collect herself. "I found him in the bathtub. He'd slashed his wrists." She swallowed hard. "He was only twelve."

For a long moment, Mrs. Lang sat quietly. Shivering. Then suddenly she let out the most horrifying, spine-chilling scream I had ever heard. It reverberated around the room. I thought she might never stop.

I gripped the arms of the rocker so hard I thought they would break. I rose then leaned down and hugged Mrs. Lang.

Her shoulder blades were brittle. They felt like the wings of a wounded bird. She pressed face against my shoulder and squeezed me tight. Her tears soaked my jacket.

"I will expose Hunter," I said, whispering in her ear. "You have my word. I promise."

Mrs. Lang pulled away and looked at me.

"I miss Billy so much," she said, whimpering. "So, so much."

Her words made me think how much I missed my parents. Sadness, I can tell you, is relatively short, but the grieving never ends.

"Please," she said, tears streaming down her cheeks. "Please. For my Billy."

"Yes," I said, thinking how now that I had Mrs. Lang's testimony, my case was gaining momentum. It was a great feeling to have. "Yes, for Billy."

She squeezed me even tighter, as if never intending to let me go. Stroking her back, I realized, as I often did in my work, that people aren't born sad or unhappy. It's a hard life that makes them that way.

When I walked down the broken stairs a few minutes later, I thought of that skinny, happy kid in the photographs hugging his basketball. I felt rage rushing from the pit of my stomach to my watery eyes, which were now bolts of anger.

To say I had hatred in my heart would have been a gross understatement. What I had was sheer abhorrence.

As I got to my car, I could still hear Mrs. Lang weeping.

CHAPTER
TWENTY-NINE

Monique and I were at my house, listening to Louis Armstrong. Candles were lit. They smelled of lavender. On the table before us was a bottle of Joseph Phelps cabernet and a box of pizza.

"How was your trip?" Monique said.

"Depressing."

'What'd you learn about Hunter," Monique said.

"A lot."

"From your voice I can tell it wasn't good."

"It was not," I said, thinking how I used to believe that the world was a place where good and bad could easily be deciphered and decoded. Not anymore. The world has changed. It's become polluted by dissension, polarization, and abomination. Understanding how things work anymore is getting harder and harder. Where have you gone, Joe DiMaggio? Our nation turns its lonely eyes to you.

I picked up a slice of pizza, folded it, pulled it toward my mouth but didn't take a bite. I laid it back down on the plate.

"Not hungry?" Monique said.

"No," I said, feeling tired, dispirited, and unsettled.

I got up from my seat and looked out the picture window. The sky was dark, the clouds ominous, as if a storm was brewing.

"Have you heard back from the producer?" I said, returning to my seat.

"About?"

"The movie role."

"I have."

"And?"

"Looks like I got the part. My agent is negotiating."

"Fabulous," I said. "Congratulations."

Monique smiled.

I leaned over and kissed the top of her head. Her hair smelled clean and crisp, like freshly washed linen.

I said, "We should celebrate. Go someplace nice."

Monique's eyes glowed like sapphire pearls.

"How about Napa Valley?" I said. "We can stay at Auberge du Soleil and hit some wineries."

"Sounds perfect."

"We'll go after I wrap up the Malone case. I'll need a break."

"Of course. First things first."

Monique lifted her glass. We clinked. Sipped.

After a minute, I put my wine glass down, got up again, and looked out the window, my eyes studying every person in the park.

"Why do you keep staring out the window?" Monique said.

I took a minute to think. I didn't want to scare her, but I felt she should know what I knew. For her own sake.

"I saw a guy yesterday staring up at our building. He was tall, white, built, and wore a black hoodie."

"So?"

"It sorta fits the description of Teddy Malone's shooter."

"You think it . . . it could be him?"

"Could be. Or maybe it was just someone admiring the building's beauty. Hard to say."

"Should we inform the police?"

"No. We just need to be vigilant."

Monique's eyes met mine and hers were vivid with hesitation and fear, a deep, consuming fear.

"Are our lives in danger?" she said.

"Whaddya mean?"

A small quiver rippled the skin at the base of her throat. "You know what I mean."

"No," I said, trying to be comforting. "Our lives aren't in danger."

"Sometimes I wish you had a different job. I get so tired of being scared and worrying about you."

"I know," I said, thinking how there were days that even I got tired of dealing with psychos, liars, and murderers.

We sat quietly. Monique picked at her pizza. I sipped my wine.

"It's confirmed," I said, my nerves settled. "Hunter's a pedophile."

"Got proof?"

"Confirmation."

"From?"

"Two people."

I told her about Jimmy Leonard and Mrs. Lang. She listened hard as she always did, as if everything depended on what I might say next.

"The kid really cut his own wrists?" Monique said, closing her eyes briefly.

"He did," I said, my voice breaking. "He was only twelve years old."

"Jesus," she said, "this is a nightmare."

"Yes, it is."

Monique reached over, put a hand on mine, and squeezed it. Her fingers were smooth and silky.

"I need to find more kids," I said.

"That Hunter molested?

"Yeah."

"Isn't two enough?"

"It's really only one," I said. "Mrs. Lang's testimony could be termed as hearsay. And I'm not sure Jimmy Leonard could handle going public."

"Do you now think Corsito knows?"

"I'd be surprised if he didn't," I said. "If I know nothing else about Corsito it's that he's a control freak. He knows everything that goes on in his program."

"You going to confront him?"

"I am.

"When?"

"Tomorrow."

"How do you think he'll react?"

"Who knows? He's unpredictable."

"You believe Hunter molested Teddy Malone?"

"It's more than possible."

"And you still think Hunter may have had Teddy killed?"

"Maybe. But I still can't discount Smith, Mitchell, Roth, Grimes, Blake, or even Corsito." I purposely left out Catalano's nephew, Anthony.

"If you had to guess, who do you think it is?"

"I'm still thinking Smith."

"Did you ever find out where Smith was the night of the shooting?"

"Not yet. But I will."

"I'm confused. Why would Smith shoot Teddy?"

"If he did shoot him, I would assume it's because he has some kind of connection to Hunter. It was Hunter who got him the job at St. Stephen's."

"Have you discounted the gambling angle?"

"Pretty much."

"What about the fentanyl?"

"What about it?"

"You think that had anything to do with his murder?"

"My guess is no. I imagine he was taking it to deal with whatever pressure he was under. Probably from being molested. Trying to forget, to go numb."

Monique shook her head. "What a case."

"Maybe the worst one I've ever been on. Or the best one, or the most important one. Depending on what happens."

We fell silent for a while. The candle was close to burning out, and a bubbly trail of wax was dripping down the sides.

Monique was letting me marinate my thoughts. I took a sip of wine and looked at her. Physically, she is breathtaking and flawlessly put together, her whole package a cluster of constellations. But what has always impressed me about her is less her beauty and more her person. I love her directness and attentiveness. I never get tired of seeing her, talking to her, or listening to her. I like how she drinks, how she laughs. How she throws caution to the wind. I've often thought what my life would be without her. Answer: Meaningless.

The Armstrong CD ended. I got up, ejected the disc and replaced it with another one.

"Who's this singing?" Monique said.

"Diane Schuur."

"Great voice."

"Few singers better."

The song "By Design" played.

"Who's singing with her?" Monique said.

"José Feliciano."

"They sound beautiful together," she said.

Wanting to put my thoughts of the case aside for a minute and give Monique a moment she deserved, I said, "Care to dance?" Monique loves to dance. Even more than singing.

"I'd be delighted."

We stood. Embraced. Began slowly dancing to the song's lyrics: "Falling in love with you was by design/Our love was meant to be, destiny."

"You know how much I love you?" Monique said, whispering in my ear.

"No, tell me."

"A million, gazillion."

"That's a big number."

"You're a big guy."

She nibbled my ear.

"Are you biting me?" I said.

"Just chewing."

"Still hungry?"

"Only for you."

"You are one sweet talkin' mama."

"I learned from the best."

"Who?"

"You."

We kissed.

"Think we'll ever get married?" Monique said.

"To each other?"

"No, knucklehead. To strangers." She smirked. "Of course, us."

"I don't know. What do you think?"

"I believe we're doing damn good the way we are."

"Can I tell you what I believe?"

"Please do."

"I believe you make me whole. Make me a better person in ways I never thought possible."

"You mean I enhance your life?"

"I mean . . . you are my life."

We held each other tight as if it were the last dance we'd ever share.

"My father once told me dancing brings two hearts together in one rhythm," I said.

"Spoken like a true jazz musician. You think we have good rhythm?"

"I think we make beautiful music together."

Monique kissed me full on the mouth.

"If that's the case," she said, "strike up the band."

I then scooped Monique up and carried her into the bedroom. Making love to her took my mind off the case. But when I woke up the next morning it was still there.

CHAPTER THIRTY

We got out of bed late. I showered and dressed quickly. So did Monique. I only had enough time for a cup of coffee before leaving to confront Smith. I strapped on my shoulder holster and grabbed a sport coat. I had to assume now that Hunter suspected I was on to him, and that if Smith was involved, there was no telling what he might do.

Outside, it was another hot day. No clouds. No wind. High humidity. The sun torched the street.

Monique was wearing a white, sleeveless dress. Very tasteful. Cute. Looking at her, my heart did a somersault.

She said she needed to run some errands in Manhattan before going to the theatre. I said I'd drop her off. When we got to the Mustang, I opened the door for her and spun around to kiss her when I heard a bang. Monique yelled. Her knees buckled. She crumbled to the ground.

"What's the matter, babe, what's wrong?" I said, trying to process what just happened.

"I . . . I . . . ," she gasped for air.

I reached under her armpits and attempted to stand her upright.

It was then that I saw blood on the front of her dress, the stain slowly expanding. She'd been shot. Anger tore through me like wildfire.

"Aw, fuck," I said, laying her back against the car seat.

Monique was moaning, her eyes closing. Except for her whimper, everything around us was quiet, as if the whole world had suddenly ceased breathing.

"Stay with me, babe," I said, staying calm but quivering with rage. "Stay with me, stay with me."

I pulled out my cell phone and dialed 911 with one hand while pressing the other on her chest. Blood came out between my fingers.

An operator answered.

"A woman's been shot," I yelled. "Washington and Third Street. Need help immediately."

A crowd gathered. Some neighborhood people recognized Monique; they offered help. What could they do?

"Elg . . . ," Monique said in a weak voice. "I'm . . . I'm cold."

Heart racing, I took off my sport coat and covered her.

"Hang in there, sweetie," I said, kissing her sweaty forehead. "I'm here, baby, I'm here. You'll be fine."

In the distance, I heard an ambulance raging.

"C'mon, c'mon!" I shouted in its direction.

When it arrived, three emergency medical technicians quickly jumped out the back door and asked me to "move aside." Just then the police arrived, local beat guys I knew. I shouted that I hadn't seen the shooter, and I'd talk to them at the hospital.

The EMTs put an oxygen mask over Monique's face and tried to stem the bleeding by applying compresses. After a time, they put her on a gurney and carefully lifted her into the ambulance.

"I'm going with her," I said.

"Of course, sir," an EMT said. The cops nodded.

I hopped into the ambulance, sat alongside Monique, holding her free hand while the EMT hooked her up to an IV and a blood pressure cuff. She started to lose consciousness. I looked at her chest going up and down, counting each breath. I never in my life had felt such unequivocal helplessness.

The ambulance took off, siren blaring. It weaved through Hoboken headed to St. Mary's Hospital. When we finally got there, the technicians lifted her out of the ambulance and wheeled her into the emergency room.

Doctors and nurses rushed to her side. They guided her into a treatment room. I asked if I could go with them. They said no.

An administrator came over to me and said, "Best you wait in the waiting room. I'll keep you posted."

"Please do," I said, trying to keep panic from my voice. "The minute you know something."

He nodded.

The waiting room was crowded. I sat alone in a corner, feeling as if my heart was hemorrhaging. Rage was festering inside me like a sick growth. I suddenly hated everyone and anyone who practices violence willingly and joyfully, who push people off subway platforms or ambush cops or execute hostages or rape children. I was sick and tired of their cruelty, their hatred, their disregard for life. What the fuck is wrong with people?!

The minutes dripped by. I gave a uniformed officer a brief statement and said I hadn't seen the shooter, just heard the shot. I wasn't even sure where it came from; I'd never taken my eyes off Monique. He started to ask me more questions, but I told him to back off. My world had already been turned inside out. He told me not to leave until the detectives arrived.

I nodded. My head throbbed. The only other time I felt such excruciating pain was the day my father was murdered.

But even then, I didn't quite feel the hostility that was now surging though my veins.

I vowed right then and there that someone would pay for this. And pay dearly. Vengeance was mine.

A television, mounted high on a wall, was tuned to the noon news. The lead story was about Monique.

The anchor, Bob Roberts, said, "This morning popular Broadway star, Monique Montgomery, was shot down while leaving the Hoboken apartment of her longtime boyfriend, ex-NBA star and current private investigator Elgin O'Brien. Police say they have no motive for the shooting at this time and are asking anyone with any information to call their hotline 212-555-7070."

The anchor took a breath. Gave a deadly serious look into the camera, then continued.

"Our reporter, Josh Clayton, is outside St. Mary's Hospital in Hoboken with the latest information. Josh, what can you tell us?"

Clayton—dark hair and large eyes—appeared on the screen, holding a microphone to his mouth.

"At this point, there isn't much to tell," Clayton said. "Miss Montgomery was leaving the apartment she shared with Mr. O'Brien and was shot in the chest by an unknown assailant. Mr. O'Brien is here at the hospital, but so far he's been unavailable for comment. What I can tell you is Miss Montgomery, currently starring in *The Glass Menagerie*, was being considered for a lead role in an upcoming Hollywood movie. The title of that movie has yet to be announced."

Clayton then turned to a bystander and said, "I'm standing here with Alice Childs who was not far away when the shooting occurred." Alice was in her sixties, had gray hair and a long face. I recognized her from the neighborhood, walking her dog.

"Tell me, Alice," Clayton asked, "what exactly did you witness?" Clayton put a microphone before her mouth. "It's more what I heard," she said. "I was coming out of my apartment when I heard what I thought was a truck backfiring somewhere down the block. Then I heard a scream and saw Miss Montgomery fall to the ground. It was horrifying. Then I saw Elgin . . . Mr. O'Brien holding her, comforting her." Alice cringed. "Sad, so, sad. There was so much blood."

The camera was back on Clayton. "That's the situation here in Hoboken, New Jersey," he said, shaking his head. "This is Josh Clayton reporting for Channel Seven Eyewitness News."

The anchor, Roberts, reappeared on screen. Turning to his co-anchor, a young Black woman, he said, "This is so tragic. Miss Montgomery is one of the truly great stars on Broadway." He pursed his lips. Then turning back to the camera, he said. "We'll update you as we get more information on Miss Montgomery's condition."

I stood and clicked the television off.

Some obese guy yelled, "Hey, buddy, I was watching that."

I flashed him a threatening look. He got the message; he shut up. I sat down and put my face in my hands.

Time passed slowly. It seemed like days. I was still sitting in the waiting room when a young doctor in a white coat, stethoscope hanging from his neck, approached me.

"Mr. O'Brien?" he asked.

"Yes?" I said, standing.

"I'm Dr. Kaplan, head of the trauma unit."

"How is she?"

"She's stable. Unconscious. We removed the bullet, but she's lost a lot of blood. We're closely monitoring her. She's intubated so her lungs won't fill with blood."

"Will she survive?"

"Too early to tell."

An icy chill clawed at my inside. It took me a minute to catch my breath.

"Thankfully, the bullet missed her heart," Kaplan said. "But we won't know for a while how much damage the shock wave trauma caused to other organs. But it didn't pass through her body, so something must have slowed it down, thank God. Condition is critical. She's still being assessed."

"How soon might you know?"

"Can't really say. If we can control the bleeding and she doesn't get a blood clot, or an infection, and if there are no surprises . . . by all indications she could—should—recover."

That was a lot of "ifs." Big, frightening ifs.

I said, "Can I see her?"

"Not right now," Kaplan said. "She's still in intensive care."

"How long before I can?"

"Not for a while."

"What's a while?"

"Not sure, since COVID there are more protocols, but I will personally keep you informed as soon as I know anything more."

I nodded.

Kaplan put his hand on my shoulder.

"I strongly suggest you go get something to eat or go home or try to go about your business. It's my experience that just sitting around waiting only brings on more anxiety." He paused. "I promise that if anything changes, I will call you immediately. Just need your cell phone number."

I gave him my phone number.

"She's in good hands," Kaplan said. "Getting the best possible care."

"I'm sure she is."

A slight grin crossed Kaplan's face.

"I saw Ms. Montgomery perform a few times on Broadway," he said. "She a fine actress."

"And an even finer person," I said.

Kaplan shook my hand, turned, and headed down the corridor.

I walked to the men's room, a lightning bolt of pain detonating through my body. I was as exhausted as a marathoner at the conclusion of a race, soaked in sweat and bent over. I tried hard to get my breathing back to normal. It wasn't easy.

The hospital bathroom was clean. I stood before the sink. And for the first time I noticed there was still blood on my hands. I washed it off, then splashed water on my face and stared in the mirror.

I saw a stranger. Angry and revengeful.

I looked old.

CHAPTER THIRTY-ONE

When I came out, two detectives from the Hoboken Police Department were waiting.

I knew one of them. His name was Paul Stone, Hoboken's chief of detectives. Paul and I had worked cases together. We were friends. Occasional drinking buddies. In my line of work, it pays to cooperate with cops. You help them out, they help you out. Both parties benefit. I didn't know the other detective.

Paul was in his mid-fifties. He stood six three and had dirty blond hair. His neck was thick, his forearms buffed. He wore black boots, black pants, and a white short-sleeved shirt opened at the collar.

"Hey, Elg," Paul said. "Sorry to hear about Monique."

"Thanks."

'How is she doing?"

"Stable . . . for now, but critical. Still in intensive care. Touch and go."

Paul lifted his chin toward the other detective.

"This is my partner," he said. "Lieutenant Ray Ortiz."

I looked at Ortiz. Short, maybe five eight, he had thick black hair and a thin black mustache.

"Nice to meet you," Ortiz said. He had a slight Spanish accent. "Sorry for the circumstances."

Paul took the seat next to me and said, "Tell me what happened."

"Not much to tell," I said. "We were getting into my car when a shot rang out."

"You see the shooter?"

"No."

"You see anything?"

"No."

Ortiz said, "You have any idea who might have shot her?"

"No."

"Do you know if she was having any conflict at work?"

"None."

"How about any issues with neighbors or family?"

"Nothing."

At that moment a young cop approached. He carried a small Ziploc bag.

"Got something for you, Sarge," he said.

He handed Paul the bag. Inside was a bullet.

"It was taken from Ms. Montgomery," he said. "Looks like it's from a centerfire rifle."

"A hunting gun," Paul said.

"Can I see the bag, please," I said.

Paul handed it to me.

I examined the bullet. It was long and bronze. Nose flattened.

"These fucking things kill game," I said, handing the bag back to the young cop.

"No shit," Paul said. "With this type of gun, the shooter could've been a mile away. She's lucky though. I saw your car. The bullet clipped the door frame. Otherwise . . . "

I immediately thought of Steve Smith. A sniper during the Iraq War. I also thought of Catalano's nephew, Anthony, a former Army Ranger. It had to be one of those cowardly motherfuckers.

"Sonofabitch," I said, pounding the armrest and feeling a wave of hate rising from the numbness in my gut.

Paul stared at me, baffled.

"What?" Paul said. "What?"

"Nothing," I said.

"Had to be something," he said. "You just don't shout 'sonofabitch' for no reason."

"I'm just angry," I said. "Ignore me."

The cop standing next to Paul said, "Need anything else, Sarge?"

"No, that's it," Paul said. He handed the cop the Ziploc bag and wrote out a receipt to preserve the chain of custody. "Get this to ballistics ASAP, and make sure it doesn't get lost."

"Got it," the cop said.

He then turned back to me.

"Just so you know," the cop said, "there's a platoon of reporters outside."

"Not surprised," Paul said.

The cop left.

"Let me ask you something, Elg," Paul said. "You been working on anything?"

"Whaddya mean?"

"A big case."

"I am."

"Can you tell me about it?"

"I'm investigating the murder a few months ago of a kid from St. Stephen's University."

"Teddy Malone?"

"Yeah."

"Find anything?"

"Not yet?"

"Any leads?"

"Some."

"Care to share?"

I shook my head. I decided not to bring up Hunter, Smith, Blake, Mitchell, Roth, Corsito, Catalano, or his nephew Anthony. I wanted to deal with things on my own . . . and in my own way.

"You think Monique getting shot has something to do with your investigation?" Paul said.

"Good chance."

"You think the bullet was meant for you?"

"Yep. No way this was random." I demonstrated how I'd spun around just before the shot.

"Got any names you want me to follow up on?" Paul said.

"Not at the moment."

He paused and looked me straight in the eyes.

"If you do," he said, "let me know. Sooner is better than later."

"Appreciate it."

Just then a reporter and a camera man raced down the hallway. The reporter was holding a microphone.

"Mr. O'Brien, Mr. O'Brien," he shouted. "Got a minute."

"How the fuck did you guys get in here?" Ortiz said.

The reporter ignored him.

"Elgin, Elgin," the reporter persisted, "What happened? What happened?"

"Get these fuckheads outta here," Paul instructed Ortiz. "NOW!"

Ortiz gently pushed them toward a door marked exit.

"Fucking reporters," Paul said. "Parasites. Always sniffling around for dirt. I hate the bastards."

"Just doing their job," I said. "I'm used to them from my NBA days. The good ones are relentless. The lazy ones you gotta worry about."

Paul stood.

"As soon as you get a chance stop by the station," he said. "We're gonna need a formal statement."

"Will do."

"And keep your head down," Paul added, "your curtains closed, and your gun nearby."

"I will," I said.

"As you well know, if somebody wants to kill you . . ."

He didn't finish the sentence because he knew that I knew that if someone did wish to kill me, really kill me, there wasn't a damn thing the police, the FBI, the army, even God himself could do to stop them.

"I wish Monique the best of luck," Ortiz said.

"Thank you," I said.

Paul put a hand on my shoulder and gently squeezed it.

"You need anything," he said, "anything at all. You know where to find me."

"I do."

"Hang in there."

"What other choice do I have?"

CHAPTER THIRTY-TWO

An hour later, I went to the nurses' station and asked about Monique.

"Nothing to report," she said.

I then asked to speak with Dr. Kaplan.

"Dr. Kaplan's in surgery," she said. "I can have him call you as soon as he's available."

"That'd be great," I said. "Can you at least tell me something about Miss Montgomery's condition."

She looked through some papers.

"No change. She's still in intensive care," she said. "Being monitored closely."

"Okay," I said. "Thanks.

There was nothing I could do to help Monique by waiting at the hospital. But I had to do something, anything . . . otherwise I'd drive myself crazy.

I went back to the waiting room and paced, feeling a hurt so deep it was as if my insides had been cored out. I could not—and would not—cry. All I knew for certain is that I would do whatever it took, legal or otherwise, to bring down David Hunter and the man who killed Teddy Malone and the person who shot Monique.

I headed toward the main exit but stopped when I saw the horde of reporters and television crews hovering outside.

"Excuse me," I said to an elderly security guard. "Can you help me?"

"How?"

"See all those reporters out there," I said chin-tilting at them.

"Yes."

"They're looking to speak with me, and I'm in no mood to speak with them," I said. "Is there another way out?"

"There is."

"Can you direct me?"

"I'll do more than that," he said. "I'll show you."

"Great."

"Follow me," he said.

We walked down a corridor past private offices and patients waiting to be seen.

"I saw you play in college," the guard said.

"You a Duke fan?"

"With all due respect, no."

"Why not?"

"Didn't like Coach K."

"How come?"

"Thought he was arrogant."

"But he was a winner."

"Personally, I prefer the coach of Gonzaga."

"Mark Few."

"He runs a clean program."

"So did Coach K."

"Still don't like him."

The guard opened a door that read "Employees Only." We walked down several flights of stairs to a basement filled with furnaces and generators. The furnaces rumbled.

"This is the fire exit," the guard said, pushing open a steel door. "It leads to the employee parking lot."

"Thanks for your help," I said, shaking the guard's hand.

"Always happy to help a Duke guy," he said.

"I thought you hated Duke," I said.

"I do," he said. "Just want to cheer you up. This isn't about basketball. It's about being a human being."

I nodded and smiled.

I staggered out into the daylight and walked through the parking lot. I saw a hole in a steel fence, and I climbed through it, coming out onto a street filled with pizza parlors, dry cleaners, and Irish pubs.

As I neared my apartment, I saw another crowd of reporters and television vans. Fuck.

I pulled out my phone and texted an Uber. Return text said the driver was only a few minutes away.

I then looked at my phone messages. There were many. All, I assumed, inquiring about Monique.

The one that got my attention was from O'Meara. I called him.

"Christ, Elg," he said. "What happened?"

I told him.

"And you think this could be connected to the Teddy Malone?"

"No question."

"I got something for you."

"What?"

"I've been poking around and found out there was a kid, a few years ago, by the name of Kenny Atkins who registered a complaint against Hunter for, get this, sexual harassment."

"You're kidding?"

"I'm not."

"Where'd the kid go to school?"

"Hofstra." Hofstra was a private university in Hempstead, Long Island.

"I don't think Hunter ever coached at Hofstra," I said.

"He didn't," O'Meara said. "The incident supposedly happened somewhere else."

"Where?"

"Don't have that."

"You got a home address for Atkins?"

"I do."

He gave it to me. Atkins lived in Weehawken, the next town over from Hoboken.

"Tell me," O'Meara said. "How's Monique?"

"In bad shape."

"From what I've seen on the news she got hit with a powerful weapon."

"She did."

"I'll pray for her."

"You're a prince, O'Meara."

"More like a coach. Just keep running the break, and I'll get you the ball. Just stay in control. Don't take any wild shots."

He knew me too well.

CHAPTER THIRTY-THREE

The Uber arrived. The driver was Pakistani. The car smelled of cigarettes and gasoline.

"Gonna take us a while to get to Queens," he said. "Traffic's heavy."

"Nothing new. Let's go." I decided it was more important to confront Smith before questioning Atkins.

The Uber took off. I sat back, closed my eyes, and rested my head against the seat. I thought of Monique lying in her hospital bed. Blood surged in my veins. My heart felt as if it had been punctured.

I dialed Pat Malone.

He answered after a few rings.

"Pat," I said, "it's Elg."

"Hey, Elg," he said. "I heard about Monique. How . . . how is she?"

"She's stable," I said.

"Let's hope for the best . . . I know the feeling."

I waited a few seconds before speaking again.

"Let me ask you something," I said. "Are you aware Dave Hunter is a pedophile?"

"I . . . I . . ."

"For fuck's sake," I said. "Just spit it out."

"I . . . I . . . heard a few rumors when Teddy was being recruited. You know how it goes."

"Ever talk to Teddy about them?"

"No." His "no" didn't convince me. I had my phone pressed so hard against my ear it throbbed.

"Why not?" I said.

"I didn't think they were true."

"Didn't think they were true, huh?"

"No, I didn't."

"You remember telling me how Teddy had become withdrawn and depressed?"

"Yeah, I . . . I remember."

"My gut tells me Hunter molested him."

"I don't believe it."

"Don't believe it or don't want to believe it?"

"Teddy would have told me."

"I think he did," I said, based on nothing more than gut instinct.

Malone didn't respond but I could hear him breathing heavily. I figured he was, like many fathers in these situations, in total denial.

I said, "First time we met I asked you if Teddy had any issues. You emphatically said no. But now I know he had issues. Big issues. Enough to make him take fentanyl. So stop bullshitting me and start telling the truth. Did Hunter molest Teddy?"

I could almost feel his embarrassment through the line. He didn't say anything.

"Let me tell you something that might motivate you to be honest," I said. "It may have been Hunter who had Teddy shot. And now Monique took a bullet meant for me."

Malone let out an agonizing groan so loud I had to hold the phone away from my ear.

"Time to fess up, Pat," I said. "Tell me what you know."

"I don't . . . don't know what you're talking about."

"YES! YOU DO! YOU KNOW DAMN WELL WHAT I'M TALKING ABOUT! STOP LYING AND GIVE IT TO ME!"

Malone was quiet. The driver eyeballed me through the rearview mirror.

"QUIT STALLING MALONE! THINK OF YOUR SON! AND THE NEXT KID!"

A minute passed.

Finally, Malone said, "I . . . I was afraid."

"Afraid of what?"

"That if what Hunter did to Teddy ever hit the press Teddy would become a laughingstock, teased in every arena he'd ever play in again for the rest of his life. The kid was frantic about it."

"What exactly did Hunter do?"

"I . . . I . . ."

"Just fucking tell me," I said.

"He . . ." Malone's voice cracked, and the words tumbled out. "One night after practice, it was just Hunter and Teddy in the gym, shooting around, playing H-O-R-S-E. Afterward, Hunter suggested they go into the weight room and do some light lifting. Nobody was there. It was late. They started teasing each other and Hunter asked Teddy if he wanted to play. Then one thing led to another and the next thing you know they were rolling on a mat wrestling."

Pat fell silent.

"And then what?" I said.

Malone yelled, "THEN FUCKING HUNTER PINNED TEDDY TO THE MAT, KEPT ASKING HIM IF HE WANTED

TO PLAY, THEN TURNED HIM OVER AND TRIED—
TRIED—TO PENETRATE HIM! DOES THAT ANSWER
YOUR FUCKING QUESTION?"

The line got quiet. I counted the seconds by the thumps
in my heart.

"What happened next?" I said.

"Whaddya mean what happened next?"

"What happened after Teddy told you?"

"Against my advice, he went and told Corsito."

"What Corsito do?"

"He said he was shocked. Said he'd talk to Hunter, that
Teddy was overreacting. That he should think about the team."

"That's it? That's all he said?"

"Yes."

"Did he follow up with Teddy . . . or you?"

"He called Teddy into his office, said he spoke to Hunter
and Hunter said he was only kidding around."

"How'd Teddy react?"

"Not well. Not well at all. He told Corsito he was going
to call Mike Thomas of the *New York Post*."

"And do what?"

"Tell Thomas what had happened."

"What did you say?"

"About what?"

"Teddy calling Thomas."

"I . . . I told him it was a bad idea."

"A bad idea? Are you for real? What the fuck were you
thinking? Jesus Christ!"

No response.

"So Teddy never made the call?" I said.

"No."

"Un-fucking-believable."

A moment of silence.

"You should have told me this from the get-go," I said.

"I was embarrassed."

"Probably not as embarrassed as you are now."

I clicked off the phone. I had nothing more to say. How a father could worry more about his son's image than him being sexually assaulted was beyond me.

It took almost two hours to get to St. Stephen's. The air was steamy. Students were walking here and there. Most were wearing light clothing. A few guys had angry scowls. None of them looked like future terrorists, but you can never be sure.

I went right to the weight room. It was empty except for Steve Smith. He was wearing boxing gloves and doing combinations on the heavy bag, pounding it with a left jab, a right cross, ducking, bobbing and weaving. His tank top was drenched with sweat.

"Excuse me," I said.

He turned and dropped his hands. His eyes torpedoed me.

"Fuck do you want?" he said.

"Where were you this morning?"

"That's none of your fucking business."

"I'm gonna make it my fucking business."

"Don't push me, man," he said. "Or I'll put your fucking head through the fucking wall."

"You may know how to use a gun," I said. "But I know how to fight."

"So do I," Smith said. "You forget. I was a Seal."

Our eyeballs locked. Neither of us moved.

"You have two choices," I said. "You can answer my question, or I'll have the police here so fast your head will spin."

"On what pretense?"

"I'll make one."

"You're fucking diabolical."

"No," I said. "I'm fucking maniacal."

"Why do you give a shit where I was?"

"Because my girlfriend was just shot with a high-powered rifle . . . one a sniper might use."

"And you think I had something to do with it?"

"I don't know," I said. "That's why I'm here."

"Well, fuckhead," he said. "I had nothing to do with it."

"Then tell me where you were this morning."

He hesitated.

"Tell me," I said.

He stared at me. My blood was sizzling. I felt like a madman.

"Tell me," I said again.

He remained silent.

"FOR FUCK'S SAKE!" I shouted. "TELL ME!"

His face suddenly became gray as putty. Thick streams of sweat ran down his cheeks.

I jerked my gun from my holster and aimed it at him.

"I'll give you another minute," I said. "You don't answer my question, I'm going to put a bullet first in your shoulder and then in your kneecap. Understand me, fuckhead? Do you? Do you?"

"Okay, okay, okay," he said, putting his hands up, shoulder high. "Calm down."

"I will when you fess up."

He ran a knuckle across his dry lips.

"I . . . I was with someone," he said.

"Who?"

"A friend."

"Where?"

"In . . . in my apartment."

"Okay, what's her name? I wanna call her right now."

An awkward silence.

"What's her name?" I said again.

Still no response.

"For the third time, what's her fucking name?"

He glared at me before answering.

"It's . . . it's not a . . . a . . . she," he said, his voice shaky. "It's a . . . he."

"Fine," I said. "What's his name?"

"Why do you need to know this?"

"To check your alibi."

"Must you?"

"Abso-fucking-lutely."

"My . . . my friend has a wife."

"I don't care if he has five wives," I said. "What's his name?"

"Frank," he said, softly. "Frank Johnson."

"Where can I find Frank?"

"He lives in Greenwich Village."

"Can anyone else besides Frank verify your story?"

"Yes."

"Who?"

"My . . . my roommate. He was there, too . . . with a friend."

"Sounds like quite the fun morning."

Smith ignored my comment.

"I'll need their names," I said.

"What for?"

"To contact them."

"Do you really have to do this?"

"I do. It's either me or the police."

I holstered my gun. Took out my cell phone and Smith gave me their phone numbers.

"Satisfied?" he said.

"Not completely."

"What else do you want?"

"Text your friends and tell them to expect my call and to cooperate."

He looked like he was about to cry. He picked up his phone. I watched as he texted. When he finished, I grabbed the phone and looked at it before he sent it. I wanted to make sure he wasn't telling anyone to clam up. He hadn't.

"I assume we're done here?" he said.

"No."

"What now?"

"Take the glove off your right hand."

"What for?"

"Just take it off."

"For Christ sake," he said. "Why?"

"Just take the goddamn thing off!"

Using his teeth, he pulled off the strings on his glove. The glove came off.

I grabbed his hand and turned it over. The veins on the back of his hand were thick and bluish, but there was no basketball tattoo.

"Sorry to be such a bother," I said, letting go of his hand. "I'm just doing my job."

"Are you?"

I turned and walked out of the weight room.

CHAPTER
THIRTY-FOUR

I went outside, sat on a bench, and phoned the three names Smith gave me before they'd have a chance to talk with each other. I reached two. Both verified Smith's account. I left a message for the third. Frank Johnson. Hopefully, Mrs. Johnson didn't check her husband's voicemail.

Even if I didn't hear back from Johnson, I was pretty sure now it wasn't Smith who shot Monique. I still didn't like Smith, but at least this time he'd stopped bullshitting me.

I put Smith out of my mind and thought of Monique lying in a hospital bed, fighting for her life. No physical beating could've hurt me more than that vision.

Though I had had more than a few women back in the day, Monique was the first one I could really talk with, express my feelings to. The possibly of losing her was almost too much to bear.

I took a minute to think. With Smith now out of the picture, I turned my attention to Catalano's nephew, Anthony. Who would have hired him to shoot Monique? I assumed Catalano. But you know what they say about assumptions.

I took out my cell phone and googled Catalano Capital. Got the phone number and called it.

The receptionist who answered sounded like a teenager. Probably some twenty-something blond beauty who venture capital guys always seem to hire. She asked me my name. I said Rudy LaRusso, a former teammate of Elgin Baylor's.

"Can I ask what this is in reference to, Mr. LaRusso?"

I said, "I'm thinking of moving all my assets from JPMorgan Chase to your company."

"Certainly, sir," she said. "I can set up a meeting with you and one of our associates."

"I've been referred directly to Mr. Catalano by coach Chris Corsito. Chris said to use his name, and that Mr. Catalano would see me immediately."

"Of course," she said, her voice excited. "Of course, being a friend of the coach, I'm sure Mr. Catalano would want to deal with your personally."

"Great. Can I schedule an appointment for today?"

"I'm sorry but Mr. Catalano was unexpectedly called out of the country, exploring opportunities in the European market. I'm not sure when he'll be returning but I don't think it will be anytime soon." She paused. "Are you sure you don't wish me to set up a meeting with someone else in the meantime?"

"No," I said. "I'll wait till Mr. Catalano returns. Thank you for your time. Goodbye."

I punched my thigh. Was it a coincidence Catalano was out of the country or was it planned? I'd bet my life, it was planned . . . minutes after Monique got shot.

I called Carlo. Like everyone else, the first thing he asked about was Monique. Then he said, "Whaddya need, paisan?"

"Where can I find Catalano's nephew, Anthony?"

"No idea. But I can find out. Once I know, I'll buzz ya."

"Need it ASAP."

"I'll get it faster than you can say Rocky Balboa."

"Thanks. Bye."

I got up off the bench and walked over to Corsito's office. Anne greeted me with a smiling hello.

"He in?" I asked.

"He's on the phone with . . ."

"I don't care if he's talking to God."

I started walking past her desk.

"You can't go in there . . ."

"Watch me."

I pushed open Corsito's door. He was leaning back in his leather chair, feet on his desk, laughing.

When he saw me, he said into his cell phone "Hold a sec" then pressed it against his chest. Opening his mouth wider than a lion facing a whip and a chair, he roared, "Get the fuck out of here!"

I went over, pushed his feet off the desk, pulled the phone from his ear, and threw it against the wall. The phone shattered.

"What the fuck?!" he said.

I leaned over him and got into his face. His breath was so foul that I had to swallow before speaking.

"You knew about Hunter?" I said.

"Knew what?" he said, in a garbled voice.

"That he molests kids."

"That's . . . that's all bullshit."

"Like hell it is."

"You're making a serious allegation," he said.

"Wow! Allegation. That a big word for a guy who only reads comic books."

Corsito tried to push me away, but I pinned him to the chair.

"I've worked with Dave over ten years," he said. "And never once in all those years have I heard a rumor or an innuendo."

"You're a lying sack of shit," I said. "There's not a damn thing in your program you don't know about."

"This is crazy," Corsito said.

I released my grip. Even though I wanted to put my thumbs on his Adam's apple and squeeze it hard enough to make his eyes bulge.

"I just spoke to Pat Malone who told me Teddy complained to you about Hunter."

"I don't recall any such thing. His word versus mine."

"He also told me that Teddy told *you* that he threatened to tell everything to Mike Thomas."

"I don't recall that either," he said, studying his manicured fingernails.

"I've spoken to a guy who said he was molested by Hunter and a mother whose son had also been molested." I was referring to Jimmy Leonard and Mrs. Lang.

"If that's the case how come no charges have ever been brought against him?"

"The mother did file charges," I said, "but Queens DA did shit. Thanks to your bag man, Catalano."

"The charges were dropped because they were unfounded. No evidence."

"Don't hand me that shit."

"You go around talking this kind of nonsense you'll be hit with so many lawsuits you won't know if you're coming or going."

"You interested in talking to the mother of a kid who committed suicide?"

"A kid committed suicide?" he said.

"Yeah. Because of Hunter."

"You got proof?"

"I got the mother's testimony."

"That's hearsay."

"No, asshole, that's fact. The kid's in the ground."

Once again, Corsito studied his fingernails.

"Not only don't you have brains," I said, "You don't have an ounce of empathy."

"Show me a coach who has empathy, and I'll show you a fucking loser."

I shook my head. What a complete asshole.

"Are you telling me you never suspected Hunter?" I said.

"Suspected him of what?"

"Are you not fucking listening to me?"

Corsito jabbed a finger at me.

"Do you really think I would keep on my staff a guy who I even thought was remotely, and I mean remotely, molesting players?"

"I would hope not."

He met my anger and frustration with a smug grin. He knew I had nothing on him, just speculations and suppositions. His eyes blazed victory.

"Well, you don't have to hope. I assure you that if I had even the slightest inkling of something going on he'd be out the door in a heartbeat." He paused, then added, "Let me tell you some things about Dave Hunter. He goes to church every Sunday. He sits on a number of important boards. He's been given God knows how many awards for community service. He's been married for almost twenty years to the same woman, Marie, who worships him. She and my wife are best friends. He has two sons who are well-adjusted and successful young men. And you're telling me this model citizen is a pedophile? What drugs are you on?"

"I don't give a shit how many awards he's been given or how many times he's received communion."

"Elgin, Elgin," he said, his voice acid with contempt. "Listen to me. Listen to me. I know we have never gotten along and in fact don't even like each other, but I'm telling you Dave Hunter is not who you think he is. Furthermore, I'll say it again: If Dave ever did anything, anything unseemly, I would fire him." He put a hand over his heart. "Trust me."

"Trust you?!" I laughed. "You're the last person I'd trust."

Corsito smirked.

"Is Hunter still at the Pocono Basketball Camp?" I said.

He drummed his fingers on this desk. It sounded like pop guns going off.

"No," he said.

"Where is he?"

"On vacation."

"Where?"

He grinned. Cracked his knuckles and said, "I don't know."

"You're lying."

"Am I?"

"Yeah. You are."

"I am not. God help me."

"God is the last person who'd help you," I said. "When will Hunter return?"

"Not sure."

"You're not sure, huh?"

"No, I'm not."

"Maybe someday you'll let your conscience be your guide."

"The only guide I follow is the one that shows the way to The Final Four."

"Just so you know, I'm not going to let this drop."

"Fine. Waste your time."

"You do know Monique was shot today?"

"I heard," he said. "Sorry to hear it. Thoughts and prayers."

His insincerity was appalling. Not even a crumb of sympathy.

"Let me tell you something," I said. "I believe Monique getting shot has to do with Teddy Malone's murder and Dave Hunter's predilections. If that's true, I can assure you I will bring both you and this university down. You understand me?"

"I'm letting it go in one ear and out the other," he said. "But you continue to do what you do, Elg. You think you're the great American avenger, but the truth is you're no more than a cheap, low-rent private dick who can't get over the fact that I make more money and get more adoration than you. You're nothing more than a fucking has-been."

"Don't make me laugh, Chris," I said. "I've said it before, and I'll say it again. You're a scam artist and everybody knows it."

Corsito's eyes flashed warfare.

"Don't ever underestimate what I'm capable of," he said, his voice charged.

"What was that? Say it again."

"Don't ever underestimate what I'm capable of."

"You know, Chris, I guarantee there's a place for you in hell."

"Good. That means I won't have to wait in line."

I left the office, slamming the door behind me.

CHAPTER THIRTY-FIVE

The first thing I did after leaving Corsito's office was call the hospital again, hoping to talk to Dr. Kaplan.

I was put on hold. Minutes passed. A surge of dread. A rush of adrenalin. Hard to calm the nerves when it sends worrying signals to the brain.

"Elgin. Dr. Kaplan here."

"How's Monique doing?"

"Still in intensive care."

"Doing any better?"

"About the same."

"Is that good or bad?"

"It's neither. It's still a matter of waiting and seeing."

I didn't know what else to say. Or ask. I just felt numb. Thinking about what happened was unimaginable and incomprehensible. Monique shot because of me. I felt intense guilt.

"If anything changes," I said. "Please call me."

"Certainly."

I hung up and once again thought of holding Monique in my arms. My vision got watery. I squeezed my eyes shut.

Next, I called O'Meara.

My voice raised, I said, "I need David Hunter's home address."

"What for?"

"I wanna pay him a visit."

"You're not going to do anything stupid, are you?"

"Would I do that?"

"In a heartbeat."

"Look. I have someone in my office. Give me a few minutes, I'll get right back to you."

"Okay."

I took a seat outside the student library. How Hunter had gotten away with his antics for so long was not surprising. I knew of coaches and administrators at colleges who either didn't want to know or didn't want to believe that someone in their program was a pedophile. I recalled how in 2011, Syracuse coach Jim Boeheim went ballistic when a kid came forth accusing his longtime assistant, Bernie Fine, of molesting him.

At first, Boeheim went on the offensive. Aggressively so. In an interview with Syracuse.com, he called it "a false allegation" adding that "the kid behind this is trying to get money. He's tried before. And now he's trying again . . . that's what this is about. Money"

When many other kids came forward with similar stories and it became apparent that Fine was guilty, Boeheim, of course, walked back his earlier statements. He suddenly found the allegations "disturbing" and "deeply troubling" and he was "personally deeply shocked," and he regretted "any statements I made that might have inhibited that from occurring or been incentive to victims of abuse."

Talk about an about-face.

My cell phone rang. It was O'Meara.

"Wha'cha got?" I said.

"Want my opinion?"

"Do I have a choice?"

"Don't do it."

"Do what?"

"Whatever it is you're thinking of doing. Especially the way you're feeling."

"How am I feeling?"

"Like somebody who is out of control."

How could I calm down with so much anger boiling inside me?

"Look, Elg, I'm as upset as you are over what's happened. I just don't want you doing something you'll regret."

"For God sake, just give me Hunter's address, will ya?"

"First, tell me why you want it?"

"Corsito said Hunter was on vacation. I want to find out if that's true or is Hunter hiding in his house."

"And if he is?"

"I'll confront him."

"With your fists in your pockets?"

"With my fists in my pockets."

"That better be the case," he said. "Forty-Five Beacon Street in Jamaica Estates."

"Thank you."

"You are most welcome," O'Meara said. "What else can I do for you?"

"Keep praying for Monique."

"How's she doing?"

"The same."

"Keep the faith, brother," O'Meara said.

"I'm trying."

He hung up.

I got an Uber. It arrived within minutes. The driver, hunched behind the wheel like a troll, spoke English. A rarity.

Jamaica Estates wasn't far from St. Stephen's. It was a town of faux Tudors and Mediterranean-styled homes, all costing way over a million dollars. We drove up Midland Parkway, a four-lane boulevard with a wide and beautiful landscaped median strip. Off to the right was a leafy park with a dozen tennis courts. I wondered if that was where John McEnroe and Mary Carillo learned to play. And perhaps where another former resident, Donald J. Trump, learned to connive.

I had the Uber pull up at a corner, a couple of houses down from Hunter's. I got out and walked down the street to study the place.

Three huge maple trees obscured the house, as if trying to hide something going on inside. Behind the trees was a gray-shingled Victorian that had large fieldstone pillars on each side of the entrance. Surrounding the entrance was a wide porch with white wicker rocking chairs. At the top of the solid double front doors was a fan shaped stained glass window. Nice looking crib.

A few people were on the street, walking dogs, running, biking, chatting on their phones. If Corsito was being honest, which is always suspect, and Hunter was on vacation, I had no choice but to break in. Without being seen. Not an easy task.

I remembered something my old mentor, Sid Meyer, told me what to do in situations like this: Take a minute to think. Assess and evaluate. Make a plan.

Problem was . . . I had no plan. No strategy. No idea what to do. That is, until I spotted a Verizon truck.

I walked over to it. The air was sweltering, unreasonably intense even for this time of day.

Sitting in the truck's cab was a young guy, stocky and curly-haired. In the seat next to him was a small brown paper bag. Probably his lunch.

I knocked on the window.

He rolled it down.

"Yes?" he said.

"I have a proposition."

"For?"

"You."

"Let's hear it," he said, looking at me sideways.

"I'd like to rent your uniform."

"Rent my uniform?" he said, his voice full of skepticism.

"Yep."

"What for?"

"It's a long story and . . . "

"Let me get this straight. You . . . you want to rent my uniform. Is that what you're telling me?"

"Yes. And I'll pay you a hundred dollars."

"A hundred bucks!" he said, excitedly. "Are you fucking kidding?"

"Nope. Just need it for an hour." I pointed to the brown bag. "You can take the money and go buy yourself a nice lunch."

"Anything's better than the mystery meat my wife made," he said.

"There you go."

He ran a hand through his curly hair and said, "Whaddya you gonna do with it?"

"Play a trick on a friend."

"What kind of trick?"

"I wanna block Fox News on his TV."

He grinned.

"I get that," he said. "I hate Fox. But what you gonna do ain't illegal, is it? I don't wanna get in any trouble. Lose my job."

"You won't. I play a lot of practical jokes on my friend. He's accustomed to my shenanigans by now."

He scratched a forest of tiny moles on his right cheek.

"You look legit," he said.

"I am legit."

"A hundred smackers ain't easy to say no to."

"Sure isn't."

I pulled the money out of my wallet. The guy watched me and smiled as I counted out the bills. He had the elated expression of a lottery winner.

"Go get yourself a cold one," I said, handing him the bills.

"Already got one . . . my wife."

He zipped off his jacket and got out of the truck.

I said, "You got gloves?"

"I do."

He opened the glove compartment and pulled out a thin latex pair.

"Just leave everything on the front seat when you're done," he said. "See you in an hour."

"Sounds good."

As he walked away, I got into the truck and put on the jacket and cap. The jacket was a size too small, but beggars can't be choosy. Then I went around the back, opened the double doors, and took out his work bag and a small ladder. Hi ho, hi ho, it's off to work I go.

Whistling, I passed two young women pushing baby carriages. They smiled and said, "Good afternoon."

"And a good afternoon to you, ladies," I said, tipping my hat—cool as a proverbial cucumber yet sweating so much I felt myself in the grip of a malarial fever.

The first thing I did as I approached the property was look for an ADT sign that read THIS PROPERTY IS PROTECTED BY VIDEO SURVEILLANCE. I didn't see any. So far so good.

There was no way I could attempt breaking in through the front door. Too conspicuous. I walked up a brick path to the back of the house and tried to peer in the basement windows. They were covered with black curtains. Who puts covers over basement windows? Only someone who has something to hide.

I put the ladder against the house, climbed up it and tried to open a window. It was shut tight and locked. I did the same thing with two other windows. Same problem.

Climbing down the ladder, a hot breeze blew in my face, bringing with it a strange mix of smells, the exhaustive breath of summer.

I moved to the back door. It had a double cylinder deadbolt. Not the best kind of lock. You'd think old Hunter would have had enough bread to spring for something better, something more secure. My guess was he was so arrogant he fancied himself untouchable.

I grabbed a small jimmy from my wallet and wiggled it into the lock. When I was playing pro basketball coaches said I had "great hands." Now, as a detective, I had "great feel." It took me only forty-five seconds to unlock the door. Usually, it took thirty. I wondered if I was losing a step. Could be. I promised myself to practice more.

I took a deep breath before opening the door. If Hunter did have an alarm system, I was screwed. Bells might ring. Lights might flash. Pictures would be taken. Cops would show up and I'd be arrested. Maybe even lose my license.

Slowly, I put my hand on the doorknob. Held it for a minute. Took another deep breath. Then I turned it. Nothing. No alarms. No lights. Whew!

I stepped into a large kitchen. It had all modern appliances. Viking stove. Sub-Zero refrigerator. And a designer Rohl sink. There were no dishes in the sink. No crumbs on the table. On the counter was a bowl of fruit. I picked up a pear. It was rotten and smelled rancid.

Next to the refrigerator was a thick door. I opened it. It was a stairway leading to the basement. I clicked on a wall light. A couple of flies buzzed near the ceiling. I walked down the wooden stairs. They were mushy. They creaked. I had to watch my step.

The basement contained a water heater, an oil heater, a washer and dryer and a sink with brown grime surrounding the drain. The room reeked of mildew.

There was a door in the far back corner. I assumed it was a safe room—lot of newer homes have them. They're supposed to be a place to hide from intruders or some insurrection by nut jobs after Armageddon. Most people end up using them for storage or something else. This one was secured by a heavy vault door with a high-end built-in electric deadbolt. Ten digits, a zillion possible combinations and not even a keyhole to pick.

Not good. I cursed out loud. Oh, how I wished I had the magical words of Ali Baba, say "Open Sesame" and the lock would pop open. Fat chance.

I stared at the lock for a long time. Hadn't a clue what numbers to punch in. I thought of possibilities, the basic combinations 1-2-3-4 or 0-2-4-6. Neither worked. I tried the two seasons that Dave was the assistant coach at Carolina and the team won the NCAA tournament. No soap.

I stepped back and pondered the lock. Nothing came to me. I scratched my chin. I scratched my head. Walked around in tiny circles. Then it hit me. Dave's old number in college was six. Worth a try. I punched "six" four times. The lock buzzed. I spun the handle. The door opened. Luck of the Irish. Or perhaps that old Black magic.

I walked into the room. It had eight inches of soundproof padding. There was an area rug, a small bar, and a king size bed. Man cave. Mounted on a wall at the foot of the bed was a sixty-inch television screen. Below it was a wood entertainment cabinet with a DVD player and dozens of DVDs. I looked at the covers of the videos. They all showed men and women in various stages of undress. Hardcore porn.

I preened inwardly. More proof Hunter was a perv.

I was about to leave the room when I heard a grinding sound coming from upstairs. Fuck! I pulled my gun from my holster. Stood frozen, breathing heavy. Silent.

I listened hard, heard the noise again.

I went to the stairs and took them one at a time, slowly easing a foot onto each step while supporting my weight on the bannisters. The door at the top was closed. Did I close it?

If not, who did? Hunter? His wife? A gunman? My mind whirred faster than a spinning ride at Disneyland.

Lifting my gun, I pushed the door open and stepped out into the kitchen, ready to fire. There was no one there.

Then I heard the noise again. It was the refrigerator's ice maker.

Cold with sweat, I left the kitchen and went into the living room. It was full of modern furniture, chintz-covered armchairs, rosewood coffee tables, and gleaming chandeliers. Sitting on the fireplace mantel were tiny Lladró sculptures and porcelain figurines. Everything looked smooth and polished as if with meticulous care.

Could someone so dirty live in such a clean house? I assumed Marie hired a platoon of cleaning ladies.

Seeing nothing of interest, I ventured upstairs. There were two bedrooms, two baths, and an office. The master bedroom had a king size bed, a dresser, a closet, and a large armoire. I looked in the armoire. It was full of women's clothes. Chanel. Gucci. Prada. Louis Vuitton. I looked in the closet. Over fifty pairs of shoes. Jimmy Choo. Christian Louboutin. Manolo Blahnik. And the handbags! My God! A countless number. From Hermes and Celine and Ferragamo. Clearly, Marie liked to spend money.

Next, I scoped out the dresser drawers. Bras, panties, and more jewelry than Tiffany's. Nothing that a man would wear. Unless Hunter was into cross-dressing.

The other bedroom was Hunter's. The closed curtains were black and dusty. On the walls were colorful paintings of basketball players by LeRoy Neiman. There was a queen size bed and two closets. Both closets were jammed with clothes and sneakers from Nike and Adidas. No doubt freebies from the sporting goods manufacturers.

I went through the pockets of every pair of pants and jackets. I found nothing but lint, coins, and sticks of Juicy Fruit.

I moved to the office. It was large, had a mahogany desk and a green metal file cabinet. Photos of basketball players covered one wall. The largest picture was of Corsito hugging Hunter after their UNC team won the NCAA championship. Both had nets hanging around their necks. They looked like hangmen nooses.

On the opposite wall was a big screen television. Below it there were shelves containing a DVD player and dozens of DVDs. All about basketball. I scanned the titles. They had the names and dates of games. None looked out of place. At least not that I could tell.

I put my hands on my hips. I didn't know exactly what I was looking for. I just wanted to find something, anything, that might help my case.

I quickly flipped through every folder in the filing cabinet. Each one had information on grammar school and high school players, both in the United States and worldwide. The names were in alphabetical order. The details were extensive. Height, weight, key stats. Hunter was, if nothing else, highly organized.

I found Teddy Malone's folder. It had a little gold star on the front. I looked for folders on Jimmy Leonard and Billy Lang and Kenny Atkins; they, too, had stars. So did some others. In every folder was a picture of a smiling Hunter with his arms around the players. They all looked alike: fresh-faced, blue eyes, dark hair, big grins, lanky. They could have been cousins. Hunter went for a type. A feeling of nausea swirled around in my stomach.

I checked the time; I had another twenty minutes left, tops. I sat behind the desk and opened the drawers. The top one was filled with pens, pencils, Post-it notes, and a small magnifying glass. The second one had thick notebooks filled with diagrams of plays. Well drawn.

The bottom drawer was jammed with pictures of Hunter alongside a variety of people. Some I recognized: Coaches like Rick Pitino and John Calipari. Financier Jeffrey Epstein and the Duke of York, Prince Andrew. Mostly birds of a feather.

I kept flipping through pictures. Many of them were of Hunter with young kids and former players. A few days ago, they would have meant nothing. Now they were creepy, but none captured my attention until I got to the last photo.

The photo showed Hunter and his wife, Marie, smiling and hugging a tall, muscular white guy in a St. Stephen's jersey.

I recognized him immediately: Walter Wilson.

Wilson had played at St. Stephen's years ago. He was a skywalker, oblivious to the idea that what goes up must come down. It was when he landed that he got into trouble. Twice, after a brief career with the Los Angeles Lakers, he'd been charged with manslaughter, yet each time he made bail, pled out, and served very little time. I figured it was thanks to alumni friends in high places. Perhaps Catalano.

I held the picture up and squinted. Something in it caught my attention. I opened the top drawer, pulled out the magnifying glass and placed it over the photo. I looked at the back of Wilson's right hand.

On it was a small, round thing.

A basketball.

CHAPTER THIRTY-SIX

I put everything back but the picture, which I stuffed into my jacket pocket. I then walked back to the cable truck and was getting undressed just as the driver returned. I kept the picture, took off the jacket and hat and handed them to him.

"How'd it go?" he said.

"Fine. My friend will be lost without Sean Hannity and Laura Ingraham."

"He'll be the better man for it."

"Couldn't agree more," I said. "Appreciate your help."

"Easiest money I ever made."

"Spend it wisely."

"Gonna buy me a great big dinner at Olive Garden."

Jesus! Olive Garden!

He hopped into his truck and drove off.

I pulled out my cell phone and called St. Mary's Hospital. A nurse's aide put me through to Dr. Kaplan.

"How is she?" I said.

"Doing better," he said. "No longer critical. Still serious but trending the right way."

"Awesome," I said, feeling the weight of the world subsiding on my shoulders. "I'll be there shortly."

For the third time, I got an Uber. It came within twenty minutes.

En route to Kenny Atkin's place, I googled why someone would become a pedophile. There was no definite answer. Some psychologists and forensic specialists suggest neurological abnormalities and/or psychological pathologies. Others hypothesize that the origin is biological, that the genesis of pedophilia is prenatal, traceable to specific periods of development in the womb.

What's disconcerting is the fact that almost all therapists say the urge to molest young kids cannot be shut off, nor can it be replaced, the way methadone can be swapped for heroin.

Reading this stuff made me, on some level, feel for Hunter, but not enough to excuse his disgusting behavior. Nor that of anyone else who knew about it or enabled it.

We got to Weehawken. Kenny Atkins lived on Gregory Avenue. His house was a two-story brick job the color of dried blood. The trees on the front lawn sagged, as if exhausted from the hot, sweltering sun.

I exited the Uber, walked up the pathway to Atkins' door and pressed the doorbell. A man, dressed in blue jeans and a purple Vineyard Vines polo shirt, opened it but kept the screen door closed. He looked to be in his late twenties, early thirties. His face was thin. His cheeks were hollow and pockmarked, his eyes black holes. He sported a black Fu Manchu.

"You Kenny Atkins?" I said.

"Yes," he said, in a suspicious voice, his right eyebrow arched.

"I'm Elgin O'Brien," I said. "I'm a private investigator. I'd like to speak with you about Dave Hunter."

He shivered slightly as if suddenly shaking off a nightmare. His face got whiter than a cue ball.

"I'd rather not talk . . . "

"What I have to say to you is important. Please hear me out. I promise I won't take much time away from you or your family."

"I . . . I don't have a family."

"No family?"

"No."

Atkins eyes momentarily closed as if in pain.

"Look," he said, opening his eyes slowly, "I've said all I have to say about Hunter."

"Not to me you haven't."

"What makes you any different?"

"I'm going to expose him."

Atkins looked at me like a visitor to a zoo looks at a strange animal.

"You know how many people have told me that?" he said.

"I assume a few."

He snickered.

"How about 'many?' " he said.

I sensed he wasn't about to invite me inside, so I got right to the point.

"Based on what you just said, I take it Hunter did molest you, correct?"

"I think you know the answer to that. Otherwise, you wouldn't be asking."

"I'm only asking because I want to help you and others who he may have taken advantage of."

A brief, tight silence followed. I broke it with a question.

I said, "When did this molestation happen?"

He swallowed hard and for a moment his body went slack as if all the essential nutrients inside it were leaking out.

He coughed into a fist and said, "Freshman year. At St. Steve's."

"And where did it happen?"

He bit his lips and said in a shaky voice, "His house."

"His house?!" I said. "His house?!"

I couldn't believe my ears. The audacity of Hunter. Molesting a kid under his own roof. Where his wife sleeps and his children visit. What a dirtbag.

I struggled to speak, but somehow managed to get words out. "Is that why you transferred from Stephen's?"

"Yeah. I quit the team before the basketball season ended."

"Did you tell anybody about what happened?"

"I sure did."

"Who'd you tell?"

"The athletic director. Kent Small."

Small. Perfect name for an AD. I waited for him to elaborate. He didn't.

"What'd Small say?"

"He said he'd look into it."

"Did he?"

"Days later he called me into his office. He said Hunter denied everything. Said Hunter told him I was a cancer on the team, a malcontent who wasn't getting any playing time and causing dissension. Said I was out for revenge."

"Did you confront Corsito?"

His eyes became hot coals.

"Are you for real?" he said, harshly. "Corsito would never have believed me. He protects Hunter."

"Protects him?" I said. "Are you saying Corsito knew about Hunter?"

"I'm saying everybody in the administration knew then and probably still knows about Hunter," he said. "It's the worst kept secret on campus."

"Let me get this straight," I said. "You're telling me Kent Small knew?

He gave a bitter laugh.

"I'm telling you the fucking college president knew," he said.

Feeling my heart begin a pounding commotion, I said, "How do you know that?"

"How do I know that?" he said. "How do I know that?"

"Yeah. How do you know that?"

"I don't have to tell you. I can fucking show you."

He closed the door. I waited and watched as a pimply-faced kid, maybe eight or nine, dribbled a basketball down the block. His moves were practiced. Precise. His athletic career launching. Stay safe, kid.

Five minutes passed. Then ten. I wondered if Atkins wasn't going to reappear. Just as I was about to ring the doorbell, the screen door opened.

Atkins was holding a manila file folder.

"Just before my mother died," he said, "she wrote a letter to Benchley . . . "

"Who's Benchley?"

"President of St. Stephen's."

He opened the folder, took out a Xeroxed letter, then opened the storm door and handed it to me.

I took a few minutes to read it. As I did, my spine turned into an icicle.

The lines that froze me were: "Coach Hunter inappropriately and sexually assaulted my son. He grabbed his penis in the shower and pushed him against the wall and tried to penetrate him. I want him fired immediately or I will seek legal action."

I handed the letter back. He put it in the folder.

"Did your mother get a response?" I said.

"She did."

Atkins handed me another letter. This one was signed Mitchell Benchley, but the letterhead was from a law firm.

It began by thanking Mrs. Atkins for writing to him. It went on to say, "I have personally investigated and discussed the matter with Coaches Hunter and Corsito, along with the school psychiatrist Regina Blake. All three strongly deny your son's allegations. If you persist in making these unfounded accusations, we will vigorously defend the reputations of Regina Blake, Coach Hunter, Coach Corsito, the basketball program, the Athletic Department and the entire St. Stephen's community by every available method, including the legal system. We consider the matter closed." Underneath his signature was a column of ESQ's, all cc'd just in case she thought about suing.

I was silent for a long moment, trying to absorb as best I could all this information that validated so conclusively the suspicions I had about Hunter, Corsito, Blake, and now Benchley.

But what hit me even more was the ugly truth of the matter. I always thought the real reason sexual abuse of athletes was tolerated was because coaches and administrators needed to protect each other. But it's more than that. Much more. It's really about power protecting power, people in authority using their influence and finding loopholes and excuses and justifications to ignore the molestations and keep their lucrative jobs. How sick is that?

Will it ever change? Will the positive benefits of the college experience—given the big NIL money now being bestowed on athletes—survive and flourish while diminishing the exploitation and phony amateurism?

My guess? Probably not. Not until schools and leagues find their moral compass and point it in the right direction.

But don't hold your breath. It's gonna take a while. If ever.

I looked at Atkins and said, "Did your mother pursue legal action?"

Atkins swallowed to wet his throat, then said, "No."

"Why not?"

"She died shortly after receiving the letter." His face tightened. "From a stroke, high blood pressure."

"Sorry to hear that."

Atkins glanced sideways, then looked back to me.

"You mind if I borrow these letters?" I said.

"For what reason?"

"It's proof that people at the university knew about Hunter."

"Have you talked to anyone else?"

"About?"

"Hunter."

"I have."

"And?"

"Another kid confirmed Hunter molested him."

"Good for him," he said. "Most kids are petrified to admit it."

Atkins handed me the folder.

"Be my guest," he said. "I'm not even sure why I've kept the letters."

"Glad you did."

With the knuckle of his right index finger Atkins rubbed his right eye.

"If you don't mind my asking and you don't have to answer," I said, "but does the memory of what happened ever go away?"

"No, it doesn't. At least not for me." His voice broke. "It haunts you, but the feelings do change."

"Change? Change how?"

"You learn to deal with them. Accept what happened wasn't your fault. Somehow you pray to God and through him muster the strength to put one foot in front of the other."

"Thank you for answering my question," I said. "I know it wasn't easy."

Atkins looked at his watch.

"Gotta get to work," he said.

"What kind of work do you do?"

"I work for Goodwill."

"You enjoy it?"

A big smile. "Very much so."

I grinned. Felt enormous admiration for him seeing how he seemingly has dealt with and accepted his horrific past while inching his way out of the darkness and into the light. He was, in my book, a true winner.

"Sounds like you have a nice job," I said. "Thank you for your help."

"A lot my help is going to do for you."

"Why you say that?"

"Because Corsito is untouchable."

"Not for long," I said. "Not for long."

CHAPTER THIRTY-SEVEN

I got another Uber. It came quickly. I got inside and the car took off.

Once inside, I phoned Mike Thomas at the *New York Post*. I knew Mike from my playing days with the Mavericks. He was old school, a good reporter, fair and honest. Not a sensationalist like so many of today's sportswriters.

The first thing he said was, "I heard about Monique. How is she?"

"She's . . . she's hanging in there."

"What's the chance for recovery?"

"I'm told good . . . if all goes well."

"I'll keep her in my thoughts."

"Thanks."

"Been busy?"

"Very"

"Hot case?"

"Gets any hotter it'll sizzle."

"Don't get burned."

"Trying not to."

"What's up?"

"Talk to me about Dave Hunter?"

"Great recruiter."

"That's what everybody says. What else?"

"What else what?"

"Is he a molester?"

I heard Mike take a deep breath. "Well, there've been whispers for years, but then again there've been whispers about a lot of coaches, but no one ever says it out loud and you can never be sure if the rumors are planted to harm recruiting. You know these coaches; they don't stop at anything."

"It's more than a whisper, Mike," I said. "It's fact."

"How do you know?"

"I've spoken to two guys he molested."

"Are they credible?"

"Very."

"Talk to me."

"I will when the time's right," I said. "Answer me this. How come nobody has written about it?"

"People have tried."

"And?"

"Kids either wouldn't talk at all or go on the record."

"Ashamed?"

"For the most part. And afraid. Others feel guilty."

"Even though it wasn't their fault?"

"Some kids don't see it that way."

"You ever talk to Corsito about Hunter?"

"A couple times."

"And what he say?"

"As soon as he got my drift, he yelled and screamed and told me if I wrote such lies, he would sue me and the paper."

"What'd you say?"

"I said if I ever got evidence, I'd write the story."

"To which he responded?"

"His favorite phrase: 'Get the fuck out of my office!' "

I suppressed a laugh.

"Let me ask you this," I said. "You think there are a lot of coaches molesting players?"

"Sure as shit," Mike said. "I don't think it's as widespread or systemic as it is with priests or Scout leaders, at least I hope not, but it certainly happens a lot, especially in the youth leagues and schools where sports wag the dog. A perfect example is the former Penn State football coach, Jerry Sandusky. All the higher-ups knew he was a perv, but nobody did a damn thing about it." He paused, then added, "If there's one issue in sports that administrators don't want to deal with, it's admitting coaches molest players."

"Disgraceful," I said, thinking how so many college officials will do anything to avoid the minefields of admission. How, I wondered, do you inoculate them against cowardice? The only way is to expose them.

"No, shit. What's hard is understanding what motivates these coaches."

"Isn't it about sexual gratification?"

"To a large degree. But it's mostly about power and control. Domination. The kids look up to their coaches who they think hold the keys to their dreams, and coaches get off on that."

"It's gotta stop."

He laughed in a way that had nothing to do with being funny. "Good luck trying."

The Uber was nearing the hospital.

"You gotta understand, Elg," Mike said. "Corsito has more power and more influence on that campus than anyone else in the administration. Even the trustees ask how high when he says jump. I exaggerate not one iota when I say he's not only revered at St. Stephen's, he's deified. A king atop his throne."

"When I get through with him all the king's horses and all the king's men won't be able to put him together again."

"In all my years covering sports, Corsito is by far the most feared, the most narcissistic, self-centered, self-promoting college coach I've ever encountered . . . and I've encountered many."

"That's saying a lot."

"Yes, it is. The fact is successful college coaches, in all major sports, have become sacrosanct. If they get caught doing, shall we say, 'questionable things,' it's shoved under the rug unless the school is absolutely forced to deal with it. And, as you know, it's always the school and the players that take the rap. The coach just moves on to a bigger and better job and keeps cashing his checks."

Outside the front entrance to the hospital a crowd of reporters and photographers stood around like bored buzzards.

"Let me ask you," Mike said. "Are you investigating Corsito for something?"

"No. Why do you ask?"

"Because if you are, don't underestimate him. He's a lot smarter than you think."

"A mule is smarter than he is."

"Maybe so, but Chris is . . ."

"Is what?"

"More devious than Putin."

"Gotta go, Mike," I said.

"Need anything. I'm around."

"I'm going to call you later."

"What about?"

"Walter Wilson."

"There's a blast from the past. What do you want with him?"

"Long story. Bye."

The Uber stopped. I got out. Reporters raced toward me, pushing microphones in my face. I repeatedly kept saying "no comment."

I fought my way to the front door, feeling like I was fighting through a jubilant crowd that had just stormed the court.

A security guard saw me, opened the door, and I stepped inside.

It hit me that I might have a chance to see Monique. The thought lifted my spirits, gave me a tingling high so intense and so pleasurable it verged on euphoria. I could not have been happier.

CHAPTER THIRTY-EIGHT

A nurse told me Monique was still in ICU. I took a seat in the waiting room and after a while fell asleep. When I woke Monique's parents were sitting across from me. I jumped up and the three of us embraced.

"Oh, Elgin," said Monique's mother, Barbara, hugging me tight. She was an elegant looking woman in her sixties who had a striking resemblance to her daughter: same blond hair and blue eyes. She wore a simple, orange sleeveless dress. They had had it rough when Monique was young, but her folks worked hard and were good people. Just like their daughter.

Barbara and I disengaged.

She put her hands on my shoulders and peered into my eyes. Deep within her pupils a heavy sadness swirled in a whirlpool pattern.

"Thank you for letting us know," she said in her Midwest accent.

"Of course," I said. "You're the first call I made."

"We took the earliest flight out we could get," she said.

"Glad you're here," I said. "How you doing?"

"As best as can be," she said.

"Let's sit," I said. "Then I'll go find the doctor."

We sat. Barbara's knees were squeezed tight. Her hands held rosary beads.

"I don't understand," Monique's father, Steve, said. He was tall and heavyset. Bearded. "Who . . . why . . . why would anyone shoot Monique?"

I knew the answer, but I didn't want to get into it now. Not the right time.

"I don't know, Steve," I lied. "The city has been experiencing a lot of random shootings."

Barbara, her eyes bloodshot, looked at me and said, "I never liked this city. Never wanted Monique to move here. But Broadway was always her dream. How can you stop someone from pursuing that?"

"You can't," I said.

Steve had his arm around Barbara's shoulders. He leaned over and kissed her cheek.

"She's gonna be okay, love," Steve said.

"Yes, she is," I said. "She's a fighter."

"Always was," Barbara said.

"I understand from the news she was up for a role in a movie," Steve said. "She was superstitious, you know. She'd never tell us about her roles until she actually got the part."

"Same here."

"She always wanted to be in the movies," Barbara said, forcing a grin.

"She will be," I said. "She will be."

Steve nodded. His hands were clenched tight.

"It sure is hot in New York," Barbara said, fingering rosary beads.

"We're in the middle of a heat wave," I said. "Over hundred degrees three days running."

"We've had the same weather in Nebraska," she said, her right knee pumping.

"Lot of crazy shifts in temperatures and weather patterns," I said.

"Climate change," Steve said.

"You're right," I said, knowing this was all small talk, meant to pass time and keep the nerves at bay.

I stood.

"I'm going to look for Dr. Kaplan," I said.

They both nodded.

I walked up to the nurse's station.

"Dr. Kaplan around?" I said.

The nurse—young, glasses, friendly—smiled and said, "Are you Mr. O'Brien?"

"Yes, I am."

"I know Dr. Kaplan wants to speak with you," she said. "Let me call the ICU."

"Thanks."

She picked up the phone, dialed, and spoke.

I leaned against the counter and looked around the area. Doctors, nurses, orderlies. Coming and going. I saw elderly people in wheelchairs. I heard machines beeping, patients groaning. There was a strong scent of antiseptics.

The nurse hung up.

"Dr. Kaplan just finished surgery," she said. "He'll be down momentarily."

"Do you know if he was operating on Monique Montgomery?"

Her eyes brightened.

"The actress?"

"Yes."

"I'm . . . I'm not sure."

My tongue went dry and the oxygen in my body suddenly seemed depleted.

She said, "I saw Miss Montgomery once on Broadway."

"Really?"

"In *The Music Man*."

I tried to smile.

"She played Marian the Librarian," the nurse said. "She has some voice."

"Sure does."

The nurse sighed and put a fist under her chin.

"What I wouldn't give to have her talent," she added.

"Wouldn't we all."

"I'm sure Miss Montgomery will be fine," she said. "What would Broadway be without her?"

"Just another street."

A door at the far end of the corridor opened. Dr. Kaplan, wearing his scrubs and clogs, headed in my direction.

"Hello, Elgin," he said.

I nodded. "Dr. Kaplan."

He put his hand on my forearm and said, "Let's go to my office."

His serious tone unnerved me. Made my heart drop for a second, as if pulled down by an anchor.

I followed Kaplan down the corridor. It seemed like the longest walk of my life. My breathing was so heavy I was almost hyperventilating. I had no idea what Kaplan was about to tell me. Had something changed? For the worse? Every fiber of my body twitched fear.

Kaplan's office was large, had a big ornate desk and shelves filled with medical books. Pictures of his wife and children, all girls, were positioned on his credenza.

He pointed to a chair and said, "Please take a seat."

I sat as slowly as a corkscrew going into wine cork. Dr. Kaplan leaned forward over the desk and clasped his hands. Tight. His expression was stern.

"Here's the situation," he said. "The bullet did serious damage to her chest. For a while, it was touch and go. She hemorrhaged a fair amount, but we were able to stop it. And didn't have to remove much tissue. The bullet didn't penetrate very far. No major organs were seriously damaged . . . she's *very* lucky. We're still monitoring her, and there's always a risk of infection. She's doing well, but she's still not totally out of the woods."

I felt my breathing slowly returning to normal.

"All things considered, I'd say the chances are looking very, very good for a full recovery. If everything goes well, she could be back on the stage in a few months."

"Can I see her?"

"She's asleep now, and there's very little you can do," Kaplan said. "Perhaps later today or tomorrow you can visit. Sound good? We'll call right away if anything changes."

I swallowed the saliva that had built up in my mouth. The doctor went on to explain in more elaborate detail her surgery and her prognosis, but all I heard were "the chances are very good." When he finished, I slowly rose from my chair.

"Thank you, Doctor," I said. "I'm going to update Monique's parents."

Kaplan and I shook hands.

I left the office and walked back to the waiting room.

Monique's parents stood as I approached.

"How is she?" Barbara said. She looked as if she had aged twenty years in twenty minutes.

"She's improving," I said, a smile forming as I spoke the words. "Doc said her chances are very good for a full recovery."

Barbara put a hand to her mouth. Her eyes teared up.

"Thank God," she said. "Thank God."

Steve put his arm around Barbara's shoulders.

"I feel as if I can breathe again," Steve said.

"May we see her?" Barbara said.

"Not right now," I said. "She's still under observation. Maybe tomorrow."

Turning to Barbara, Steve said, "Maybe we should go back to the hotel. Get some rest."

Barbara nodded.

"Where you staying?" I said.

"The Marriott Marquis in Times Square."

"I'll take care of the hotel, and I'll get you an Uber."

"Thanks," Steve said.

The two of them hugged me. We held each other for a long, long time. I thought of Monique in intensive care . . . because of me. I felt reduced, shriveled, and couldn't say anything. But at least she was going to survive. I hoped.

CHAPTER THIRTY-NINE

I walked her parents out of the hospital. Reporters and cameramen descended on them, shouting questions and asking for comments. I cleared the way and put them into an Uber. As the car sped off, Barbara turned and looked at me through the rear window. She waved. Tears rolled down her cheeks.

I headed home. The reporters followed me like hunting dogs. I ignored them. I felt like I was back in the NBA, leaving an arena after a big win.

Thankfully, my car was still there. I was worried that the police might have impounded it. I ran my finger across a deep crease on the edge of the door.

I entered the house and plopped into a chair. Took a few deep breaths. I looked at a picture of Monique that was taken in Bermuda. In it, she's wearing a gauzy white dress, and her smile was brighter than the sun. I could almost smell her lavender perfume.

I kept staring at the picture, and every sight, every sound, every feeling from that time came back to me like a boomerang. I put my hands over my face. And it was only then that the tears finally came streaming out, running in warm rivulets between my fingers.

After a while, I went upstairs and took a shower. I turned the water to hot and let the jets pound my head and shoulders. Steam fogged the stall. But my eyes were clear. I pictured Monique and me in the living room dancing to Diane Schuur and José Feliciano singing "By Design" The lyrics swirled in my head: "Our love was meant to be, destiny/You and I will love eternally." The tearing started again.

I exited the shower and dried off. Put on a pair of Paige jeans and Rhone tee. Slipped on my shoulder holster and covered it with an unstructured linen sport coat.

I went downstairs and looked in the foyer mirror. My eyes resembled blisters. My skin was blotchy. I said to my reflection: "Somebody's going down. Even if I go down with them." My voice didn't sound like my own. It sounded deranged.

I called Mike Thomas.

"Where can I find Walter Wilson?"

"What could you possibly want with that lunatic?"

"I'm doing a background check," I lied. "He might have passed some bad checks. Probably nothing, but I gotta run everything down. If I come up with anything newsworthy, I'll let you know."

"Great. You know of all the kids who ever played at St. Steve's, Wilson was the best. Fans still talk about him like he's a God. It's a shame he committed so many offensive fouls . . . off the court."

"He sinned against his own talent."

"I'm shocked he's not in jail."

"So where would he be?"

"Last I heard he was strutting his stuff in Brownsville. Blair Park. You know it?"

"Yeah. I played there a few times in high school. Tough place. Lots of talented guys, who, for one reason or another, didn't make it to the NBA. Or even to college."

"No kidding," Mike said. "It is where former great players go to recapture glory. The games get quite heated."

"Trust me, I know," I said. "I had more than my share of fights there."

"So has Wilson. Once he beat a kid who blocked his shot so bad the player was hospitalized for weeks."

"Talk about a flagrant foul."

"That's only half of it. Get this—I hear Wilson likes to shoot stray dogs. For fun."

"Dogs? Really? That's a different lifestyle."

"Sweet guy. Need anything else?"

"Nope. Appreciate the info."

I hung up and called O'Meara.

"What can you tell me about Walter Wilson?" I said.

"The basketball player?"

"Yeah."

"What's your interest in him?

"I think he's the one who killed Teddy Malone and may have shot Monique."

I said "may have" because I still wasn't sure I could discount Catalano's nephew, Anthony. Nor Emma Mitchell or Adam Roth or Amare Anderson's friend, Gary Grimes. Or maybe Anderson himself. Still a lot of loose ends that I needed to be tied into a tight knot.

"Got proof?" O'Meara said.

I told him about the manager of Infernos spotting the basketball tattoo and then finding the picture of Wilson in Hunter's desk.

"Whoa. Whoa. Whoa," O'Meara said. "How'd you get that picture?" He paused. "On second thought, don't answer that."

I didn't.

"The picture is something," he said, "but it's not enough to go on. We'd need more evidence, more corroboration. And unlike some people . . . we can't break into Hunter's house without a warrant."

"I understand."

"Do you?"

"Yeah."

"Please do me the favor of remembering that in the future."

"I will."

"Now in answer to your question about Wilson," he said, "I can tell you he has a long list of priors."

"Concerning?"

"Drugs, robbery, assault, and . . . attempted murder."

"Christ! Why isn't he in jail?'

"I told you why. New York has a very liberal judicial system. Judges let more criminals out of jail than put them in jail. It's a travesty."

What's even more of a travesty, I thought, were the many shyster lawyers who go into court, stand before a judge or jury less concerned with the truth and more concerned with ripping a case to shreds. It has become so prevalent justice is no longer about guilt or innocence. It's about negotiating and manipulating. Saying and doing whatever it takes to get a plea bargain.

O'Meara said, "If you want, I can have my guys question Wilson. Roust him on something."

"No."

"Why not?"

"I'd rather do it."

"You sure?"

"I'm sure."

"Suit yourself."

"I just wanted to let you to know in case something unexpected happens."

"Whaddya mean . . . unexpected?"

"I mean unexpected."

"Appreciate the head's up," he said. "Just don't do anything foolish."

"Sometimes you gotta do the wrong thing for the right reason."

"Meaning?"

"He's gonna pay."

"Revenge gets you nowhere."

"I used to believe that."

"Listen to me and listen to me good, Elg. Wilson is still a human being . . .

"Not anymore. Not if he's the one that shot Teddy and Monique."

"You don't know for sure he's the shooter."

"You're right, I don't. But I believe what I believe."

"Look, Elg, don't be stupid. And don't make me lie . . . this conversation never happened, right?"

"What conversation?"

I thanked O'Meara and ended the call.

I got in the Mustang for the first time since the shooting. Blood still stained the seat. I covered it with a towel and looked at the scar on the door frame from the bullet. It reminded me how lucky Monique was. If the bullet hadn't clipped the door, she'd probably be dead. Perish the thought.

I drove across the Brooklyn Bridge into Brownsville, an area that had one of the highest drug and crimes rates in all five boroughs.

Despite recent attempts at gentrification, there were still lots of boarded-up storefronts, vacant buildings, and empty lots. The lots were filled with broken bicycles, cinder blocks, supermarket carts, beer bottles, and food wrappers. Mangy-looking dogs rummaged through the contents. I pictured Wilson cackling and taking aim.

I stopped for a red light. On my left were abandoned brick buildings scarred with bullet holes. On my right were pawn shops, liquor stores, pool halls, Baptist churches, burger joints, discount clothing outlets, cut-rate furniture marts, bars, and barbershops. More than a few homeless men slept in the doorways. It was, for all intents and purposes, the Boulevard of Broken Dreams at the intersection of Poverty and Neglect.

The court at Blair Park was next to a kids' playground. Monkey bars, merry-go-rounds, swings, slides. Mothers sat on wooden benches, pushing baby carriages back and forth. Elderly gents, smoking cigarettes, squatted on the ground shooting craps. Standing above them watching were younger dudes, Black and White, drinking out of paper containers. Loud Latin music filled the air. Salsa.

Even at mid-morning with the temperature in the high nineties, a full-court game was in progress. Shouts, screams, the scrape of sneakers on asphalt. Almost all the players were Black. Almost all had cuts, bruises, and scars. Stigmata from battle.

I took in the action. The game was fast and furious, sharp elbows, hip-checks, and explosive drives. The players stutter-stepped, dribbled around their backs, through their legs. A clinic on street basketball.

I watched as one skywalker rattled the rim after a slam-jam-thank-you-ma'am tomahawk dunk. The crowd hooted and hollered. High fives everywhere.

I noticed a tall, Black guy in shorts, high white Cons, and a New York Knicks jersey leaning against a fence. Styling with gold chains around his neck and big Maui Jim sunglasses, he had biceps the size of cantaloupes and hands larger than ping-pong paddles.

I sidled up to him and said, "Good game out there."

"Some serious muthafuckers be making it rain," he said in a slow, husky voice.

"No shit," I said. "You play?"

"Got next."

I extended my hand and said, "Elgin O'Brien."

He lowered his glasses. His eyes were big and brown.

"Hey, bra, I remember you," he said. "You used to be big-time."

"I still am."

He chuckled.

"Nehru King," he said. We bumped fists.

"Wha'cha doin' here, man?" he said.

"Checking out the action."

"Best comp in the city. Lot of bad-ass players."

"No question. A court of appeal."

We watched the game. We saw a Black kid, late twenties, built like a linebacker make a quick cross-over dribble, stop, and hit a long step-back three. James Harden–like.

"That boy got hisself some moves," Nehru said. "Too bad his head be screwy. Been to more junior colleges than I can count. Fucked up every time. Now he's just another street legend."

"Speaking of legends," I said. "You know if Walter Wilson ever plays here?"

"He does, man, but I ain't seen him in a while." He made a silent whistle. "Tell you what, man. That boy could play. We used to call him White Chocolate 'cause he played so much like a brother. He's another one who screwed up. He could have been one of the best. Had unbelievable hops. The joke was that if you put a dollar on the top of the backboard he could jump up, get it, and leave change." He paused, then added, "He's a head case, alright, but I'll give him credit for one thing."

"What's that?"

"Dude keeps his body in great shape. And as fucked up as he is, he still got game."

"You know where he lives?"

"On the street, man. I don't even think he has a crib. Mostly sleeps in his car."

"What kind of car?"

"An old beat-up black caddy."

"He have a girlfriend?"

"Mostly skanky crackheads."

"Really?"

"If I'm lying, I'm flying."

"Any idea where I might find him?"

"Only other place I know he hangs beside here is some pool hall in Manhattan called Chalkies. It's on"—he snapped his fingers—"on Twenty-Third Street."

We watched now as a thin, emaciated-looking kid made a beautiful pass that was less thrown and more conjured, like a magician pulling a rabbit from a hat. The crowd went wild. Cheers, applause, hoots, and hollers. Game over and done.

"It's showtime for me, my man," he said. "You stickin' 'round to watch me slay and parlay these losers?"

"You mean shake and bake 'em . . . "

"And mothefuckin' quake 'em."

"I'd like to, but . . . "

"Hey, bra, maybe I can get you in the game."

"I might get schooled."

"Then again all your swishes may come true."

"Would love to J up," I said. "But I gotta go."

"To Chalkies?"

I nodded. Tried to palm him a twenty. He kept his fist closed.

"No need, bra," he said. "Us hoopsters gotta stick together."

We slapped high fives, and I walked off the court.

As I headed to the car, I realized there was someone else I needed to confront, someone whose very existence made my entire body thrum with rage.

CHAPTER
FORTY

St. Stephen's president, Mitchell Benchley, had an office on the third floor of what was called Harris Hall. I walked up a curved staircase, the white walls decorated with framed pictures of former school presidents. They all looked as if they suffered from bad cases of constipation.

Holding Kenny Atkin's folder, I was greeted by a secretary who resembled Roseanne Barr.

"Is Benchley here?" I said.

"Yes, he's in the office," she said. "May I help you?"

"No, you may not," I said, barging into a large office where three men were sitting around a conference table the length of a bowling alley. At the head of it was a short guy with thick white hair and jug handle ears. He was wearing a light blue oxford shirt, a plaid bow tie, and sweater vest. Beneath the vest was a belly so big it looked as if pillows were stuffed inside it. A fat Muppet.

"Which one of you clowns is Mitchell Benchley?" I said.

Bow Tie harrumphed and said, "Who do you think you are barging in like this?" His voice had a lisp.

"I'm Elgin O'Brien," I shouted. 'You Benchley?"

Bow Tie looked at one of his companions and said, "Milton . . . call security."

Milton—thin, weaselly looking, no doubt a kiss-ass dean—picked up the phone.

I immediately said, "Put the phone down, Uncle Miltie, or lose a hand."

Milton dropped the phone as if it had suddenly become red hot.

I walked over and stood looking down at Bow Tie.

"I'll ask you again," I said. "Are you Mitchell Benchley?"

He didn't answer. I pounded the table. He jumped.

"I . . . I am," he stuttered.

I pointed to the other two men and said, "Get the fuck outta here."

They both rose quickly and raced out the door. Such backbones.

"What do you want?" Benchley said, cowering. "Security will . . . will . . . will be here soon,"

"I don't care. I wanna know why you've let Dave Hunter molest players."

"What are you talking about?" he said, indignantly.

I held up the folder.

"I'm talking about a letter a Mrs. Atkins wrote to you."

Benchley feigned incredulity, his mouth opening and closing like a guppy.

"Who?" he said.

"You know damn well who," I said. "She wrote you regarding Hunter molesting her son, Kenny."

"I don't remember . . ."

"Don't give me that 'don't remember' bullshit. You remember." I took a step toward him.

"Yes . . . yes," he said. "Now that you mention it, I . . . I do have a vague recollection."

I wanted to slap his face. I despise cowards.

"You did nothing," I said.

"That's . . . that's not true," he said. "I spoke with Coaches Hunter and Corsito, and they assured me nothing untoward ever, ever happened."

"You simply took their word for it, huh?"

"I . . . I . . ."

"You never even spoke with Atkins, did you?"

"I . . . I did not."

"No, you didn't. You just washed your hands over the matter. A regular Pontius Pilate."

"We . . . we did, however, refer Kenny to the school's psychologist . . . "

"Who like *you*, knew about Hunter, but like *you* did *nothing* about it."

"I can't speak for Dr. Blake."

"You don't have to," I said. "Her lack of action on Kenny's behalf speaks for itself."

Benchley slumped in his chair, seemingly shrinking before my eyes. He kept glancing at the door hoping security would come and save his pompous ass.

"I'll tell you some other facts," I said. "I think Hunter molested Teddy Malone, and when Teddy threatened to go public, Hunter or maybe Corsito had him murdered. Then one of those jackals hired someone to shoot me but instead shot my girlfriend."

Benchley closed his eyes and pressed trembling fingers to his forehead.

"I . . . don't know what you're talking about," he said.

"Yeah, you do."

"I run a top-flight university here," he said.

"No, you don't," I said. "What you run is a sports factory. And like most college presidents at big-time programs, you haven't the balls to reign in your out-of-control, all-powerful coaches . . . like Hunter. Like Corsito."

"You're wrong," he said. "They're no different from any other faculty member."

I laughed. Was this bozo kidding or what? Did he not realize the horrible fraud he was perpetrating on higher education?

"Wake up, Fatso, willya?" I said. "You've either been asleep at the wheel or sitting up here in your ivory tower sucking your thumb and not caring about the abuse that's happening in your athletic program. Which makes you in my eyes . . . pathetic."

Fear distorted Benchley's face. Looking at it, I wondered how someone like him got to his position. You wonder where he came from and what were his credentials. But you probably really don't want to know. If you did, you'd no doubt vomit.

"Let's . . . let's talk about this," he said.

"There's nothing to talk about."

I reached down and took hold of his bow tie. It was a clip-on. I ripped it from his shirt collar.

"How a man of your, I assume, intelligence became such a lapdog for an asshole like Corsito and a molester like Hunter is beyond me. You're a disgrace to academia."

Benchley gave me the look of a man about to face a firing squad.

Just then two security guards burst into the room. One was short, the other tall. Both had beer bellies dripping over their belts. One fumbled his nightstick, and it fell to the floor.

"No worries, gentlemen," I said. "I'm leaving. And not soon enough."

As I was headed out the door, I turned and said to Benchley, "You haven't seen the last of me, Fuckhead."

I tossed his bowtie in a trash can.

FORTY-ONE

I got back in the Mustang and drove off campus. A few miles along the Van Wyck Expressway, traffic came to a total standstill. I pounded my fists on the steering wheel until they throbbed.

Thoughts bounced around inside my head like popcorn in a popcorn maker. I thought of Monique in the hospital. I thought of coaches who abused and molested kids. I thought of administrators like Benchley who allow such despicable behavior to fester. I thought of the NCAA that fails repeatedly to punish coaches who blatantly break the rules.

Big-time college sports is a cesspool. It was a little better when I played, but now it's all about money. Big money. Winning at all costs. Even if you must cheat to reach your goals. Bottom line: Higher profits are much more important than higher education.

Need proof? Just look at March Madness. It's a game show. A cash cow. Maybe instead of hiring Jim Nantz and

Grant Hill to announce the games, CBS should hire Vanna White and Ryan Seacrest.

I still get a chuckle thinking about the college president I heard years ago say, "When it comes to sports and education, I want a college the basketball teams can be proud of." Kidding or not, it was an outrageously ridiculous thing to say. But I believe he meant it.

A big part of the problem is that athletic directors and college presidents are only ass-kissers, accomplices, and apologists for powerful coaches who have become masters of deceit and negotiators of long-term lucrative contracts.

Despite their lofty rhetoric, most college coaches, especially those running the football and basketball programs, don't care if a player attends class or gets a degree. Players are nothing more than commodities, bought and sold to the fans. They're exploited and told by ass-chewing, profanity-shouting coaches that if they don't reach their potential and win, they're betraying the fans and themselves. I heard that malarky myself countless times.

I love it when I hear coaches talk about building character when, in fact, they wind up building characters who believe, foolishly and unrealistically, that the only thing that matters is paying the price for stardom—at the expense of their physical and emotional well-being.

What's worse is how these same coaches are revered, adored, and admired by fans and alumni—and put on a pedestal. Often, they're called great. Heroic. Trust me, they're not. Heroes are those men and women who have something dangerous at stake, who put their lives on the line to save others, like doctors and nurses, cops and first responders. The only thing coaches put on the line is their dirty laundry.

Traffic inched along. As I got near LaGuardia Airport, I saw yellow cones and a giant blinking white light merging traffic into one lane. A truck had overturned and two cars were badly damaged.

Dozens of cops were directing cars. There were flashing red lights. Medical personnel, in bright white uniforms, carried someone on a stretcher.

Seeing the stretcher made me think of Monique. If I hadn't been assured that she was doing okay, I might have broken down and cried.

My cell phone rang. It was Carlo.

"Got bad news for you, paisan. Word is Ant-knee blew town. Nobody knows where he is. Or if they do, they're not saying."

"Thanks for checking," I said, almost certain the shooter was Wilson. "But I don't think I need to find him anymore."

"Oh, sure. You send me on a wild goose chase."

"What can I say? I owe you a cannoli."

"Cannoli, my ass. Front row tickets to a Knicks game would be much more appreciated."

"I do my best," I said. "Ciao, brother."

I hung up. A minute later, the phone rang again. This time it was Paul Stone, Hoboken's chief of detectives.

"Sorry about Monique," he said.

"Thanks."

"How's she doing?"

"Better. I think she's going to make it."

"Glad to hear it," he said. "Just wanted to update you."

I eased the Mustang from the center lane into the left lane. Traffic was beginning to move. Slightly.

"We've spoken to a number of people who were near or around the area at the time of the shooting," he said. "One person, an elderly man who was walking his dog, said he saw a man running away out of a rehabbed building down the block just after he heard the shots being fired."

"Could he describe the guy?"

"Yes and no. Yes, insofar as he said the guy was tall but, no, inasmuch as a facial description. Couldn't tell if he was Black, White, or Chinese."

I glanced out the window and saw a tow truck arriving at the accident scene.

"Another witness," Paul added, "a young gal on her way to the PATH station, said she also saw a tall guy running and jumping into an old beat-up Caddy."

"What color?"

"Black."

I immediately thought of Nehru King telling me Walter Wilson drove an old beat-up black Caddy.

"Beyond those two wits," Paul Stone said, "We have nothing. We're trying to run down the car . . . but there are a lot of old black Caddies, and she didn't get a plate number, or even the state."

I moved past the overturned truck. Its cab was crushed. I hoped the driver survived.

"Bottom line," Paul said. "We don't have much to go on, but we're still pursuing leads. My guys will continue to check the security and Ring cameras from every shop and building in the vicinity of your house."

"Great."

"Is there anything else you remember that could help us?"

"No," I said, "But I'm following up on something."

"Care to share?"

"Not right now."

"Want our help?"

"I'm good."

"I know you're good," he said. "Just don't go off half-cocked."

"Would I do that?"

"Yes."

"If I need you, I'll call."

"Great," Paul said. "Keep me posted."

"Will do."

"See ya, buddy," he said, then hung up.

Now I was more than sure Wilson was the shooter.

But I still needed an answer to the biggest question: Who hired him?

CHAPTER FORTY-TWO

halkies was hidden beneath a dilapidated three-story building that was held together by bird dung and exhaust fumes. There was no sign out front. The entrance was a dark hole down a few cracked steps. I didn't know if Wilson was there, and if he was there, would I come out in one piece. If I came out at all. There should have been a sign outside that read: Abandon all hope, ye who enter here.

But I never worry about danger. Or pressure. Didn't as a basketball player and not now as a private investigator. I guess it goes back to a conversation I once had with my father.

I said, "Dad, what's the toughest thing you've ever done?"

"That's easy, son," he said. "It's getting out of bed every morning."

At the time he said that—I was maybe nine—his words flew over my head like a kite going skyward. It was only when I got older that I understood what he meant: How tough it was for a Black man to exist in a White world.

Compared with the taunts and threats, the injustices and humiliations, the stabbings and beatings that my father endured growing up in New Orleans, my life was a piece of cake.

I took the gun out of my holster, broke the cylinder, spun it, and looked through the chambers. Fully loaded, I jerked my wrist and snapped the cylinder shut.

A voice in my head suddenly said, "Don't give this asshole a chance. Provoke him, then shoot him. If I don't and he goes on trial, New York's liberal judicial system will have him back on the street in no time.

But a dissenting voice countered: Calm down. You're pissed off. Half-crazed. Don't do anything stupid. Anything that would jeopardize your career and life.

I closed my eyes. Saw Monique getting shot. Her pain. The bleeding.

Fuck it, I said, this motherfucker is going down.

I opened a heavy wooden door. It shut behind me with the thud of a guillotine's blade.

The room was foul with the stench of rotten eggs and stale beer. Cigarette butts littered the grimy tile floor. Neon beer signs covered some walls. High in one corner was a security camera. The only real lighting in the place came from the green conical fluorescent lamps that hung over a half dozen pool tables. The room resonated with the sound of clacking balls.

Players were either standing upright holding pool sticks or hunched over about to take shots. I watched one guy walk around a table, studying the layout of balls. He'd stop and look. Stroll. Stop and look. Stroll. All the while chalking the tip of his stick.

He finally bent over, called his shot, aimed and scattered some balls. Two colored ones dropped into corner pockets. Minnesota Fats would have approved.

Sitting at small metal tables and watching the shooters were a handful of big, scar-faced Black and White men. If I had to guess, they were drug dealers, pimps, gamblers, killers who were pregnant with menace and contaminated by evil. Humanity's headaches.

They were all wearing ripped jeans and dirty tanks. Smoking cigars. And joints. A couple of them eyeballed me as if I was some Martian who had just dropped in from space. Their angry faces appeared consumed with suppressed violence. Although a dingy sign on the wall said, "All Players Welcome," I knew that certainly didn't apply to me.

Ignoring them, I looked at the back of the bar. A slender, skanky Hispanic-looking gal wearing white shorts that barely covered her butt and a revealing blouse that exposed large breasts, was seated next to a tall, well-built White guy.

Walter Wilson.

Smoking a cigarette and sporting baggy knee-length black shorts and a black sleeveless tee, he had the body of a heavyweight fighter. His biceps were huge. His neck was thick. I figured he was all 'roided up. Just looking at him, I could tell he was a deadly force.

I slowly walked toward him, stepping over a guy who was either asleep or dead on the floor.

I got within inches of Wilson's face.

He said, "What'cha lookin' at, asshole?"

"Nothing much."

He cupped a hand behind his right ear. "What'd you say?"

"You heard me."

He took his hand down. "Ain't sure I did, muthafucker."

"Yeah, you did."

His eyes narrowed, pulsing with homicide.

"Please don't tell me you don't remember me," I said.

He shifted in his seat. As he did, I noticed a gun sticking out of his waistband. It looked like a .45. The kind that killed Teddy Malone.

"I'm still alive and well," I said.

Wilson stood. He was one tall drink of water. Had me by a few inches.

"Beat it," he ordered the girl.

She didn't move.

Wilson slapped her across the face and pushed her off the chair.

"Screw, bitch," he hollered. "Screw."

The girl ran away, shouting obscenities in English and Spanish. The pool shooters paused for a few seconds, then resumed their games.

Looking at me, Wilson said, "I advise you, muthafucker, to get lost." His voice was just as the manager at Infernos had described: clogged as if full of phlegm.

"You killed Teddy Malone," I said.

His expression didn't change. Looking at him was like staring deep into the eyes of a vampire bat.

"I ain't killed anybody," he said.

"Yeah, you did."

"Prove it."

I pointed to the tiny tattoo of a basketball on the back of his right hand.

"Manager at Infernos remembered you getting into an argument with Malone," I said. "He saw the tattoo."

"Don't prove a thing," he said, smiling. His teeth were rotted.

"You also shot my woman."

He cocked an eyebrow. "As if I give a shit."

"Well, I give a shit."

He stood there, his dead eyes never leaving mine.

"What'd you gonna do about it?" he said.

"Make you pay."

He blew cigarette smoke in my face.

"Telling you one more time, man," he said, his voice rising. "Leave now or in a hearse."

The room got quiet. There were no clacking balls. The only sound came from the low hum of the fluorescent lamps.

Wilson tossed his cigarette on the ground and squashed it as if it were a cockroach.

"You're asking for it," he said, after hacking up a wad of phlegm.

I grinned.

Wilson pushed me backward.

I grinned wider.

Wilson pushed me again. Bad idea.

I quickly kicked him in the groin. He groaned and doubled over. Clasping my hands, I reached up and pounded the back of his neck. He stumbled backward. Then he straightened up and came at me, wildly throwing punches. I sidestepped them and hit him with a right hook to the kidneys, followed by a left jab to the stomach.

Those punches could have flattened a rhino. But not Wilson. He countered with a solid smack to my face. I never saw it coming. My head snapped back.

We circled each other, sweat pouring down our faces.

Wilson took a deep breath and rushed me again. He was like a wild animal, crazed and dangerous. He threw a haymaker. I ducked. He missed. I rose and hit the side of his head with everything I had. It felt like I hit a brick wall. My hand was numb.

Instead of going down, Wilson backpedaled and reached for his gun. I went for mine.

I was faster. I shot him in his right bicep. Wilson yelped and his gun went off into the ceiling. I fired again. Same spot. Wilson's face contorted. He dropped the gun, and I quickly kicked it away. The air stung with the acrid smell of cordite.

I took a quick glance around. The room had emptied. Except for Wilson's girlfriend who was now racing toward me . . . holding up a butcher's knife.

"Stop right there," I shouted, my gun dead-aimed at her.

"I keel you!" she screamed.

"Be cool," I said.

"I keel you! I keel you!"

"Chill out, lady."

She raised the knife above her head.

I fired a bullet at her feet.

"GET THE FUCK OUT OF HERE!" I yelled, fueled by the rage and fury that burned deep within me.

She jumped. Glared hatred at me.

"Don't make me tell you again," I said. "Drop the FUCKING knife or I drop YOU."

Her hand shaking, she finally let the knife slip from her hand. Then she turned and ran out the front door screaming, "Murderer! Murderer!"

I glanced back at Wilson. He had ripped off his shirt. Blood streamed down his arm.

"Don't kill me, man," he whined. Mr. Tough Guy suddenly looked about twelve years old. He tried to stand, stumbled and fell.

I pulled back the hammer on my gun. It made a hard metal crack.

Wilson flinched. His eyes were the size of radial tires. Fat beads of sweat washed his face.

"Please don't kill me, please don't kill me," he said again.

"I'm going to ask you some questions," I said. My voice sounded cruel, cutting, hateful. "If I think you're lying to me, I will keep shooting you and shooting you until I get the answers I'm looking for. You understand me?"

Wilson groaned and howled like a demented wolf.

"Let's start with an easy one," I said. "Did you murder Teddy Malone?"

He didn't answer.

"DID YOU MURDER TEDDY MALONE?" I shouted.

Still no answer.

I curled my finger around the trigger.

"Last chance. Talk or die, asshole. Your choice."

He stared at me with his soulless eyes.

"Okay, okay," he said. "I did. I did."

"Did what?"

"Shoot the kid."

"Why?"

"Five large."

"Hunter gave you the five large?"

"No, no. She gave . . . "

"Waitaminutewaitaminutewaitaminute. Whaddya mean she? Who's she?"

Silence.

"Who the fuck is she?"

"Marie."

"Marie?! Marie Hunter?!"

"Yeah, man. Yeah. She said the kid was just some faggot who was going to tell the press about her husband was a . . . a fuckin' perv."

A horse's kick in the head would have seemed like a love tap compared to that bombshell. It took me almost a minute before I could speak again.

I said, "You're telling me it was *Marie Hunter* who paid you to shoot Teddy Malone? Is that what you're telling me? Is it? Is it?"

He didn't respond.

I fired a bullet near his right leg. He cowered and closed his eyes. A wet stain appeared on his pants between his legs.

"ANSWER ME!" I shouted, feeling as vindictive and vengeful as I ever felt.

"Yeah. Yeah," he cried, his eyes wild with fear. "She . . . it was her. It was her. That cocksucker Hunter even tried to do me when I was there."

"And did she also pay you to shoot me?"

"Yeah, man, yeah . . . gave me even more money. Ten grand."

My gun hand wobbled. I lowered my gun inches from Wilson's forehead.

"Please," he said for the third time. "Please don't shoot me." He was drooling with fear.

Oh, how I wanted to. How I so wanted to blow his fucking brains out. But I knew that if I did it would make me no better than him.

Wilson, holding his bleeding bicep, was now crawling backward like a giant centipede.

"Hey man," he said. "Show me some mercy?"

"Sorry," I said. "I'm fresh out."

Outside, I heard police sirens. Minutes later, a slew of cops rushed in, pointing their weapons and screaming.

A big, overweight one, holding his gun with two hands, shouted at me. "Put the gun down!"

"I'm a private investigator," I said.

"I don't give a fuck if you're Sam Spade," he said. "Drop the gun. Now!"

"Not until you call Sergeant Bill O'Meara."

The cop blinked. The nameplate above his shirt pocket read: Madsen.

"O'Meara?" he said, his voice rising.

"Tenth Precinct."

"I know."

"Call him."

"Not till you lower your gun."

"Not till you call him."

It was a standoff. Like two cowboys at high noon.

Wilson was still writhing and moaning.

"Shut the fuck up," I said, waving my gun at him.

"No need to drag this out," Madsen said.

"Call O'Meara," I said. "He knows the situation."

Madsen exhaled, then turned to a young officer, his gun still pointed at my head.

"Get O'Meara on the horn," he said.

"Yes, sergeant," the officer said, pulling out his cell phone.

Wilson was now bucking on the floor like a bronco and yelling about needing a doctor.

Everyone ignored him.

The officer handed his cell phone to Madsen.

"It's O'Meara," he said.

"Bill," Madsen said into the phone. "It's Jack Madsen. I got a guy here holding a gun by the name of . . . " He lowered the phone and said, "What's your name?"

"Elgin O'Brien," I said.

Madsen said my name into the phone. He then listened for a second. "It appears he shot somebody."

"In self-defense," I said, pointing to a security camera. "The video will prove it."

Madsen took a quick glance at the camera, then said into the phone, "I'll ask."

He looked at me and said, "Who's the guy on the floor?"

"Walter Wilson," I said.

Madsen passed the name onto O'Meara. He then nodded and nodded.

"Got ya," he said. "Thanks." He handed the cell phone back to the young officer.

"Okay, O'Brien," Madsen said. "O'Meara vouches for you. You lower your gun, and I'll lower mine. Deal?"

"Deal."

I lowered mine. Madsen lowered his. Two officers quickly rushed to me and took my gun. Three others pulled Wilson to his feet.

One then grabbed a towel off the bar and wrapped it around Wilson's bloody bicep. Using latex gloves, another cop picked up Wilson's gun.

"This man tried to kill me," Wilson shouted. "Tried to kill me. Shot me twice."

Madsen ignored him. He turned to the officers cuffing Wilson and said, "Get him the fuck outta here."

"Got it," an officer said.

Three cops then escorted Wilson out of Chalkies. He ranted and raved the entire time.

Madsen approached me.

"You're the basketball player, right?" he said.

"Used to be."

"I heard about what happened to your wife . . . "

"Girlfriend."

"Your girlfriend who was shot. Sorry to hear it."

I nodded.

"The guy you shot," he said. "He the shooter?"

"Yes. He admitted shooting Teddy Malone and Monique Montgomery."

A drop of sweat fell off Madsen's nose.

"Okay," he said. "Let's go."

"Where?"

"To the station house."

"Am I under arrest?"

"No."

"Thanks."

"Don't thank me. Thank O'Meara."

"Will do."

CHAPTER FORTY-THREE

The next morning found me in O'Meara's office. My face hurt and the area around my eye was black and blue.

"You have a helluva shiner," O'Meara said, sitting behind his desk. He was wearing a white shirt with a gold shield over the pocket.

"Wilson got me good," I said, touching the skin above my eye with my swollen right hand.

"You got him one better. I saw the video."

"I was faster."

"A real Dirty Harry."

"Thanks for keeping some information out of the papers."

"Like I had a choice. The chief just loves it when a private dick pulls strings. Besides, we don't want to tip any one off until we've got more evidence and can make some arrests."

O'Meara reached across his desk and picked a cashew out of a tiny glass bowl. He chewed it and said, "We've interrogated Wilson."

"And?"

"At first, he gave us a sob story about how he was innocent."

I snorted.

"He was adamant he had nothing to do with shooting Teddy or Monique," O'Meara said.

"I assume you pressed him?"

"We did more than that," O'Meara said. "We told him ballistics compared the bullets from his gun with the bullets that killed Teddy Malone."

"I'm guessing they match?"

"Sure do."

I grinned.

"Got something even better, I just spoke to your buddy, Paul Stone. He said he tried to get ahold of you, but of course you were busy shooting Wilson. Anyway, his detectives got some footage from a bodega down the street from your place showing Wilson buying a soda and carrying a large duffel bag, which, by the way, was also in his caddy. Dollars to donuts the bullet taken from Monique will match the bullets taken from the rifle."

I grinned wider.

"Are you surprised it was Marie Hunter and not Dave who ordered the hit?" O'Meara said.

"I was, although some coach's wives are scarier than Hannibal Lecter."

"At least they don't eat their adversaries."

"No. They just have them shot."

O'Meara chuckled.

"Are your guys out looking for Dave and Marie?" I said.

"Better believe it."

"Corsito said Hunter was on vacation."

"Where?"

"Didn't say."

"Alone? Or with the missus?"

"Don't know."

"Here's another thing you don't know. Wilson's other priors are still felonies."

"This would be his third major offense."

"Correcto mundo."

"You remind him of that?"

"I mentioned how a third offense carries a mandatory prison sentence of twenty-five years to life." He paused and grinned. "I also said that if he turned state's evidence, admitting his guilt and testifying as a witness, his sentence might be reduced."

"What he say?"

"He said a lot. Admitted to both shootings . . . at the request of one Marie Ruggiero Hunter."

"Here's something *you* don't know," I said. "Since the shooting I did an online background check on the lovely Marie Ruggiero. Wanna guess who her uncle is?"

"No idea."

"James fucking Catalano."

O'Meara's eyebrows shot upward. "Jesus Christ."

"That's just half of it," I said. "Get this. Maria's father, Vince Ruggerio, had a sister. Take a shot at who she married?"

"Who?"

"A guy by the name of . . . Carmine Corsito."

O'Meara made a whistling sound by sucking air through his front teeth.

"You . . . you mean it's . . . it's Chris's . . . "

"Yep. Chris's father. Marie is Chris's first cousin."

O'Meara aggressively scratched the back of his neck as if he had an intense itch.

"Quite the tangled web," he said.

"Back when Chris was being investigated by the NCAA for recruiting violations at Carolina, I'm guessing it was Marie who called Uncle Jimmy and had him pull strings to get Corsito another job—the job, of course, being St. Stephen's—for, I might add, a helluva lot more money." I paused, took a breath. "Of course, I assume Jimmy made sure Dave and Marie were also taken care of. By that, I mean Corsito hiring Dave at St. Steve's."

"This is nuttier than a Hitchcock movie."

"It's a family affair," I said. "A very dysfunctional incestuous family affair."

"Makes the Rupert Murdoch clan seem like The Osmonds."

"Justice does prevail," I said.

"Not always."

"But it has in this case," I said, thinking how closing an investigation like Teddy Malone is what keeps me going.

"Yes, it has."

O'Meara's smile was brighter than a magnesium flash. He grabbed another cashew and popped it into his mouth.

"I'll let you know when we apprehend the Hunters," he said.

"Please do."

"Until then, we're going to keep much of what we know under wraps," he said. "Anything else I should know about?"

I told O'Meara about the letter Kenny Atkin's mother had sent to Mitchell Benchley.

"Are you're telling me that not only the university president, but also Corsito knew Hunter was a perv?" O'Meara said.

"And let's not forget about the athletic director, Kent Small, and the school's psychologist, Regina Blake."

O'Meara pressed bunched fingers and a thumb to the bridge of his nose.

"Guess I'll have to bring Corsito in for questioning," O'Meara said.

"He'll deny knowing anything about Hunter or the letter to Benchley."

"We'll question Benchley as well, along with Small and Blake. New York is a mandatory reporting state. Even if they deny, we can make trouble. Can I have the Atkins letter?"

"Not yet."

"Whaddya mean not yet? It's evidence."

"I just need it another day."

"What for?"

"Can't tell you. You're just going to have to trust me."

O'Meara reached for a cashew but didn't pick one out.

"Against my better judgment," he said, "I'll give you twenty-four hours. Then I need the letter. Am I clear?

"Crystal."

I stood and extended my hand.

"Thanks, Bill," I said.

We shook.

"Tell me," he said, still gripping my hand and putting his other on my shoulder. "How's Monique?"

"She's coming along," I said. "I'm heading over to see her next."

"God be with her."

"I think she'd prefer to be with me."

CHAPTER FORTY-FOUR

Dr. Kaplan, wearing a white coat, black clogs, and stethoscope, met me in the lobby of St. Mary's.

"She's doing great," he said, grinning. "She's on pain medication and she'll have some dietary restrictions for a while and might need follow-up surgery if there are any complications or to remove scar tissue, but overall, she'll be fine. In time."

I gave a sigh of relief.

"Can I see her?" I said.

"You can."

My heart hurdled.

We took an elevator up to the intensive care unit. It smelled of ammonia and disinfectant.

I walked into Monique's room. She was in a gown and lying in bed, still hooked up to an IV. Above her head, monitors were beeping.

She looked at me and smiled. It was as bright as sunlight coming up on a dark morning.

I grabbed her hand, leaned down and kissed her forehead.

"Hey, gorgeous," I said. "How are you feeling?"

"I've felt better."

"I'm sure you have," I said. "You look good."

"Liar, liar, pants on fire."

"Seriously," I said, "You look great, given the circumstances."

She shifted. Grimaced.

"You, on the other hand, look like hell," she said. "Nice shiner. What happened?"

"Got hit with a pool cue."

She gave me a funny look.

I pulled over a chair and sat beside her bed.

"Think I'll leave you two alone," Kaplan said. He then smiled at Monique. "Glad you're doing so well."

"Thanks to you," she said.

Kaplan patted my shoulder.

"Be seeing you, Elgin," he said.

"When can she be released?" I asked.

"A nurse should be coming by shortly to move her into a private room," he said. "If all systems are good, and there are no complications or infection, she can be out of here by next week. She's very, very lucky."

I nodded and thanked him.

Kaplan left.

I squeezed Monique's hand tighter and kissed her on the lips.

"You've had quite the ordeal," I said.

"At least now if I ever get a role as a dying patient, I'll know how to play the part."

"Typical actress," I said. "Always thinking of their next role."

Monique reached over and gently touched my shiner.

"Tell me," she said, "How are *you* doing?"

"Now that I'm with you, I'm doing great."

"You sure don't look it. Aside from your battered face, you look exhausted."

"I am."

"That bullet wasn't meant for me, was it?"

I shook my head.

"It was intended for you," she said.

I nodded.

She adjusted her pillow. Her face crunched. Seeing her look of pain tore at my insides.

"God, how I wish you would quit this job," she said. Her words were less a statement and more of a plea.

"We can talk about that when you get home."

"Please," she said. "It's important."

"I know."

"Do you?"

I nodded.

"Why can't you just let this business of finding murderers go?"

Thinking of my father, I swallowed and said, "because the business won't let go of me."

There was a momentary silence. Only noise came from the beeping monitors.

Monique said, "Did you find who killed Teddy Malone?"

"I did."

"Who was it?"

I gave her a thumbnail, told her how it was Marie Hunter who had hired Walter Wilson.

"You're kidding me?" she said. "Hunter's wife was behind all this?"

"Yep."

"And was it Wilson who shot me?"

"It was."

I decided not to get into how Marie was Corsito's cousin. Information overload.

"You owe me, big boy."

"For what?" If nothing else, I'm good at playing dumb.

"For what? For what? I took a bullet meant for you."

"How can I ever repay you?"

She put a finger to her lips.

"Let's see," she said, contemplating. "You could buy me dinner at Carbone's."

"I can."

"Or you could take me to Bermuda."

"I can."

Taking the finger down from her lips, she said, "Or, better still, you could buy me a Birkin bag."

"Whoa, Nelly," I said, raising a hand. "You know how much one of those Hermes bags cost?"

"I do," she said. "It's the least you could do . . . considering what I did for you."

"You drive a hard bargain," I said. "But you've earned it."

A young nurse entered the room.

"You look tired," she said to Monique. "You should rest."

The nurse checked Monique's vitals. All good.

"You'll be back dancing on the stage in no time," the nurse said.

"I hope so," Monique said.

I stood, leaned down and once again kissed Monique.

"Love you," I said.

"Right back at you."

"You know something," I said.

"What's that?"

"In this world of very special people, I'm glad there is you."

"Ah, Chet Baker."

"I should have sung it."

"Thank God you didn't. That would have really caused me pain."

"Still the sassy lassie."

"You expect me to be any different?"

"No. And I wouldn't want you to be."

Monique winked.

"Did Corsito know about Hunter?" she said.

"He knew."

"Then do me a favor."

"Certainly."

"Get him. At least then I'll know all this was not for nothing."

"Your wish, my command."

"One last question," she said.

"Which is?"

"You ever going to tell me how you really got that shiner?"

CHAPTER
FORTY-FIVE

I went home, feeling like a wave of exhaustion had finally washed over me. I felt calm. Relaxed. For the first time in days, I was able to get a good night's sleep.

The next morning my phone rang almost a minute after I woke up. It was O'Meara.

"How's Monique?"

"She's gonna be fine," I said. "She'll be released in a few days unless there are complications."

"Let's hope there's none."

"Yes, let's hope," I said. "What's up?"

"Turn on the television," he said. "Tongues are wagging. Channel Seven."

"Why?"

"Don't ask any questions. Just do it. Talk later. Bye."

I reached over, grabbed the remote, and clicked on Channel Seven Eyewitness News.

Standing outside the St. Stephen's Arena where hundreds of fans had gathered, reporter Josh Clayton was talking "And right now we are waiting to hear from coach Chris Corsito. Dave Hunter, Corsito's longtime assistant, is wanted for questioning by the police. He has been accused of not only molesting players but is now suspected of hiring former St. Joseph star Walter Wilson to shoot Teddy Malone and Monique Montgomery. Corsito has often referred to Hunter as his best friend and right-hand man. Certainly, the two of them have been successful together, winning two NCAA championships at the University of Carolina."

The face of studio anchor Bob Roberts appeared on a spilt screen.

"Josh," Roberts said. "Have you spoken with Coach Corsito?"

"Not yet. He's expected to address the media soon."

"How about the athletic director, Kent Small?"

"Small has been unavailable for comment."

"Is he on campus?

"Nobody knows where he is." Typical athletic director. When the going gets tough, the AD runs away.

"What about President Benchley?" Roberts said. "Has he made any comments?"

"Just a written statement saying that he's shocked by the allegations against Hunter and will immediately request an investigation."

"There's been an allegation that the school psychologist, Regina Blake, was aware of Hunter's activities. Do you know anything about that?"

"All we know is that late last night Ms. Blake resigned her position."

"I understand there have been calls in the media for Corsito to resign. What can you tell us?"

"Yes, there have been some calls for him to resign. But if my cameraman can pan to my right, you'll see there's hundreds and hundreds of students and fans here supporting Corsito."

The camera then showed hundreds of fans holding signs saying "We Love Corsito" and "Corsito Is Great." As soon as they saw the camera, everyone started cheering and hooting. A bunch of shirtless fraternity bros flexed before the camera, each with a letter painted on their chest spelling out C-O-R-S-I-T-O. Dumbnuts.

"Okay Bob," Clayton said. "Back to you in the studio."

Roberts's face filled the screen.

"Now to the war in Ukraine," he said. "Ukraine appears to be ramping up its counteroffensive after a pummeling a key Russian hub and claiming . . . " He stopped, touched his earpiece. "Oh, we have some breaking news from St. Stephen's University. Let's go back to our reporter on the scene, Josh Clayton. Josh, what do you have for us?"

"Coach Corsito is expected to appear momentarily," Clayton said.

Behind Clayton, viewers could hear fans chanting, "We love Corsito. We love Corsito."

"I see Coach Corsito is about to take the podium," Clayton said. "Let's listen."

The camera followed Corsito as he strutted up to a podium looking like a man with a chip on his shoulder the size of a California sequoia.

Wearing an open-collared white shirt, he had a large gold cross lying in his throat instead of his usual gold chain. He waved to the crowd like a politician at a rally, all his rough edges smooth and lacquered.

"Good afternoon, everyone," he said, smiling and silencing the crowd with a wave of his hand. "Thank you all for coming on such short notice. I have a few comments to make and perhaps answer some questions."

He pointed to someone in the crowd and gave the thumbs up sign. I had to laugh. Coaches like Corsito don't just make waves, they make a fucking typhoon.

"Let me start by saying Dave Hunter is one of the finest men I've ever had the pleasure to know," Corsito said. "He has given his time and his money to many charitable organizations. He has been honored by God knows how many businesses. He's a devoted husband to his wife, Marie, a wonderful father, and my best friend in the world."

Corsito paused. "Now let's me address the disgusting and despicable rumors surrounding Dave. They are totally and unequivocally untrue. Let me say that again, and you can underline it and tattoo on your forehead: totally and unequivocally untrue. What is happening here is a witch hunt. It's a smear campaign manufactured by the phony press. What's most upsetting is that David is being condemned as guilty before innocent. Shouldn't it be the other way around? I think so, and I'm sure when Dave returns from vacation he'll be vindicated. I also think that events that occurred years and years ago are being brought back up by discontented and malicious former players who wouldn't pay the necessary price to succeed and now see a payday at the end of the rainbow of lies. They should be ashamed of themselves and so should anyone who falls for such"—he paused for effect—"fairy tales."

He fell silent for a minute, head bowed as if in prayer, hands clasped. Loud cheers erupted from the crowd surrounding him.

"Okay," he said. "I'll take a few questions.

He pointed to Clayton.

"Coach," Clayton said. "Why do you think players are making these accusations? What's their motivation?"

"That's an easy one," he said, smirking. "They're doing it for money. I mean, what other reason could there be? Mark my words, they'll get some unscrupulous lawyers who will try to sue the school for millions of dollars. Book it."

Corsito pointed to another reporter.

The reporter asked, "What do you think of your former player, Walter Wilson, allegedly saying he was paid to kill Teddy Malone and Elgin O'Brien?"

Corsito listened. You could tell he wasn't happy with the questions. He was clearly hearing the words but no doubt envisioning vultures.

"As we all know, Walter has had a rough time," Corsito said. "As I understand it, he's a gangster, and probably a drug addict, who since leaving St. Stephen's has been in jail for more things than I can remember. He's a perpetual liar who will say anything to stay out of jail except the truth. Next question."

"Why would he lie about Hunter?" the reporter said.

"Because he's a liar," Corsito answered.

Corsito then pointed to a young, female reporter.

"Yes, young lady," he said, grinning widely. "Your question."

"I'm curious," she said. "Why would Hunter allegedly pay Wilson to shoot former NBA star, Elgin O'Brien. Can you comment on that?"

Corsito gave a malicious snort.

"First of all," he said, "it's a mistake to categorize O'Brien as a star player . . . "

"He did make the NBA all-star team twice," she said.

"How that happened is laughable," Corsito replied.

The crowd cheered wildly.

"What's your feelings about the shooting of Monique Montgomery?" she asked.

"Who?" Corsito said.

"The Broadway actress. O'Brien's girlfriend."

"Right, right," Corsito said. "I heard about that. Anytime somebody is senselessly shot my thoughts and prayers go out to their family."

Again applause.

"One last question," Corsito said.

He pointed to Mike Thomas of the *New York Post*.

"This should be an interesting question, for as we all know Mike writes for that rag called the *Post*," Corsito said. "They don't cover sports. They cover scandals. Personally, I use the newspaper to light my fireplace. So, Mike, let's hear your negative question."

"My question is a simple one . . ." Mike said.

"Not surprising coming from a simple man," Corsito said, flashing a big smile.

"It's my understanding that Elgin O'Brien has a letter from the mother of a former player Hunter molested that was sent to the university's president, Mitchell Benchley," Mike said,

"So?" Corsito said.

"So your president wrote back saying he spoke with you about Hunter's behavior. Is that true?"

"Is what true?"

"Did Benchley address the accusation with you?'

"No. No, he did not."

"Never?" Mike said.

"Did you not hear my answer?"

"Are you saying the president lied?"

"What I'm saying is—ask him."

"One last question."

"Thank God."

"A reliable source . . . "

"Didn't think the *Post* used reliable sources, Mike."

"I'm told Marie Hunter, your cousin, may also be implicated in this scenario. Is that true?"

"I'll tell you what's true," Corsito shouted. "This press conference is over."

Corsito stepped back from the podium. The crowd roared and applauded. He lifted both his arms and flashed the signature "V" sign he often gave after winning a big game.

I watched him and thought: In all my years in sports, I never met a coach who always needed a close-up on the soundstage of life.

Josh Clayton was back on the screen.

"There you have it," Clayton said. "Coach Chris Corsito is standing firmly behind assistant coach Dave Hunter. He's making the case that the accusers are making these accusations for money and that Walter Wilson, his former player, is a drug addict who lies."

Bob Roberts now appeared on the spilt screen.

"You think there's any chance Corsito might get fired?" Roberts asked.

"The only way that would happen is if overwhelming evidence is presented that Corsito knew about and was covering for Hunter," Clayton said. "The odds of that happening are slim and none. This is Josh Clayton reporting for ABC Channel Seven Eyewitness News from the now scandal-ridden campus of St. Stephen's University. Back to you, Bob."

Roberts turned to his co-anchor and said, "This is a very troubling situation."

His partner, a young, attractive Black woman in her forties, said, "It is, Bob. Anytime you're talking about molestation and sexual assault it makes you cringe."

"Well," Roberts said. "Corsito has been in trouble before, and he's always escaped punishment. We'll see what happens now."

Yes, I thought, we sure as hell will. I turned off the TV.

CHAPTER
FORTY-SIX

My phone rang. I figured it was O'Meara and didn't check the number. It wasn't.

"Is this Elgin O'Brien?" It was a voice I hadn't heard before. Deep and rich.

"Yes."

"My name is Peter Dunne."

"Yes."

"I've been reading about you in the papers," he said.

"Don't believe everything you read."

"Usually I don't," he said, "but in this case I do."

"Have we met?"

"No."

"What can I do for you?"

"It's what I can do for you."

"What's that?"

"Provide you with something."

"Regarding?"

"David Hunter."

"What is it?"

"Enough to put him in jail. I guarantee it."

So far, the guy sounded legit, and the cops needed more evidence to charge Hunter. I was willing to hear him out.

"We need to talk," Dunne said.

"I'm listening."

"Face-to-face."

"Okay. You know Pete's Tavern?" I said, thinking it best to pick a public place, neutral ground, just in case. I mean, I didn't know this guy from a hole in the wall. He could easily be a "friend" of Catalano's luring me out with some phony story.

"In Gramercy Park?" Dunne said.

"Yeah."

"Can you meet me there in, say, an hour?"

"I'll be there."

The minute I hung up, my cell phone rang again.

This time it was O'Meara.

"You watch Corsito?" he said.

"I did. Typical phony performance."

"He sounds believable. Always does."

"That's his gift," I said. "He should have been a politician."

"Got news for you."

"Shoot."

"We got him." he said.

"Hunter?"

"Yep."

"Where?"

"A palatial home in . . . Palm Beach, Florida. Guess who owns it?"

"James Catalano."

"Bingo."

"Was Marie there?"

"No. We're still looking for her."

"She could be in Europe with Catalano."

"What makes you say that?"

"His secretary said that's where he was."

"We'll check it out," he said. "If all goes well, we'll have Hunter transported up here tomorrow."

"Then what?"

"He'll be questioned and booked."

"Followed by a hearing?"

"I've spoken to the Leonard kid, and he's agreed to testify against Hunter. Between his testimony and Kenny Atkins' testimony, we should have enough to convince the DA to charge Hunter with assault. It'd be nice if more kids came forth."

"I'll see what I can do. Is Wilson at Rikers?"

"The infirmary, at least until some scumbag attorney gets him out on bail."

"Is that possible?"

"Sadly, it is."

"Know what bothers me?"

"The Kardashians?"

"Aside from them," I said, "everybody is going to be held accountable except . . . Chris Corsito."

"That's because we got nothing directly implicating him . . . to a cover-up. Or the shootings."

"I can't stomach the idea of him once again escaping punishment."

"Then get me some evidence and I'll nail his ass."

"I may have something," I said, thinking and hoping that whatever Dunne had to show me was actionable.

"Whaddya got?"

"I'll know soon."

"I suggest you hurry. And don't forget. I need the Atkins letter."

"I'll have it for you tomorrow.

"Why not today?"

"You're pushy, you know that?"

"That's what my wife says. Talk soon."

I hung up, strapped on my shoulder holster, and then went outside and got into the Mustang.

Pete's Tavern is the oldest operating bar in New York City. Opened in 1864, it has brick walls, wood tables, sawdust floors, and Guinness on tap.

I liked the place because aside from its ambiance—brick walls, checkered tile flooring, old black-and-white photos—it had a literary history. The author O. Henry, who lived down the street on Irving Place, wrote his famous work "Gift of the Magi" there. Being a fan of O. Henry's short stories, I always hoped I'd see the ghost of him sitting at a table, dipping his quilled pen into an ink bottle, and scribbling away.

I slid into a booth across from the bar and immediately a waitress wearing a white apron around her waist approached. She was young, probably a college kid, with skin pink as Spam and hair as yellow as a banana. It was pulled back in a ponytail.

"What can I get you?" she asked. She had a thick, Irish accent.

"A Guinness."

"You got it."

Somebody had left behind a copy of the *New York Post* on the seat. I picked it up and read the front page. There was a picture of Hunter with a headline above it that read, disgustingly, "The Back Door Man."

You could always count on the *Post* to write a catchy headline. I still chuckle at "Headless body in topless bar."

I flipped to the story inside. It was written by my friend Mike Thomas. It was factual and accurate.

Also in the paper were pictures of Monique from different Broadway shows. I looked at them, then put the paper aside.

The waitress returned and put down the pint of Guinness. I took a big sip.

"Anything else?" she said.

"Not for the moment."

She left.

The front door opened, and a big guy entered. Bearded and bald, he was wearing blue jeans and a yellow linen shirt. Hanging off his right shoulder was a canvas bag.

He came directly to my table.

"O'Brien?" he said.

"Yep."

He slid into the booth. I studied his body for a hidden gun, just in case. He didn't seem to have one.

"Thank you for meeting me," he said.

"My pleasure," I said. "Care for something to drink?"

"Think I will. It's hot out there."

"Hell on earth."

I signaled the waitress. She came over and asked Dunne what he wanted.

He looked at me and said, "What are you having?"

"Guinness."

He smiled at her and said, "I'll have the same."

"I love Guinness," I said. "In Ireland they call it the cure."

"Cure for what?"

"Everything that ails ya."

The waitress brought Dunne's drink. He took a sip and said, "Aah. That's nice."

I nodded.

"I congratulate you on outing Hunter," he said, after wiping some foam from his lip.

"It's long overdue."

"Yes, it is."

"What I need now is proof that Corsito knew about Dave."

"That's why I'm here," he said. "I think I can help."

"Whaddya got?"

"A tape."

"Of?"

"My son . . . with Hunter."

My mouth dropped.

"What's your son's name?"

"Eddie."

"How old was Eddie at the time?"

"Eighteen. A freshman in college."

"What college?"

"University of Carolina."

"My rival."

He grinned.

"I forgot," he said. "You played at Duke, right?"

"I did."

"Great school."

"Was Eddie a basketball player?"

"Yes. He went to Power Memorial here in the city before going to Carolina to play for Corsito."

"And Hunter was his assistant?

"Yes, he was. Also recruited him. Almost lived at our house Eddie's senior year."

I took a sip of beer.

"It was Corsito's first year at Carolina," Dunne said.

"Okay," I said. "Tell me what you got?"

"I'll get right to the chase. One night Eddie came home and told me Hunter told him his wife was out of town and invited him to his apartment for pizza. He said he was going to show him some game films, which he did, pointing out what he needed to do to be a starter and a possible NBA prospect. The typical bullshit. But as the night progressed, Hunter started feeding him booze and put on some porno. Midway through the film, Hunter pulled his dick out and told Eddie to suck it if he wanted to be a star."

"How'd Eddie react?"

Dunne picked up his glass. He took a big gulp, draining his drink.

"You gotta understand," Dunne said, "Eddie thought that everything he ever wanted was on the table, all his dreams. He was drunk and . . . and, well he ended up doing it."

My chin sank to my chest. The audacity of some college coaches. They think because they have power, they can take advantage of vulnerable kids. No different than priests.

The waitress came by.

"Can I get you guys anything to eat?" she said.

Neither of us had an appetite. We both said no.

I pointed to Dunne's glass.

"Want another?" I said.

"More like I need another," he said.

I ordered two more drinks.

"Eddie was devastated," Dunne continued. "He adored Hunter who, to be fair, had put in a lot of time helping Eddie refine his game. I think they call that 'grooming.' "

"Did you register a complaint with the school? Call the cops."

"I wanted to, but Eddie pleaded with me not to," he said, shaking his head. "So . . . I didn't."

I squeezed a napkin.

Dunne expelled a long breath that seemed to leave him depleted.

"Just so you know," he said, "I'm a video technician. Mostly freelance, industrial shoots, and I've done surveillance for private dicks—er, investigators like you." He paused and grinned. "I even did some jobs back in the day for your old boss . . . Sid Meyer."

"Really?" I said, getting a quick flashback of Sid. If Sid engaged Dunne to do work for him, then Dunne had to be good. Damn good. Sid only hired the best. "Small world."

"Ain't it?" Dunne said. "Anyway, after what happened to Eddie, I wanted to go and kick Hunter's ass but Eddie, who was so ashamed, begged me to leave what happened alone. But, or course, I wouldn't."

He got quiet for a moment. A long moment.

"Please continue," I said.

"I concocted this plan," he said. "I . . . "

The waitress returned with our beers. Dunne quickly took a sip, then heaved a slow, ample sigh.

"Go on," I said.

"At the time, Eddie was living off campus with two other guys who were hardly ever there because they were always shacking up with their girlfriends. I went down to North Carolina with a bunch of equipment and convinced Eddie to let me rig up this video recorder in his living room."

"To do what?"

"I know this sounds crazy, but to invite Hunter over and hope he'd make another play on Eddie."

"Risky."

"Very. But I told Eddie that if we didn't do something about Hunter, he'd probably never leave him alone and possibly pull his stunt with other players."

"Let me get this straight," I said. "Eddie agreed to this?"

"He did. Reluctantly. Very reluctantly."

"Wow. Okay. What happened?"

"After practice one day, Eddie told Hunter his friends were out of town and he invited Hunter to stop by. Needless to say, Hunter was thrilled. I was outside, just in case. Anyway, Hunter shows up and after having a beer, Hunter pulls out his laptop and suggests he and Eddie watch a video. The film was of two guys making it. At some point, Hunter unzips his pants and tells Eddie to go down on him. This time Eddie says no. Hunter grabs him by the neck and tries to push Eddie's head down. Eddie runs out of the house. But get this . . . Hunter doesn't leave. He stays and starts jerking off. That's where I come in. I was listening to everything from my van."

I was almost in disbelief of the story. But if I'd learned anything in my career as a detective it's that people do the strangest things. Especially when it comes to revenge.

"When Eddie left the house, he ran to my van. I then went inside and confronted Hunter. Well . . . more than confronted him. I caught the sick bastard with his pants down around his ankles and I slapped the shit out of him. He ran outta the apartment still zipping up his fly."

"Then what happened?"

"The next day I called Corsito and told him what transpired."

"What Corsito say?"

"He said I was full of shit. To which I said come to my hotel and watch the video."

"He said no. He wanted me to bring it to his office. I said not a chance. We bickered. Finally, he agreed."

"Why were you so adamant about him going to your hotel?"

"I wanted to tape his response."

"Good thinking."

"I thought so."

We both drank at the same time.

"So Corsito comes to my hotel room," Dunne said. "I show him the video. He freaks. He says it's all a big mistake, a misunderstanding, that my son was gay and Hunter had been counseling him and my boy had come on to Hunter, that Hunter was as much a victim as my son. I laugh in his face. He then says he knew Hunter had a problem with 'boundaries,' but he'd make sure something like that would never happen again. He then tells me that we should work something out. He said that if the tape got out it would ruin his career. He offered to make, what'd he called 'restitution.' "

"What kind of restitution?"

"Cash money."

"What did you say?"

"I said I'd talk to my wife and Eddie."

"How much was he offering you?"

"I'll get to that," he said.

"This is one wild story."

"Yes, it is."

"And you have all this on video?"

"I do."

"Mother mercy."

"Anyway, a few days after I met with Corsito, before I went back to New York, I was visited at the hotel by two men representing him. They offered me two hundred thousand dollars cash. At the time I was barely making fifty grand a year. I wasn't sure I wanted to take the money, but my wife and Eddie convinced me to do otherwise . . . largely because of my wife's condition—she had all these autoimmune diseases. So . . . I took the deal."

He cringed and looked away. Seemed crestfallen with guilt. He brought one hand up and rubbed his face. He kept it over his eyes when he spoke. "Am I proud of myself for taking it? Not in the least. But I justified it under the guise of my family getting what they deserved."

"Did you video the money men as well?" I said.

"Sure did," he said, taking his hand from his face.

"Did these men ask for the tape?"

"They did. And remember, this was years ago. I had it on cassette."

"You give it to them?"

"I did."

"What then do you have for me?"

"The original."

"The original?"

"Yeah."

"I figured you gave them the original."

"You figure wrong," he said. "What I gave them was a copy."

"Did they ask you if *you* had a copy?"

"Of course, they asked."

"And what did you say?"

"I said I didn't because I didn't. I had the original."

"And they believed you?" I said, stupefied that anyone could be so dumb.

"Obviously, they did."

"Whoa . . . whoa . . . whoa . . . time-out," I said. "Why'd you keep the original?"

"In case I ever had to go to court," he said. "Copies usually aren't admissible. Sid taught me that."

I put a hand on my head.

"Holy shit," I said.

Dunne finished his beer.

"Eddie is married now, has two boys," he said. "He's had a lot of therapy. A lot. Ate up most of the money. He has told his family about what happened, and they understand."

"Why bring this out now?" I said.

"Simple. Eddie read the stories in the paper about Hunter molesting those kids and he wants him punished."

Dunne opened his shoulder bag, took out a small box and handed it to me.

"Time stamped and everything," he said. "It's high-quality, still good. It's yours."

"In return for what?"

"Nothing."

"Nothing?"

"I just told you. We gotta put a stop to these pedophile coaches."

I took a long look at the tape in my hand.

Holding it up, I said, "Is this the original?"

"No."

"No?"

"It's a copy," he said. "I thought it best if I kept the orig-inal. See, when this happened, I even taped myself making the copies, one for me, and one for the money men. I marked them both, then sealed the original in a box and sent it to myself via registered mail." He grinned. "It's another trick Sid taught me."

"For what reason?"

"For the cops . . . someday."

"Where's the original now?"

"In a safety deposit box. Still sealed."

"Good thinking. Smart."

Dunne nodded.

"I so appreciate you giving me this tape," I said. "You sure there's nothing I can do for you?"

"Not a thing," he said. "Just use it as you see fit."

"Even if it exposes and embarrasses you and your son?"

"Even if it exposes and embarrasses us."

Dunne stood and shook my hand.

"Thank you for your time," he said.

"No," I said. "Thank you."

Dunne left.

I sat for a while, staring at the tape. I finished my beer and thought of something Sid Meyer often said to me. He said, "No matter how much time and energy you put in on a case sometimes the whole thing turns on a bit of luck." Thanks to Dunne, I just got lucky.

I signaled for the check. The waitress waved me off. On his way out, Dunne had picked up the tab.

CHAPTER FORTY-SEVEN

I immediately drove home and took out my old Sony VHS recorder, the one that Monique always called "the dinosaur." I kept it around to watch some old movies that never came out on DVD or streamed. I viewed Dunne's tape. Carefully. The picture and sound were clear. Everything he told me was there. Conclusive evidence. Corsito knew. That slimy sonofabitch.

I called Corsito's office. His secretary Anne answered.

I gave her my name. The line immediately went dead.

I quickly left the house. It was brutally hot and blindingly bright. The glare that came off the hoods and windows of cars damn near burned my retina.

I got in the Mustang and drove to Corsito's home in Kew Gardens. I knew where it was because he had invited me to a Christmas party there many years ago. Why he invited me I still have no idea. Probably just to show me how big his house was.

It was monstrous, Scarlett O'Hara's mansion on steroids. The grass was better manicured than Wimbledon. The lawn had more flowers than Brooklyn's Botanical Garden. There was a long gravel driveway and white Doric columns. The roof was steeply pitched, the windows leaded glass, the chimney red brick.

I walked up a flagstone path flanked by rose bushes. The front door had a brass knocker with a lion holding a ring in its mouth. It struck me as the perfect metaphor for Corsito.

I rang the doorbell. An attractive woman who looked like a 1970s Miss America contestant opened the door. She had heavily sprayed bleached blond hair and big, brown eyes. Her face was powdered like a geisha and her forehead was unnaturally smooth. Botox. She had a slim waist and large breasts. Countless diamond bracelets and diamond rings. Lady Gaga would have been envious.

"Hello, Betty," I said.

As the expression goes, if looks could kill . . .

"What do you want?" she said. There was a hardness to her voice that matched the hardness in her face. She was fashioning white tennis shorts and a green-sequined blouse. Not exactly the kind of blouse you wear on the court.

"Is Chris here?" I said.

"You got some nerve showing your face here," she said, her voice sharper than a saber sword.

Before I could respond, Betty added, "Why are you doing this?"

Betty, it was said, protected Chris the way a bodyguard protects a Mafia chief. Even slight criticism sets her off.

Once as a joke, a reporter wrote that one winter's night in bed, Betty said, "God, your feet are ice cold" to which Chris replied, "When we're home, honey, you can call me Chris."

Betty had a shit fit. She demanded the reporter be fired. He wasn't. But she never stopped trying to get him axed.

"Tell me," I said. "What exactly am I doing?"

"Trying to destroy Chris. And Dave and Marie."

"I . . . "

"Chris has told me how jealous you are of his success and what he's achieved. You're nothing more than a cheap detective."

"I'm not cheap," I said. "I spend money pretty freely."

Her face squeezed tight. In the distance, I heard a church bell. Probably a funeral mass.

"You think you're funny, don't you?" she said.

"At times."

"Well, let me tell you something mister jokester," she said, her voice getting louder and louder. "There's not a chance in hell you're going to destroy Chris' career. Chris is a great coach and a great man. He is adored by the fans, by the school, by the alumni, by the entire St. Stephen's faculty. The basketball world loves him."

"By your measure," I said. "He probably should be canonized."

She scoffed. Behind her I could see into the large living room. Everything was green and gold. The color of money.

"Don't you care that your husband protected a child molester?" I said.

"Dave is no more a child molester than I am," she said. "Poor Marie is sitting in my kitchen right now. The girl has been crying her eyes out for hours. She's absolutely devastated. All these allegations come from spoiled brats looking to make a quick buck."

"That's not true."

"It sure as hell is. And let me tell you, we're not giving up without a fight."

"I wouldn't expect anything less."

"We've already hired some killer criminal defense attorneys. They're not only going to exonerate Chris, Dave, and

Marie . . . but we're also going to sue your ass and make damn sure your license gets revoked."

"Happy hunting."

Betty lifted her hand as if she was going to slap my face. But she didn't. She just screamed at the top of her lungs, "STOP THIS! FOR THE LOVE OF GOD, STOP THIS! HAVEN'T YOU HURT CHRIS ENOUGH! ENOUGH ALREADY! ENOUGH!"

I had no response.

"I want you off my property," she said, her face swollen and red. "Or else I'll have you arrested."

"Fine," I said. "By the way, tell your buddy Marie the police are looking for her."

Just then Marie appeared, standing aside Betty.

"Let 'em fucking look," she said. Her voice was cruel and hard. Ugly.

Marie had the same plastic look as Betty, only her hair and skin was darker. She was wearing a too tight and too short black dress and four-inch pumps. Her eyes were the same as Walter Wilson's: empty and soulless. And they sure didn't look like she'd been crying.

"Don't think you're gonna get away with this shit," she said, her fists closed tight.

"What shit?"

"Your fucking lies!" she yelled. "You're going down, buster. Down, down, down."

"As per Uncle Jimmy?"

She pointed a finger at me. Her fingers were long and spindly like the Wicked Witch in *The Wizard of Oz*. On her fourth finger was a diamond ring the size of a golf ball. Bet that cost old Hunter a pretty penny.

"My uncle will do whatever I ask him to do," she said.

"What? Shoot me?"

She smiled. Teeth like a crocodile.

"Trust me, honey," she said, "someday they'll be a knock at your door . . . "

"You're amazing, Marie," I said. "You make Catherine de Medici looked like a pussycat."

"Don't compare me to some cheesy Italian broad from Jersey."

Marie tried to move a step closer to me, but Betty put her arm out like a semaphore and stopped her.

I gave Betty a quick look. When I did, Marie spit on my shoes. Classy.

Betty then shut the door with the slow deliberate care of someone closing a coffin lid.

I got into the Mustang and was just about to start it when I noticed the door to Corsito's garage was open. To the right of a sleek blue Mercedes sport car was a line of golf bags. I remembered that Corsito was a golfing fanatic. It was often said that if he wasn't on a basketball court, he was on the golf course.

I knew from reading the papers that he played at the prestigious Jamaica Hills Country Club, an exclusive resort where the initiation fee started at $150,000 and the annual dues were $20,000. Supposedly, Corsito was given a freebie to attract boosters who would pay full fare just to play a few rounds with him. Hero worship.

I drove to the club, stopped at the main entrance and was immediately greeted by a young valet dressed in a bright white uniform.

"Afternoon, sir," he said, opening my door.

"Afternoon," I said, still in my seat.

"Love your Mustang," he said. "What year is it?"

"1989."

"Nice. Must be worth a fortune."

"Must be," I said. "Is Coach Corsito here?"

"If it's Saturday and it's off-season and the weather's good, he's here."

"I take it he's here," I said. "Has he been here long?"

"Might just be teeing off."

I got out of the car and walked into the clubhouse. Wide planked floors, white wicker furniture. There was a gift shop and a dining room. On the walls were colorful photos of Tiger Woods and Phil Michelson and Jon Rahm. I was very proud that I never belonged to a country club nor ever would. Too hotsy-totsy for this Harlem kid.

I walked to the attendant—fifty, short hair, golden tan—who was guarding the door leading to the course. He regarded me like something stuck to the bottom of his shoe. Guess I didn't look like the country club type. Thank God.

"What can I do for you?" he said in a synthetically snobby voice.

"I'm looking for Coach Corsito," I said.

"May I ask what this is about?"

"It's a very personal matter," I said. "And very important."

Probably afraid to risk dealing with Corsito's ire, he said, "Coach just teed off."

I wiped imaginary sweat off my forehead.

"Whew! Got here just in time," I said.

"Well, I'm not supposed to allow nonmembers on the course," he said, "but since it's for Coach Corsito . . . " He pointed to French doors. "Go right through there."

I went through the doors and headed toward where Corsito, along with three other guys, were on the putting green, studying the balls.

When I got within ten yards of the green, I shouted, "Hey, Chris!"

Corsito, wearing white pants and blue polo shirt, was bent over in a putter's stance, practicing his swing. He turned and froze.

I continued walking toward him. Around me birds swooped and squealed. It sounded as if they were making a distress call.

Corsito's three buddies immediately blocked my path.

"Get the fuck out of here," said a guy who had the face of a drunken scarecrow.

"Yeah," said another, "get lost." This dude had blotchy cheeks and runny eyes. "We don't want your type around here."

"What type is that?"

"Troublemaker."

I started to walk around them. Both men got in my face. So close I got a whiff of their breath. Smelled like pumpernickel. Probably from bourbon.

"Let the asshole through," Corsito said.

The men parted. I moved past them.

"Whaddya doing here?" Corsito said.

"We need to talk."

Corsito made a farting sound.

"Got nuthin' to say to you," he said, and started to walk away. I followed him.

"But I have something to say to you."

"There's nothing whatsoever you could say that would interest me."

"I know that *you* know Hunter is a pedophile."

"For Christ's sake, Elgin, give it up, willya? And keep your voice down."

"Sorry, Chris, I have proof."

"Proof, my ass. You ain't got shit."

I took a few seconds before speaking again.

"Dunne," I said in a soft voice that had all the weight of a hard shout.

"Done what?" he said, misinterpreting the word.

"Eddie Dunne," I said.

Corsito turned. His face was a mixture of anger and concern.

"What about Eddie Dunne?" he said, his voice low.

"His father came to see me."

"So what?"

"I'll tell you so what. He gave me a video of you admitting you knew Hunter was a molester."

"Bullshit!" he screamed.

His buddies raced to his side. Corsito waved them off.

"The video is quite damning," I said. "In fact, I'd go so far as to say your career's over."

He snorted. "Fuck you talking about? You can't end my career."

"I don't intend to. You're going to do it yourself."

Corsito exhaled a puff of pain. I got the sense that something was sinking in, moving him into a cold, frightened state. He paced back and forth like he was on the sidelines five points down and the clocking ticking.

"You want to talk about this here?" I said. "Or should I call the police?"

Corsito glared at me. Wiped a layer of sweat off his forehead. Flies and mosquitoes swarmed around him like tiny demons.

"Here," he said.

"Good. I suggest you put down your putter and follow me."

Corsito handed his putter to the scarecrow.

"There's been an emergency," Corsito said. "I gotta go."

He then turned to me and said under his breath, "You know if I want, I could have you killed."

"By calling Catalano?"

He smiled.

"Must be nice to have a rich, vicious lapdog."

"Comes in handy."

"To clean up you messes?"

"No. To eliminate them."

CHAPTER FORTY-EIGHT

We entered the dining room. It smelled of whiskey and beer. There were golfers sitting at various tables, sporting brightly colored Ralph Lauren shirts and slacks, their legs stretched out, ankles crossed, sipping cocktails. No doubt captains of industries.

Many of them waved to Corsito or shook his hand and offered some words of support. A few said what was happening to him was a disgrace and eyed me suspiciously. Corsito kept calling it "a witch hunt."

We took a table in a far corner, out of earshot.

"What exactly do you have?" Corsito snarled through gritted teeth.

"Eddie's father was a video expert. He rigged up a camera that shows not only Hunter with his pants down trying to molest his son, but also of you apologizing about his behavior."

Corsito put his head back and glanced at the ceiling. Pissed.

I said, "Then there's the footage of some Carolina alumni offering the father two hundred thousand bucks . . . in cash."

His head dropped and he grinned, the tip of his tongue appearing briefly, then quickly withdrawing with reptilian rapidity.

"I'm aware of all of this," he said in a strong voice. "But that tape was destroyed."

"Not the original."

He snorted. "We destroyed the original."

"What you destroyed was a copy," I said. "Dunne was no dummy. He kept the original."

For a moment, Corsito smoldered like a tree struck by lightning. His eyeballs smoked.

"Your millionaire friends were so stupid," I said, "they actually believed Dunne had given them the original."

Corsito leaned back in his chair, his scorched eyes fixed on me.

"Fuck you want?" he sneered.

"Excuse me?"

"How much?"

"How much what?"

"Money."

"You think I'm bribing you?"

"Why else would you be telling me this?"

"Because I got you by the balls."

"You think?" he said, his lips curling with scorn.

"I know."

"You know, do you?"

"Check."

Corsito suddenly started laughing like a loon, his eyes lighting up like candles on a birthday cake.

"You're so fucking delusional," he said. "Here's what's gonna happen. I assume you'll make the tape public, right?

I will go before the press and say the tape recorded by some player's father, a damn video expert, in order to blackmail me and swindle money—a couple hundred grand—from me. Since there's no check, he can't prove where or how he got the money. I'll also say that I did admit to Hunter's behavior but that I thought it was only a one-time thing and that he was drunk. I'll add that I spoke to Hunter, and he swore he'd never do it again, that he'd been molested as a child and has since undergone counseling and stopped drinking—Regina Blake will back me up on that. And as far as I knew, he never did anything else to any other kid until you came along and dragged up these baseless allegations from the past and gave everybody the idea they could make a big score. Trust me, Elgin, I'll beat this thing sure as I've beaten every other false allegation against me."

"What about the video showing the alumni guys offering him money?"

"I'll just say I knew nothing about that," he said, a diabolical grin on his face. "Who do you think the public will believe? Me or some dopey blackmailing video technician?"

I was silent. A tiny tremor corkscrewed in my bones. Corsito was doing what he did best: concocting a plan to get himself out of trouble.

He wasn't finished. "The worst—the worst—that will happen to me is I'll get fired. But the school, after we go to court, will wind up paying me millions in severance. Why? Because they knew all about Hunter the whole time and they'll want to cover their asses. What happens after that? Another college will hire me. Or I'll coach overseas for a year or two then come back to the states and get an even better job." He moved his hands as if adjusting levers. "If I know anything about college presidents and athletic directors it is that they will forgive anything as long as you win and make their school money. And I make schools money. Big money. Endowments have tripled since I came to St. Stephen's. And money talks, baby."

Corsito shut one eye and squinted with the other as if he were looking through the barrel of a gun.

"But I got an idea that might benefit us both," he said, his voice softening into conspiratorial hush.

"This should be good."

"Listen, I know I can beat this, but I'd rather not have any more bad publicity," he said, hunched forward like an eager salesman trying to strike a deal. "I got a team that can win a title next year and I sure as hell don't want a public scandal, if I can avoid it. So? How's this? I denounce Hunter, admit that I suspected him of molesting players but could never prove it. And then I'll throw him under the bus and say he admitted to hiring Wilson . . ."

I cut him off. "It wasn't Hunter who hired Wilson. It was . . . your cousin Marie."

He tried hard not to react. "Doesn't matter, I'll still say I knew nothing about her or the shooting. But I will say Hunter told me about it just before he took off to Florida. And I was so shocked, so distraught, so concerned it took me a day to process things. That I was all set to go to the police but then they arrested him."

He lifted his right index finger. "Here's the catch. All you gotta do is admit that you coerced these players into making false allegations. Why? Because you were jealous of my success. And I'd want all this in writing." He paused. Seemed pleased with himself. "So? What do you think?"

"I think you're fucking crazy."

"Not if I get you a million, even a few million, bucks." Another pause. Dramatic. "Cash," he added. "Cash."

I pursed my lips. Loud laughter exploded from golfers at a nearby table. I heard the clicking of glasses, the clanging of silverware.

"Look," he said, "Whaddya make a year?

"Over a hundred grand."

"How much you have in the bank?"

"Not much, but I own my place."

"Yeah, in fucking Hoboken. With a few million bucks you and your lady friend could live a life of luxury."

"We live pretty well now."

"But you could live larger."

"Larger isn't always better."

"From what I'm told, Monique hates what you do for a living. She'd give anything to see you quit, wouldn't she?"

You had to hand it to him. He knew, somehow, where I was most vulnerable.

Thinking of Monique in the hospital with a bullet meant for me, I said, "Suppose, just suppose, I did take the money. Isn't it going to look strange me suddenly coming into such a windfall?"

"Who the hell's going to care? Or know?"

"The IRS."

Corsito's fingers danced on his thighs. His eyes shifted back and forth like an oscillating pendulum.

"Got it," he said. "I'll have some alum buy your business."

"Buy my business?"

"Yeah. You could say you were tired of detective work and wanted to retire. Especially in light of what happened to your girlfriend."

I scratched my stumbled chin.

"You have existing contracts with some companies, right?" Corsito said.

"I do. Handling security."

Corsito shut his eyes and squeezed the bridge of his nose with a finger and thumb. After a minute, he beamed with confidence and said, "Your P&L will justify the money. It's untraceable anyway. You won't even have to report it."

I took a minute to digest his offer. I thought of Monique, how she hated and worried constantly about me getting hurt, even killed. I thought, too, about how keeping her safe was a dialogue I had in my head almost every day since I met her and almost every minute since she was shot. I don't think I could handle her ever getting hurt, never mind getting shot again . . . because of me.

In my mind's eye, I saw her lying in the hospital bed, virtually pleading with me to quit my job. After all she'd been through, how could I deny her request? How could I be so selfish? Isn't it more important to care about someone else rather than yourself?

That's what Monique's done for me. She's given me the greatest gift one person can bestow on another: a love of life and a life of love. Without Monique, my existence would be impoverished. Empty. Dark. I've often told O'Meara I'd rather face my own death than survive hers.

So . . . what if I quit? Hadn't I put enough bad people in jail to justify getting revenge for my father's murder? Hadn't I risked my life for people who sometimes failed to thank me or pay me? Isn't it a fact that as I've gotten older, the criminals have gotten more violent, more deranged, more ready to put a bullet in your head? Is that anyway to live?

The options riffled through my head like a deck of cards. If I left the detective business, I could start a new chapter in my life. I could become a security consultant. Or perhaps go back to school and get a master's degree in English. Teach. Write a novel. I did, after all, major in journalism at Duke.

I also pondered the reality of exposing Corsito, the Donald Trump of college basketball. Like Trump, he would take cover behind his power and no doubt find a way to beat the system. He always has and I suspect he always will, largely because he admits nothing and denies everything.

At the very least, Chris Corsito is a devious monster of evil genius. What fans don't understand about him is this: Yes, he cares about winning and losing. But the fact is what he *really* cares about is glorification.

And it's not just Corsito I was thinking about. It's gotten to the point now where most college coaches can get away with and be forgiven for almost any financial or sexual violations. As long as their team is winning big games and generating big money, the worst penalty they get is a slap on the wrist and a golden parachute.

I caught a reflection of Corsito and me in a mirrored beer sign hanging on the wall. Corsito was grinning, smug and satisfied. We looked like we were on the same team.

I suddenly wanted to vomit. FUCK HIM! Fuck him for making me even think about giving up a job I love and taking his dirty money. FUCK HIM!

I said, "Can I think about this?"

"Yeah, yeah, sure," he said. "You got one fucking minute." He licked his lips like a tiger ready to devour a deer.

I looked out onto the golf course. Foursomes. Carts. Soaring balls. I was happy I never took up the sport.

"Well?" Corsito said.

"I'm thinking."

"Time's up. I want your answer. We have a deal or not?"

"Okay," I said, forcing a smile. "I accept your offer. But I'll need a mil cash up front and a signed purchase agreement for the balance."

Corsito clapped his hands with the enthusiasm of a trained seal.

"Done," he said. "Where's the video?"

"At my house."

"The original?"

"Yeah."

"I want it today."

"Today?"

Corsito looked at his watch.

"I'd like to finish my round," he said.

"You can get the cash that fast?"

He chuckled.

"I know people who have resources," he said, snapping his fingers at a young waiter who sprinted over faster than Noah Lyles.

"Yes, Coach, what can I get for you?" He spoke with such reverence it was as if he were addressing the King of England.

"How about a Remy Martin XO Excellence," he said, grinning. "And put it in a Waterford snifter."

"Whatever you want, Coach," he enthused like a kid ga-ga over his favorite player. "You got it. You got it."

Corsito then pointed at me and said to the waiter, "While you at it, get one for my partner here as well."

Partner, my ass.

The waiter raced off as if his shoes were on fire. Less than a minute later, he was back with the snifters. He handed each of us a glass. Beaming, Corsito swirled his brandy and took a big gulp. I barely touched mine.

"Ah," Corsito said, holding the glass high and staring into it. "A winning drink for a victorious guy." He lowered the glass. "Where can I get the video and the letter?"

"How about we meet at my house," I said. "Say four o'clock."

"Fine. I'll be there."

"Okay. In case I'm on the phone or something I'll leave the front door unlocked. Just come on in."

Corsito drained his drink and licked his lips.

"I'll have everything ready," I said.

He slapped his palms on his knees, stood and said, "Damn right you will."

I glanced at an inspirational poster on the wall, a golfer ankle deep in a sand trap. Above him were the words "Play it where it lays." It made me think of something Arnold Palmer once said: "If you're in trouble, eighty percent of the time there's a way out." Words to live by.

Corsito said, "Let me assure you of one thing."

"What's that?"

"You do anything stupid and you're a dead man."

I didn't react. Didn't respond.

"And you know what else, Elg?" he said, flashing the kind of phony smile movie stars give on the red carpet, "You just confirmed to me something I always believed."

"What's that?"

"Anyone can be bought off."

Almost, I said to myself, almost.

CHAPTER
FORTY-NINE

I drove home, listening to CBS news. I was just about to turn the car off when the newscaster said, "In unrelated news today, Emma Mitchell, daughter of famed pianist, Michael Mitchell, was arrested this morning along with former hoop star Gary Grimes in a sting operation near the Baychester Middle School for selling drugs in a school zone. Both are currently being held in a Bronx detention center, although Mitchell is expected to make bail and be released later today."

Shaking my head, I thought: Such an odd couple to be doing such dirty work. Maybe some jail time will straighten their crooked lives out. Then again, I doubted it.

I turned the key in the ignition, went upstairs, and showered. I wanted to wash off the guilt of even momentarily considering Corsito's offer.

I dressed quickly, then returned some phone calls, mostly to clients who I hadn't been paying attention to during the past week. I also rang Mike Thomas, Paul Stone, and Bill O'Meara. We chatted for a while and made plans for getting together soon. I owed all of them big. I appreciated them asking about Monique and congratulating me on the case.

I laid on the bed and wrote the letter Corsito requested, hating every word I wrote, but now those words had a purpose.

When I finished, I looked at the wall clock. It was two o'clock. To take my mind off Corsito, I turned on the Turner Classic Movie channel. It was showing *On the Waterfront*. I had watched it dozens of times, but it suddenly hit home as never before. I was transfixed as Brando's character, Terry Malloy, was savagely beaten by Mob boss Johnny Friendly's thugs. Bleeding profusely and barely able to walk, he wouldn't give up, wouldn't give the thugs the satisfaction of quitting until he could testify in court to the Waterfront Crime Commission.

Watching the movie made me think about Teddy Malone. Made me realize that this case wasn't just about murder or sexual molestation, any more than *On the Waterfront* was just about the killing of Joey Doyle.

In truth, my case was really about the molestation of an entire industry, college sports, the corruption of the game, perpetrated by coaches who have lost sight of their mandate to turn boys into men. Yes, it's good, even admirable, that a coach helps his players achieve their athletic potential. But it's more important that he provides guidance and assistance to players who struggle with academics, adolescence, and fame. That's what real coaching is all about. Winning—and money—should be way down on the list.

I always get sad when I think how unscrupulous coaches, snakes in the athletic garden, hide behind their power and escape severe punishment time and time again. Sure, they sometimes face disgrace, but more often than not, they rebound. That's just how it is in big-time college sports today: coaches lying, cheating, stealing, and pocketing the most outlandish remuneration—all in the name of victory.

The bottom line is big-time college basketball and football have become nothing more than a minor league preparing players for the pros.

As shitty as I felt about considering Corsito's offer, at least I could take solace in the fact that now I was going to pull off one of the rarest of feats—making a corrupt college coach accountable.

When *On the Waterfront* ended, I stood and applauded. Good for you, Brando. Standing up for that which is right. Whatever the cost.

I went downstairs to the office. Looked at my watch. It was now three-thirty. Almost game time. Or, as sports announcers like to say, crunch time.

I expected Corsito to be late, as was his annoying custom. But to my surprise, he arrived fifteen minutes early. Guess he was anxious to consummate the deal. Even though I had told him that I would leave the front door open, he rang the bell. I hit the buzzer.

He came into the office, carrying a large duffel bag. Dressed in black pants and a black shirt, he wore a black baseball cap and big black Ray-Ban sunglasses. Camouflage. He looked like Darth Vader—minus the hood and cape.

"Hope you don't mind me coming early," he said. "I've been sitting in my car for a while watching the building just in case you tried anything."

"Only thing I've been doing is watching a movie," I said, sitting behind the desk.

He put the bag on the floor and said, "Stand the fuck up."

"What for?"

"I don't trust you not to pull some kind of stunt. Now get up, turn around, face the wall and spread 'em."

"You gotta be fucking kidding me."

"Do it."

"No."

"DO IT!"

I shook my head.

"Don't fucking shake your head at me," he said. "You want this deal or not?"

I had no choice. I had to follow orders. I turned, put my hands on the wall and faced it. Corsito started patting me down. When he got to my pants, he reached inside one of the pockets and pulled out . . . a tiny recorder.

"I knew it," he said. "I fucking knew it."

All I could do was look at him. White-faced. Humiliated.

"You think you could fool me. ME! CHRIS CORSITO! THE GREATEST AND SMARTEST COACH IN COLLEGE BASKETBALL! DID YOU?! DID YOU?!"

"I . . . "

"Did you really think you could get away with this?"

"I . . ."

"You stupid motherfucker you," he said, tossing the recorder on the floor and stomping on it as if he were squashing grapes. "Now give me the fucking letter."

I sat. Took the letter from a desk drawer and handed it to him. Reluctantly.

He took off his sunglasses and snatched the letter from me like a starving dog seizing a long-awaited treat. He then plopped down in the wing chair, put on a pair of bifocals and took his time reading.

When he finished, he removed his bifocals and held the letter up as if it was a winning lottery ticket. He kissed it, folded it and put it in his pants pocket.

"You write well," he said. "I almost believe this shit myself."

"Glad you approve."

His irises gleaming with cold satisfaction, he crossed his legs and grinned. Cocky as hell.

"I told my wife about our deal," he said, his voice acid with scorn. "Know what she's said?"

"No. Tell me."

"She said she always thought you were a phony." Then he cackled.

I didn't respond.

Corsito moved his hands as if he were shaking maracas.

"Gimme me the video," he said.

"In a minute."

"No . . . NOW!"

"I have some questions."

"About?"

"Why'd you let Hunter get away with molesting kids."

"Stop with this shit, will you?"

"No. I want to know why."

"For Christ's sakes, you know why."

"I don't."

He rubbed his eyes with the heels of his hands.

"I'll just say this. Dave is a great recruiter, the best in the business. As good a coach as I am, and I am one of the greatest, if not *the* greatest ever, I can't win without talent. Year in and year out, Dave gets me the best."

"Doesn't it bother you that he molested kids?"

"Of course, it did and does," he said, shrugging. "But look, most of these kids wanted to have their dicks sucked anyway. And the others that didn't, well hell, they probably discovered they were gay."

"I take it then that you were aware Dave sexually assaulted Teddy Malone."

He rocked his head, hesitated, as if not wanting to answer me.

"What do you want me to say?" he said.

"The truth."

"The truth, Elg, is an elusive target."

"Only for you."

Corsito tilted his chin upright like someone who was about to have a medal placed over their head.

"Okay, okay," he said. "Yeah, I knew. So what? Teddy complained to me about it, but I told him to keep his mouth shut. I said that if he did, I'd make damn sure he'd be the star of the team next year and then jump to the NBA. I told him to get over it and go speak with the school's psychologist."

"Blake?"

"Right. Regina Blake. Good lady."

"Blake was aware that Hunter had molested Teddy?"

"What do you think?"

"I think she did. But she didn't do much to help him, did she?"

"She did what she could. Teddy was weak, which is why I tried to toughen him up."

"I see."

Corsito shifted in his seat.

"Enough chitchat," he said. "Gimme the fucking tape and I'll be on my way."

"One final question."

"What's that?"

"Were you aware that it was Marie Hunter . . . with Dave's consent . . . who hired Walter Wilson to murder Teddy and kill me?"

"I don't know anything about that."

"Yeah, you do."

"I don't."

"Yeah, you do."

"I don't."

"Bullshit."

"Bullshit yourself."

"For your information," I lied, "Wilson told the police that Hunter broke down and told you all about Marie's plan."

"That stupid prick said that?" he said, rearing back in his seat. "He's lying."

"He put it in writing."

"What a dumb fuck."

"You did know then about Marie hiring Wilson, didn't you?"

"Why you wanna know this shit?" he said. "It's water under the bridge."

"I want closure."

"Closure?"

"Yeah, closure."

Corsito clasped his hands behind his head and stretched out his legs. He resembled a man on the beach sitting in a sling chair catching rays.

"Listen," he said, his eyes glistening. "Believe what you want."

"Then the deal's off," I said. "I go to the press with what I have and let the chips fall where they may." I paused. "That just might—just might—prevent you from getting that lucrative lifetime contract you've been angling for."

The look in his eyes changed. His pupils now glinted like razors.

"It's your call," I said. "Your career."

Corsito unclasped his hands and leaned forward as if to tell a deep dark secret.

"Look," he said in a totally exasperated tone, "I . . . I . . . only learned about it when Dave came into my office and started crying like a baby. He couldn't believe it when he found out that Marie had hired that idiot Wilson. He felt guilty, okay? Does that fucking satisfy you?"

"To a degree."

"For fuck's sake. What do you want?"

"I want you to admit that you knew Marie was going to have Teddy Malone killed."

Corsito shook his head as if being attacked by a host of bees.

"I'm not going to admit that," he said.

"Then give me back the letter," I said, extending my hand.

He gripped his knees. Tight.

"The letter," I said, my hand still extended. "Give it over. Then I'm going to call Mike Thomas."

I grabbed my cell phone and started dialing. It was a theatrical move meant to unsettle him.

Corsito looked at the phone, and his face became a mixture of surprise and irritation.

"You're bluffing," he said.

"Am I?"

He closed his eyes, his lips moving in muted anger.

"Okay, okay, okay," he said, flapping his hands in the air. "I knew. Satisfied?"

"Not entirely."

"For Christ's sake what else you wanna know?"

"Why you did nothing to stop it," I said, putting the phone aside.

"Because by the time Dave told me about the plan it was already in place. What could I do?"

"Squash it."

"It was too late."

"No, it wasn't. You allowed it to happen. Just like you allowed Monique to get shot."

"Look, I'm sorry about Monique. Dave didn't tell me that was part of the plan. Monique was collateral damage." He paused. "You can blame yourself for that."

"Don't worry . . . I do."

Corsito stood and said, "Are we fucking done here?"

"Almost."

He put out his hand.

"The video," he said.

"Not till I see the money."

"It's right here," he said, handing me the duffle bag.

I flipped it open and peeked inside. There were stacks and stacks of wrapped bills. I picked up a bundle and riffled through the currency with my thumb. All hundreds. Along with the cash was a folder. Inside was a notarized purchase agreement signed by some fat cat.

Corsito pulled his phone out and snapped a picture of me holding the money.

"Okay, smartass," he said. "You got your fucking money, and now I have proof you took it. I even recorded our conversation on my phone. Try going to the press now, hotshot." A satanic grin. "And for the last time gimme the goddamn video." He glanced at his watch. "I wanna get back to the club and get in a few rounds."

I smiled into Corsito's ugly face. It represented to me every deceit, cheat, and betrayal I had ever experienced. He made Bernie Madoff seem like a boy scout.

I reached into a desk drawer, pulled out the video and handed it to him.

"Appreciate it," he said, looking at it the way I assume Sir Galahad did upon finding the Holy Grail.

"One more thing," I said, suddenly feeling ebullient for the first time since I took this case, my contained emotions on the point of release, like a bird fleeing its cage or a horse leaving the starting gate.

"What's that?" Corsito said.

A moment of silence. Then heavy footsteps could be heard slowly coming down from upstairs. Seconds later, Mike Thomas and Paul Stone appeared, just as we planned when I phoned them earlier. In Paul's right hand was a digital recording device. I'd left my office intercom on, and they heard the whole thing on the speaker upstairs.

Corsito's eyes got wider than hubcaps, his complexion whiter than a marshmallow. He blinked rapidly as if trying to erase the people standing before him.

"I think you know Mike Thomas from the *New York Post*," I said. "The fellow with him is Paul Stone, chief detective of the Hoboken Police Department."

Corsito stiffened, as if someone touched the back of his neck with a huge ice cube. Outside, in the distance, the bells from St. Anthony's Catholic Church rang cheerfully. How appropriate.

Paul approached Corsito and said, "You're under arrest for obstruction of justice. I'm sure the DA will add charges regarding withholding evidence, child molestation, and murder." He then read Corsito his rights. Corsito listened with a clenched face.

Paul then looked at me and said, "Thanks for the tip."

"Thank *you* for getting here on such short notice," I said.

Corsito started to speak, but Paul silenced him by saying "Turn around." Corsito turned. Paul cuffed him.

Just then O'Meara walked into the room, took in the scene, and chuckled.

"Happy to be standing after sitting on my ass the past few hours watching the front door," he said. "But I'm glad I took the day off." He pointed at Mike and Paul. "Starsky and Hutch here showed up only minutes before Mr. Dough Boy pulled up for his half-hour stakeout."

Both Paul and Mike didn't react. I think maybe they might have preferred being compared to Crockett and Tubbs. A much cooler duo.

Mike got into Corsito's face and said, "Got any comment . . . Coach?" He said the word "Coach" with as much sarcasm as he could muster.

Corsito ignored him and glared at me.

"Have you gone m-m-mad?" he stammered.

"Mad? I've been mad ever since I took this fucking case."

"You're making a big mistake," he said.

"I've made many mistakes, but this isn't one of them."

"I don't deserve this," he said, his lips moving like a second-rate ventriloquist. "I don't deserve this."

"Yeah, you do," I said. "You committed too many flagrant fouls."

Corsito shot me the frightening look he used to intimidate his players. I couldn't help but think of the big bad wolf huffing and puffing and threatening to blow the house down. Laughable.

"Whatever happens," he said. "I'll destroy you. My friends will make damn sure you never work in this or any other town again."

"Pardon me if I don't faint."

Perhaps realizing his bravado wasn't going to score him points he spoke in a voice so low I could barely hear it. He said, "Elg, can we talk?"

"No can do, Chris," I said. "It's all over."

"What's all over?"

"Everything but the shouting . . . and a soon-to-be headline on the back page of the *New York Post*."

He faltered like a scarecrow cut from its post. Dark shadows of pain appeared beneath his eyes like scabs. Looking at him, I thought he could almost have been heroic—if he wasn't so tragic.

Paul grabbed his forearm, steadied him, and led him out of the house while carrying the duffle bag which also contained the video.

"Chris," I said.

Corsito turned. His eyes were dead.

"You were wrong," I said.

"About?"

"Not everybody can be bought off."

CHAPTER FIFTY

Early the next morning, I gave Kenny Atkins's letter to O'Meara and told him where he could find Marie Hunter. Then I went back home and watched the local news. Every station started their broadcast showing Corsito and Dave and Marie being taken into custody. In one shot Betty Corsito hung onto her husband's neck as if he was a human life preserver.

There was also footage of the chairman of the St. Stephen's Board of Trustees saying he was asking for the resignation of the athletic director, Kent Small, and president Mitchell Benchley. A reporter noted that James Catalano had resigned as head of the booster club. He released a statement saying he "was deeply disappointed by the allegations about Marie." I had to laugh.

Someone got to Kenny Atkins and put a microphone in front of him. He spoke openly and candidly about what happened with Hunter, even suggesting that Marie was not only in the house when the sexual assaults took place, but he believed that she was more than aware of what was happening.

As he talked, tears rolled down his cheeks. It was chilling.

Once again, reporter Josh Clayton of ABC Eyewitness News, was reporting from the St. Stephen's campus.

"There are hundreds of people out here, protesting the arrest of coach Chris Corsito," Clayton said, holding a microphone. "Many are calling it a witch hunt. One student told me that he was transferring from St. Steve's because he couldn't remain at a school that wouldn't support a great man like Corsito.

"The former athletic director and the former president have said, through intermediaries, that they were unaware of Hunter's behavior and have also made it clear they will not be available for any interviews on the advice of their attorneys.

"From what we've gathered, Corsito is denying any knowledge of Hunter molesting players, despite the report of a video that reportedly shows him apologizing for Hunter's behavior. We've subsequently learned Corsito has hired the law firm of Kaplan, Cohen, and Simon, arguably Manhattan's most powerful legal team, to represent him.

"It will be interesting what's ahead for the coach. We do know he's told friends that he's sure he will be back coaching sooner than later."

Clayton paused, touched his earpiece and said, "I've just been informed that since the arrest of Hunter as many as a dozen more players have come forward, alleging that Hunter molested them at a kids' basketball camp up in the Poconos. From what we've learned, these supposed episodes happened between 2008 right up until today. They allegedly include children as young as ten years old. This is shocking and terrifying news."

Clayton inhaled, then added, "This is Josh Clayton, Channel Seven Eyewitness News reporting from the riotous campus of St. Stephen's University."

I turned the television off the television and smiled. Sometimes all the pieces of a puzzle do come together.

Monique called just before noon. She was anxious to leave the hospital, even though Dr. Kaplan thought it best if she'd remain hospitalized a few more days.

But Monique has a stubborn streak, and I knew trying to convince her otherwise would be foolish.

To accommodate her I called Visiting Nurses of Hoboken and arranged for someone to check in on her starting tomorrow. I knew her parents would be extending their stay so I was confident Monique would be in good hands.

I left the house. Outside, the heat wave had finally broken. Thunderstorms had moved in overnight, and the morning air was cool and refreshing. It was as if the rain had cleansed the town.

I started walking toward the Mustang when I noticed a short, potbellied guy leaning against a Honda SUV. Pat Malone.

He cleared his throat, extended his hand and said "Hello, Elgin."

I kept my hand in my pocket.

He pointed to my black-and-blue eye.

"What happened to you?" he said, his voice as nervous as a truant kid facing the school principal.

"Got into a fight," I said.

"Looks . . . looks," he stuttered, "like . . . like you got hit hard."

"You should see the other guy."

Malone licked his lips. They looked dried than sandpaper.

"I'm sorry I didn't tell you about Hunter from the get-go," he said.

"You should be sorry," I said. "It would have saved me a lot of time and prevented my girlfriend from getting shot."

His wrinkled face squeezed tight. He looked away for a moment, his lifeless hands hanging at his side.

"I'll never forgive myself for what happened," he said.

I nodded.

"I just wanted to stop by and give you something," he said.

"I don't want any money." I remembered his retainer check was still in my wallet. I took it out and tore it up. "You don't owe me a thing."

He opened the door to his minivan, reached inside and pulled out a St. Stephen's basketball jersey.

"This was Teddy's," he said, his voice breaking. "He always said he would give it to me when he became a pro." He swallowed hard. "Since he'll never be one, I thought it best to give it to someone who was a pro. And who acts like a pro."

He handed me the jersey. Number 12.

"That was my number at Duke and Dallas," I said.

"I . . . I know," he said. "Teddy was a big fan of yours. O'Meara was always telling him how you played the game the right way. That's why when O'Meara recommended you, I knew I was talking to the right guy."

"Thank you," I said, holding up the jersey and feeling myself tear up. "I appreciate this . . . but he was your son. You should keep it." I handed the jersey back to him.

His lips quivering, Malone took it and held it to his chest as if it were a baby.

"Again, Elgin, my apologies," he said. "Thank you for what you did . . . for Teddy."

I looked at him and thought of something my father once told me. He said one should always forgive and forget. Grudges weren't good for the soul. In my father's honor, I extended my hand. Malone quickly grabbed it. We shook.

He started to speak, but no words came out. After a few seconds, he slowly turned, got into his minivan and gave me one last look. His face was that of a dead man.

I stood there for a while, thinking how lucky I was to have a father who didn't care if I played basketball or the piano. All he cared about was making sure my life would be fulfilling. Happy and content. How fortunate was I?

I got into the Mustang and drove to the hospital. To avoid reporters, Monique, wearing sweats, was at the back entrance, sitting in a wheelchair, her parents beside her.

When she saw me, her face broke into a big smile. As did mine.

Dr. Kaplan, along with some nurses, were circling her and wishing her a quick return to Broadway.

I thanked everyone and told Monique's parents to stop by later. I then wheeled Monique to the car. She bent to get inside. Grunting.

"So nice to be out of there," she said, as we drove down Washington Street.

"So nice to have you out of there," I said.

When we got to the house, I helped Monique get out of the car. She moved gingerly, small steps at a time. I escorted her into the living room where she lay down on the couch. I put a pillow behind her head and a blanket over her legs.

"Comfy?" I said.

"Yes. Though my body hurts like hell."

"Not easy taking a bullet."

"Especially when it wasn't meant for me."

"Yeeessss," I said. "Can I get you anything?"

"A hug in a cup would be nice."

"Earl Grey? English Breakfast?"

"Earl Grey."

I went into the kitchen and brewed the tea. I returned minutes later and handed her a mug decorated with a picture of a heart.

"Thank you, my dear," Monique said.

"Anything else?"

"A little music wouldn't hurt."

"You got it."

I flipped through my CDs and selected one I thought appropriate to the occasion: Chet Baker singing "There Will Never Be Another You."

"Good choice," Monique said.

"I think so."

We sat quietly and listened to Baker, Monique sipping her tea and me holding her hand.

"I won't be able to dance for a while," she said, putting her cup down.

"Doesn't matter."

"Probably can't drink wine like I used to."

"Don't care."

"Might even take weeks before we can make whoopie again."

"Guess we'll just have to find a new way to harmonize."

"You mean like this."

Monique lifted her face slightly. I bent mine down. She then gave me the longest, most passionate, kiss ever.

"Better watch out, girl," I said, my lips still on hers. "You keep kissing me like that we may be back in full harmony sooner than you think."

Monique laughed. It was a good laugh. Full of energy. Pure joy. I could tell she was feeling better.

So was I.

Acknowledgements

I'd like to thank Pat Murphy, Carmine Curcio, Steve Romano and Jean McDonald for their brilliant editorial insights and suggestions. Thanks, too, to my former college teammate, Ray Kelly, for his basketball advice and musical selections. I'm much obliged and very grateful for the educational lessons given to me by Hubie Brown and Bradley Siegel, both of whom I admire for their preparation, dedication and devotion to their crafts. A tip of the fedora to my gangster grandfather who often told me, "Good times never last, but guys with big balls and extreme chutzpah always carry the day." That piece of advice was inevitably followed by another of his crazy aphorisms: "When the going gets tough, the tough gets going—to the nearest gin joint". I genuflect before Mike Sager for his professionalism and Pat Jordan for his inspiration. Without Pat, I would never have had a writing career. He's not only a mentor; he's a friend. Not to mention, he's one of the best, if not THE best, sportswriter ever. Last, and most important, I pay homage to my wife, Tracey, who put up with my endless impatience, frustrations and technical deficiencies.

Love you all!

—Richard O'Connor

Thanks to Richard O'Connor for trusting me.

—Glenn Stout

About the Authors

Richard O'Connor is a former high school All-American basketball player who later became the captain and leading scorer of a Duke freshman team that is the only freshmen basketball team in Atlantic Coast Conference history to go undefeated. After a brief professional basketball career, he turned to writing and became an award-winning journalist who wrote for dozens of publications, including *GQ*, *Esquire*, *People*, *Sport*, *Sports Illustrated* and *The New York Times*. His memoir *Taking a Shot* was called, by Hall of Fame NBA coach Hubie Brown, "A moving coming-of-age memoir about a kid who made a tough decision, took risks, faced challenges and wound up scoring big points in life."

Glenn Stout is an author and editor of more than 100 books. Founding editor of *The Best American Sports Writing* and *The Year's Best Sports Writing*, his biography of Trudy Ederle, *Young Woman and the Sea* has been translated into four languages and in 2024 was made into a major motion picture of the same name by Disney. He is also author *of Tiger Girl and the Candy Kid: America's First Gangster Couple*, *Fenway 1912*, *Nine Months at Ground Zero*, *The New York Times*' bestseller *The Pats*, and many others. A longtime editor and writing coach, he is director of the Archer City Writer's Workshop at the Larry McMurtry Literary Center. A graduate of Bard College and Simmons University, he is a dual citizen of the United States and Canada and lives in Vermont.

About the Publisher

The Sager Group was founded in 1984. In 2012 it was chartered as a multimedia content brand, with the intent of empowering those who create art—an umbrella beneath which makers can pursue, and profit from, their craft directly, without gatekeepers. TSG publishes books; ministers to artists and provides modest grants; and produces documentary, feature, and commercial films. By harnessing the means of production, The Sager Group helps artists help themselves. For more information, please see TheSagerGroup.net.

www.ingramcontent.com/pod-product-compliance
Lightning Source LLC
Chambersburg PA
CBHW061041310726
48969CB00004B/1033